Brook Benton

THERE GOES THAT SONG AGAIN

Brook Benton

THERE GOES THAT SONG AGAIN

Herwig Gradischnig
& Hans Maitner

MUSIC MENTOR BOOKS
York, England

BROOK BENTON (1931-1988)

Management	BROOK BENTON	Exclusive Agency
VARIETY Mgt.Corp.	OKEH Recording	GALE
1619 B'way New York City	Artist	48 W.48th St.New York City

Acknowledgements

The biographical essay about Brook Benton could never have been accomplished without the assistance of the singer's family. Thanks are due to Brook's widow, Mary Benton; sister, Ruth Springer; brother, Richard Peay; nephew, Brook Grant; Sony-BMG A&R Manager Jeff James; and especially Brook's daughter Vanessa for the willingness and patience with which they answered questions in personal meetings, on the phone or by letter. Their friendship and love accompanied this project throughout and ultimately made it possible.

Herwig Gradischnig

I am very grateful to the following people for their contributions to the *Discography*.

Special thanks to Frans Andree, Dr Michael Arie, Ottilie Gradischnig, Jeff James (Sony-BMG A&R Manager), Johann Linder, Eveline Maitner, Gerd Miller, Dieter Moll, Dr Friedrich Mühlöcker, Dr Konrad Nowakowski, Mag Reinhard Stockinger and Werner Wöhrer.

Thanks also to Peter Amesmann, James Austin (Rhino A&R), Albert Bernard, Rosemarie and Ferdinand Bröthaler, Walter Buczolich, the Chilf family, Peter Chromy, Bill Dahl, Colin Escott, the late Gunther Fritz, Marv Goldberg, Enoch Gregory, Daniel Gugolz, Jeff Hannusch, Herbert Hawle, Kurt Hriczucsah, Ira Howard, Keiji Inagaki, Steve Kasmiersky, Terry Kay, Barry Lazell, the late Bernhard Liebe, Mike McDowell, Bill Millar, Herbert Mrak, Alex Novak, Clyde Otis, Don Ovens, Leopold Penzenauer (Rock Shop, Vienna), Robert Pruter, Georg Ramsmeier, Bob Rolontz, Norbert Ruecker, Roy Rydland, Werner Siegmund, Tom Simon, Margie Singleton, Linda Solomon, Roger St Pierre, Alfons Svoboda, Wolfgang Sturmberger, Günter Tollhammer, Walter Uhlich, Billy Vera, Georg Weiss, Herbert Weiss, Elizabeth Wenning, Chris White, Julius Witek, and Brigitte and Rudolf Ziermann.

Hans Maitner

Foreword by Hans Maitner

Brook Benton has an important place in my life, in that I have been fascinated by his wonderful voice since childhood. However, it was never my intention or ambition to collect all of his recordings. It was only when my long-time friend Walter Buczolich decided to transfer all his Brook Benton records onto CD and put them up for sale that I acquired the LPs I was missing. As a result, my interest in Brook Benton increased greatly, and I now wanted to find out as much as possible about the musical and personal history of this artist. In the course of my research, I was astonished to discover that there was neither a proper Brook Benton biography, nor a serious discography of this singer's extensive musical legacy anywhere in the world.

During a visit to my very good friend, Dr Friedrich Mühlöcker, he showed me his newly installed computer, and I asked him and his son to search for the term 'Brook Benton'. I was surprised and at the same time overwhelmed by how many entries appeared under this name.

One of these Internet results particularly intrigued me: a certain Dr Herwig Gradischnig from Kapfenberg declared himself to be a serious and knowledgeable fan of Brook Benton, and I got my friend to send him an email in my name, asking him to contact me by telephone. Later that same day, shortly after returning home, I received a call from Dr Gradischnig and there began a lively and free exchange of ideas. As time went on, the two of us became friends and we decided to work on a Brook Benton biography and discography. Herwig took on the former, while I concentrated on the latter.

In the summer of 2003, Herwig and his wife visited Brook Benton's family in New York. His widow, Mary, and daughter Vanessa helped get our project off the ground by loaning us Brook's scrapbook, which contains a vast collection of reviews of his artistic endeavours, as well as details of his many and varied private and social activities.

Fortunately, my long-time friend Dr Konrad Nowakowski also took pleasure in our project and was able to support us with valuable information about Brook Benton gleaned from the Internet. I must also mention Frans Andree, a Dutchman living in Spain who has created a private Brook Benton website, to whom we likewise owe a debt of gratitude for his suggestions.

If you have any comments, corrections or additional information about Brook Benton, we would be delighted to hear from you. Please contact: **Herwig.Gradischnig@gym-kapfenberg.at**.

Contents

PART I

ATTEMPT AT A PORTRAIT (Herwig Gradischnig)

Introduction 17

1 Childhood and Move to New York 21

2 Clyde Otis, Dave Dreyer and Mercury Records 37

3 Brook Benton the Recording Artist 41

     Mercury 43

     RCA Victor 76

     Reprise 85

     Cotillion 88

     MGM 99

     Brut (All Platinum) 102

     Stax 104

     All Platinum 105

     Olde World 108

     HMC 112

4 The Voice 115

5 Brook Benton on Stage 119

6 Style and Stagecraft of Brook Benton the Entertainer 143

7 TV Shows and Film Projects 151

8 Brook Benton's Personality 161

9 Brook Benton the Family Man 163

10 Brook Benton's Social Commitment 171

11 Brook Benton and Civil Rights 179

12 Brook Benton's Character, Likes and Interests 193

13 Brook Benton's Legacy 203

PART II

DISCOGRAPHY (Hans Maitner)

Recording Sessions 1949-88 213

US Releases.. 267

    Singles 267

    EPs 276

    LPs 278

    Selected CDs 293

    Downloads 295

    Tapes 296

    Jukebox Records 302

    Radio Spots and Transcription Discs 304

    Bootlegs 312

UK Releases 313

    Singles 313

    EPs 318

    LPs 319

    CDs 324

    Tapes 324

International Releases 326

    Angola 326

    Argentina 326

    Australia 327

    Belgium 330

    Canada 330

    Chile 333

    Denmark 333

    Finland 334

    France 335

(West) Germany 337

Greece 341

Hong Kong 341

India 341

Iran 341

Ireland 342

Israel 342

Italy 343

Jamaica 344

Japan 344

Korea 345

Mexico 346

Netherlands 346

New Zealand 351

Norway 353

Philippines 354

Portugal 354

Peru 354

Russia 355

South Africa 355

Spain 357

Sweden 358

Taiwan 359

Thailand 360

Turkey 360

Uruguay 360

Yugoslavia 360

APPENDICES

I	Unissued and Rejected Titles	363
II	US Picture Sleeve Singles	367
III	Brook Benton's Hits	371
IV	Brook Benton the Composer	381
V	Sheet Music	385
VI	Brook Benton Songs recorded by Other Artists	389
VII	Films, Videos and TV Shows	393
VIII	Notable Early Live Appearances	399

Bibliography 401
Index of People's Names 405
Index of Songs & Album Titles 409
Index of Films & Shows 413
Index of Recordings 414
Illustrations & Photo Credits 426
Song Lyric Credits 427

Part I

ATTEMPT AT A PORTRAIT

Herwig Gradischnig

Introduction

Countless books and essays have been written about poetry and songs, and their creators and performers, many of them academically orientated. But behind all the scholarly endeavour, the principal motivation to write about songs and poems is a feeling that each writer can describe, according to their own experience, as exhilaration, awe or amazement; something that stirs a reader or listener deep within and impels them to find out more about this phenomenon, to reflect upon it, and to write about it.

In this bio-discographical work about the singer Brook Benton, the discographical part will satisfy the academic requirements. Hans Maitner, an expert on blues and related musical forms, and additionally a great devotee of Brook Benton's vocal artistry, took on the task of collecting all of the singer's records and listing them in accordance with established discographical criteria in a comprehensive discography. Our years of research brought one surprise after another and raised new questions, which, barring a few exceptions, we were able to resolve. While current commentaries mention about 300 Brook Benton recordings, Hans has been able to account for more than 660, including many titles which were remade at different times. We do, of course, possess all the released titles, but there is also a wealth of unissued material, especially on Mercury and Cotillion.

The biographical essay about Brook Benton's career and artistic legacy stems from the aforementioned 'awe' of the author at the vocal and interpretative art of this extraordinary singer. Over the decades, this awe has developed into a feeling that one can perhaps best convey via the word *love*. Now, loving something also means embellishing the object of one's love, not in the sense of *admiring* it or *talking it up*, but in the deeper sense which subsists within the word *loving* – namely drawing close to something to understand it, to appreciate it, and to embrace and immerse oneself in the entire beauty and meaning of that which is perceived to be *worthy of love*.

From this standpoint, the career-related biographical outline of Brook Benton cannot avoid a certain degree of subjectivity. As an aficionado and collector of recordings by all the great popular singers – male and female – the author trusts that any subjectivity on his part will be outweighed by the objectivity of a comprehensive musical and general aesthetic knowledge, which will hopefully preclude any subjective misjudgements or totally incorrect assessments. The appraisal of aesthetic phenomena, particularly within the sphere of poetry and songs, always has certain emotional components and is also the product of what is known as 'taste'. Knowledge, education, and the taste that results from them are criteria for the choices of both consumers and reviewers of works of art, regardless of the genre. Seen in this way, judgments of taste are not just something arbitrary, but first and foremost expert judgments.

Jean-Paul Sartre's proposition that the reader is the creator[1] applies not only to linguistic art, but also to the fields of visual arts and music, where the listener is the creator. Through their devotion and understanding, their education and their intellectual-emotional capacity, and ultimately through their *love* of the work, listeners able to elevate music to the height it deserves, and perhaps was also intended by the artist.

Brook Benton is a kind of musical cosmos within the world of popular music. This is something which purists in particular should bear in mind, as they have a fondness for pigeonholing artists and attempting to categorize them using terms like crooner or pop-, soul-, country- or jazz singer, and are rarely prepared to consider previous opinion. Naturally, there are different styles of art, forms and means of expression which are separated by historical development, yet develop simultaneously. Connoisseurs know about the close ties which lie within the depths of art's creative process. Nothing is excluded; rather, it is a mutually dependent juxtaposition or progression, which very often develops into a union.

In popular music, different terms are used in an effort to express this fact of reciprocal relationships and conditions. 'Fusion' or 'crossover' are common expressions for this. In jazz, for instance, the most diverse directions and styles – albeit with certain common qualities – are subsumed under the term 'mainstream'. The term 'crossover' is also applied to Brook Benton's music. If one looks at the singer's chart entries, he can be found under the heading 'R&B' as well as 'Pop'. Yet there is a string of recordings, singles as well as albums, that eludes such clear-cut categorization.

What exactly is Brook's incomparable interpretation of Tony Joe White's 'Rainy Night In Georgia'? Is it a form of blues? Is it soul? Where does the superb album, *There Goes That Song Again*, recorded with the Quincy Jones Big Band, belong? Is the *On The Countryside* LP what might be termed country music? How does one evaluate the wonderful *That Old Feeling* album, a collection of standards sung to the highest standard? Isn't there more to the five brilliant Cotillion LPs than just the cliché of 'soul'?

---

[1] Jean-Paul Sartre, *Was ist Literatur?* (Rowohlt, Hamburg) 1960.

In 1983, Brook recorded an album of Christmas songs which included a new version of 'This Time Of The Year', which he had previously recorded for Mercury. How should this swinging cut actually be categorized, given its arrangement and execution?

The singer felt he would achieve success if he created music that deejays of all musical persuasions, rock-crazy teenagers, and also students who treasured ballads would find appealing.[2]

Perhaps 'crossover' is indeed the label that best describes Brook Benton's oeuvre. Defining the art of greats is fundamentally problematic, as artistic endeavour often defies clear classification. Brook is always blues, he is soul, and he swings most elegantly where the material demands it. His masterful phrasing makes this rhythmic tension, which characterizes the swing feeling and stems from the time ratio between the beat and the vocal, noticeable on slow songs too. He is creative and spontaneous. Thanks to his exquisite voice and polished technique, he can go out on a limb singing both highs and lows *bel canto*, but can also sing expressively where the material demands it. Furthermore, there is his remarkable empathy with the lyrical message of a song, which allows him to develop and, above all, convey highly individual interpretations of even well-known songs. Behind Benton's vocal artistry are feeling and intellectual control, the necessary ingredients of high-class performance.

Let the title track of the album *There Goes That Song Again* be the rallying cry for many music lovers to discover or rediscover Brook Benton's vocal legacy. I'm not just talking about the well-known hits, but about becoming acquainted with the mass of little-known material by this exceptional singer and possibly introducing it to a wider audience.

Let's keep Brook Benton's music alive!

---

[2] *On The Flip Side*, probably 1959.

CHAPTER 1

Childhood and Move to New York

'I was blessed with the gift of music... I sang in the choir of my church and I sang with my family. I enjoyed singing more than anything else. I found out I could express myself in song. It brought me an inner peace. It was a sensation of satisfaction. I can't put it into words. I didn't dream of being wealthy, because, you see, I was already wealthy. When I sang, I felt like a millionaire. I dreamt of someday being able to sing for all the people. Not only for Negroes[3], but for everybody... I wanted to sing. I wanted to make people happy.'[4]

Brook Benton was born Benjamin Franklin Peay on 19 September 1931 in Lugoff near Camden, South Carolina. He was the fourth child of William and Mattie Peay. Brook had seven siblings, six sisters and one brother. His father, a bricklayer by profession, was also choirmaster at the Ephesus Methodist Church in Lugoff. Naturally, all the members of the family were in the choir.

The surname Peay derives from the French farm on which Brook's ancestors toiled as slaves. All of them had music and singing in their blood, and that was the reason why the family was always able to stay together. Exceptional singers were always required for church services and other festive occasions, and the owners of the farm therefore decreed that no member of the family was to be sold. Thus Brook's forebears were spared the lot of other slave families, many of whom were broken up in that way.

Their descendants continued the family singing tradition, and Brook received a solid training in gospel and spirituals in the church choir of his home community. Young Benjamin and his family sang in churches, at social events, at school functions and at various celebrations. Brook never forgot his first performance with the ensemble... because it never actually happened. A quartet had been formed from the ranks of the choir for an Easter programme. At the start of their performance, Brook got the jitters and none of the fourteen choir members could manage to persuade him to sing. Thus the quartet quickly became a trio.[5]

---

[3] Whenever the term 'Negro' is used within this work to signify an African American, it is a literal quotation from a contemporary source whose authenticity is important to appreciate.
[4] *Hit Parader*, 4 August 1963.
[5] *New York Daily Mirror*, 8 January 1960.

Brook Benton got his start as a singer in the choir of the Camden Methodist Church in South Carolina. Brook is second from left in this picture which was taken in 1946.

Brook recalled that his father would have liked him to become a minister, but he preferred to be like him: 'When I'd see him stand before the congregation in a little Methodist church, open the hymnal and ask the choir to rise, I thought my father – a choir leader – owned the whole world. I knew that life was for me.'[6] Music was the most important thing in his family. 'We are all deeply religious and we celebrate our faith through music. My father, who was a choir director for over 25 years, is exceptionally musical,' he added.[7]

Brook had been singing spirituals for as long as he could remember. Like many black singers, his musical roots lay within the realm of gospel and spirituals, with their endless possibilities for expression and close relationship to the blues – whether in slow, sustained-note form (*sostenuto*), or accentuated with rhythm and swinging, vocally exploiting the broad spectrum from *bel canto* to *espressivo*.

Years later, when he was an established singer and entertainer, Brook confessed that the spirituals he had heard and sung as a boy were still within him. He still sang them because he felt them, and he loved them because he felt them. The choir at his church had also given him the courage he needed to leave the Lugoff-Camden

---

[6] *New York Telegram and Sun*, 29 July 1960.
[7] Unknown source, 1959.

area and seek his fortune in the big city. In an interview after his breakthrough at Mercury, he revealed the gratitude he still felt in his heart for the choir and its members: 'I want to do something for the people who actually gave me my start. I'm referring to the people in that church choir. Not long ago, I had a heart-to-heart talk with Irving Green, the president of Mercury. I told him how much I appreciated all the good things that have happened to me, and we discussed the idea of my going back to Lugoff and making a spiritual album with the present choir of the Ephesus Methodist Church. A portion of my royalties from the album would be donated to the church... I've been wanting to do something for that church and that choir for a long time. This is my opportunity... Whatever I am today, I owe to the good friends who helped me in my hometown.'[8]

From the age of ten, Benjamin had been 'putting words together' – i.e. writing poems which then evolved into songs. Initially, he didn't even notice that it was actually songs that he was creating, not poems. Well, poems are basically songs. Tone and rhythm are both essential ingredients of poems, and even the concept of a 'lyric' references the musical element in these poetic creations. Brook appositely noted that the texts and melodies of his songs emerged simultaneously.[9]

Many of the songs he wrote for himself and later recorded for Mercury – among them 'It's Just A Matter Of Time', 'So Close' and 'Kiddio' – evolved out of these early poems. In an interview for the Unistar radio network[10], he affirmed that he had written these poems and songs purely for himself and no one else – which provides a clue to the basic lyrical tone of the composer and his creations: lyricism is subjective, emotional and experiential.

With ten mouths to feed, life certainly could not have been easy for the Peay family. In retrospect, however, Brook felt they had actually been better off than many others – this despite the fact that every day had been a struggle for survival.

To help support his family, Benjamin began working at the age of twelve, delivering milk for the Camden dairy. The young lad would sing while he worked, though he was the only one who heard it. Throughout his life, Brook remembered two of the songs he sang at that time: 'Take My Hand, Precious Lord' and 'Black Rat'. He later recorded the former for his *Gospel Truth* album on Cotillion.[11] Brook also revealed that he was attacked by dogs more than one hundred times while delivering milk – which he could evidence by five scars on

---

[8] *Hit Parader*, September-October 1962.
[9] Unknown source, 1959.
[10] *Solid Gold Scrapbook: Birthday Salute*, Unistar, broadcast 19 September 1990.
[11] See pages 95-6 and 255.

his legs.[12] Additionally, all the other members of the family worked in one way or another to contribute to their livelihood. According to Ruth Springer, one of Benjamin's sisters, unity and loving togetherness within the family were among the most valuable things the children received at home.

At the age of thirteen, Benjamin formed a quartet, the Camden Jubilee Singers. The group sang at parties, church socials and later could also be heard on the local radio stations, where they enjoyed great popularity. Their repertoire included spirituals, hymns and also popular songs. Brook felt that, at the time, they really did everything that was possible in a small town like Camden. A promoter who had heard them on the radio wanted to make some recordings of the quartet. Benjamin tried to progress the matter on his own, and the promoter really did want to record some of his songs – but only in return for a fee! The singer later recalled asking himself at the time why he needed to pay anything if this agent thought that he could sing: if this man has such a small record company that one has to pay to record there, then he, Benjamin, should be looking for a big company that is able to give him money for singing.[13]

Ultimately, nothing came of the proposed recordings. The Camden Jubilee Singers stayed together while all the members were still at high school. It was only when Benjamin decided to try his luck as a singer and songwriter in New York and other members of the group were drafted that the ensemble split up.

Brook remembered that, at the time, there were hardly any recreational activities for young people in Camden and the surrounding area. The choir and attendance at church on Sunday were a welcome change. Going to church also offered a chance to meet up with a girl that may have taken one's fancy. Brook later wrote a song about this with Clyde Otis entitled 'I'll Meet You After Church Next Sunday', a brief excerpt of which runs as follows:

> *I'll meet you after church next Sunday.*
> *Please say you'll be there.*
> *'Cause I'd like to take you walking*
> *If the weather is fair.*

It's a simple song which originated from within Benjamin's daily life, no big deal, nothing that would have turned the music world upside down, but it is nevertheless a lyrical creation that is capable of touching a listener by its simplicity and naïveté. However, the earnestness with

---

[12] *World Telegram*, 22 October 1959.
[13] *New York Daily Mirror*, 8 January 1960.

Bill Landford & The Landfordaires
ca. 1950 (from poster).

which Brook delivers it[14], without great pathos, prevents it from descending into kitsch.

Opportunities for the talented young Benjamin soon became too limited in Camden and the surrounding area. He knew that he would only really stand a chance of getting to the top if he went to New York, where he might be able to gain a foothold. In a US radio network interview broadcast on 4 October 1986, Brook recalled that he saw he would never get anywhere in a small town like Camden, so he started looking for a better place from which to keep an eye out. New York seemed to be the best place for that, so he went to the city in 1947. One of his sisters, Willie Lee Dixon, was already living there, so he had a place to stay. Despite this, his first visit there was only brief and he returned to Camden rather disillusioned.

Upon his return to the city in 1948, Benjamin joined Bill Landford[15] & The Landfordaires, who sang spirituals and gospel music. A former member of the Golden Gate Jubilee Quartet, the legendary group who pioneered the rhythmic spiritual ('singing with a beat') and more recently the Southern Sons, Landford had now formed his own outfit in their image. Benjamin toured with the Landfordaires for three years. They appeared in California and then in the southern States, singing in churches, halls and clubs. Their first engagement earned him $10, which he donated to their travelling fund. Brook later recalled that they were paid 'weekly – very weakly', and would get $40 for the

---

[14] Clyde Otis later included the song on a double LP of Brook's demo recordings (see page 35).
[15] His name is variously spelt Langford or Landford.

whole group for a performance if they were lucky. On one occasion, they even had to sing without being paid anything at all.

On a back road somewhere in deepest Georgia, their dusty old jalopy was in desperate need of fuel and just before darkness fell they found a gas station. 'We were out of the car, stretching our legs,' Brook recalled, 'when suddenly a mean-looking guy stepped out of nowhere. "Sing!" he growled. And we saw that he was keeping one hand in a lumpy-looking pocket. Man, you never heard a quartet vocalize louder, faster or longer! We never knew how he knew we were singers, or whether he really did have a gun – at a time like that you just don't put out a questionnaire. We sang our whole repertoire before he clumped back into the darkness.'[16]

Peay and the Landfordaires made some recordings for Columbia in late 1949: 'Touch Me, Jesus', 'Lord I've Tried' and 'Troubled, Lord I'm Troubled' are slower, sustained-note songs; 'Trouble Of This World', 'Run On For A Long Time' and 'You Ain't Got Faith' are rhythmically-accented gospel numbers performed by a vocally proficient, swinging group unobtrusively accompanied and rhythmically supported by a single guitar.

In 1951, Benjamin decided to throw in his lot with the Jerusalem Stars, and subsequently with the Harlemaires. Although neither group made any recordings, he did, however, rejoin the newly renamed Bill Landford Quartet in time for their May 1953 session for RCA in Nashville, which produced 'Jesus, Lover Of My Soul', 'The Devil Is A Real Bright Boy' and 'I Dreamed Of A City Called Heaven'. A promotional photo of the group (see next page) confirms Brook's presence in the line-up at that time. What is more, he can be heard here for the first time as a soloist on a released recording. He sings the introduction of 'Jesus Lover Of My Soul' and captivates as a soloist on the four choruses of 'The Devil Is A Real Bright Boy'. He sings the whole of 'I Dreamed Of A City Called Heaven' solo. His mellow baritone carries the song easily, and he swings most elegantly throughout. According to Jeff James, A&R manager for BMG Music Group (now Sony Music), the quartet cut fourteen titles in total. It is also worthy

RCA VICTOR
RECORD PREVUE
DISC JOCKEY SAMPLE
NOT FOR SALE
RCA VICTOR DIV. CAMDEN, N. J.
RADIO CORPORATION OF AMERICA

P. D.
E3-YB-0647   (20-5459)

I DREAMED OF A CITY CALLED HEAVEN

BILL LANDFORD QUARTET

Time: 2:58

---

[16] Unknown source.

RCA Victor promo shot of the Bill Landford Quartet, 1953.

of mention that, on all their RCA recordings in Nashville, they were accompanied by Chet Atkins on guitar.

Neither the recordings, nor his live appearances with Bill Landford's groups brought Benjamin any nearer to his goal of establishing a career as a singer in New York; his dream was not to be fulfilled for several more years. In retrospect, Brook felt that, while New York naturally offers all kinds of opportunities, one needs to know what one is doing in order to successfully capitalize on them: 'New York... was worse than home the first three years... It took that long... to find out what was happening there, being a greenhorn – which I was.'[17]

To secure his material existence in the big city, Benjamin took a range of different jobs. He worked as a chauffeur, in a grocery store, ironed clothes, washed up at the Copacabana and drove a truck for the Garment District. Singing while driving the noisy truck reputedly strengthened his voice. His baritone, which would later be described as rich, warm and irresistible, rang out loud and clear in the canyons of

---

[17] Unknown source, ca. spring 1960.

7th Avenue in Manhattan. But neither the traffic cops, nor cab drivers, nor pedestrians heard him.[18] In order to try to seize one of the opportunities he'd been dreaming of, Benjamin would go from door to door before and after work to demo his songs and his voice to people in the music business. Everywhere he went, nobody wanted to listen. He lost several jobs because, from time to time, he would take a day off to introduce himself to managers instead of going to work.

It should also be added here that it took Brook several years to develop his vocal characteristics: the contrasting of highs and lows, and a rich, velvety baritone voice which can grace both tenor and bass passages and can be employed both expressively and *bel canto.*

As Mary Benton, the singer's widow, recalled, Brook never took any singing lessons in all the time she knew him. His voice was quite simply a gift from God. He did, however, take elocution classes to improve his enunciation. In fact, at one point he even considered becoming an actor. Naturally, Brook practised singing at home, for which used a tape recorder. He constantly worked to improve himself. Composer/producer/singer Jerry Chesnut's assertion that Brook Benton sought perfection in everything he did is absolutely right.[19]

Although the ambitious Benjamin had sung at every job he'd had, it was while working as a truck driver that he first seriously started writing songs. He would drive his vehicle at breakneck speed to deliver all the goods as quickly as possible, and paid all the kids he could find to help him unload. He could use the remaining time for composing. According to Brook, the place where he always found most inspiration was the corner of 24th Street and 9th Avenue (although on occasion he also said it was 30th Street).

Benjamin had a simple method for working out which of the countless songs in his head were the best ones. If it was a good song, the words would flow easily one after another; however, if he got stuck when stringing words together, the song was no good and he would discard it. Brook also mentioned that, while working as a truck driver, he was occasionally given time off by his boss, a Mr Bernard Goldstein, so that he could sing in nightclubs, at parties, etc, for which he earned $15 per appearance. One evening, when he was singing outside a house with four other guys, he was heard by Bill Cook, a black deejay who was to have some influence on the subsequent career of Benjamin Peay. Cook offered them a group contract, but they did not find success. Brook later recalled that their first record only sold about ten copies.[20]

Peay and Cook, who was always fair to his artists, became

---

[18] *Rock & Roll Magazine*, 1959.

[19] Jerry Chesnut's homepage, 002.

[20] *New York Daily Mirror*, 8 January 1960. The name of the group and the record are both unknown.

friends. There's an interesting quote from Cook about his new discovery: 'I've had the honour to work with, and for, many of the great names in entertainment. Roy [Hamilton], of course, was the one I believed in and worked hardest for... but when I first I heard [Brook] I knew that he had the talent it takes to be a truly sensational star.'[21]

Cook introduced Benjamin to Marv Halsman at Epic, a subsidiary of Columbia. It was through Halsman that the singer got his first recording contract. Roy Hamilton, who at that time was a very well-known singer, was also signed to Epic. Benjamin immediately felt drawn to him and they remained close friends until the latter's death. So close, in fact, he christened his second son Roy Hamilton. The singing star later recorded several titles penned by Brook, including 'I'll Take Care Of You', 'The Same One', 'Looking Back', 'It's Just A Matter Of Time' and 'Will You Tell Him' for MGM and Columbia. His sad fate affected Brook deeply. Aged just 40, Hamilton suffered a stroke in 1969, from which he died on 20 July that same year. Brook was shocked by the high cost of his friend's medical care and confided to his friend and contemporary, the famous R&B singer Ruth Brown, that he would work for as long as he could to ensure that he was financially prepared for any such eventualities.[22]

In 1954, Adriel McDonald, the former bass of Decca's Ink Spots, assembled a vocal group called the Sandmen which included himself, tenor Walter Springer, and Furman[23] Haynes, a baritone. Springer, who happened to be married to Benjamin Peay's sister Ruth, recommended his brother-in-law for the lead. Springer, Haynes and Peay were all former gospel singers.

On 14 December 1954, the quartet cut three titles at Columbia's studios in New York: 'When I Grow Too Old To Dream', 'Somebody To Love' and 'I Could Have Told You'. Quincy Jones was arranger and bandleader on all three recordings. They returned three days later on 17 December to back Chuck Willis on his recording, 'Lawdy Miss Mary'.

The Sandmen's 'When I Grow Too Old To Dream' and 'Somebody To Love' appeared in April 1955 to good reviews. Interestingly,

---

[21] Marv Goldberg's R&B Notebooks: *The Sandmen*, 2002.
[22] Ruth Brown with Andrew Yule, *Miss Rhythm* (Donald I. Fine Books, New York) 1996.
[23] Some sources spell his name 'Thurman'.

Columbia issued the recordings on OKeh, rather than Epic, because they were considered to be primarily R&B material with little chance of making the pop charts. 'I Could Have Told You' remains unissued, though Brook subsequently re-recorded the number in 1959 for his first Mercury album, *It's Just A Matter Of Time*.

On 'Somebody To Love', Benjamin Peay can be heard for the first time as a soloist on a secular release. Vocal group specialist Marv Goldberg opines: 'If you've never heard "Somebody To Love", do yourself a favor and try to get a copy of the recording. It's a wonderful ballad and would have made the charts, if only OKeh had pushed it.'[24]

Indeed, the song reveals an admittedly youthful, but already mature singer, whose voice possesses that soaring element which is the hallmark of all great voices. Peay effortlessly sings long vowels in a sustained-note ballad and varies the motifs. The beautiful song gains in substance and excitement through the singer's interpretation, and his feel for the poetic message and the 'touch of blues' within him. This largely unknown waxing is an early gem whose beauty is worth discovering.

Despite their lack of commercial success, these recordings resulted in several bookings for the group in New Jersey and Pennsylvania. However, a projected tour with Savannah Churchill never materialized.

The Sandmen were soon back in the studio again. On 4 February 1955, they cut four titles as backing vocalists for Lincoln Chase, including 'That's All I Need' and 'The Message'. Both are R&B numbers and were released in March on Columbia. The vocal introduction to 'The Message' especially sounds really 'black' and is very interesting. On 21 April, they again sang backup on a Chuck Willis session. The song, 'I Can Tell', was issued on OKeh in May. Both these releases likewise received good reviews.

As time went on, tensions must have developed within the Sandmen. Benjamin had emerged as a wonderful, expressive baritone who stood out conspicuously from the many tenor voices of the era. It is easy to understand why OKeh were interested in releasing some solo recordings by him.

The Sandmen's next session,

COLUMBIA

Copyrighted. Made in Canada. "Columbia" and ⊕ Trade Marks.

40475
(4-55)   (BMI) 2:09

THAT'S ALL I NEED
(Chase)
LINCOLN CHASE and The Sandmen
Orchestra under the direction of
Ray Ellis
(CO 52939)

---

[24] Marv Goldberg, ibid.

on 26 May, yielded 'Ooh' and 'I Was Fool Enough To Love You', the latter of which remains unissued. On 2 June, Benjamin made a solo recording of 'The Kentuckian Song', the theme of the movie of the same name starring Burt Lancaster. This happened without the knowledge of the other members of the quartet.

And something else happened too. In August, OKeh released 'The Kentuckian Song' *b/w* 'Ooh' under Benjamin's new stage name, Brook Benton, on which the Sandmen's only role was as background singers on 'Ooh'. From this point on, Benjamin Peay was known as Brook Benton – a name reportedly thought up by OKeh A&R man Marv Halsman. McDonald, Springer and Haynes split from Brook, who now made an attempt to launch a solo career.

Initially, this enterprise enjoyed relatively little success, with releases on OKeh and then Columbia's pop subsidiary, Epic, turning out to be flops. That may come as a surprise, given that the arranger and bandleader on both sides of Brook's first solo release was none other than Quincy Jones. 'The Kentuckian Song', a sustained-note number, is hardly enough to make one jump out of one's seat, but it does nevertheless demonstrate that the young singer had enough talent and ability to perform a slow song without boring the listener.

By way of contrast, 'Ooh' is a rhythmically accented number which demonstrates Brook's affinity for swinging material. The beautiful clarity of his vowels and his accurate intonation, as well as the swinging treatment of a song, are qualities that the young singer brought with him from his thorough training as gospel singer. The tenor solo in 'Ooh' is slightly reminiscent of the saxophone solos common in rock'n'roll, which was beginning to blossom at that time, albeit with a little bit more of a jazz feel.

At this point, the Epic LP, *Brook Benton At His Best*, needs to be mentioned. Although this album wasn't released until 1959, the recordings on it were all made between 1955 and 1957. The first track on it is 'The Wall'. Originally released as a single on Epic in February 1957, it is the Benton number which first attracted the attention of Clyde Otis. Brook later joked that it only sold about fifteen copies. The song goes:

> *There's a wall between us…*
> *Can you tear down the wall*
> *And mend my aching heart?*

'Well, there was a wall all right', Brook later said, laughing, 'but the record buyers didn't try to climb over it!'[25]

---

[25] *Detroit News*, 18 March 1964.

His other Epic single, 'Give Me A Sign', was another bomb: one of those 'hits' that only his brothers and sisters bought. As he ironically remarked afterwards: 'I have a very large family and they all were behind me.'[26] The singer also gave away a few copies.[27]

Upon closer examination, the Epic LP does have some qualities which make it abundantly clear that none of the cuts on it could ever have been a hit in any chart. The material comprises a mixture of slow ballads and several numbers with rather more accentuated rhythm, which one could categorize as 'slow rock'. The arrangements reflect the style of the times, and the many beautiful saxophone solos are more than just fillers. Brook once again demonstrates his talent as an interpreter of ballads – he had long since acquired the necessary vocal wherewithal. He also completely masters the medium-paced rocking tempo of several songs. His voice is soft and flowing – something that would later come to be identified as a trademark of Brook Benton the mature singer. What are still missing are the dramatic 'dip downs' that would become the defining feature of the great Brook Benton.

On two songs on the LP, Brook makes vocal concessions to contemporary taste, as defined by rock'n'roll's protagonists – Buddy Holly would provide a model for this later on. The hard and disjointed singing of several notes on one vowel is striking, especially on 'Love Made Me Your Fool' and 'Give Me A Sign'. It is very different to the familiar soft, melismatic tone and the way of handling vowels that the singer usually likes to employ, even on his swinging material. Rock'n'roll basically swings hard, and the hiccuping singing style of many rock'n'rollers made it easier for them to accentuate the offbeat. As a mature vocalist, Benton would never again succumb to this mannerism.[28]

An expanded CD version of the Epic LP including the single cuts 'Ooh' and 'All My Love Belongs To You' was reissued by Sony/BMG in 2005. The producer of this compilation, Jeff James (A&R Manager at Sony/BMG Music), intimated to the author that a complete set of Brook Benton's Columbia sessions may be on the cards, though this has yet to surface.

In 1955, Brook made a number of highly acclaimed appearances in Cleveland, Ohio. Galen Gart listed these in his book, *Rhythm & Blues in Cleveland: 1955 Edition*. At the start of September, Brook appeared along with other entertainers at the Ebony. The show was advertised as probably the biggest nightclub revue of the season. 'Brook will sing several songs that the audience will enjoy. He will be

---

[26] *Boston Traveler*, 17 April 1964.
[27] *Baltimore Afro-American*, 10 July 1962.
[28] Listen to the 1959 Mercury hit, 'Hurtin' Inside'.

accompanied by the Joe Cooper Orchestra,' stated 'On The Town'.[29] A poster for the event had already defined him more precisely as a baritone. A little later, from 19 September onwards, Brook began an engagement at entertainment mecca the Chatterbox, where he was billed as 'OKeh Records' new super-baritone'. He was backed by the Ralph Wilson Orchestra.

Benton was to remain in the programme until 2 October. In a preview for the string of appearances, the reviewer was convinced that the singer would leave the Chatterbox and the management of the Jambi Rooms satisfied. He was described as handsome with a really good baritone voice (which could be heard on his records) and a repertoire which encompasses ballads as well as numbers from the blues domain. Although his engagement turned out to be rather shorter than planned, his appearances must nevertheless have been very successful, because he was back on the Chatterbox stage again from 11 December, with Ralph Wilson once again providing the accompaniment. This time, Brook was billed as an 'outstanding baritone'. 'On The Town' speaks of a baritone ballad singer who had been such a big hit, first at the Ebony and then at the Chatterbox, that his latest engagement became a reality due to public demand.

Brook's appearances at the Ebony and the Chatterbox brought him great popularity in Cleveland, though they had no appreciable effect on his subsequent career as a record star. At the Chatterbox, he found himself in good company. He remained at this establishment until the end of the year, where he shared the stage with Linda Hopkins. 'On The Town' announced that 'On January 1, the great Billie Holiday will have the honor of appearing with Brook Benton' (note the form of wording), and a little further on it states that all three singers (Holiday, Benton and Hopkins) will be on stage for the New Year's Day show.

In 1957, Brook made a fresh attempt to break into the record business and switched to RCA Victor. His recordings for the RCA R&B subsidiary Vik are well-documented, most notably on the 2001 CD, *The Essential Vik and RCA Recordings*.

The first two numbers pressed by Vik were 'Come On, Be Nice' and 'I Wanna Do Everything For You', both of which conformed to the rock'n'roll idiom popular at the time. 'I Wanna Do Everything For You' in particular is a lively rock number mildly reminiscent of Elvis Presley (as is 'Hurtin' Inside', which Brook later cut for Mercury). Elvis and Brook did actually have some contact, as is evidenced by the famous photograph of them backstage in Memphis in 1957, so it can be surmised that the two singers influenced each other to some extent.

Brook's debut release on Vik is also the first instance of his

---

[29] *Daily News*, date unknown.

cooperation with Clyde Otis, which, as far as the production is concerned, places Benton in focus as the singer. They co-wrote both songs. More will be said later about the Otis-Benton connection, especially with regard to Mercury, the label where Benton spent his golden years. His second Vik release, 'A Million Miles From Nowhere' – a somewhat bombastic dramatic song with a powerhouse vocal – was a minor success. However, it didn't advance his career.

In 1957, Brook also got the chance to appear in the movie *Mister Rock and Roll*. The musical director of the project was Lionel Hampton, deejay Alan Freed appeared as himself, and the featured acts included greats like LaVern Baker, Chuck Berry, Clyde McPhatter, Little Richard and Ferlin Husky. World boxing champion Rocky Graziano also had a role. Two songs by Brook can be heard in the film – both Vik recordings. He is shown singing (or rather, miming to) 'If Only I Had Known', while 'Your Love Alone' is played as background music. If the Paramount release increased Brook Benton's prominence, it did not result in him breaking through into new dimensions in music and show business.

As is evident, Brook's career as a singer only made very laborious progress, despite the fact that he made many recordings between 1955 and 1958. It has already been mentioned that, at the beginning of his time in New York, the aspiring artist had to take on many different jobs in order to keep his family's heads above water.

However, he was very soon able to rely upon other activities that were more in keeping with his artistry and would ultimately advance it in a decisive way.

He wrote songs and worked as a demo singer. To gauge whether a particular song might be a success, record companies would first circulate some recordings of it. These productions were made as cheaply as possible – i.e. with minimal instrumental accompaniment, for instance a piano with a rhythm section. They were mostly done without background singers, but on the other hand they needed vocalists who could sing very well and were also not expensive. Brook felt he had found some really good work here. He did not yet consider himself to be a great singer, but he saw that his style, the way he sang, was catching on. Brook estimated that he cut over 500 such solo demo recordings during this period. It would not be a big step from cutting demos to making records in his own right.

In 1972, Clyde Otis released a selection of these demos on Trip, among them also some of the singer's subsequent successes. The double album, which was released under the title *Ain't It Good*, contains 24 tracks.[30] Songs like 'Doggone Baby, Doggone', 'Ninety-Nine Percent', 'I'll Stop Anything I'm Doing', 'Ain't It Good' and 'You're Movin' Me' are swinging numbers with simple patterns and reveal Brook Benton as a singer straddling R&B and rock'n'roll. 'Ninety-Nine Percent' is made of exactly the kind of material from which Brook's hits, such as 'Hotel Happiness', could later be fashioned: namely an urbanized blues mood with a swinging rhythm.

'Next Stop Paradise' is reminiscent of the work-song genre, while 'Walking Together' and 'Everything Will Be Alright' clearly show Benton's gospel past. It's a pity that Mercury didn't record Brook doing these songs. 'Everything Will Be Alright' in particular had hit qualities. Even in demo form, it's a beautiful, bluesy number, delivered by the singer with intensity and early mastery. Similarly, 'The Rest Of The Way' definitely had what it would have taken to give Brook Benton a hit. Perhaps more could have been done with these songs, as was the case with 'May I' and 'Nothing In The World', which Benton later recorded for Mercury. (Incidentally, the latter was also waxed by Diane Schuur and Nat 'King' Cole.) On the demos of 'This Bitter Earth', a song which later resurfaced on an LP of the same name, and 'Don't Walk Away From Me', Brook presents himself as a singer eminently capable of deploying mature vocal resources and interpreting the musical material.

Contained within this recorded legacy were countless songs

---

[30] This album was reissued in November 2014 on the Jasmine 2-CD, *The Early Years: 1953-1959*. However, 'Devoted' and 'You're For Me' are the later RCA recordings.

from the pen of Brook Benton. Composing had become another mainstay of the ambitious young singer. By his own account, Brook wrote over 300 songs. Clyde McPhatter's 'A Lover's Question' and Nat 'King' Cole's 'Looking Back', both huge successes, are Benton compositions which were also recorded by him as demos. But it was only after their success could be predicted with a degree of certainty that the two established singers accepted his material. In 1958, Clyde McPhatter spent 24 weeks in the *Billboard* pop charts with 'A Lover's Question'. The record went to No. 6, and also spent 23 weeks in the R&B charts, where it reached No. 1. Similarly, Nat 'King' Cole enjoyed a No. 5 pop hit that year with 'Looking Back', which stayed on chart for 19 weeks. It was also a No. 2 R&B hit, charting for 16 weeks.

Brook and Clyde Otis also wrote 'Thank You Pretty Baby' for Nat Cole. Cole was taken with the song and recorded it, but his label didn't release it at the time.[31] In the summer of 1959, Otis decided to record it for Mercury as a duet by Brook and Dinah Washington. They rehearsed the number, and a recording session was duly arranged. On the night of the session, Dinah turned up with a sore throat. Rather than having to send the musicians home and reschedule, Brook sang it alone, and so well – straight, without technical gimmicry – that Mercury released his version as it stood. The song, a bluesy ballad with a moderate beat, became one of his biggest early hits.[32]

By this time, Brook had already been working with Clyde Otis for quite a while. Together they penned an attractive rock number, 'Doncha Think It's Time', which was recorded in 1958 by Elvis Presley. The label of the single and later Elvis literature both show the composers as 'Otis-Dixon'. This is because Brook also composed under the pseudonym 'Willie Dixon', which was the married name of one of his sisters (although some sources claim the 'Willie' was after his beloved and revered father).

Irrespective how much or how little record success he'd had up until now, Brook had nonetheless started to make a name for himself in the business after ten years of hard work, many setbacks, disappointments and privations, and having to take on jobs and activities far removed from his hopes and wishes in order to provide for his family and himself. With such auspices, what could possibly go wrong with the budding career of the ambitious young singer? A great – in Bill Cook's words, *sensational* – career seemed ready to take off. It just needed a spark to light the fuse.

---

[31] Capitol, Cole's label, actually released an album in 1967 titled *Thank You Pretty Baby*; however, the song was not released as a single until 1968.

[32] *Sunday Star*, Washington, DC, 16 August 1959.

CHAPTER 2

Clyde Otis, Dave Dreyer and Mercury Records

In January 1959, Brook Benton's first hit stormed the charts, capturing the hearts of millions. The long-awaited success had finally arrived. It really had been just a matter of time, and it was the song 'It's Just A Matter Of Time' which catapulted the young African-American singer up into the stratosphere. It was co-written by Brook, Clyde Otis and Belford C. Hendricks, the composer, arranger and bandleader who would be responsible for a whole string of Benton hits in the ensuing years. Hendricks had already co-written Nat 'King' Cole's hit, 'Looking Back', with Benton and Otis, and he and his orchestra had accompanied Cole on various occasions. He had also arranged such popular records as 'Dear Lonely Hearts', 'Ramblin' Rose' and 'When You're Smiling'.

The collaboration between Clyde Otis and Brook Benton has already been mentioned. But how did it actually come about? After cutting 'The Wall', his last recording for Epic, Brook requested a meeting with Otis, who had already written a number of successful songs. They were finally introduced to one other through Roy Hamilton's manager, Bill Cook. Brook showed Otis some of his songs. Clyde laughed at them, and thought them amateurish. Hurt, but not discouraged, Brook offered to bring more of his songs. Although Otis wasn't very impressed, he agreed, as he was sure he would never see Brook again. But Brook's songs kept getting better and better, and he was eventually able to sell some of them to him. Otis then introduced Brook to publisher Dave Dreyer, who felt that they should work together. This partnership yielded well over 150 compositions.

Brook describes his collaboration with Dave Dreyer as the first big step towards his desired goal. He repeatedly attributes a large part of his success to his former manager, the publisher and composer of big hits like 'Me And My Shadow', 'Back In Your Own Back Yard' and 'Cecilia'.[33] It was Dave Dreyer who was initially responsible for bringing about the extremely productive collaboration between Brook Benton and Clyde Otis. Their first hit together (co-written with Belford

---

[33] *Long Island Press*, 12 August 1962.

Clyde Otis *(left)* and Brook Benton in the studio, early '60s.

Hendricks) was Nat Cole's 'Looking Back'. One success led to another. Eventually, Otis became the leading A&R man at Mercury Records, and Benton was signed to the label as a recording artist.[34]

'It's Just A Matter Of Time' was his first hit for the label, and was followed by many others up to 1961. (In this context, it should be noted that some of the recordings released from 1959 onwards had actually been made years earlier – namely in 1955 ('It's Just A Matter Of Time', 'Hurtin' Inside') and 1956 ('So Close', 'How Many Times', 'So Many Ways', 'Endlessly').[35]

Now let us give Brook Benton a chance to speak. In an interview broadcast in early October 1986 on various US radio stations, the singer recollected how he had cut a demo of one particular song, 'It's Just A Matter Of Time', which became his first big success: 'I wasn't sure that they were gonna allow me to record this song as an artist, so I used two renditions. One demonstration record I made with the low notes, and the other one I used my voice ordinarily. The publisher, who was my manager, said he wouldn't let anyone hear

---

[34] 'Brook Benton Bulletin', *Hit Parader*, September 1961.
[35] The exact details and recording and release dates of these records, insofar as they are known, appear in the *Discography*.

this song. And that's what he did. Atlantic called me and wanted me to demonstrate some things, and I demonstrated that low-note rendition – in person of course. But, doing this, I got into very big differences with Clyde.' The 'low notes' mentioned by Brook would become one of the trademarks of his vocal art.[36]

At the end of 1957, a vocal group called the Diamonds had a No. 4 pop hit with 'The Stroll'. Clyde Otis and Belford Hendricks were credited on the label as the song's composers. At a concert in 2000, their lead singer, Dave Somerville, talked about its genesis and identified Clyde Otis as the writer and the young Brook Benton, who at that time was still waiting for his first hit, as vocal coach. Brook had also made a demo of the number, on which he experimented with low notes for the first time. This mannerism is widely regarded as a legacy of early R&B giant Percy Mayfield. In a 1983 interview for Radio London, Brook cited Louis Jordan, Percy Mayfield and Ivory Joe Hunter as his early role models. Blind Boy Fuller was the first blues singer that he consciously listened to. However, it was the deep voice of Percy Mayfield that he had especially admired as a youngster and hoped that he too would be able to sing those low notes one day. So, he began working at it and cultivating this style, albeit without consciously trying to copy Mayfield.[37] Benton's vocal arrangement was adopted by the Diamonds, and close listening to their version clearly bears that out. However, it appears that he also contributed his own ideas to the Diamonds' worldwide hit.

Brook continues: 'Through "The Stroll" Clyde got a position with Mercury Records. Naturally, he took me along and said he could get me to go along. And then I made a choice where I should go: to Atlantic, or go to Mercury with Clyde, and naturally I went with Clyde.'

Here, Clyde Otis, who one of the absolute greats of American popular music, needs to be looked at in greater detail. Born in Mississippi in 1924, he became the first African-American A&R boss of a major label. He too had struck out to New York to try to fulfil his musical ambitions. Like his later musical partner and protégé, Brook Benton, Otis worked different jobs during the daytime and composed at night. His ascent finally began in 1958, when he joined Mercury – together with Brook Benton, of course. Otis worked with greats like Dinah Washington, Sarah Vaughan, Timi Yuro, the Diamonds and others, in the course of which he became the first producer to use string arrangements for black vocalists. The overemphasis of the string section by African-American arrangers that some critics find fault with was without a doubt a consequence of the new possibilities opened up by Clyde Otis.

---

[36] Benton's voice is examined in greater detail in *Chapter 4*.
[37] *Now Dig This* 212, UK, November 2000.

It is also worthy of mention that Clyde Otis was the first African-American producer to win a Country Music Award: he organized and produced sessions for country stars in Nashville. Elvis Presley, Aretha Franklin, Johnny Mathis, Patti Page and others recorded his songs. The first phase of his collaboration with Brook Benton ended in 1961 with the latter's greatest-ever chart triumph, 'The Boll Weevil Song'.

The years that followed turned out to be so successful for Brook Benton that he could scarcely have imagined them in his wildest dreams.

CHAPTER 3

Brook Benton the Recording Artist

Brook Benton's early attempts in the recording business were discussed in detail in *Chapter 1* and are therefore not covered below. All his known recordings are listed in the excellent *Discography* compiled by Hans Maitner that constitutes the second half of this book. Most of the records that Brook Benton made during his career were cut for Mercury between 1959 and 1965. In fact, this period can be described as his golden years. Between January 1959 and March 1965, the singer took 38 songs into the charts.[38]

The intention of this chapter is principally to review Brook's albums, and also particular songs out of the mass of over 660 recordings which are of greater artistic significance, in order to define his status as a singer and interpreter of popular music. As part of this, close attention will be paid to Brook's voice, his vocal technique and the manner of his interpretation. The *Golden Hits* and *Golden Hits (Volume 2)* albums will not be examined separately, as they have already been the subject of countless compilations and reviews. Instead, the reader is referred to the Mercury, Rhino and *Millennium Collection* anthologies, the last two of which extend beyond Benton's Mercury recordings.

Just how much of an impression Brook Benton made on music fans with his first hits is indicated by an open letter to the singer published in the *Hit Parader* magazine of August 1959, eight months after the release of 'It's Just A Matter Of Time' and 'Hurtin' Inside', and five months after 'Endlessly' and 'So Close'. One Sandra Townsend wrote:

Dear Brook,

I've been a record buyer for several years now, and for those several years I've always looked for the same things in which records to purchase – I look for sincerity and warmth in the performance of the artist.

---

[38] For details see *Appendix III*, page 371.

The first time I heard 'It's Just A Matter Of Time', I knew this was a record I must have and that you, Brook Benton, were to become a star that the nation must have. Now your recording of 'Endlessly' only further proves that I was correct in my judgment. Your style, your warmth, your sincerity – not to mention your inimitable talent – can only soon make you one of the greatest stars the American music scene has ever known.

Welcome, Brook Benton, to the land of stars.

There are two important things which can be deduced from this letter. The author of this heartfelt message must be (or must have been) a music lover whose taste in music is embodied by feeling and intellect. Secondly, Ms Townsend cites warmth and sincerity as being the most important characteristics of Brook Benton's vocal art for her. Both these quality criteria assign Brook Benton to an audience possessed of a certain maturity, serenity and musical knowledge, an audience which has an ear for really good singing and which is also ready for, and receptive to the nuances in this singer's interpretations.

Mercury

It's Just A Matter Of Time

Soon after his first big hit, 'It's Just A Matter Of Time', a Benton LP of the same title came onto the market. However, the title track is the only number on the album from the writing team of Benton, Otis and Hendricks. 'Tell Me Your Dream' was arranged by Brook and Bert Robinson. The rest of the material consists of standards, on which the Belford Hendricks Orchestra accompanies the singer throughout.

Brook Benton's attempt to establish himself as a ballad singer through a body of well-known songs was without doubt a success. Accompanied by a large orchestra with horns and strings, he works with predominantly smooth material. None of the songs demands Benton's wide vocal range, and they develop softly and pleasantly. Occasionally, he plays with his low notes, adding individual colour to the songs. Brook demonstrates a solid vocal mastery. His intonation, modulation, timbre, phrasing, and a wealth of variations reveal a magnificent singer who demonstrates his ability to swing on numbers like 'Tell Me Your Dream' or 'Love Me Or Leave Me', but who can also endow slow songs like 'I'll String Along With You' or 'The Nearness Of You' with rhythmic tension. This ability to build rhythmic tension despite long vocalized syllables is one of the trademarks of Brook Benton's vocal art. The swing element often pushes him away from short final syllables into the middle of entire phrases or polysyllabic words with long and also short vowels, which he always spreads over several notes.

This technique is undoubtedly a legacy of African-American

hymnal music: the gospel music and spirituals which constitute Brook Benton's musical foundations. Benton realizes his particularly elegant brand of swing simply through perfect timing, first delaying the start of his vocal – which stretches the interval between the beat and deployment of the voice – then accelerating the vocalization as is necessary. It was not without reason that the English music critic Ray Coleman wrote of the 'inherent swing' of Brook Benton's music. By that he meant that Benton always swings, even on slower, rhythmically calm material, by varying individual passages which he infuses with his characteristic way of building up the tension on the offbeat. This fact is evidenced by countless examples of Brook's work. One needs look no further than the transition in 'The Nearness Of You' and the lines *'When you're in my arms / And I'm feeling close to you'* for immediate confirmation of the aforementioned. Passages from Brook's wonderful 1966 album, *That Old Feeling*, which contains only slow standards, demonstrate time and again his ability to also imbue slow-paced songs with rhythmic tension. Another case in point is the Joe South composition, 'Don't It Make You Wanta Go Home', which Benton recorded in 1970 for Cotillion. Thanks to his phrasing towards the end, this restrained, slow number becomes an extremely swinging affair.

Another aspect of Brook's approach to singing which is conspicuous from the outset is the care with which he embraces each individual word, every syllable, wrapping his voice around them, differentiating them tonally and handling them sensitively in order to convey the lyrical message of a particular song. The art of song is the art of sound, and because of that, every aspect of text that is set to music is important. The pretentious treatment of words and syllables sometimes results in a rather overstylized mode of singing, a type of mannerism which one may now and then feel is exaggerated, but which was also preformed within African-American religious music and from there went on to greatly influence black secular music – notably the many forms of jazz, blues, R&B, soul, etc.

Brook Benton will later develop his style and voice further; however, the singing technique described here will remain one of his trademarks. Irrespective of what material he works with in future – pop, standards, blues, country, soul, even something jazzy – it will always be Brook Benton, not some poor imitation or concession to the tastes of the day, that serious devotees of his music will get to hear and treasure. His first LP holds a promise of further artistic development that cannot be rated highly enough.

Endlessly

Brook Benton's second album appeared in 1959 and, like the first, was named after one of the singer's big hits at the time. As before, the title song is the only one on the LP co-written by Benton; the remainder are once again all standards. This second Brook Benton album is structured more or less along the same lines as his first, though it is rather more rhythmically accented. The title song, 'Endlessly', possesses significantly more of a tempo than 'It's Just A Matter Of Time', while 'People Will Say We're In Love', 'Blue Skies' and 'Around The World' are truly rhythmically propelled numbers. The sleeve notes make reference to this and, using the example of 'Around The World', rather vaguely point out Benton's own unique rhythmic treatment of a song: he keeps the beautiful melody alive, yet puts the drive of an express train behind it, belting across the message in a dynamic way.

Benton is even described as the greatest rhythm singer of all time. Now, while there is no 'greatest' or 'best' within any art form, it is possible to speak of 'greats' whose work may be on a similar level, even though there may be differences in content or form between them. Overall, the record is a beautiful concoction and, like his first album, also needs to be viewed as an attempt to position Brook Benton as a ballad singer in contrast with the prevailing rock'n'roll idiom. Songs like 'Because Of You', 'More Than You Know', 'Time After Time', 'A Lovely Way To Spend An Evening', 'The Things I Love' and 'May I Never Love Again' – material that constitutes part of the body of classic American songbook – support this claim. In the arrangements, string instruments strongly dominate the proceedings. In this, the album differs somewhat from Benton's first, where the sound picture is partly defined by horn sections.

I Love You In So Many Ways

Comments regarding the musical style of this 1960 album are similar to those applied to both its predecessors. This LP, which was again named after one of Benton's current hits, consists entirely of slow, stately music, although this time the majority of the songs selected are not standards. George & Ira Gershwin's beautiful classic, 'Someone To Watch Over Me', is contrasted by new material: eleven songs, seven of them co-written by Brook. In the commentary on the record sleeve, Lou Sidran emphasizes the mastery with which Brook handles the words of a song, and suggests that his senses in that regard may have been sharpened by his occupation as a songwriter. He also stresses the many possibilities for expression within Benton's voice that enable him to alter his delivery within a song without jarring either the ear or the pulse of the audience. The writer cites Brook's performance of 'Someone To Watch Over Me' as an example of his outstanding interpretative skill. In particular, the singer's treatment of the middle section demonstrates that he has genuinely understood what Gershwin was trying to convey through this song.

Two numbers on the LP (the title track, 'So Many Ways', and 'So Close') also made the singles charts. In many places, the latter song reveals a singer who understands how to sing expressively and whose repertoire does not need to be built solely on melodious sound. All the other songs on the album feature smooth singing, which makes for pleasant listening, but is hardly likely to take the listener's breath away, while the ending of 'In A Dream' exhibits a noticeable pull in the direction of operetta.

Two more Brook Benton albums were released in 1960: *The Two Of Us*, which includes amongst other things the legendary duets with Dinah Washington, and *Songs I Love To Sing*. Because the musical structure of the latter fits the same framework as Benton's previous LPs, it is discussed first.

FOOLS RUSH IN
IT'S BEEN A LONG LONG TIME
THEY CAN'T TAKE THAT AWAY FROM ME
BABY, WON'T YOU PLEASE COME HOME
I DON'T KNOW ENOUGH ABOUT YOU
WHY TRY TO CHANGE ME NOW
OH! WHAT IT SEEMED TO BE
SEPTEMBER SONG
MOONLIGHT IN VERMONT
I'LL BE AROUND
LOVER COME BACK TO ME
IF YOU ARE BUT A DREAM

Songs I Love To Sing

Brook personally chose all the material for this album while he was convalescing in hospital. In doing so, he selected songs which he regarded as being among the most important within the American musical canon. The result was this wonderful collection of standards, which was reissued by Verve in 2003. The CD was accompanied by a string of well-meaning reviews which put the high musical quality of the album into perspective. The similarity between Brook Benton's and Nat Cole's vocal styles is cited, but it is also appositely noted that Benton proves that great singing doesn't depend on the material.[39] *All Music Guide's* Joe Viglione also thinks that Brook sounds like Cole on some recordings on the album. The similarity in phrasing and vocal structure are astonishing. The high regard which Benton's version of Rube Bloom & Johnny Mercer's 'Fools Rush In' engenders is also interesting. His performance is described as 'classic', and the entire record is rated as something special.[40]

'Fools Rush In' also made the charts. The number stands out markedly from the rest of the material on the album because of its tempo, and also contrasts with other popular versions of the song. The many monosyllabic words in the lyrics incline towards a swinging

---

[39] David Rickert, Internet.
[40] Joe Viglione, *All Music Guide*.

interpretation and may have prompted the arrangement of the song conceived by Benton and Clyde Otis. All the previously mentioned characteristics of the singer's swinging style are present here: the delay before he comes in with the vocal; the amazing drawing-out of vowels and the subsequent acceleration in articulation; the creation of an offbeat feel by the corresponding singing of several notes on one vowel, etc.

In a 1984 interview, Brook explains the concept behind his arrangement of this song. 'Fools Rush In' was always given a ballad treatment, and it was one of the first songs that he consciously remembered hearing. But he didn't see the song as a ballad. *Only fools*, he thought, *rush blindly into something* – so he wanted to do the song as an uptempo version, and not as a ballad. He set the song to a faster tempo, and it was successful for him.[41] Although they are performed at a more moderate pace, 'Lover Come Back To Me', 'Baby Won't You Please Come Home' and 'They Can't Take That Away From Me' are other thoroughly rhythmically tight, swinging numbers.

Overall, the LP reveals a singer who has attained maturity. His voice has become fuller, his intonation is perfect, he effortlessly holds the long vowels, his vibrato is elegant and unobtrusive, and his variation of the musical material is executed in a playful manner. The opening track, 'Moonlight In Vermont', ranks among Benton's most outstanding vocal performances on the album. It is a pearl amongst all of his recordings up to that time. The mellowness of his singing is like the mildness of moonlight which lends soft contours to the surroundings, but without making them indistinct. The intonation of the word *bend (in the road)* and the last syllable of the word *hypnotized (by the lonely evening)* in the bridge, and the straight singing of the written note over the span of an octave prove that Benton is an accomplished singer.

Brook's beautiful, sensitive whistling is also to be heard here for the first time. Other songs such as 'It's Been A Long Time', 'If You Are But A Dream', 'Why Try To Change Me Now', 'September Song', 'Oh! What It Seemed To Be', 'I'll Be Around' and 'I Don't Know Enough About You' similarly place high aesthetic demands upon the listener. In Joe Viglione's opinion, Brook's rendition of 'September Song' should have been included on one of the Kurt Weill tribute albums.[42] Throughout the entire LP, Benton's voice is again reminiscent of Nat Cole, and its quality has variously been described as velvety, silky or mellow. This classification has become a kind of hallmark for Benton's singing; an unimpeachable seal of quality, notwithstanding the fact that

---

[41] *Solid Gold Scrapbook: Birthday Salute*, ibid.
[42] Joe Viglione, ibid.

his voice is capable of much more nuance and expression than reviewers generally give him credit for. As an artist, Brook Benton operates on two levels. He enjoys great success as an interpreter of hits mostly co-written by himself, which cause a stir in both the pop and R&B charts. However, the singer's albums contain rather different material, in that they don't have the same kind of mass appeal as his hit singles, but showcase a vocalist who can handle the most diverse material and who cannot simply be catalogued as a pop singer. It is nevertheless astonishing how much favour Brook managed to find with the public – and this during a period principally dominated by rock'n'roll.

The musical character of each of the three albums discussed so far is broadly the same: each LP contains one or other of the singer's hits, but predominantly features standards known to the listener in both vocal and instrumental versions: smoothly flowing music interrupted from time to time by a swinging number.

**The Two Of Us
(Brook Benton & Dinah Washington)**

Content-wise, the LP does not deliver what it promises. Only four of the twelve songs are actually duets; the remaining eight numbers are split evenly between Brook and Dinah. The duets are 'Baby (You've Got What It Takes)', 'A Rockin' Good Way (To Mess Around And Fall In Love)', 'I Do' and 'I Believe'. The most successful of these was 'Baby', which reached No. 5 in the *Billboard* 'Hot 100'. 'A Rockin' Good Way' registered at No. 7. Both are uptempo numbers created from the

Above and right: Brook and Dinah rehearsing at the *Two Of Us* session.

same mould. 'I Do' and 'I Believe' are catchy but slower recordings which did not achieve the same popularity as the two rockers. The remaining songs on the LP are also predominantly slow material, except for the mid-tempo 'Because Of Everything', a solo performance by Brook.

During the recording of 'Baby (You've Got What It Takes)', an argument blew up between the two artists, which it is difficult to know what to make of. The cause of it was a part of the song which was intended for Dinah, but which Brook barged in and took instead. Brook spoke about this incident on a number of occasions. Dinah had trouble remembering the words, so he had supported her during rehearsals by loudly recapitulating her lyric. In doing so, the exact sequence of their respective cues slipped his mind, and it so happened that, during their recording, Brook suddenly began singing one of her parts. Dinah immediately screamed, 'You're in my spot *again*, get out of my spot!'

To Brook, that was a distortion of the facts, as it had never happened before, and he laughed about it. In his own words, he almost exploded with laughter. Clyde Otis recorded this mistake. Brook was ready to repeat the whole thing, and even pushed for it, but Clyde just said, 'We've got it, we've got it!' Brook complained about the error, but Clyde stuck with his 'We've got it, we've got it!' Brook's artistic

perception drove him to repair mistakes, but Clyde did not correct what Brook had termed a mistake. The record was a success, selling a million twice over.[43]

After this incident, Dinah was no longer willing to continue working with Brook, and so the proposed joint album became an LP which contained more solo numbers than duets. Whether there were also other reasons for her attitude – say, some competitiveness she would not admit to – is difficult to establish. Considered objectively, the short-lived nature of the Clyde Otis-initiated project was a loss to the music world, as well as for the two protagonists.

Benton, who sings with greater stamina and a more flexible voice than Washington, was more than simply a congenial partner for

---

[43] US radio network, 4-5 October 1984.

the Queen of the Blues. On the two rocking numbers, 'Baby' and in particular 'A Rockin' Good Way', Brook, with his mellow voice weaving around the basic melody and his special way of swinging, is the ideal foil for the more abrupt, drier, harder-singing Dinah and her dramatic accenting. The two could quite effortlessly have created not just one album together, but also at least a second. If one listens to the songs which Dinah recorded solo not long after – say 'Early Every Morning' or 'We Have Love' – and compares them to the similarly styled duets on *The Two Of Us*, one can clearly sense how these and other titles might have succeeded, had they been recorded as duets by Brook and Dinah. Moreover, it is evident how greatly Brook's elegant vocal artistry inspired Dinah's way of singing.

There is a discussion of the *Two Of Us* album on the Internet by Kohji 'Shaolin' Matsubayashi.[44] Technical data for the entire production are meticulously listed. The Belford Hendricks Orchestra supplied the instrumental accompaniments for all the duet recordings. Joe Zawinul's piano contribution is singled out for special mention. (Zawinul confirmed his presence on the session in an interview with Hans Maitner at a concert in Vienna in 2004.)

The review of the album by Shaolin suffers from a rather clumsy judgemental comparison of the two vocalists. Shaolin reckons that Dinah Washington is, without a doubt, the Queen who can sing everything, and that she sings much better than Brook, as evidenced by the ballad 'There Goes My Heart'. That the reviewer chose to prove his point with a song which Brook didn't record until six years later for RCA with the Billy May Big Band suggests a certain lack of awareness on his part. The comparison 'better' or 'worse' is misplaced when it comes to greats like Dinah and Brook. The assertion that Dinah sings much better than Brook is both unobjective and incorrect. Nevertheless, Shaolin does concede that Brook Benton possesses a mellow but deep vocal texture.

In reality, Washington must have been a very unbalanced individual. Ruth Brown recalls that, in the '50s, she was once invited up

---

[44] shaolin@microgroove.jp, 18 March 2004.

on stage by her at Birdland. The audience demanded that Dinah let Ruth sing, and she agreed. While Ruth was singing, Dinah disappeared to her dressing room. When Ruth had finished her song and was being loudly applauded by the audience, Dinah stormed back on stage and chased her off. After the concert, when Ruth and her husband paid their respects to the eccentric Dinah, the Queen told her fellow performer, 'Well, I will take the time to give you my autograph, Ruth, 'cause the truth of the matter is you can sing. But you ain't s'posed to come on other folks' shows an' take over – 'specially my shows!'[45]

It would be very easy to blame Dinah's insecurity and unacknowledged over-competitiveness for her disproportionate reactions. But the disagreements between her and Brook conducted in the public gaze went further. On one occasion, Brook was booked to appear at the Regal Theater in Chicago. Dinah at that time was running a club in the city called the Roberts Show Lounge, and Brook, Ruth Brown and other artists from the Regal show visited Dinah there. Dinah was on stage and began introducing the various performers. When she invited Brook to come up on stage and they began singing their recently recorded duet, 'Baby', a problem arose. Brook, who was feeling mischievous, changed the lyrics and sang, *'Baby, you've got what it takes... 'cept I wonder why you can't hold a man.'* As he did so, he looked her straight in the eye. Dinah stormed off stage through the swing door, came back a few seconds later with a meat cleaver and went after Brook. He reportedly took one quick look and fled for his life![46]

Dinah's sixth marriage had recently failed, and if Brook knew about it, then his joke was hurtful and in poor taste. Washington's reaction was in keeping with her impulsive character, but at the same time exposed her vulnerability and insecurity.

Clyde Otis gives a somewhat different account of this incident, which Robert Pruter included in the booklet he wrote for the expanded reissue of the album in 1994: he and Brook had gone to the Roberts Show Lounge, where Dinah was performing. The pair's duets went really well that night, but while Dinah was singing she made some reference to 'that dumb so-and-so who couldn't sing the duets right'. Brook immediately leapt out of his chair and called her a bitch or something similar. Ray Charles, who was also there, jumped in to berate Brook for his language and calm everyone down.

The owner of the club, Herman Roberts, paints a really good picture of Dinah's contradictory personality. According to him, Dinah

---

[45] Ruth Brown/Andrew Yule, ibid.
[46] Ibid.

was both vain and insecure. She especially displayed her insecurity in her dealings with Brook Benton, who was a great singer. She and Brook could have recorded together with great success. They could have made a fortune, but Dinah never worked with him again. And every time Brook came into the club, she made a big commotion in order to avoid having anything to do with him as a fellow artist. Her psychological problems constantly stopped her from becoming one of the greatest singers of the era.[47]

Of course, nowadays everyone knows that Dinah without doubt ranks amongst the great female singers. We can only dream of what artistic heights a longer collaboration between Dinah and Brook might have led to.

Benton's nephew, Brook Grant, does not think there was any real hostility between Dinah and Brook, and that a lot of it was just played up. The events which followed Dinah Washington's untimely death in 1963 testify to his statement. Brook happened to be booked to perform at Basin Street West in Los Angeles. When the club closed in remembrance of Dinah until the Friday of the week of her death, he flew to Chicago to attend the funeral ceremony. Upon his return to LA, he dedicated a special memorial show to her.

Despite all the fussing and fighting between them, Brook and Dinah had enjoyed a long friendship. At a press conference held at the time Brook opened his engagement at Basin Street West, he told several disc jockeys of plans he'd made to record new material with Dinah, and of other plans for including her in numerous projects of his Brook Benton Enterprises.[48]

Unfortunately, the life of Brook Benton Enterprises proved all too short. However, Brook was able to render one final service to his deceased colleague as a pall-bearer at her funeral. The song 'This Bitter Earth', which Brook recorded for Mercury in 1964, is his homage to Dinah Washington. He chose it because it was one of Dinah's favourites, and, in his opinion, one of the songs into which she poured all the soul and feeling that were pent up in her heart.[49]

Brook's granddaughter, Ammayeh Yisrael, first heard her grandfather sing the Clyde Otis composition when she was seven years old. The music inspired her to write a poem with the same title, which was later published in a book called *Enchanted Dreams*. It is a touching little work of art which expresses pain, fear and hope, and does justice to both artists' personalities – Dinah's as much as Brook's:

---

[47] Dempsey J. Travis, *An Autobiography of Black Jazz* (Urban Research Institute, Chicago) 1983.
[48] *Los Angeles Sentinel*, 19 December 1963.
[49] *St Louis Argus*, 3 April 1964.

This Bitter Earth

This bitter earth,
Here I stand.
This bitter earth,
I love to hug.
This bitter earth,
Till heaven awaits.
This bitter earth,
May bless us all.

If You Believe

This 1961 LP is Brook Benton's first album of spirituals. It contains everything that the average 'divine music' listener could hope and wish for: the sounds of timpani, bells and harps, a powerful choir behind the soloist, and above all music that trickles like liquid wax into the listener's ears. The accompanying sleeve notes describe in rather exaggerated fashion the reaction of the participants and those in charge after the end of the recording session: there were engineers and music experts on hand in the recording studio who felt the same feeling of elation and excitement that must have been felt by the engineers and experts at Cape Canaveral when America's first manned space vehicle roared off the ground successfully. One can accord with the statement that this spiritual album is sung with an intensity of feeling rarely experienced before. Gospel aficionados might perhaps criticize this record for a lack of originality and insufficiently ecstatic expressive power, and for polished arrangements and a smoothness that prevent expressive and spontaneous utterances, which are an essential defining characteristic of this music, from emerging.

These reproaches to the album and its musical conception are partially deserved. However, one ought not fall into the trap of comparing live gospel music – such as that heard at a gospel meeting – with a gospel or spiritual concept album that is to go on sale and has to appeal to a wide range of public tastes. What record productions are not subject to commercial imperatives determined by the industry? When appraising this album, one must also bear in mind that Benton was a Methodist, and thus belonged to a religious community whose faith manifests itself more quietly and calmly than, for example, that of the Baptists. This fact certainly fed into the conception of the album and helped to determine its style. Additionally, *If You Believe* was the first Benton album not to feature strings. All the songs on it including 'The Lost Penny' were arranged and adapted by Brook Benton and Malcolm Dodds.

As a singer, Brook performs at the highest level on this production. The heights he attains on the well-known 'Go Tell It On The Mountain' surpass anything he had previously recorded. In Benton's version, the song develops into a swinging, expressive hymn that lives up to the genre's name. In particular, the multiple repetitions of *'Go (and) tell it'* towards the end of the song are almost unsurpassable as far as what one expects from gospel ecstasy. Swinging elegantly, Brook interprets 'Shadrack' with a shot of humour.[50] Several other songs on the album likewise offer undivided pleasure, for example 'Going Home', 'Steal Away', 'Remember Me', and especially his heartfelt rendition of 'Just A Closer Walk With Thee'. Paul Newman performed this song in the peerless film *Cool Hand Luke* (1967) in the same laid-back manner as Brook Benton – or, more precisely, delivered it in a breathy *Sprechgesang*[51]. They both succeeded, in their own way, to articulate the longing of being closer to God that is intrinsic in the song.

After completing the *If You Believe* album, Brook expressed satisfaction with his life so far and with his new spirituals LP. He said he loves singing, no matter what style it is, and is very happy with all the songs he has written and recorded. He said he experienced the greatest satisfaction of all from his new spirituals album.[52]

---

[50] The song was also included in the *Golden Hits (Volume 2)* anthology.
[51] A style of singing which is between speaking and singing.
[52] *Hit Parader*, September 1961.

The Boll Weevil Song and 11 Other Great Hits

From the very beginning of his career, Brook Benton had been treated as a ballad singer, and the 1961 *Boll Weevil* LP is absolutely the singer's ballad album. One characteristic of ballads is their story-telling nature, and in this album twelve stories are told which are distinctive from each other in their lyrical content. Benton presents to the listener tales which are ironic and humorous, sad, dramatic and tragic; tales which radiate hope, and which occasionally deal with almost-abstract events. He matches his style of singing to each type of material: there are pop-styled numbers and country music, as well as blues-inflected and swinging songs.

The title track gave Brook the highest chart placing of his career: No. 2 in the *Billboard* 'Hot 100'. Related by the singer in *Sprechgesang*, this ballad, an argument between a boll weevil and a cotton farmer whose fields have been invaded by the pest, belongs to America's musical tradition and has been interpreted by many artists. The idea to adapt the song came to Brook while he was driving to California. He would sing it while travelling, but never seriously thought about recording it. When he did, it became a smash hit.[53]

Brook explained the story in more rather detail in a radio interview. At one show he did, the audience demanded an encore, for which he wasn't prepared, so he started singing 'The Boll Weevil Song'. He played with the song and the audience, and changed the lyrics – which of course is permissible in a live show. The crowd laughed and were delighted with it. Initially, Brook didn't realize how much audience appeal the number had. He later told Clyde Otis about

---

[53] *Hep*, December 1963.

it, and after he had demonstrated the song, Otis thought they simply had to record it.[54]

Brook's daughter, Vanessa, recalls that her father was an admirer of the blues singer Huddie Ledbetter *aka* Leadbelly. Indeed, if one compares Leadbelly's 1945 version of 'The Boll Weevil Song' to Benton's, there are striking similarities. One can imagine that Brook had Leadbelly's version in mind while he was working on his adaptation.

The manner in which Benton performs this number is a mixture of rhythmic *Sprechgesang*, which advances the content of the dialogue between the farmer and the boll weevil, and a very swinging sung refrain, in which he additionally demonstrates his effortless ability to spontaneously vary the constantly repeated line *'We have/We've got a home'*, in which he not unintentionally stresses the word *home* with a low note. The vocalization of the narrative part of the lyrics through rhythmically accentuated *Sprechgesang* is an early anticipation of what eventually turned into that we now call rap. The entire recording sounds playfully spontaneous, exploding with musical creativity and musicianly joy that the listener can barely tear himself away from.

After 'The Boll Weevil Song', Clyde Otis parted company with Mercury and Brook Benton. He was replaced by Shelby Singleton, under whose tenure Brook would make subsequent recordings and albums for Mercury. The numbers 'Honey Babe', 'Frankie And Johnny' and 'The Intoxicated Rat' evince a swinging style similar to the title song. The story of the drunken rat comes closest to 'The Boll Weevil Song' in its structure. Here too, there develops a sequence of narrative rhythmic recitations and a sung, more strongly accented swinging refrain. Through his interpretation, Brook succeeds in making clear the message hidden between the lines: drink a little alcohol, and you become a different person; you are uninhibited and no longer able to correctly gauge your behaviour.

The most swinging number on the album is the tragic love story 'Frankie And Johnny', whose narrative and musical development progresses in parallel, as it were, from a certain epic dimension to a tragic climax which painfully lingers on during the song's fade-out. Incidentally, 'Frankie And Johnny' was the first recording Brook made with Shelby Singleton.

A very special gem to be found among the material on the album is 'It's My Lazy Day', a casually rendered number in which Brook seems to yawn the final *'It's my lazy day'*, making the attuned listener yawn as well – not because the song is boring, but because yawning is so contagious.

---

[54] *Solid Gold Scrapbook: Birthday Salute*, ibid.

Another highlight of the LP is Benton's version of Big Bill Broonzy's 'Key To The Highway'. Brook turns the rhythmic blues, as conceived and performed by Broonzy, into an internalized song, very bluesy, with overtones through which he – in contrast to the optimistic title – conveys the sadness and loneliness of the subject of the lyrics. During the fade-out, Brook turns in a beautifully whistled solo based on the musical theme, proving himself to be a genuine exponent of the multi-faceted blues genre. The song belies the *'And Eleven Other Great Hits'* part of the title. What Benton delivers on this album, also on the likes of 'A Worried Man', 'Johnny-O' and 'Four Thousand Years Ago', is magnificent interpretive singing and outstanding musicality that rise above any suspicion of wanting to be considered simply a collection of so-called hits.

In this, we should also not overlook the contribution of Stan Applebaum, who arranged all the material on the album and also conducted the musicians. Applebaum was responsible for the arrangements on many other artists' hits, as well as composing for famous big bands and symphony orchestras.

There Goes That Song Again

Following this album's release in 1962, there was immediate high praise from the critics: Benton proves again why he is one of the top male singers. His versatility knows no limits. Whether it is a swinging number or blues ballad, Brook Benton comes up with a winning combination of voice and talent.[55] Benton's extraordinary, thrilling voice

---

[55] 'Album Picks', *Music Vendor*, May 1962.

coupled with the tasteful musical accompaniment of the Quincy Jones Orchestra affords absolute listening pleasure. The album should appeal to a large number of the singer's fans.[56]

Brook Benton and Quincy Jones with his orchestra: this is a combination that only those in the class of musical genius could have conceived. The gifted singer, whose name alone evokes sound pleasures, teams with the talented young arranger and big band leader to present a dozen great standards that have never sounded like this before. Brook Benton's way with the ballad has established him as one of the country's top vocalists. With this album he also demonstrates his creativeness, giving a vibrant approach that introduces him as a swinging Brook Benton. Quincy Jones's provocative arrangements are showcases for Benton, and add tasteful musical backings to the singer's heartfelt performances... From their easy, swinging performance, it is obvious that Benton and Quincy enjoyed this recording session. There is no question that the listener will, too.[57]

The *Sunday Star*'s J. Sasso feels that Brook and Quincy, inspired by these twelve songs, have both delivered their best work so far. The reviewer calls them 'a powerhouse singer-arranger duo' and states: 'We're looking for top action on this one.'[58] In their 'Album Scoop' section, *Music Reporter* rates *There Goes That Song Again* as the best record.[59]

Brook had already been able to demonstrate his versatility with a countless succession of hits and the albums which were released in parallel with them. However, the 1962 LP with Quincy Jones and his orchestra was a new challenge for the singer. The record's sleeve note states very matter-of-factly that Benton reveals another aspect of his multi-faceted vocal style here: a creativeness that enables him to infuse familiar standards with an excitement and freshness that makes them sound new all over again. He accomplishes this with a vibrant, individual approach that will win him new followers in both the pop and jazz fields.

The album is a swinging, jazz-oriented production which has lost none of its exhilarating and exciting freshness in the 40-plus years since its creation and release. Quincy Jones's arrangements are timeless. They do not overwhelm the singer, but instead give him space to find complete vocal expression. And so, the entire work is filled with stupendous musicality, and one can sense the delight that all those involved in the production of this album experienced.

---

[56] 'Popular Picks of the Week', *Cash Box*, May 1962.
[57] 'On The Records', *Tan*, Chicago, September 1964.
[58] *Sunday Star*, 5 August 1962.
[59] 'Album Scoop', *Music Reporter*, May 1962.

It does, however, seem barely credible that Brook's shout, 'Quincy, let's do it – again!' at the end of 'All Of Me' was totally spontaneous, or that the repetition of the final chorus also just happened without having been rehearsed, as the record's sleeve note would have us believe. Then again, Jones did standardize the arrangement of 'All Of Me': an instrumental version of this number performed at a concert at the Sands Hotel in Las Vegas by Frank Sinatra and Count Basie and his orchestra is essentially the same.[60] It could, of course, also be that Quincy and his gifted musicians actually did respond so quickly and flawlessly to Benton's request. A discussion about this would be superfluous, since the entire album is characterized by spontaneous creativity, mainly thanks to Brook's vocal mastery. The orchestration and Benton's interpretations result in an unbelievable synthesis of musicality, joy in the melody, and swing.

Benton sings *bel canto*, expressively, he goes out on a limb with highs and lows. He sings spontaneously throughout, playfully improvising and always thrilling the listener. His dialogues with trumpeter Joe Newman during the fade-outs of many of the songs are musical gems. Simply listen to 'There Goes That Song Again', 'I Love Paris', 'Breezin' Along With The Breeze' or 'I'll Get By', and you will have to agree.

Most of the numbers on the album are structured and arranged so as to lead up to a climax at the end. 'When I Grow Too Old To Dream', 'There Goes That Song Again' and 'I Love Paris' are fine examples of this. In line with the instrumental introduction, Benton starts the latter in a minor key while improvising and changing the opening melody. After a brief, epically wide-ranging passage, he delivers the line '*I love Paris in the summer, when it sizzles*' in an extremely swinging manner, in his familiar *Sprechgesang* style. For a while, his voice continues the narrative in parallel with the orchestral arrangement, then, after an instrumental interlude, leads up to a swinging finale and a final switch to a major key. The big band in all its glory and Benton's powerful voice let the listener experience the rousing excitement of swing. The conclusion, featuring the swinging musical interaction between Brook and Joe Newman, has already been mentioned.

Purists may find fault with the dominant use of strings in the middle section of the song. In doing so, they overlook the fact that it is precisely through the use of strings and harmonica that a sound-picture is created which lends the song its special Parisian atmosphere. In actual fact, Jones had formerly studied in Paris under the renowned Nadia Boulanger.

---

[60] *Sinatra At The Sands* (Reprise 2FS-1019) 1966.

Strings also introduce the album's title track, whereupon Brook weighs in with an almost-unsurpassable intensive swing on the first two lines of the song. The not-too-short singing of monosyllabic words is, again, characteristic of Benton. As has already been outlined, the rhythmic tension is generated by his unique timing. The delay in the start of the vocal and the way in which Brook handles vowels result in lengthier sung syllables, and words and entire lines being charged with rhythmic tension. In order to keep the whole thing swinging, however, it is of course necessary to sing the occasional monosyllabic word in a very clipped way.

Let us consider the first four lines of the verse:

There goes that song again.
We used to call it our serenade.
We fell in love
When we heard it play.

Out of these 21 words, 19 are delivered monosyllabically, and all of them are drawn out apart from *fell*, which Benton curtails so much that it fuses with the following *in*. This way of swinging makes it possible for him to employ his vibrato whenever he thinks fit. Thus, he is able to demonstrate the mellowness and flexibility of his voice on any kind of musical material. In this respect, Brook differs significantly from Frank Sinatra, who essentially sings final syllables in straight time on swinging material, employing vibrato for the most part only at the end of a phrase or a line.

The *There Goes That Song Again* album offers an abundance of musical highlights out of which no song can be ranked above the others. The gloriously swinging opener, 'When I Grow Too Old To Dream'; the interesting, strongly swinging version of 'I Didn't Know What Time It Was'; 'Trouble In Mind', carried by Brook's powerful voice; the uptempo arrangement of 'Blues In The Night'; the painful 'I Don't Know Why (I Just Do)'; the refreshing 'Breezin' Along' With The Breeze, with its beautiful fade-out; the incredibly tense 'After You've Gone'; 'I'll Get By', which radiates peace and serenity; and the song which Brook adopted as a motto for his life, 'Let Me Sing And I'm Happy'; Brook Benton stamps his character on all of these and imbues them with inimitable qualities.

Let us now allow our Internet friend, Shaolin, who has already been quoted in connection with *The Two Of Us*, have his say. For this record too he supplies some detailed discographical information, but is again unable to refrain from making a judgement based on his personal taste. This time, he calls Brook a great singer 'who sings so mellow and smooth'. He describes the record as 'the singer's nice

Quincy Jones.

album'.[61] Of course, Brook was not a jazz singer, but he did have a deep understanding of each individual song. Shaolin's closing admission that he really loves this album 'too much' is also worthy of note.

Of course, some objections could be voiced regarding a certain superficiality in this assessment. However, any possible inaccuracies in this review are outweighed by the openly expressed undivided joy in this wonderful album, which can without any doubt be placed in the front row of all other relevant productions. It is a pity that the managers, the producers, or even the singer himself did not continue working in this direction. What magnificent musical fruits might have borne by a collaboration between Benton and Nelson Riddle – something that would have been more than possible during Benton's time with Reprise (see pages 85-7). Brook said that Riddle's orchestra was his favourite band.

Similarly, the opportunity to team Brook with small jazzy combos was never taken. The pressure of constantly having to produce hits undoubtedly prevented much, as far as artistic potential within the US music scene is concerned, from coming to fruition. Not without reason does a single released by Brook in the same year as *There Goes That Song Again* – 'Hit Record' – claim that a hit is the key to success.

According to Brook Grant, Quincy Jones apparently wanted to produce Brook Benton again. However, Brook was unhappy with the concept of the project he proposed, and so unfortunately the two never got to work together again. If this information really is correct, then one must certainly reproach Benton for being short-sighted.

It is a rather sad fact that, in his biography, Jones only mentions Brook Benton peripherally, in the same breath as many artists who have contributed to American culture. Brook was one of the first vocalists with whom he worked in the recording studio. During the time Jones was one of the top men at Mercury, he had been very close to the singer, made a great album with him, and rated him as a vocalist. Quite why Brook only gets a passing mention in his autobiography, only Quincy himself can explain.

---

[61] shaolin@microgroove.jp, 18 March 2004.

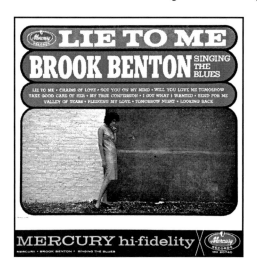

Singing The Blues

Also recorded and released in 1962, the album *Singing The Blues* (commonly known as *Lie To Me*) includes several numbers which are among the most-played Brook Benton songs worldwide. These include the magnificent opening track, 'Lie To Me', a very bluesy version of 'Chains Of Love', 'Got You On My Mind', 'My True Confession' and 'I Got What I Wanted'. 'Lie To Me', 'My True Confession' and 'I Got What I Wanted' also achieved some very respectable singles chart placings.[62]

The *Washington, DC Star* published a very interesting note regarding the album's genesis. Brook Benton's ability to swing had brought him success. Shelby Singleton, who was responsible for artists and recordings at Mercury, had been trying for months to persuade him to record in the relaxed surroundings of the southern city of Nashville. However, Brook was reluctant to record in the 'easy atmosphere' of Nashville for two reasons. Firstly, it meant there would be no written arrangements, and secondly, much of the material that was coming out of Nashville was not really his style. But Singleton won through, and the singer from South Carolina spent three days in Nashville, where he recorded several singles and an album. During the session, Brook was far from satisfied with the material that had been prepared for him. Because of that, he and Singleton's wife, Margie, stayed up all night writing 'Lie To Me'.[63]

Brook later explained in an interview exactly what happened. He came up with the title, then he and Margie began working on the

---

[62] See *Appendix III*, page 373.
[63] *Washington, DC Star*, 21 September 1962.

Brook with Margie Singleton.

song. They had never worked together before, but the ideas flowed quite easily. Nevertheless, he was under a great deal of pressure. They needed the song for the following day, and the worry of it not being ready on time was very stressful. Brook said that, at that time, he did not appreciate the meaning of 'Lie To Me', only that it meant not knowing the whole truth at a particular moment. He added that, financially speaking, the song had been successful for him.[64] The deeper meaning of 'Lie To Me' became clear to him later. He no longer wanted to sing the song – which is one of his best – in front of

---

[64] *Solid Gold Scrapbook: Birthday Salute*, ibid.

audiences, because he himself had been lied to far too often.

The outcome of the session overall prompted Brook to make some interesting comments. The musicians in New York come in, play their arrangements cold and collect their cheques. They have nothing in common with their southern counterparts. The musicians in Nashville, on the other hand, are accustomed to following the singer and capturing their mood. Everything is relaxed, and the result was a wild, swinging session.[65] Despite the swing feeling that pervades the LP, it consists predominantly of slow numbers, although 'My True Confession' and 'Send For Me' have faster tempos. Interestingly, Brook also included 'Looking Back', one of his biggest composing successes, which gave Nat Cole a No. 5 pop hit in 1958.

One can agree with the sleeve notes, which, in a brief review of the individual songs, describe 'Valley Of Tears' as probably the best cut on the LP. Fats Domino's simple rendition of the song simply burbles along rather insignificantly. Benton's version, by contrast, is conceived as a very slow number, but, thanks to the singer's renowned method of producing rhythmic tension, also swings powerfully. The offbeat feel is strengthened by hand-clapping, which accentuates the second and fourth beats in 4/4 time. The creation and augmentation of rhythm by hand-clapping is a favourite device in popular music. This method of producing a rhythm can also be found on other Brook Benton hits like 'I Got What I Wanted', 'Hotel Happiness' and 'Another Cup Of Coffee'.

Brook's interpretation of the song, realized here particularly through voice colour and articulation, allows its lyrical message to emerge very clearly. The highly musical and bluesily whistled passages fit harmoniously into the intended design concept of the recording. The underlying dark-blue-to-black feeling which runs through the song is palpable.

This unity of an intrinsic message and appropriate vocal realization applies equally to other songs on the album, especially to those numbers overflowing with self-doubt (Carole King's 'Will You Love Me Tomorrow' and 'Tomorrow Night') or expressing deep longing and devotion ('Pledging My Love').

In a Mercury Record Corporation PR release, Quincy Jones said of the album, 'Brook can do everything, and *Singing The Blues* proves it. They are not old, worn-out blues. They swing with a new style of phrasing and beat. The versatility makes for a refreshing new opportunity.' There remains just one question: Why did Quincy never again work with Brook?

---

[65] *Washington, DC Star*, ibid.

Best Ballads Of Broadway

1962's *Best Ballads Of Broadway* signifies another step in the development of Brook Benton's career as a singer. After the three earlier albums of standards, as well as the LP with Quincy Jones, which was likewise oriented towards standards, it became obvious that Brook Benton, like many singers before him, was now ready to take on Broadway musicals. From this point on, he would travel down at least two different musical paths. As before, Brook was able to continue adding to his string of hits with singles like 'Hotel Happiness' and 'Two Tickets To Paradise', while on the other hand he also recorded albums whose content was intended for a mature, consciously listening audience and only yielded an occasional hit every now and then. As was previously noted, the efforts of Benton's management to secure the singer's position as an acknowledged interpreter of classic American popular music certainly played a part in this.

Benton himself had never kept his fondness for this music a secret. The fact that, in doing so, he might have upset many fans who principally concentrated on his hits should not simply be dismissed. In 1983, Brook recorded a Christmas album which included a very swinging, sparsely orchestrated version of his 1961 release, 'This Time Of The Year'. In an Internet forum, a purchaser of the album who was surely a fan of his complained that this recording was jazz and had nothing to do with the original Christmas song. As is evident, Brook did not make it easy for his fans, especially if they did not really develop further, to follow him down this road to different material and its corresponding forms of expression.

If one were to advance one slight criticism of the *Best Ballads Of Broadway*, it would be that there is something of an imbalance in the relationship between the rhythmic and slow numbers. Four elegant and lightly swinging numbers pep up the album, but stand alongside eight slow-paced sustained-note titles. The sequences of three slow songs in a row on both sides of the LP can become tiresome, and of course bypass one of Brook Benton's outstanding talents, namely his feel for swing. The fact that this talent was utilized so little is an unforgivable failing on the part of those managers and producers who accompanied Brook on his way as a recording artist.

Be that as it may, Benton turns each of the numbers on the album into a true *song*, meaning he finds every note that conveys the emotional situation of the subject of the lyrics. And once again it is an entire palette of feelings that is woven through these songs: happiness ('Make Someone Happy'); inner joy and a sense of good fortune ('I've Never Been In Love Before'); sadness and serene wisdom rooted in personal experience ('Hello Young Lovers', 'Love Look Away'); and absolute emotional security ('If Ever I Would Leave You'). Brook makes all of this clear in his interpretations mainly through the colouring of his voice in each instance.

The arrangements by Luchi De Jesus are tasteful, but the choral accompaniments could perhaps have been deployed rather more sparingly, so as to distract as little as possible from the intimacy of his voice; for this body of songs in particular demands sensitive vocal treatment – something Brook attached great importance to. These songs express the mental state and frame of mind of particular characters from musicals in dramatic situations and may be likened to operatic arias. Like them, they are found at particular points within the plot and in each case represent an emotional or dramatic climax. Take the ending of 'Hello, Young Lovers', for example. If one grasps the intensity of the feelings expressed by Brook in the lines

> *I've got a love of my own,*
> *I had me a good love of my own…*

then one will understand what they mean. Benton makes the pain of lost love audible and palpable, but over-the-top arrangements can diminish this effect.

This extraordinary emotional intensity is an essential quality of this album which music lovers and experts appreciate, yet it makes no concessions to the audience who like Brook Benton as a hit singer. It demonstrates that the current assessment of Benton, which attempts to reduce him almost exclusively to the role of a hit singer, is incredibly short-sighted and completely overlooks his artistic potential.

Born To Sing The Blues

On 27 and 28 November 1963, Brook Benton recorded another album of high musical quality which one can likewise assume was in no way intended to be a hit, *Born To Sing The Blues*. And this record really does offer the blues, although on the one hand the substantial financial investment and the refined instrumental and choral accompaniments rather bypass the innermost essence of the genre, while on the other were scarcely necessary for an expressive singer like Benton. De Jesus again creates a tapestry of background music out of the choral and string arrangements against which Brook's voice is able to unfold. In front of this sound texture, he places solo instruments like the guitar, piano and woodwind – and especially the saxophone and clarinet. These create a truly bluesy mood in a swinging, groovy way, with the most versatile instrument, tonally speaking – the clarinet – contributing some particularly interesting and expressive blues elements on 'After Midnight', 'I Worry 'Bout You' and 'I'll Never Be Free'.

As good as the choral and string arrangements are, the grand overall concept at times comes across as overblown and could also have been planned around one voice – especially one like Brook Benton's. African-American arrangers have rightly been accused of the occasional excessive use of strings. The fondness for larger string ensembles has a socio-historical basis: it wasn't until the '50s that string players could be incorporated into recordings by black singers. We know that Clyde Otis was the first arranger to use black musicians in his string sections, and many successors of this great of African-American music let string orchestras in their arrangements swell to ever larger proportions. In truth, Brook Benton did not need any of that at all. On this LP, he sounds best when he is accompanied as sparingly

Brook chats with Luchi De Jesus during a break in recording.

Luchi De Jesus and Brook at the September 1963 session with Damita Jo.

as possible and is able to impart that which we call the blues in the most authentic way. On the Irving Berlin composition 'Nobody Knows', the deployment of the orchestra sounds almost like interference with Brook's performance, which, after the choral and instrumental introduction at the beginning, has developed into a dialogue between the singer and the lead guitar. At the bridge, the song reaches its climax. Brook sings *'I'd rather be'* with all the power his voice can muster, almost without any accompaniment, then artistically reduces the volume in the passage *'a sinker on a fishing line'*, at which point the orchestra comes in again behind the vocal. His near-solo vocal on 'Since I Met You Baby' is nicely bluesy and intimate, backed only by piano and clarinet, before first the choir and then the whole orchestra take over the accompaniment. On 'Every Goodbye Ain't Gone', the orchestra swings along with Brook's vocal in a perfectly fitting manner, but even so one can't escape the feeling that a proper big band might have been able to give the number even greater power.

The quality of this album, its concept and its musical realization needs to be acknowledged, for it contains some real highlights for the listener to discover, with Big Bill Broonzy's 'The Sun's Gonna Shine In My Door', Billie Holiday & Arthur Herzog's poignant 'God Bless The Child' and Benjamin & Weiss's 'I'll Never Be Free' conveying an absolute blues feel.

On The Countryside

Brook Benton's affinity with country music had already become apparent prior to this 1964 album. One only needs to think of 1962's 'With The Touch Of Your Hand', a slow waltz that would have fitted into any country hit parade, or the same year's 'Dearer Than Life', whose ingredients similarly pointed in the direction of this musical style. It therefore came as no surprise when the singer released a whole album of country classics. Good country music is always sustained by a shot of blues and swing, and, in an appropriate form, can most definitely be related to one part of the music Brook Benton had made up until that point.

The material for this LP originates from well-known greats of this musical style including Johnny Cash, Ernest Tubb, Bob Wills, Jenny Lou Carson, Faron Young, Rex Griffin, Eddy Arnold and others. Luchi De Jesus was again responsible for the arrangements and for conducting the orchestra. The parallels between the overall sound of *Born To Sing The Blues* and *On The Countryside* are obvious. The choir and orchestra accompany the singer, replacing the characteristic country fiddle; however, the jazzy rhythm section is a new element. The piano switches between country and gospel styles. The voice is always Brook Benton: there are no signs of the nasal, from-the-throat singing cultivated by many country singers at that time. Brook shows off the entire spectrum of his vocal power of expression: high notes from the chest, but also in a sustained head voice; low notes; vocal passages which are clear and clean are supplanted by guttural singing. He varies musical motifs, and one can feel his joyous creative will as he builds up the rhythmic tension ('Faded Love', 'All Over Again', 'Letters Have No Arms'), shines as a wide-ranging and epic balladeer ('My Shoes Keep Walking Back To You'), does justice to simple songs with his melodious voice ('Everytime I'm Kissin' You'), appositely conveys the inner pain of lost love ('I'm Throwing Rice', 'I'll Step Aside') and sings the darkest of blues ('I Don't Hurt Anymore', 'I'd Trade All Of My Tomorrows', 'Going, Going, Gone', 'Just Call Me Lonesome'). His version of the Johnny Cash number 'I Walk The Line' comes from the same session. However, it wasn't included on this LP, but appeared later on a Pickwick compilation.[66]

On The Countryside is a mixture of various forms of musical expression: country, pop, blues and even elements of jazz are to be found in this beautiful, high-quality synthesis which reaches its peak with the swinging, spontaneously sung 'All Over Again'. Its opening track, 'Going, Going, Gone', achieved a singles chart placing. This success was followed by a booking on a show at the New York Apollo commencing 14 February 1964. There, Brook appeared alongside Aretha Franklin, Irwin C. Watson and others.[67]

Paul Contestable of the *Catholic Courier-Journal* gives *On The Countryside* an exceptionally good review. Most of the songs on the

---

[66] See *Discography*, pages 237 and 281.
[67] *Famous Apollo*, February 1964.

album are highly enjoyable. He finds Brook's rendition of 'Faded Love' particularly impressive, and that other tunes ('Just Call Me Lonesome', 'I Don't Hurt Anymore', 'All Over Again' and others) are presented in a most provocative and enjoyable manner. Contestable says it is a special treat to hear some of these fine songs done without the cornball backing vocals that are so prevalent at this time.[68]

In the years that followed, Brook Benton would from time to time return to country music. In 1966, he released an album called *My Country* with the Anita Kerr Singers on backing vocals, and his proposed 1988 comeback was also to be initiated partly down the country music route.

This Bitter Earth

This LP was Brook's last on Mercury. *The Special Years*, which was to have followed it and includes seven (so far) unissued recordings, was never released.[69]

As mentioned earlier, Brook recorded the title track of this LP after Dinah Washington's death as a homage to the singer. The focus of the album is, again, the blues in Brook's unique interpretative style. Expressive singing alone is not Benton's thing, though he is undoubtedly capable of immense expressiveness, which he refines and ennobles with a polished vocal technique. Along with all the expression, the joy of melodic singing, care in the articulation of

---

[68] *Catholic Courier-Journal*, Rochester, NY, 6 August 1964.
[69] See *Discography*, page 280. The authors have found a single-sided test pressing of Side 1. This contains six tracks, including the previously unissued 'I'll Always Love You', 'On My Word' and 'Our Hearts Know'.

emotion within the lyrics, and, of course, a kind of mannered vocal shaping of the material can always be observed. It is a smooth form of blues, albeit one which always complies with the requirements of this musical form. The arrangements, again by Luchi De Jesus, are deserving of unreserved praise. As the singer's melody-giving dialogue partners, the rhythm section, guitar, harmonica and piano create the dynamic framework for almost all the songs. Only 'This Bitter Earth' and 'It's Too Late To Turn Back Now' have big string arrangements. The trio of female voices is used in a way which accentuates the drama of certain numbers, but never to the extent that the vocal arrangements appear overdone. This may be experienced to particularly good effect on titles like 'Don't Do What I Did (Do What I Say)', 'Please, Please Make It Easy', 'What Is A Woman Without A Man' and 'What Else Do You Want From Me'.

The record was rated excellent by the *Long Island Advocate*: 'Brook Benton, who possesses one of the smoothest and most appealing voices in popular music, sings as if nothing else in the world mattered in a soul-satisfying blues set that has success assured. Anyone who has ever before been impressed by a Benton performance will be very pleasantly moved by the artist's distinct treatment of the material on the album. An enjoyably spent 30 minutes.'[70]

In her review, Martha Jean (The Queen) refers to the sleeve notes, and at the end of her statement affirms that, in her opinion, Brook is back on the road to success.[71] Indeed, three numbers from the album – the bluesy 'Lumberjack', the Clyde Otis composition 'It's Too Late To Turn Back Now', and the rocking, swinging 'Do It Right' – did make the charts.

Two other songs with a swinging feel rank among the absolute highlights of the album. One of these is 'Fine Brown Frame', a modernized interpretation of an old song, where the piano and harmonica only have a function of short response and the chorus develops into an unobtrusive tapestry of sound in the background. This in turn gives Brook exceptional opportunities to assert his guttural, bluesily smoky voice. The refrain is again brought to life by the singer's richly varied stylings.

The second, 'What Is A Woman Without A Man', is similarly arranged. It is Brook's own composition, in which the singer humorously relates the story of Adam and Eve's creation and banishment from Paradise. It is only after the Creator takes Adam to task about the apple and Adam attempts to excuse himself with *'No, Mister Maker, that was Miss Eve'* that one realizes that the title 'What Is A Woman Without A Man' is injected with a good shot of

---

[70] *Long Island Advocate*, 7 December 1964.
[71] *Michigan Chronicle*, 26 September 1964.

irony: in truth, the object and subject ought to be exchanged here. We are already sufficiently familiar with Brook's swinging way of recitation from the *Boll Weevil* album, but the linguistic mastery with which he respectively intones the parts of the Lord and Adam reveals a considerable degree of acting ability on the part of the singer. All in all, the song ranks as one of his most noteworthy recordings.

'Do It Right' could be described as a very swinging, smooth rock'n'roll or R&B number. A finely tuned rhythm section lays down the foundation over which Brook's voice, swinging and dancing, is able to find expression in conversation with the guitar. The pain-filled 'What Else Do You Want From Me' and 'Learning To Love Again', a song in 6/8 time, are followed by 'I Had It', a number that fits within the genre of R&B. The final track on the album, 'It's Too Late To Turn Back Now', is reminiscent of country music's leading lights.

The contract between Mercury and Brook Benton was not renewed when it expired in 1965. It had been known for quite some time that this would happen. There had been a legal dispute between Mercury and the singer at the beginning of 1963. Brook had sued the company for breach of the contract he had signed on 23 October 1958. The amount claimed exceeded $750,000 in respect of copyright and other payments which the singer alleged the company owed him. On top of that, popular music tastes in America had changed since 1964: with the success of the Beatles, everything English became the preferred style, and many heroes of rock'n'roll and rhythm & blues were forced out of the market. Although he was a crossover artist, Brook Benton was also significantly affected by these changes, and the new managers at Mercury didn't want him any more.

Given the circumstances, Brook and Mercury could no longer work together, even though the company still had a catchy vocalist with wide appeal. Between March 1963 and July 1965 Brook had eleven songs in the *Billboard* 'Hot 100' – among them singles like 'Another Cup Of Coffee', a number based on the successful formula of 'Hotel Happiness'; the theme song of the film *A House Is Not A Home*, which was rated higher musically than Dionne Warwick's version[72]; the beautiful 'Lumberjack', on which Brook demonstrated his rich voice; and 'Love Me Now', his last chart placing for the label. An exceedingly productive collaboration between a singer and a record company had come to an end. Despite making great recordings, Brook Benton would never again be able to emulate the commercial success he had enjoyed during his time with Mercury. Between 1965 and 1970, he only managed eight singles chart entries, of which 'Rainy Night In Georgia' became his biggest international hit.

---

[72] *California Sentinel*, 5 November 1964.

RCA Victor

New Bag

Clyde Otis (left) and Brook Benton were caught smiling during their recent West Coast date for RCA-Victor. The sound that they worked with, with an LP in mind, was country music. Seems that everything came out fine.

In the liner notes of the excellent Rhino compilation, *Endlessly: The Best of Brook Benton*, Billy Vera writes somewhat superficially that Brook and Clyde Otis found a home at RCA Victor in 1965, where they managed to eke out one mid-level chart record, 'Mother Nature, Father Time'. In other words, they took the money and ran.

This terse statement demands a correction. Brook Benton signed with RCA Victor for three years in October 1965, but a little over two years later producer Jimmy Bowen already signed him to Reprise.

As well as the single 'Mother Nature, Father Time', the collaboration between Otis and Benton also yielded an album of the same title. Other fruits of the renewed cooperation between the two were the albums *That Old Feeling* and *My Country*, two musical productions of the highest artistic quality. There were also several noteworthy singles.

Mother Nature, Father Time

Essentially, this 1965 album offers the kind of fare that one was frequently accustomed to hearing from Brook Benton. The back cover includes the revealing wording *'Brook Benton – The way you like to hear him'*, a sort of programme of the musical material to be found on the record and its vocal realization by the singer. The majority of the tracks are bluesy ballads, interspersed with a few rhythmically stronger numbers.

A very objective and apposite review of the record may be found in the *Negro Digest*. It concludes that the album is a mixture of highs and lows. Brook invests the power of his pleasant, natural voice in a selection of songs, some of which, like 'You're Mine' or 'It's A Crime', are rather weak. The record's low point is an Elvis Presley-oriented rock number titled 'Foolish Enough To Try'. Since 'Kiddio', it has been known that Benton does not have to remain limited to ballads, but he surely is deserving of better uptempo numbers than those on offer here. Highlights of the album are the blues numbers, especially when Benton displays his talent for storytelling, adding not only the characteristic quality of his voice, but also a great deal of personality to such songs. Overall, it is not Brook Benton's best album, but the weaknesses are only to be found in the material. The voice can, as always, be relied upon.[73]

There is not much to add to this perceptive review. The quality of Brook's voice reveals itself on several recordings. It has a supple capacity, demonstrates expressive power, and the singer exposes himself through the emotion of his performance. 'Mother Nature, Father

---

[73] *Negro Digest*, July 1966.

Time' charted, and a Scopitone film for jukeboxes was produced.[74]

Perhaps the best number of the whole session is 'While There's Life (There's Still Hope)'. After a very bluesy instrumental introduction by a tenor saxophone and trombone, Brook comes in on the same note. Almost throughout the entire song the choir and strings create a continuously flowing sound which is accented during transitions by rhythmically arranged horn passages and a dialogue with the piano. At the bridge, the song is carried to a higher plane by Brook's soaring voice but returns to the tonic keynote at the end, whereupon the singer adds weight to the last word *hope* through his singular vocal treatment of the stressed vowel.

'The Song I Heard Last Night' is also deserving of mention. It is, to all intents and purposes, a trivial outing that works principally on account of its melodious sound. Brook stretches beautiful, long sound arches over individual single words (*wooooorld*), and in the first line (*'The song I heard last night, play it again'*), sings the last word *again* in the lowest note he has ever committed to wax, namely low D. He later sang an entire song in the same low key: the spiritual 'Going Home In His Name', on 1971's *The Gospel Truth*.

That Old Feeling

Released by RCA in 1966, this excellent Brook Benton album consists exclusively of standards. Here, Brook presents himself at the absolute peak of his development as a singer. His rich baritone voice unfolds

---

[74] This type of film can be described as the forerunner of video clips, without which popular music – particularly that for young people – is nowadays rarely marketed.

into highs and lows as he masterfully interprets musical themes without neglecting a single word of the lyrics. In doing so, he lifts these frequently sung and instrumentally played songs within the public domain from the level of the prosaic to a higher sphere of fully matured vocal and interpretative art. If they are just what RCA Victor ordered to provide new life for this bevy of familiar tunes, as the liner notes state, then Benton fulfils this task in the most wonderful way. His voice soars above the lowlands of ordinariness and takes the sensitive and cognisant listener on a journey of the highest musical enjoyment. Brook creates musical motifs out of single words and even syllables, and skilfully integrates them into the whole composition. He changes parts of individual songs without abandoning the basic melody, thereby engendering a curiosity as to how he will further develop the composition. 'Blue Moon' and 'Love Is A Many-Splendored Thing' are good examples of this. Meanwhile, his characteristic building-up of rhythmic tension can be clearly experienced on 'Peg O' My Heart' and 'Moon River'.

It is not easy to spotlight individual songs, but 'That Old Feeling' with its heavy emphasis on the lyrically significant word *old* at the end, and the intonation of the second syllable of the following word, *feeling*, is a real gem. Equally good are 'Call Me Irresponsible' and 'The Second Time Around'. 'A Nightingale Sang In Berkeley Square' is perhaps the most beautiful recording on the album. It is a song that plays with memory:

> *That certain night, the night we met,*
> *There was magic in the air.*
> *There were angels dining at the Ritz*
> *And a nightingale sang in Berkeley Square.*

The uniqueness of those two people meeting corresponds with the extraordinary fact that angels were dining at the Ritz and above all that a nightingale was singing in Berkeley Square. The brilliant vocal styling of the song befits the exclusivity of the situation, and through Benton's repetition the keywords *nightingale* and *sang* become separate, musically distinct motifs. The speaker in the form of the singer reflects on an event that is already imperfect: by the subtle nuancing of the words *good night* – they are initially sung on the same note – the artist makes it clear that, in his opinion, the encounter has turned into a relationship that still echoes. However, the way in which these two words are handled at the very end of the song follows a natural speech pattern, with the sound curve sinking between *good* and *night*, but references the ending of the song rather than an exit from the love story.

That Old Feeling was reissued on CD in 2004 along with another of Brook Benton's RCA albums, *My Country*, and left a lasting impression on music lovers. One fan writes in an Internet forum that he considers Brook Benton to be one of the best interpreters of romantic ballads he has ever heard. He describes *That Old Feeling* as his absolute favourite Benton album. His rich, seductive baritone caresses each song and transforms it into a classic of his own. Every single recording is flawless. 'Moon River' is described as the definitive version of the Henry Mancini classic. Finally, our music fan invites listeners to close their eyes and let themselves be carried away by Brook Benton's beautiful voice. There is nothing left to add.

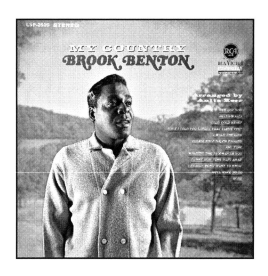

My Country

My Country, another RCA LP released in 1966 and again produced by Clyde Otis, contains – like *On The Countryside* – material from the realm of country music. However, the character of this record differs fundamentally from the Mercury production. Whereas that is structured around grand orchestration, a powerful choir and a stylistic mix of pop, country, blues and jazz elements, this album captivates with its leaner, but no means less consummate, arrangements and Brook Benton's intimate vocal artistry.

My Country was arranged by Anita Kerr. As leader of the Anita Kerr Singers, Kerr made many quality recordings with her choir. Additionally, the group were very busy providing backings for vocalists in the Nashville country hit factory. They can be heard on countless recordings by Bobby Bare, Hank Snow, Skeeter Davis, Porter Wagoner and others. On Benton's *My Country*, this choir is a style-forming element of a musical production which cannot be described as typical country music. As Harold Stern appositely remarks in his commentary on the record sleeve, 'When you buy Benton, you get Benton. You get a singer who puts his own stamp of individuality on every number.'

Brook turns all the material into standards: songs which one could also include in an American Song Book. As on many Benton albums, slow numbers, which are particularly suitable for interpretation, predominate. Two titles give Brook the chance to swing. Johnny Cash's march-tempo 'I Walk The Line' – which he also wrote – is turned into a highly elegant, swinging affair. In similar fashion, with rhythmic accents and also a shot of blues, Brook delivers the well-known 'Walking The Floor Over You', on which the Anita Kerr Singers swing no less elegantly than the soloist. These magnificent versions of two well-known numbers make one long for more, but unfortunately there are no others like them on the album. The majority of the songs are about lost love, and Brook puts all the sadness in the world into songs like 'Cold, Cold Heart', 'He's Got You', 'I Really Don't Want To Know' and 'Hello Walls'. The darkest of the songs is 'Gone', though Anita Kerr's arrangement places greatest importance on a pleasant sound. The simple song is full of resigned pain and cannot help but move every listener.

Benton creates a complex emotional mix of uncertainty and fear, as well as confidence and hope, that is palpable in songs like 'Please Help Me, I'm Falling', 'He'll Have To Go' and 'Have I Told You Lately That I Love You?'. Of course, none of these carefully selected songs crafted to the highest musical standard became a hit. Although country hits were produced in Nashville at the time, Benton's reworkings of country classics yielded nothing more than a listenable album of excellent interpretations. The entire long-player is infused with the aura of a mature vocalist, who, irrespective of what type of material he works with, produces something outstanding.

An impartial music fan who purchased the '2-on-1' CD reissue of *My Country/That Old Feeling* wrote of *My Country* in an Internet review: 'This is the best edition of old-time music that I have ever heard. The texts and singing, supported by the singer, are very pleasant and enjoyable to listen to. I recommend this album to all of those, young and old, who appreciate listening to authentic love songs.'

In his sleeve-note commentary, Harold Stern expresses the opinion that Brook, more than anyone else in today's popular music, seems destined to inherit the mantle of greatness worn by the late Nat 'King' Cole.

Sings A Love Story

This album was released in 1975 and contains previously unissued recordings from the sessions Brook cut for RCA Victor in 1966. These were variously arranged by Bert DeCoteaux, Ray Ellis and Billy May. All the material from *That Old Feeling* and *Sings A Love Story* was released in 1989 on the RCA CD, *This Is Brook Benton*. As well as the songs which are stylistically similar to those on *That Old Feeling* (of which 'More' is the most memorable), the numbers with Billy May and his big band are especially interesting. The record contains five titles by Billy and Brook, namely 'There, I've Said It Again', 'I Only Have Eyes For You', 'Unforgettable', 'There Goes My Heart' and 'Just As Much As Ever'. A further two titles with May – 'Sweet Georgia Brown' and 'Beyond The Sea' – appeared in 1991 on a Curb CD compilation titled *Greatest Hits*.[75]

May was a well-known and sought-after arranger and bandleader, and his arrangements for Benton are solid. However, they lack the spark, the electrifying swing, that Quincy Jones created, which in part is also down to the material. 'There, I've Said It Again', 'Unforgettable', a melody that is inseparably associated with Nat 'King' Cole, and 'There Goes My Heart' are all songs with a measured tone and not really suitable for swinging arrangements. However, the other two numbers offer more, rhythmically speaking. Despite the medium-paced tempo, 'Just As Much As Ever' swings intensively, and the Billy May Big Band joins in with this rhythmic feel with musical delight. Vocally and instrumentally 'Sweet Georgia Brown' and 'Beyond The

---

[75] See *Discography*, pages 247 and 293.

Sea', which were also recorded at these sessions, are executed reasonably well enough, but are unlikely to make anyone leap out of their seat.

Brook Benton – The Billy May Way [unissued]

The discovery of an entire album of RCA material, *Brook Benton – The Billy May Way*, in the UK in 2006 was a sensation.[76] The recordings were made in Hollywood and the record was pressed in the UK as a demo. There is a note on the label to the effect that these recordings may not necessarily be representative of the finished record and must not be used for review purposes. The album contains different versions of the five Billy May titles included on the 1975 LP, plus five others: 'Lover Come Back To Me', 'Makin' Whoopee', 'It's Been A Long, Long Time', 'I'm Beginning To See The Light' and 'Sentimental Journey'. The most notable difference is in Benton's vocal. Brook sings more softly throughout the entire album, with more of a sustained head voice; the vocalization emerges more freely and spontaneously; the feeling of openness – improvised singing and jazzy echoes – is noticeable. Moderate-tempo numbers with a heavy swing feel like 'I'm Beginning To See The Light', 'Makin' Whoopee' and 'Sentimental Journey', and especially the fast and very swinging 'Lover Come Back To Me', with superb accompaniment by the swinging Billy May Big Band, head in this direction. The relaxed, playful elegance with which Benton approaches the musical material is striking. The way in which he abandons the original notation of 'I'm Beginning To See The Light'

---

[76] For details see *Discography*, page 320.

in order to create his own song, as it were, lest he should return to the written melody again, is great improvisational class. All in all, this record, which is completely unknown even to the most serious Benton fans, is a treasure that shows yet another facet of this exceptional singer, and picks up again from that which was started with Quincy Jones on the album *There Goes That Song Again*, but was never taken any further.

Brook also recorded a string of singles for RCA, of which 'Keep The Faith, Baby' *b/w* 'Going To Soulsville' must be mentioned: two very bluesy numbers that he could really get his teeth into, which he sings with pleasure and expertise. This material also includes two Christmas songs, 'Our First Christmas Together' and the well-known Austrian carol, 'Silent Night'. Benton's version of 'Silent Night' may come across as slightly pompous, however the recording not only demonstrates his vocal capabilities, but also presents itself first and foremost as a genuine and convincing proclamation of the glad tidings of the birth of Christ that goes straight to one's heart.

Last but not least, the humorous tale related by Brook in the 'Roach Song' should not be overlooked. The content of this number and its elegant execution in rhythmic *Sprechgesang* with a heavily swinging sung refrain are reminiscent of the legendary 'Boll Weevil Song', but it did not become the blockbuster that was anticipated.

Reprise

Lining up in Las Vegas: the all-star cast at Reprise.
Left to right: Sammy Davis Jr, Bing Crosby, Frank Sinatra, Brook Benton,
Dean Martin and manager Finis Henderson.

Even before his contract with RCA had ended, Brook was signed to Reprise by Jimmy Bowen. Together with Buddy Knox, Bowen had emerged in the '50s as a singer in the rock'n'roll style, but with a country music orientation. His biggest hit was 'I'm Sticking With You', released in 1957.

Ten years later, as a producer for Reprise, he was hoping to take Brook Benton down the same road to success that Dean Martin, Sammy Davis Jr and Frank Sinatra were going down at Reprise, each of course with their own unique material. The solitary *Laura* album and a handful of singles were the fruits of this short-lived liaison. As one might expect, the producer's and singer's hopes remained unfulfilled, although Brook, as always, delivered some excellent work.

Laura, what's he got that I ain't got

The album's title track, 'Laura', a number with country roots, was the only Brook Benton Reprise recording to make the charts. Here Brook displays his strengths: a full, rounded voice, an absolute feel for swing with an ability to create a bluesy sound, and above all the ability to tell a story behind which the personality of the narrator can be sensed. A similar observation can be made with regard to 'Ode To Billie Joe', which was a hit around that time for Bobbie Gentry. It is interesting to note how the volume of both the vocal and the instrumental backing increases as the song progresses, and with it the drama. Sound-wise the final chord leads back to the beginning again.

 'Stick-to-it-ivity' is a truly beautiful number – the story of two frogs with different characters. They end up in a terrible situation that only Sam, who never gives up, is able to extricate himself from. It was the latest in a succession of similarly styled numbers ('The Boll Weevil Song', 'The Intoxicated Rat', 'The Roach Song' and others) which Brook relates humorously, ironically, but also with the necessary seriousness. The recitation of the epic tale and the swinging refrain alternate back and forth, and together with the great arrangement by Ernie Freeman result in a number that is exceptionally listenable. Naturally, the successful Sam also reflects a fair bit of the (slightly smug) American self-image.

 Other songs on the album that undeservedly attract scant attention are '(There Was A) Tall Oak Tree', whose content deals environmental problems; the beautiful medley, 'I Left My Heart In San Francisco–San Francisco (Be Sure To Wear Flowers In Your Hair)'; the country song, 'You're The Reason I'm Living'; and especially 'The Glory Of Love'. The way in which Benton slightly alters the melody, and plays with highs and lows in a rather mannered way – especially on the climax in the bridge (*'Hey, hey, we've got each other's arms'*) – is truly classic. In doing so, he fashions a work of art out of a simple pop song from Louisiana.

Overall, the album suffers somewhat from a sound that one was used to hearing particularly with Dean Martin, which strongly permeates several tracks. As a result, the old 'This Is Worth Fighting For' and particularly James Last's 'Lingering On' turn out as smooth, in part operetta-like pop numbers. 'Here We Go Again', a Ray Charles composition, was likewise deserving of a better arrangement.

Brook's view that he made good recordings at Reprise can be endorsed without reservation. Three further recordings which appeared on singles, 'Weakness In A Man', 'Instead (Of Loving You)' and 'Lonely Street', offer good music, even if it is principally oriented towards a melodious sound. The composer of 'Weakness In A Man', singer-songwriter and Grand Ole Opry member Jerry Chesnut, made some noteworthy comments about Brook's version of his song.

Jimmy Bowen produced the record on the West Coast, with the Hollywood Strings providing the backing. Jerry had just purchased a stereo system and when he got the recording and played it, he was overwhelmed. 'It was like taking a country songwriter's music to another level,' he writes. He was so overcome, that he actually had tears in his eyes as he listened to it. It was like having one of his daughters crowned Miss America, he said.

Brook performed the song to perfection, but this was how he always did things. Jerry adds: 'I loved this when he did this, and now, many years later, I still do.'[77] Brook later recorded a great version of another Chesnut composition, 'Woman Without Love'.

It is difficult to comprehend why Brook did not record any more material for Reprise. Perhaps there were reasons other than commercial ones which led to the termination of the contract between the singer and the company. At that time, the label's owner was Frank Sinatra, whose fellow Rat Pack members Dean Martin and Sammy Davis Jr were also on its roster. It would have been of great interest to Brook to work in the musical sector which Frank Sinatra serviced: swinging material with big band accompaniment. Indeed, he expressly named Nelson Riddle's band, who at the time accompanied Sinatra on most of his recordings, as his favourite orchestra. A tie-up between Riddle and Benton could definitely have yielded high-class musical results. Perhaps the shadow of a social issue in the broadest sense of the word had fallen over the relationship between Brook Benton and Reprise and outweighed a temporary financial setback?

---

[77] Jerry Chesnut Homepage, 02.

Cotillion

Brook Benton recorded his final single for Reprise in 1968. That same year, he began a collaboration with the Atlantic Records subsidiary Cotillion which proved exceptionally fruitful from an artistic standpoint. The offer from Atlantic had been on the table since 1958 – remember he recorded a demo of 'It's Just A Matter Of Time' for Atlantic as well as for Mercury – and this time Brook took Jerry Wexler up on it and signed on the dotted line. At the time, the company was enjoying great success with soul music. Brook Benton can, along with others, be described as one of the forerunners, developers and role models of soul.

To do this view justice, one must consider African-American music in its multiplicity of forms as the base from which soul would emerge as a specific musical direction. Between 1968 and 1972, Brook recorded a string of singles and five albums on Cotillion which rank among some of the best they ever released. Jerry Leiber, Mike Stoller, Garry Illingworth and most notably Arif Mardin worked on them as producers and arrangers, all with extraordinary skill and sensitivity. Everyone who was anyone was pulled in to assist: Cissy Houston, Myrna Summers, the Sweet Inspirations and others as backing vocalists; the Dixie Flyers (Mike Utley, electric piano and organ; Jim Dickinson, guitar and keyboards; Tommy McClure, bass; Sammy Creason, drums and percussion); King Curtis – the tenorman had previously played on Brook's first Mercury sessions in 1955; George Dorsey and Pepper Adams (reeds); Joe Newman and Neal Rosengarden (trumpets), Romeo Penque (flute), Benny Powell (trombone), Cornell Dupree and Jimmy O'Rourke (guitars), Dave Crawford (piano), Chuck Rainey (bass) and Billy Ziegler (drums) among others.

Benton himself took another step towards singing perfection and set a new standard for musical creative power with his voice. The recordings for Cotillion demonstrate that he is in a position to take on new challenges and further enhance his abilities as a vocalist and interpreter. Brook's collective output for Cotillion shows us a complete palette of his mature vocal possibilities. These include unbelievable high notes sung from the chest; intimately vocalized high passages in a sustained head voice; extreme lows, alternately *bel canto* and pure expression; and an incredible diversity of tone colours in his voice. Extraordinary phrasing, perfect timing, elegant swing, lyrical subtlety and an epic dimension to his storytelling are already familiar qualities of this singer, which he endeavours to further refine. Behind all of this can be discerned the personality and life experiences of an artist whose sung messages stir the heart and soul of all those who have the ability to listen to music in a serious way.

Artistic significance and commercial success diverge where Benton's Cotillion recordings are concerned. Out of approximately 60 released titles, just six made it into the charts, namely 'Do Your Own Thing', 'Nothing Can Take The Place Of You', 'Rainy Night In Georgia', 'My Way', 'Don't It Make You Want To Go Home' and 'Shoes'. Only 'Rainy Night In Georgia' was an international success.

Do Your Own Thing

This 1969 LP, half of which consists of singles, doubtless conformed with the musical notions Atlantic had associated with Brook. Thanks to his expressive and ecstatic delivery, 'Touch 'Em With Love', 'Nothing Can Take The Place Of You', 'Woman Without Love', 'Break Out' and 'She Knows What To Do For Me' present themselves as absolute soul numbers. But Brook wouldn't be Brook if he didn't stray from the beaten path time and again. 'Destination Heartbreak', wonderfully powerfully sung, is a song one would sooner attribute to the blues genre. Conversely, 'Set Me Free' could readily be classified as country music, for which the piano part used throughout the arrangement argues. 'Do Your Own Thing' is a sophisticated tune with an interesting harmonic structure. Sung by Brook with restraint, but also with intensity, it in no way degenerates into a cliché. 'Hiding Behind The Shadow Of A Dream' and 'I Just Don't Know What To Do With Myself' are two lyrical creations whose tenderness and deep sadness respectively are made audible and tangible by Benton in different styles determined by him, but with unerring emotionality. During this, the echoes of hymnal music forms in gospel and spirituals are obvious.

This brief portrayal of stylistic differences between the various titles on the album should be understood as an indication that narrow definitions in the field of art are no more than aids at best, which apply to a greater or lesser extent in individual cases. Brook Benton is unquestionably a soul singer, yet cannot be defined by this style of music alone.

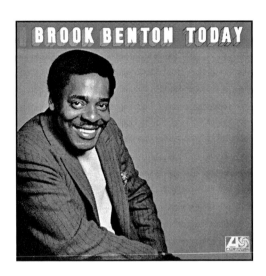

Today

This 1970 album includes two titles co-written by Brook Benton: the swinging 'Where Do I Go From Here' and 'Baby', a song also released by Joe Williams. Not every song on this album is first class, but some are unrivalled masterpieces. Specifically, the LP contains Brook's rendition of Tony Joe White's song, 'Rainy Night In Georgia', which is arguably the definitive version. During a 1975 UK tour, Brook revealed in an interview for *Blues & Soul* magazine that White had sent him hundreds of songs, and that 'Rainy Night In Georgia' was exactly what they had been looking for at the time.[78] It rightly became a huge international success for him and no anthology of Benton can be taken seriously if it does not include 'Rainy Night In Georgia'.

The record is a gem and was highly praised by the critics. If one starts from the premise that the art of song is a subjective expression of feelings which likewise communicates itself to those who resonate with it, then the composer, Tony Joe White, and its interpreter, Brook Benton, along with the musicians and arrangers, attained perfection here. The song's content, sound and rhythm create

---

[78] *Blues & Soul* 321, UK, December 1975.

an indissoluble unity which transfers itself in vibrations and waves to the listener, for the moment moulding and shaping his spirit, his emotion and the overall state of his personality. As always, Benton makes monosyllabic words as long as possible:

> *Neon signs are flashing,*
> *Taxi cabs are passing through the night...*
>
> *Find me a place in a box car...*

He lets them float, creates musical motifs from them, but knows to build up a close tension between them, which, together with his already present blues and soul feel results in a vocal art that cannot be classified under one simple label.

Brook also delivers a very individual interpretation of Paul Anka's 'My Way'. The song became the more mature Frank Sinatra's signature tune, so to speak, and his version has also become *the* interpretation of this title as far as the public are concerned. In contrast to Sinatra's reflective, even slightly complacent performance of 'My Way', Brook offers a completely different interpretation. In his hands, the song becomes an almost-despairing existential message that lays bare the self-doubt of the speaker, as to whether what he did was right or not. The elaborately arranged number, performed with a swinging rhythm, did actually make the charts, but was not the success for him that it deserved to be. Indeed, Brook personally believed that his 'My Way' was superior to 'Rainy Night In Georgia'. The orchestration, like his singing, was considerably more sophisticated, yet no one noticed that.[79]

'I've Gotta Be Me', a song discussed in more detail in the chapter on Civil Rights, is also commended here to the reader. Brook's interpretation of this title again diverged from the usual treatment and turned it into a lyrical gem whose beauty discloses itself to those who listen attentively and in doing so are able to discern the singer's intention.

Two very expressive numbers on the LP are 'Life Has Its Little Ups And Downs' and 'Desertion'. On both of these bluesy songs, Brook attaches less importance to beautiful singing, and more to the expressiveness of his voice. In the former, the singer exposes himself on the high notes, at times in a shrill tone, in order to do justice to the subject. 'Desertion' is the blackest number on the album. Brook relates a sad story in a blues style and with expressive singing. The dominant horn section in the background amplifies the dramatic tone of the ballad, while the low notes with which he operates here add further

---

[79] *Blues & Soul*, ibid.

intensity to this feeling.

The recording as a whole radiates soulful blues, or bluesy soul. 'Can't Take My Eyes Off You' is a fluently sung and free-flowing song. Benton's voice dances around the basic melody without really changing it. The pairing of Brook's voice with Cissy Houston's makes the performance somewhat over-emotional. A contrast to this is provided by the forceful, rhythmically accented 'We're Gonna Make It'. The triumphant *We*, sung long and high, followed by a strongly emphasized *gotta*, create a brilliant climax at the end of the song.

All in all, the album offers some very beautiful music and an excellent singer. It was not without good reason that it was reissued together with *Home Style* on a Rhino 2-CD in 2004. A Japanese issue of this album appeared in 2007 (see *Discography*).

Home Style

This album, which was also released in 1970, is one of the finest that Brook Benton recorded during his career. All the material selected for the LP is worth listening to because of the treatment Brook gives it, and several recordings are of the highest order, although they never became hits – possibly for that very reason. As ever with Benton, close listening is a must. The beauty and extravagance of his vocal performance reveal themselves to the cognisant listener and bestow upon them unexpected aesthetic, emotional and spiritual pleasures.

Brook again contributed a song to the album: the jazzy, swinging 'Let Me Fix It'. On this track, Brook simply glows with the joy of singing. His swinging dialogue with Mike Utley's organ, in which

Cissy Houston also participates in the background, now and again becomes a duet between Cissy and Brook. In one raggy, soulful final sit-in, a grooving rhythm section, the organ as solo instrument and creator of the basic rhythm, and lastly the Sweet Inspirations, together create a number to make the heart of any music fan beat faster.

Highlights of the album include three songs which again originate from the pen of Tony Joe White. 'For Le Ann' begins after a spoken introduction with a metaphor which reveals the composer to be a poet:

Memories of your smile rolled 'cross my mind

Brook's vocal realization and the arrangement correspond to the intentions the composer put into the song. Sadness and loneliness become palpable through the reflection of the speaker:

Why must it be so lonely together

Lost love affects him more than the pain of separation; it leads to the loss of his own soul:

I'll be a song without some soul.

The varied and persuasive continued repetition of this final line serves as a description and reinforcement of the emotional state expressed throughout the song. However, the notion that he could play in a mannered way with the word *soul* to allude to an analogous style-characteristic of soul appears not to have been in Benton's mind. Brook empathizes with the affected person – the subject of the lyrics – and speaks and sings from that standpoint, thereby making the listener conscious of his suffering.

'Willie And Laura Mae Jones' is a rhythmically vibrant, wonderfully swinging song. Brook again delivers it as if he were the individual affected, and one can truly believe every word. A time of carefree and unprejudiced coexistence and work:

We worked in the fields together.
We even learned to count on each other.
When you live off the land
You don't have time
To think about another man's color.

The mutual assistance and celebrations together have irrevocably come to an end. The happiness of the first three verses gives way to the more sombre tone of the fourth. The refrain

> *The cotton was high and the corn was growing fine,*
> *But this was another place and another time.*

is a kind of pictorial description of this unpostponable parting. The musical joy in the performance of all those involved stops the pain of separation from becoming too painful. The need for change is accepted.

'Aspen Colorado', also written by Tony Joe White, deals with various topoi of popular American music. Being born into modest circumstances:

> *I was born into a simple life*

The suddenly awakened need to get up and go:

> *Then there came a time in autumn I had to leave*

The time of restless wandering and a mostly futile search for work:

> *Tried to get a job in Alabama,*
> *But the man said he didn't need no one today,*
> *So I made my way home down to Memphis*
> *And stayed a few days.*

The unsuccessful plea of a mother to her son to come home, and the hero's goal to find himself:

> *There'll come a time in everybody's life*
> *When you have to search for peace of mind*

And finally the compulsion to move on, despite or because of the futility of all one's efforts:

> *So I might go (I'm going) to Aspen Colorado*
> *To spend some time, I hear it's fine.*

Apart from the occasional low note, Brook sings the song in a reserved manner, mostly with a sustained head voice. He sings soulfully, swings, and his vocal performance exhibits the highest elegance and a playful ease which are shaped with great interpretative ability. He highlights key words within the lyric by giving them special emphasis. Thanks to Brook's elongation of the word *leave*, the *'I had to leave'* at the beginning of the song becomes a necessity. A similar function is carried out by *everybody's*, which is demonstratively elevated to a high note, and the doubling and tripling of the word *search*. Not to mention the mother's imploring *'But please come home'*. Out of this beautiful song Brook creates a universe of hope, doubt, longing and reflection. He stresses the reflective tone in the final lines – especially on the word *hear* – thus conveying the ambivalence of the speaker's feelings.

Benton gives a very different treatment to Bob Dylan's 'Don't Think Twice, It's All Right', resulting in a version that could be described as a mixture of soul and country. After a very swinging transition introduced by Joe Newman, the closing horn passage is reminiscent of the historic New Orleans style.

'Born Under A Bad Sign' and 'Don't It Make You Wanta Go Home' are discussed elsewhere. During the fade-out of the Joe South-penned 'Don't It Make You', we again get to hear – for the first time in a long while – Brook's very musical spontaneous whistling. The versions of 'Whoever Finds This I Love You' and 'It's All In The Game' which are to be found on the previously mentioned Rhino CD reissue of the album are different takes to those on the original LP. The instrumental and choral arrangements are identical, but Brook's singing is excessive as regards his handling of the vowels. They appear to be early attempts (very interesting for the collector) and are more tailored to soul. 'Willie And Laura Mae Jones' is also slightly different. Brook comes into the fifth and final verse (*'Years rolled past our door / We heard of them no more'*) differently than he does on the Cotillion LP.

The Gospel Truth

Ten years after *If You Believe*, Brook Benton released a second album of gospel songs and spirituals. It includes his composition, 'If You Think God Is Dead', and his arrangement of 'Precious Lord', as well as newer compositions and traditional material. The album starts with a tremendous opening number, 'Let Us All Get Together With The Lord', an invocation used at the beginning of a church service. It is an immensely swinging song with a very exposed, hymnally singing Brook backed by a large choir. The rhythmic acceleration at the end of the song demands from the singer high singing and articulation at a very fast tempo. Brook has to push his vocal capabilities to the limit, but through this the song gains its crucial ecstatic tone.

One of the most beautiful performances on the album is 'Oh Happy Day'. Brook turns the well-known popular song into an internalized message of joy. At the bridge, the feeling of happiness which believers associate with the birth of Jesus Christ breaks through forcefully, but is then softened in an elegant way, so that the general mood upon which the song is predicated remains intact. Brook again demonstrates his great musicality through his empathetic whistling at the beginning and towards the end of the song. Also notable is the fact that he sings various high and low voices in the background vocals. Reviewer Bernd Grimmel considers Benton's version of 'Oh Happy Day' to be a unique arrangement of this classic that is worth hearing. Furthermore, he describes the whole album as a most remarkable gospel LP.[80]

Vocal contrasts shape both 'Going Home In His Name' and 'Take A Look At Your Hands'. The first song is pitched very low, and here Brook frequently sings his lowest note, low D. Conversely, 'Take A Look At Your Hands', features the highest chest note that he has ever committed to record. In the refrain at the end of the song, he sings the word *hand* four times in B1. In other words, the vocal range utilized by Brook on his recordings spans two octaves and a quinte.

His composition, 'If You Think God Is Dead', reveals itself to be a slowly rendered tune which develops almost like a prayer. The focal point is the title line, which recurs at the end as a refrain during which Brook shapes each repetition differently – an approach we are already familiar with from other songs by the singer. Of the traditional gospel numbers in the last third of the album, 'I Dreamed Of A City Called Heaven' is the most pleasing in its rhythmic execution. Despite high-quality performances by the musicians and choir, and Benton's committed singing, 'Doing The Best I Can' and 'Precious Lord' come out a little long-winded, although Brook's voice, accompanied only by a piano on 'Precious Lord', exhibits immense expressive power.

---

[80] www.gospelszene.de.

Story Teller

This 1972 LP also marks the end of Brook Benton's association with Cotillion. Brook made the singles charts for the last time in his career with the song 'Shoes'. It's a good, soulful number and skilfully produced, but is not the best cut on the album by a long way. That honour should probably go to the opening track, the poignant 'Movin' Day'. The song is lyrically and musically a small work of art and goes straight to the core of the thoughts and feelings associated with a break-up and especially with a farewell. The vocal power, wisdom and philosophical world view of a man who has come to know such emotions make the doubt, sadness and uncertainty engendered by such a situation comprehensible to the listener, although the musical execution and realization of the song place high demands on them. The plaintive sound of guitar and clarinet in the instrumental interlude intensify the feeling of the pain of parting which permeates the song. The arrangement of the fade-out is masterful, with Brook characteristically repeating the main theme, *'Movin' day'*, but varying it each time, making the drama of the situation tangible.

'She Even Woke Me Up To Say Goodbye', 'Sidewalks Of Chicago' and 'Country Comfort' are musically similar numbers. Stylistically, they could be described as crossover country, carried by a magnificently singing Brook, who portrays the emotional state of each song in the most beautiful way. A couple of careful listens are probably required to comprehend the true beauty of 'Poor Make Believer', as Brook relates the story of the self-deceiver in a very low-key, casually swinging way. There is no excitement here, no loud sounds disturb the intimate self-confession, which again ends in a fade-out with multiple variations.

Although the vocal of 'Willoughby Grove' is similar in style, the song itself is slower and more measured. Its content deals with a return to a home changed by modern times. The theme of environmental issues was very topical in the '70s and there is a similar rendition of this song by Sammy Davis Jr.

'Save The Last Dance For Me', a hit from the well-known Doc Pomus & Mort Shuman song factory, is considerably altered by Benton's treatment. Brook forgoes the meat of the song to a large extent, instead making it a platform from which to demonstrate his vocal artistry. The constant alternation between high and low notes is breathtaking. For that reason, it isn't immediately catchy. Once one becomes accustomed to the divergence of the melody from that of the original, then it's possible to appreciate Benton's version. In particular, the plaintive tone he adopts in his appeal, *'But don't forget who's taking you home / And in whose arms you're gonna be'* will intrigue the listener.

'Big Mable Murphy', the tragic ballad of Big Mable and Little Melvin, is imparted in a very swinging way, and in his customary manner: stirring, tinged with a touch of irony, not overlooking the drama of the event.

All in all, the LP contains a selection of catchy tunes including several songs of great lyrical potency. Benton reveals himself to be a singer beyond all reproach. The fact that Atlantic did not want to maintain their ties with him can only be explained by the fast-moving nature of the recording business, where commercial success – or lack of it – is constantly taken into account. For his part, Brook felt that, aside from 'Rainy Night In Georgia', his association with Atlantic had not exactly been a very felicitous one, and stated that he did not intend to renew his contract.[81]

---

[81] *Blues & Soul*, ibid.

MGM

In the same year that Brook's last LP for Cotillion was released, he made some recordings for MGM. However, by 1973 the association was already over. All that Brook and MGM managed to bring to market was one album containing ten tracks, two of which were also released as a single (see *Discography*).

Something For Everyone

Benton produced two of the titles on this 1973 LP, 'Alone' and 'Send Back My Heart', together with Al Rosenstein. These two bluesy ballads, along with 'Remember The Good', are among the best that the album has to offer. The song 'Sweet Memories' and the medley 'For The Good Times–It's Just A Matter Of Time' herald the fact that one can't necessarily expect something new on this record. The unbiased listener will note that the material here is familiar to a greater or lesser extent, nothing that will bowl anyone over, but nevertheless still delivered by Brook in a quality way, as ever. The frequently noted fact that Brook Benton was often better than the material he was given – for which he must also bear responsibility to some extent – is conspicuous here.

On this album, Brook repeats musical forms and modes of expression which are backward-looking. Though there are a few nice numbers, there is nothing here that surpasses or even equals the high quality of many of the Cotillion recordings. It seems no one bothered to go to the trouble of producing a conceptualized, well-thought-out album that would have been able to show off more of the singer's artistic ability. The fact that no fewer than four arrangers worked on the material for the LP is evidence of this.

The song 'If You've Got The Time' attained a particular significance for Brook. A number of years earlier, he had created an additional source of income for himself as an advertising vehicle. In 1963, the Liggett & Myers Tobacco Company had recruited him to publicize their products. Around the same time, he also made a commercial for portable radios which went: *'Hi, this is Brook Benton. Take a lively companion wherever you go, take a portable radio! I'll be there right with you.*[82]

Along with Count Basie and others, Brook also promoted Pfeiffer Beer (*'Pfeiffer is my kind of beer, you'll like it too'*).

In 1971, he was engaged by the Miller Brewing Company, who launched a nationwide campaign in the US for their 'High Life' brand under the slogan, *'If you've got the time, we've got the beer'*. Brook participated in this campaign along with the Troggs and a country singer named Johnny Mack. He recorded five different promos for Miller based on the melody of his MGM recording, 'If You've Got The Time', with emphasis on the line *'If you've got the time, we've got the beer'*. The titles of these are 'All Vocal Jingle' (*aka* 'Straight Jingle'), 'City People', '5 O'Clock World', 'Heading Home' and 'Orange Candles'. These recordings were not produced for radio broadcast, but were intended to be played in bars where Miller Beer was served in order to subtly influence the drinking habits of the clientele.

According to his nephew, Brook Grant, Brook also made a commercial for Michelob Beer in the mid-'70s as part of their *'Weekends were made for Michelob'* campaign, but sadly this could

---

[82] Radio spot, unknown source.

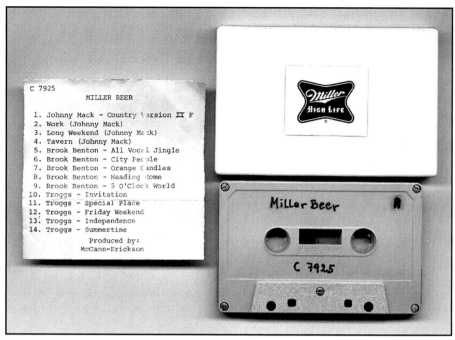

Cassette version of the Miller Beer promotion with additional tracks
not on the EP discovered at a Texas record dealer's.

not be traced.

Clearly, there wasn't a great deal of money to be earned from such contracts, but they could potentially help artists achieve greater prominence. At the time, this was not especially necessary in Brook's case, as he had only recently been in the charts. A few years later, however, this initially negligible aspect of his career did take on a degree of importance for the singer. In 1977, when he was travelling with some other people in an elevator, a woman thought she recognized him, but wasn't sure. She nudged her male companion, who squinted at the tall, dark figure and showed a glimmer of recognition. 'Brook Benton,' someone informed the inquisitive couple. 'Right!' the woman exclaimed, looking closely at the singer. 'I thought I knew your face... you're in the beer commercials!' Despite the somewhat backhanded compliment, Brook smiled graciously and thanked the lady for her attention.[83]

---

[83] *Ebony*, May 1978.

Brut (All Platinum)

Shortly after the interlude at MGM, Brook Benton signed with Brut, the men's fragrance division of the perfume and cometics giant Fabergé, who wanted to get involved in the record business. The singer recorded a number of titles for them in 1973 and 1974, which yielded two singles: 'Lay Lady Lay' *b/w* 'A Touch Of Class' and 'South Carolina' *b/w* 'All That Love Went To Waste'. The proposed album was never released because Brut abandoned the project immediately after the recording work was completed and withdrew from the music industry. A compilation of ten Brut recordings simply titled *Brook Benton* was subsequently issued in 1977 by All Platinum, for whom Brook briefly recorded in 1976 (see pages 105-7).

Brook Benton

Brut did not spare any expense or effort to produce a good album. Elaborate arrangements with big orchestration and choral accompaniment were deployed in the hope of landing a hit of one sort or another. Indeed, the record contains potential hit material throughout. A very beautiful, typical Benton version of Bob Dylan's 'Lay Lady Lay' could readily have made it into the charts if the single had been properly promoted. The same goes for his treatment of John Lennon's 'Jealous Guy', 'On Your Side Of The Bed' and the oldie, 'A Touch Of Class'. Benton is committed to these songs, feels his way into them, and transforms them in his familiar manner into ballads with a lot of blues feel. As always, he attaches importance to good singing, showcases his big voice, and nuances the material as necessary with articulation and phrasing.

'South Carolina', a homage by Brook to his home state, is a number worth listening to, as he understandably puts a great deal of emotion into it. 'When Summer Turns To Fall' can be ranked as a wonderfully sung classic Benton ballad, though the instrumental break in the middle with a female vocal lead perhaps turned out rather too sweet. Conversely, 'Sister And Brother' is a song which very tenderly and sensitively deals with the secret love of two individuals. The swinging 'A Touch Of Class', arranged over dominant horns, ends in a brilliantly intensified climax. The same can be said of 'The Night Has Many Eyes'. The repetition of 'Lay Lady Lay' in a longer version at the end of the LP may be very interesting for Benton's serious fans, but is also an indication that Brook and Brut had reached the end of their joint enterprise.

Though it remained largely unknown, the album turned out very well as regards its musical structure and unquestionably deserved more attention than it received.

Stax

The association between Brook Benton and Stax could have given rise to great hopes. Stax was a label that could have embraced his unique style and offered him further opportunities to develop. The deal was brokered by Brook's long-standing partner, Clyde Otis, in 1974.

Otis had a production agreement with Stax, and he included Brook in it. Unfortunately, the hope Brook put behind his signature on the contract was never fulfilled. Due to a series of setbacks, Stax became his biggest-ever disappointment: he had a contract with the label, but was unable to make any recordings. Co-owner Al Bell had signed Brook just as Stax's financial problems were beginning. When it became clear that Bell could not sort out the situation immediately, he called Brook into his office and explained the position to him. During the meeting, Bell asked him if he wanted to be released from his contract. He could have frozen Brook's contract, but instead gave him the chance to look for new opportunities and continue his career. Brook swore that he would never forget that.[84]

Brook managed to record four songs for Stax, two of which, 'The Winds Of Change' and 'I Keep Thinking To Myself', were released as a single in 1974. That was the sum total of a liaison which could have delivered so much more. Both numbers have since appeared on various CDs. In 1998, his two unissued Stax cuts, 'These Arms You Pushed Away' and 'You've Never Been This Far', surfaced on a Tring International compilation.[85]

---

[84] *Blues & Soul*, ibid.
[85] *Endlessly* (Tring International GRF-164) UK, 1998.

All Platinum

Following the turbulence at Stax, Brook was left without a contract for a short time. In 1975, having considered various options, he decided to give All Platinum a try. Chuck Jackson, another veteran who had sold millions of records, had also gone to the label. Brook had not yet entered into a contract, but Joe and Sylvia Robinson, who headed the company, appeared to have a philosophy of the music business that was a perfect match for the ambitions of an artist such as Brook.

A session in New York with Sammy Lowe resulted in 'Mr. Bartender', a song with real hit potential. Brook describes very clearly the conundrum he and his producers faced: should they stick with their core business and go all out to make a disco-type record, or take a chance with a higher-quality production that would not sell as easily. Brook, of course, was willing to compromise, but not at the expense of losing his artistic identity. As he explained to *Blues & Soul*, he could never just go in and shout out a song. He has his own way of doing everything and would not be interested in sinking below what he considers to be his own level or standard. He would never sacrifice style just to get a hit, because it wouldn't be him.[86]

Brook eventually signed a contract with All Platinum, who released the LP *This Is Brook Benton* in 1976, as well as several singles (see *Discography*). The album was repackaged for the European market as *Mister Bartender*, with a different running order plus two additional tracks which had appeared on singles in the USA, 'Mr. Bartender' and 'Taxi'. In 1977, All Platinum released a second LP simply titled *Brook Benton*. This was a ten-track compilation of material the singer had cut for Brut in 1973-74 (see pages 102-3).

Sadly, the All Platinum label failed to achieve any great prominence within American popular music and remains largely forgotten today.

---

[86] *Blues & Soul*, ibid.

This Is Brook Benton / Mister Bartender

This album was produced at considerable expense, and is indisputably of high musical quality. Strings, horns and a choir are Benton's accompanists on his musical journey, during which he introduces both old and new material. Brook has not lost any of his vocal faculties. It is conspicuous that he sings with more of a sustained head voice on this album than on other productions. On the one hand, this can be ascribed to the choice of songs, and on the other, to the prevailing style at the time.

The title song, 'Mr. Bartender', and numbers like 'It Started All Over Again', 'Weekend With Feathers', 'You Were Gone' and 'Taxi' reveal a laid-back Brook Benton who nevertheless strives to project great emotion in his voice. 'Can't Take My Eyes Off Of You', previously recorded for Cotillion, acquires a new emotional quality in the All Platinum version, and the classic 'A Nightingale Sang In Berkeley Square'[87] is a vocal and interpretative highpoint of the album. The treatment of the key word *sang* and the rhythmic tension which Brook builds up around this word through special intonation of the vowel is high vocal art. However, it is incomprehensible why the beautiful alto sax solo in the interlude had to be marred by a rather kitschy pizzicato.

There is nothing to be said against a good disco version of the well-known Rodgers & Hart song, 'My Funny Valentine'. However, the fact that the number is extended by identical repetitions by the rhythm section makes it boring and detracts from Benton's good singing. The arrangement of the recording is a clear concession to the disco style of the time.

---

[87] Shortened to 'Nightingale In Berkeley Square' on the US pressing.

The overall impression of the album is similar to that of Brook's other long-players, but on various numbers it leans more towards the popular disco style than one might have expected from a highly individualistic stylist such as Brook Benton. Of course, the album is also not short of bluesy or swinging numbers. With their keenly tailored horn arrangements – albeit also slightly oriented towards the disco beat – 'Now Is The Time' and especially 'I Had To Learn (The Hard Way)' are good examples of the swinging Benton. Both songs attach great importance to the refrain – an idiosyncrasy of his interpretative approach. As always, Brook brilliantly varies the repetitions, changing the melody or stressing other words within the lyric. This should not be dismissed as mannered posturing, but rather ought to be appreciated as the singer's attempt to express the diverse and most intimate nuances from the world of emotions that a song possesses.

Last but not least, there is Stevie Wonder's 'All In Love Is Fair', which is given a very noticeable tragic turn by Benton in a beautiful and interesting interpretation.

In summary, it can be attested that *This Is Brook Benton/Mister Bartender* is an album of great musical quality. The material, arrangements and musical interpretation are, as reflected in Benton's previously stated intention, hardly formulated simply to create hits. Like almost all of his LPs, this album appeals to a mature musical public or to music lovers who have travelled a long way with the singer and understand his artistic achievement, and can get something out of it. Be that as it may, the record did nothing to advance his career.

Olde World (Sounds of Florida)

A real fresh start seemed to open up for Brook Benton with the Olde World label, especially as it once again involved a collaboration with his legendary partner, the composer, arranger and producer Clyde Otis. Benton himself admitted the relief he felt after he signed with Olde World in 1977, which ended a long lean period during which he kept his head above the water with demo records, advertising contracts, club appearances and even tours of Europe.[88]

In a long interview with *Ebony* magazine, Brook clarified his situation at the time. There had been several reasons for the silence, including personal issues and contractual problems that prevented him from recording for three years. A couple of record companies had told him that he was too old: 'I was just wondering if Frank Sinatra was too old, or if Dean Martin was too old. Bing Crosby wasn't too old, and Elvis Presley wasn't too old... I'm not going to be "over the hill" just because somebody says that I am.' Fortunately for Brook, songwriter Bennie Benjamin introduced him to Olde World Records.[89]

The managers at Olde World were very optimistic. Scott Lovin, president of the label's parent company, Galaxy Communications, enthused: 'Brook has had 18 gold records in his career. This new record[90] is taking off now, and we feel that we can get 20 more. Things are just beginning to happen. We are saying: "Watch out, World! Brook Benton is back!"'[91] Wally Roker, president of Olde World, was equally upbeat: 'Brook is a phenomenal recording artist and one of the few who are still around. I think he can go farther today than he did before, because considerably more people are ready to accept him now, and the recording industry itself has grown three times or four times larger.'[92]

Unfortunately, these optimistic expectations were to remain unfulfilled. Olde World, and subsequently Sounds of Florida, managed to release a handful of Brook Benton singles and two LPs, *Makin' Love Is Good For You* and *Soft*, the latter of which duplicates some of the titles on the former, albeit with slightly different vocals.[93] None of these productions achieved satisfactory sales.

---

[88] *Soul* 10, 3 July 1978.
[89] *Ebony*, May 1978.
[90] The single, 'Makin' Love Is Good For You'.
[91] *Ebony*, ibid.
[92] Ibid.
[93] See *Discography*, pages 260-2 and 283-4.

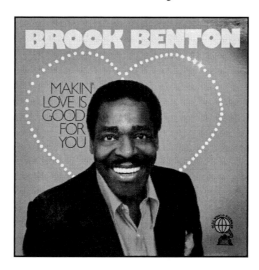

Makin' Love Is Good For You

It is telling that only the title track of this 1977 LP generated any kind of reaction. A Tony Joe White song, it does not, however, measure up artistically with the great numbers Benton made out of other White compositions like 'For Le Ann', 'Willie And Laura Mae Jones' and, of course, the peerless 'Rainy Night In Georgia'. However, Brook did once again draw attention to himself with 'Makin' Love Is Good For You', even though this was from a younger audience only interested in a (short-lived) disco hit. He also went on tour across the USA to promote the single and album.

The most beautiful number on the album, 'Let The Sun Come Out', remains largely unknown. It is again a product of the highest lyrical quality, in which the harmony of the composition and interpretation express the appeal for togetherness and its associated sentiment of hope in the most wonderful way. This song is comparable to the celebrated 'Rainy Night In Georgia' in the density and intensity of its impression and expression, and could alone have justified the entire album, on which yet more beautiful material waits to be discovered: 'I Keep Thinking To Myself', 'Better Times', 'Til' I Can't Take It Anymore' and others. 'A Lover's Question', written by Benton and Jimmy Williams, had already attained a degree of importance before Brook recorded it for Olde World. Thanks to his meticulous discographical research, Hans Maitner has been able to account for over 40 cover versions.

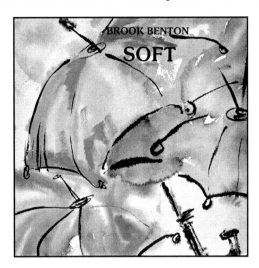

Soft

Released in 1984 by Clyde Otis[94], this album duplicates some of the numbers on the Olde World LP, albeit with slightly different vocals over the same instrumental backing tracks. The record is a mixture of rhythmic and slower-paced numbers, of which 'You're Pulling Me Down' and 'Love Is Best Of All' stand out. 'You're Pulling Me Down' yet again showcases the singer's low register throughout, while on 'Love Is Best Of All' Brook particularly works with the weighting element, i.e. the expression of the underlying feeling through the refrain or with refrain-like repetitions. 'Glow Love', from the 1983 film, *The Big Score*, is another beautiful song.

Brook and Clyde Otis made a host of very fine recordings for Olde World which received neither the necessary promotion nor distribution, and were only released years later on various compilations. Numbers like 'You've Never Been This Far', 'These Arms You Pushed Away', 'Old Fashioned Strut', 'Trust Me To Do What You Want Me To (And I'll Do It)' and the touching 'A Tribute To "Mama"' belong to that body of songs in American popular music which are beyond comparison. Benton's imitation of voices and vocal peculiarities (Jimmy Durante, Sammy Davis Jr) on 'Old Fashioned Strut', and his imitation of instruments (trombone, bass) during the fade-out reveal what vocal surprises still remained hidden within his broad chest.

'A Tribute To "Mama"' is a song that can reduce the listener to tears. Naturally, it is very emotionally charged, as is characteristic of the genre, yet does not slip into being trite or kitschy. A story is related

---

[94] See *Discography*, page 284.

here, succinctly and sensitively, which many of the older generation have experienced in their own lives: a deprived but secure childhood in a family held together by a mother following the death of the father; a longing for the big, wide world; sadness about the disappointment there:

In the pictures the city looked so warm

but, despite everything, mother's reassurance that

Life is pretty much what you make it,
So get up kids, we got to make it through another year.

The words and music of this lyrical treasure are brilliantly implemented through Benton's wonderful internalized interpretation, so that the merging of memory, security, longing, disappointment, sadness and confidence within this ode develop within the listener at the same time. It is a pity that this song was only accessible to an extremely small audience, because a track on a record is only as good as its promotion allows it to be.

It has to be conclusively stated that Brook Benton recorded some real pearls of American popular music for Olde World, some of the most beautiful of which we have the writing team of Clyde Otis and Duncan Cleary to thank for.

It would be years before Brook entered a recording studio again.

HMC

HMC Records were based in Charlotte, North Carolina. Producers Nick Hice, Reese Culbreeth and Duke Hall were planning to make a record of Christmas songs and chose Brook Benton as the singer for the project. The LP was recorded in 1983 and was released that same year. It was Brook's final album and the last artistic highlight in his recording career.

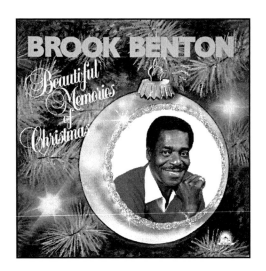

Beautiful Memories of Christmas

Over the years, Brook had recorded the occasional Christmas song, including the famous carol, 'Silent Night'. *Beautiful Memories of Christmas* is, however, the only Christmas concept album by the singer. *All Music Guide*'s Andrew Hamilton gave it a brief but very nice review: 'This aptly titled season's greeting features Benton's affable low-baritone-ish tenor rejoicing the precious holiday with songs that pay homage to the birth of Jesus.'[95]

Considerable effort was put into the production of the record. The tight rhythm section (keyboards, drums, bass) is augmented by three guitarists, nine horn players and ten violinists. In addition, Brook is supported by an eight-strong choir and two children's choruses. Producer Duke Hall wrote the horn and string arrangements and contributed the song 'Christmas Makes The Town (Such A Happy Place)'.

The result of all these endeavours is a truly beautiful album

---

[95] Andrew Hamilton, *All Music Guide*.

which strikes the right tone for this special time of year. In this, it differs from many better-known stateside Christmas productions, which are loud, noisy and brash. Benton's Christmas album is, by contrast, sensitive and touching, and once again demonstrates this singer's wonderful ability for putting feelings into words. Happiness, joy and hope, but also sadness, which for many people is the dominant feeling at this time, can be sensed in these songs. Brook has lost none of the expressive power of his voice, or its lyrical tenderness, epic range or rhythmic elegance. It is hard to comprehend that a singer with such vocal and interpretative capabilities would soon no longer be heard.

The album's title track, 'Beautiful Memories', is a fitting introduction. After introducing it with a spoken monologue, Brook begins to sing, summoning up memories of Christmastime from his own childhood. The song is a gem, intensifying the thoughts and feelings one associates with Christmas.

Benton originally recorded 'This Time Of The Year' in 1961. Here, he delivers an elegantly swinging update of this song. The swinging piano, Brook's vocal performance and his graceful whistling demonstrate his affinity to elements of jazz. 'Merry Christmas All' also swings with a refrain artistically shaped by the singer, particularly on the rapid succession of changes from high and low notes, which he intones perfectly. 'I Wish Everyday Could Be Like Christmas' is an exceptionally beautifully crafted song. According to Leonard Bernstein, a song must rise up on wings once the theme has been introduced. Here, Brook's voice seems to hover around a reference point during the introduction before rising on wings to the heavens, carrying its wishes with it.

'Blue Decorations' has the Christmas of a lonely man as its theme. He decorates the tree in blue and hangs gifts on it for the person he is missing. The song is the first of a succession of numbers which could be described as catchy, in which Brook demonstrates his mastery of creating musical motifs out of words through the way he handles vowels to create a mood.

'I've Got The Christmas Spirit' once again picks up the motif of memory:

When December snow used to take my breath away...

and connects it to the theme of loving devotion, probably the most precious gift a person can give:

The greatest gift I've got to give is love.

With great musicality and profound sensitivity, Brook turns the entire line containing the keywords *gift* and *love* into a sort of 'song within a song'. He does the same with 'Decorate The Night'. He ennobles the song with his beautiful voice, again emphasizing two particular words in an atmospheric line through his vocalization to create an atmosphere rich with feeling:

December snow *is falling down...*[96]

Brook also gives a special twist to the words *falling* and *down*: he sings *falling* low and lets the word *down* soar. Through this device, he conveys the feeling of happiness and high spirits associated with the falling of snow at Christmas. 'Decorate The Night' stands out from the mass of average American Christmas songs as a lyrical creation of high emotional intensity, and of beauty in both form and vocal realization.

On the final track, 'When A Child Is Born', Brook yet again exhibits the power and expressiveness of his voice. His joyful and vocally confident proclamation of the hope which accompanies the birth of a child painfully underscores the fact that he would from now on fall silent on record.

---

[96] Boldface is the author's emphasis.

CHAPTER 4

The Voice

In 1993, Johnny Otis wrote that it would be valuable to expose some of the current crop of young singers to the understated magic of Billie Holiday or Brook Benton, who epitomize artistic discretion and balance. 'This would help counter the present-day tendency of young singers, some of whom are blessed with sensational voices, to overscreech and squall, and use ill-advised pop mannerisms and gimmicks.'[97]

The first time that *Scoop USA* reporter W.M. Barnes heard Brook's voice was when he was invited to Wildwood, near Pittsburgh, where the singer and his friends happened to be staying. He recounts his impressions under the heading 'Soul and Brook Benton'. Brook's younger brother Richard was serving cocktails when all of a sudden Barnes was captivated by a thrilling sound emanating from the suite next door. Never having heard Brook's voice before in the flesh, it took his breath away. At first, it was pleasant and gently caressing, then it soared and finished in complete abandon.

Brook was working on a song called 'Lumberjack', which had not yet been released. Barnes confesses to being completely overwhelmed by a vocal talent of such magnitude.[98]

The singer's vocal skill and capabilities, the way in which he used his voice and his characteristic traits had essentially already been worked out. Soft, velvety, silky, mellifluous, syrupy, but also husky and guttural are the attributes most commonly associated with Brook Benton's voice. Sometimes, even figurative periphrasis is employed to convey particular characteristics: it is rich and soft, and Brook has a way of using his voice that makes a sound like a breeze through a field of cello strings.[99] Critics also cite the warmth and intimacy of Benton's voice – qualities which touch the heart and soul of the listener through their ears. More precise appraisals of his vocal art cite the singer's vocal range; his ability to employ his voice in a variety of ways; the delicacy and precision with which he treats individual words within the lyrics; a feeling for the blues; and the inherent swing in his singing (see

---

[97] Johnny Otis: *Upside Your Head! Rhythm & Blues on Central Avenue* (University Press of New England, Hanover, NH) 1993.

[98] 'Soul and Brook Benton', *Scoop USA*, 29 August 1964.

[99] *World Telegram*, 22 October 1959.

above). Ron Drain describes Brook Benton's voice in even greater detail, acknowledging its earthy, exuberant, poignant, relaxing, romantic, sentimental, slow, soft, sophisticated, soulful, storytelling, sweet and upbeat qualities.[100]

All these characteristics which are attributed to Brook Benton's voice are correct as to detail, but it is also notable that the qualities 'soft', 'velvety' and 'silky' are most frequently used to describe it. This undoubtedly stems from the fact that the majority of reviews originated during Benton's golden era at Mercury, which is also where this classification of his voice makes its first (though by no means only) appearance.

As a singer, Brook Benton commands various techniques of voice formation and vocalization, and deploys his voice in accordance with the requirements of his interpretative approach to the song in question. In this, his vocal options extend from *bel canto* to *espressivo*. Benton sings with a full chest voice, frequently changes to a sustained head voice, and occasionally also sings falsetto. His actual vocal range is astonishingly wide and extends from low D/E♭ to B1. The way in which he plays with the notes, contrasting the very high ones with very low ones is characteristic of his singing technique.

Another essential characteristic of Brook Benton's singing is the way his voice floats, allowing him to ennoble songs, while at the same time making it virtually impossible to emulate. To one Midwest deejay, however, Joe Henderson and Brook Benton sounded so much alike that he reportedly played Henderson's latest disc for several hours before he realized that it wasn't Benton who was singing.[101] This, however, only demonstrates that the deejay in question had never learned how to listen properly. Henderson tries to imitate Brook's singing style, especially in the alternation of low and high notes in the transition from tonic to dominant. He can replicate it in form up to a certain level, but from the perspective of vocal ability, it is nothing more than a poor imitation of what Benton can offer. To continue with the 'floating' metaphor, Henderson's voice languishes at ground level, moving between notes without ever coming close to the light, soulful floating of Brook's, which so often forsakes the flatness of the familiar and the ordinary. It is more than a big misunderstanding to mistake Henderson's 'Snap Your Fingers' for a Benton hit.

It is instructive to listen to Sammy Davis Jr's version of this number. The way he sings 'Snap Your Fingers' moves his singing much closer to Brook Benton than the many deliberately Benton-styled songs of Joe Henderson. Brook also named the prodigiously talented

---

[100] 'A Rainy Night In Georgia', epinions.com, 13 June 2003.
[101] *St Louis Argus*, 15 June 1962.

Davis as the artist who had the greatest influence on him.[102]

Brook once remarked that he was irritated with having so many imitators. Amongst others, he cites Ben E. King as sounding more like him than he did himself. In truth, with his wide array of options for vocal expression, Brook Benton was nearly impossible to copy. Conversely, he himself was in a position to imitate many of his distinguished contemporaries to perfection. He could impersonate Nat Cole, Louis

---

[102] *Journal Americana,* New York, 26 January 1964.

Armstrong, Ray Charles, Sam Cooke, Jackie Wilson, Frank Sinatra and also Sammy Davis Jr deceptively well. He particularly liked to do this while performing his famous 'Boll Weevil Song', in the course of which several of the aforementioned celebrities would make an appearance. Additionally, Brook would also imitate on stage the gestures, facial expressions and intonation of various actors, for example Walter Brennan.

Brook Benton's voice is, without a doubt, an exceptional phenomenon within popular American music. Its versatility, suppleness, and subtlety of expression and timbre amazes listeners, and forces new, interesting approaches even to familiar songs.

CHAPTER 5

Brook Benton on Stage

We have already heard that, while he was still young and barely known as a recording artist, Brook Benton made successful live appearances. His second engagement at the Chatterbox in Cleveland, which primarily came about because of popular demand, is a case in point. After Brook scored a hit with 'It's Just A Matter Of Time' and was as a result able to appeal to different audiences, the doors of show stages, clubs, theatres and concert halls opened up for him. He was a much-booked entertainer who could thrill audiences and cast his spell over them. As a result, he was often away from home for weeks on end performing in all the big cities across the USA, as well as touring outside the United States.

Brook Benton's live concerts were of a very high standard from the outset, and he was a top star within black popular music from the beginning of his career to the end.

Stars of the blues, rhythm & blues and doo-wop scenes, as well as vocal and instrumental protagonists of jazz and pop, were the support acts for his live shows. The following list of names, which in no way pretends to be complete, testifies to this: Jimmy Reed, Eddie Boyd, Clarence 'Gatemouth' Brown, Wilbert Harrison, Etta James, Bobby Freeman, Ruth Brown, Jesse Belvin, LaVern Baker, Fats Domino, Marie Knight, King Curtis, the Platters, the Flamingos, the Drifters, Shep & The Limelites, the Coasters, the Meadowlarks, Roy Hamilton, Maxine Brown, Leonard Reed, Billy Butler & The Enchanters, Andy & The Bey Sisters, Inez Foxx, Nipsey Russell, Timi Yuro, Ben E. King, Bunny Briggs, Dee Clark, Willie Lewis, Curtis Lee, Aretha Franklin, Lloyd Price, Bruce Channel, Della Reese, Joni James, Buddy Lester, Damita Jo, Jackie Wilson, Phil Upchurch, Chuck Jackson, Dion, Del Shannon, Johnnie Ray, Paul Anka, Lesley Gore, Trini Lopez, Lonnie Donegan, Bobby Rydell, the Righteous Brothers, Al Hirt, Milt Buckner, Joe Williams, Ella Fitzgerald, Ray Charles, Dinah Washington, Nancy Wilson, Art Farmer, Benny Golson, Maynard Ferguson, Gerry Mulligan, Dizzy Gillespie, Cannonball Adderley, Count Basie, Lambert, Hendricks & Ross, Nina Simone, Carmen McRae, Betty Carter and Jerome Richardson's All Stars. All these artists' reputations speak for themselves.

Brook Benton with his tour bus, 1959.

A comprehensive portrayal of Brook Benton's live performances is neither possible nor necessary within the scope of this work, so only significant appearances within and outside the USA will be cited and described. It must also be stated in advance that, towards the end of the '70s and throughout the '80s, at a time when he no longer featured in the charts, Brook was still a popular live attraction. That he had lost none of his vocal qualities is demonstrated by his stage performances in Hollywood in 1982, in the UK in 1984, and in New York in 1987. He was also enthusiastically embraced by country music fans who saw him perform on Opryland's *General Jackson Showboat* in early 1988 and on the live *Nashville Now* TV show just a few weeks before his death.[113]

In his autobiography, *It's Sid Bernstein Calling...*, the legendary US promoter succinctly describes the situation around the beginning of Brook's career: 'Shaw Artists had a young black singer who had been playing the chitlin' circuit – the numerous night, supper and dance clubs in the black urban areas of America. He was on the road to stardom and, in my opinion, ready for a major coming-out in New York. So on the heels of Miles Davis, I booked Brook Benton into the Apollo.

---

[113] Peter Grendysa, 'Brook Benton', *DISCoveries* 25, October 1998.

Left to right: Dave Dreyer, guitarist Billy Johnson and wife Pat,
Brook Benton and wife Mary, Minnie Dreyer and an unknown man, 1959.

Lucky for me, Brook had just released 'It's Just A Matter Of Time'. The record was peaking, and everybody wanted to see him. Brook Benton sold out the Apollo for the week.'[114]

There is an anecdote regarding Brook's first Apollo engagement. The show's promoter, disc jockey Tommy Smalls *aka* Dr. Jive, had to act as a referee between Brook and Wilbert Harrison when a big argument erupted over who was to close the show. Benton won out on the basis of his four current hit records.[115]

In the years that followed, Brook appeared at the Apollo time and again, always as top of the bill. His support acts included greats like Valerie Carr, the Shirelles, the Drifters, Andy & The Bey Sisters, Maxine Brown, Ruth Brown, Irwin C. Watson, Aretha Franklin, Major Lance, the Flamingos, Jimmy Reed, Bobby Ephraim, King Curtis, the Reuben Phillips Band and many others.

As early as 1959, he was booked in Washington, DC for guest appearances at various establishments. Here too, he was the headliner, with top-class supporting programmes provided by the likes

---

[114] Sid Bernstein, *It's Sid Bernstein Calling...* (Jonathan David, New York) 2001.
[115] Unknown source, ca. 1959.

Photomontage of a live appearance at the Apollo.

of Ruth Brown, Bobby Freeman, Jesse Belvin, the James Moody Band and others. On 12 February 1960, Brook appeared at the Washington Regal as 'Mercury's New Recording Champion' along with Ruth Brown, James Moody and his orchestra, Eddie Boyd and others. In August that year, he again appeared at the Regal as 'Mercury Records' Hottest Star' alongside top-notch acts like Andy & The Bey Sisters, Sammy Turner, Ben E. King, LaVern Baker, the Red Saunders Orchestra and others.

In the ensuing years, Brook would spend some 30 to 40 weeks each year on tour. The places he appeared at, as well as concert reviews, will serve to emphasize the high artistic standing that should be accorded to this singer and entertainer.

In March 1960, Brook made his debut in Los Angeles. A.S. 'Doc' Young's report from the *Los Angeles Sentinel* reveals how much the critics, as well as the public, were taken with the artist's performance and his show as a whole.

The audience sat down and waited for him to inspire their applause. But on being properly inspired, as they soon were, they latched on to him and were reluctant to let him go. The result was: he sang and sang and sang and sang. Brook came onstage meticulously dressed and opened with a number called 'This Could Be The Start Of Something Big'. He belted out a spiritual called 'Good News', which he said was his mother's favourite song. This was an audience-participation number, carrying a beat that set up an involuntary mass snapping of the fingers, patting of the feet, and rhythmic nodding of the heads.

Finally, Young offers his impression of Benton, which is that he can sing, and that he possesses a distinctive style. As a composer turned performer, his rendering of lyrics – his true interpretation of lyrics – is superb. He notes that the orchestral backings, conducted by an outstanding pianist named Luchi De Jesus, contributed much to the making of Brook's rousing act, and that the entire Benton production rolled on smoothly, merrily, wonderfully from 'Ol' Man River' to the spiritual, and on to the recorded hits. The multitude listened, liked what they heard, and repeatedly clamoured for 'More! More! More!'

The reaction of prominent showbiz contemporaries who witnessed Brook Benton's performance is also of interest. Among those at the second house that evening, which Brook opened, were Louis Prima, Keely Smith, Gary Crosby and Walter Winchell. Louis sat quietly, listening like a student, applauding politely. Keely was lavish in her approbation. Gary dug Brook from the first to the last. Walter was, at first, quite reserved about it all. But as Brook delivered song after song, he got the message, began to snap his fingers and join the beat with head and feet. On his way out of the club, Winchell enthused about Benton: 'He's got what it takes all right!'[116]

Brook could be seen all over Los Angeles, at the Beverly Hilton, the Cloister Club, the Palladium on Hollywood's Sunset Boulevard, the Moulin Rouge in Hollywood, and elsewhere. March 1962 witnessed his debut in Las Vegas, in the Driftwood Room of the Flamingo Hotel.

---

[116] *Los Angeles Sentinel*, 31 March 1960.

Although it was his first appearance in the city, it would not be his last. It was also here that Brook later apparently became an innocent victim of organized crime – an unfortunate affair which certainly had a negative influence on his career, as well as imposing a heavy burden on his family.

Two of Brook's early appearances must definitely be mentioned here, as both brought a large number of the most prominent vocal and music stars onto the same stage. On 15 April 1960, the Brooklyn Paramount hosted the *Easter Parade of Stars*, billed as 'The Greatest Easter Show Ever Presented on Stage'. This event featured Brook, Dinah Washington, the singing trio Lambert, Hendricks & Ross, Art Farmer & Benny Golson, Maynard Ferguson and others. On 13 October 1961, the Uptown Press Club presented the *Biggest Show of Stars for '61*, again with Brook Benton as the headliner, along with the Platters, the Drifters, Curtis Lee, Phil Upchurch and others.

Brook's engagement on 7-9 February 1963 at Oklahoma City's Warner Theater is another appearance which unquestionably demands attention, as it was the first time a black singer set foot on a stage in Oklahoma to give a show. In the media, Brook was heralded as one of the best ballad singers of the recording, theatre and club world. It was the first appearance in Oklahoma by Benton, who had already presented his impressive show in all the major cities including New York, Washington, DC, Chicago and Las Vegas.[117]

Also impressive are the names of the black musicians and singers booked to appear in Oklahoma City soon after, for whom Brook undoubtedly paved the way: Dinah Washington, Ray Charles and Louis Armstrong.[118]

Live performances did not always pass off smoothly, and there were also times when Brook travelled in vain. In the summer of 1962, he was scheduled to appear in Twinsburg Township, a small town near Cleveland, to sing at a *Steer Roast Day* picnic there. Having arrived in Cleveland the night before, he waited in vain that night and endlessly

---

[117] *Los Angeles Sentinel*, 31 January 1963.
[118] *Oklahoma Times*, 29 January 1963.

the following day for the promoters, who never showed.[119]

The life of a wandering minstrel was not what Brook had been striving for, as it separated him far too often and for too long from his beloved family. In addition, there were the difficulties and reprisals to which black artists were exposed, which likewise represented an enormous potential for stress for him. Of course, he was aware that records alone were not enough for a proper career. Meeting his public, talking to them, which surely has to be the outcome of every truly successful show, was not just a necessity for the singer; he needed and liked this means of communicating with his fans, and relished the opportunity to do so. The following episode provides a good indication of the ambivalent feelings he must have had towards his life in show business.

A few weeks after his successful guest performance in Oklahoma City, Brook was involved in an extremely unpleasant incident in St Louis. He was attacked in the dressing room of the Riviera Club by two unknown assailants, sustaining cuts and a severe injury to his ear. It started because he did not want to sing any more with the band, who were unable to read music. He was also critical of the microphones. 'The people kept screaming they couldn't hear me', explained Brook, 'and I could not do my act because incompetent musicians couldn't do their job.'[120]

Brook performed blues and jam numbers which did not require any music-reading ability on the part of the band. After the first show, he angrily left the stage and told his pianist, Cliff Smalls, that there would not be a second show. A man over six feet tall came with deejay George Logan and urged him to continue. Brook agreed, but wanted his money upfront, as someone in St Louis had previously attempted to cheat him. The promoter, Melvin Strong, paid him $1,500. After that, Brook went to his dressing room, and while he was alone an unknown man came in and punched him. He then demanded the money. Immediately after that, the six-foot man reappeared and also began

---

[119] *Jet*, 30 August 1962.
[120] *Amsterdam News*, 23 February 1963.

beating him. Brook was covered in blood. The noise attracted other people, who came down the basement stairs and held Brook down while he was being hit. The people were all hostile to the singer, and some yelled for him to be shot. Brook was rescued from this situation by the intervention of the promoter and a woman, who took him to the office. The police officers who came to the crime scene made no attempt to support the singer, or to assist him with regard to his rights to protection or legal redress. On the contrary, they wanted to take action against him for bad behaviour. After Brook finally made it back to his motel room, he telephoned four different doctors seeking treatment, but was refused each time.[121]

If one gives this scandalous incident due consideration, one is led to conclude that the disagreement about carrying on with the stage show and about the money can be viewed as being representative of the outbreak of latent racial tensions during the '60s. Hate-filled whites could easily take out their anger on the black singer, as they were in a safe majority in this particular situation.

Eventually, Brook rang his manager, Irving Siders, in desperation. Siders immediately flew to St Louis and brought him back to New York, where he was treated by Dr Gerald Friedman.

The Riviera Club in St Louis was well known at the time and most of the top black entertainers played there. Benton and Siders both sought legal advice in St Louis. The singer stated that he also intended to sue the club, as he felt that what happened that evening was an attack on all members of the theatrical profession and an insult to their dignity.[122] In the wake of this brutal assault, he was forced to cancel five further shows in cities on the West Coast.

Just how stressful, even unhealthy, it is for an artist to get up on stage virtually every day for weeks on end is attested to by the problems Brook experienced at the Flame Show Bar in Detroit. Following a sensational ten-day guest residency at this establishment, he wanted to cancel his performance on the last day of this engagement, which was a Sunday. Brook had played four additional shows over and above his contract, and had made yet another television appearance to promote the club. He had overexerted himself, had laryngitis, and had been treated by a doctor who recommended that he take a break from work for a few days.

After some negotiations with his manager, Herb Wright, the club initially agreed to his request. They could book Jackie Wilson as a replacement for Brook. However, cancellations by many people who knew about the possible substitution changed the minds of the Flame

---

[121] Ibid.
[122] Unknown source, February 1963.

Show Bar's management. They insisted that Brook fulfil his contract, or they would not pay him. It was only after he had explained the situation to the crowd that they agreed to waive his appearance and pay him his fee. Later on, Brook apologized for the unedifying affair. He had heard that all the fuss had caused Ms Eileen Lewitt, one of the club's managers, to have a heart attack.[123]

Brook disregarded his doctor's advice to have a few days off. Instead, he used the free day to rest his voice and fly to New York. There, he opened Basin Street East, which also proved to be a huge success for him. Trumpeter Al Hirt had been booked to headline the show, however, by the end, Brook had the crowd completely on his side and was acclaimed as its star.[124]

From time to time, it is opportune for an artist to feign illness to prevent him or herself from becoming sick, as is illustrated by an episode involving one of Brook Benton's concerts. He was singing at the Star Theater in Paramaribo, Surinam (Dutch Guiana). The air conditioning had broken down, but the house was jammed full for three performances. Brook had to pretend he had laryngitis in order to get off the stage.[125]

In the summer of 1963, Brook's eagerly anticipated first UK tour was finalized. Along with Dion, Timi Yuro, Lesley Gore and Trini Lopez, he was to play various concerts in London in the autumn of that year, as well as taking in a string of radio and TV appearances including *Sunday Night At The London Palladium*. The tour was scheduled to run for ten dates and then move on from Britain to Paris, Munich and Rome. Several Scandinavian and Dutch cities were also on the itinerary.

In one British newspaper, music critic Ray Coleman previewed Brook's UK debut. Coleman states that he is certainly one of the greatest single talents in show business today, and that it is one of the unexplained mysteries of popular music that Brook Benton has failed to 'arrive' in the big time of the British scene. If he gets half the admiration for his in-person appearances that millions of LP collectors have lavished on him – it says in the article – then Benton is due for a hero's welcome. 'It's Just A Matter Of Time', 'So Many Ways' and 'Baby' (with Dinah Washington) have provided him with million sellers in America. Yet his dent on the British chart has been negligible. Coleman wonders why, and suggests it is maybe because Benton is simply too good.[126].

There is some truth behind this statement. In 1963, the Beatles

---

[123] Unknown source, April 1963.
[124] See also page 148.
[125] *Jet*, 9 August 1962.
[126] Unknown source, first week of October 1963.

Brook and Dinah Washington at the Brooklyn Paramount, 1960.

were on top in the UK. A new trend in music began to develop with quasi-explosive force, with many similarly styled English groups following in their wake. Certainly, it is necessary for a listener to concentrate more and pay greater attention to a ballad singer of Brook Benton's quality in order to appreciate his vocal performance in all its richness – unlike the Beatles, whose songs anyone could sing along to without much difficulty. Therein also lies the importance of this quartet, and the quality of many of the Beatles' songs should on no account be denied. Many of them have become public property and have been absorbed into the repertoires of well-known greats in the world of popular music.

Coleman explains the phenomenon of Brook's poor showing in the UK charts in a different way. It is foolish to assert that Benton has written too few songs that one can hum along with. One is forced to assume that his image in Britain has not been built up effectively enough. When it comes to singles, these are the days of the personality cult. Alas, no Benton personality has pervaded his work on singles.[127]

Coleman's statement should not be misinterpreted as an indication that Brook Benton's personality was lacking in some way; rather, as Coleman had already previously intimated, the problem was a shortfall on the PR side. In Britain, Brook Benton had been too vaguely promoted, or not at all, either as a personality or as an artist. Also, his humorous, quiet, religiously inclined and socially competent personality would not have been easy to market in Britain during the Beatles era. There may have been similar issues with Brook in the USA too, as it was around this time that his managers began thinking about how to reposition him as a personality and an artist.

Coleman now turns his attention to Brook Benton's vocal qualities. 'Ask around for an evaluation of his vocal worth, and the praise runs in,' writes the critic. His albums sell excellently, and Screaming Lord Sutch and disc jockey Brian Matthew both rate him as their favourite singer. Coleman briefly but appositely sums up Brook's vocal qualities and technique, citing his strong, masculine-plus timbre, his jazzy phrasing, his warmth, his human interpretation of lyrics, his built-in swing, his devastating range, and his depth. He names Dinah Washington, Ella Fitzgerald and Pat Boone as Benton's favourite singers. His favourite band is the Nelson Riddle Orchestra. Coleman closes his article by extending a warm welcome to the UK to Brook Benton.[128]

In his statement, the music critic not only demonstrates a thoroughly expert understanding of the mechanics of the music industry, but also delivers in summary one of the most penetrating analyses of Benton's vocal artistry. Although Brook was unable to perform on the first night of the tour due to illness, his subsequent appearances were tremendously successful. Peter Thompson noted that, at the London Palladium, the Beatles like many others were knocked out by Brook's professionalism. After the concert, however, a mass of teenagers stormed the site to try to get to the Beatles.[129] Ringo Starr's assessment of Brook Benton is most interesting. In a handwritten letter from 1962 that was put up for auction in December 2006, the Beatles' drummer ranks Brook, along with Chuck Jackson

---

[127] Ibid.
[128] Ibid.
[129] Unknown source, 26 October 1963.

and Dinah Washington, among the singers that he rates most highly.

Brook Benton's appearance at the Finsbury Park Astoria proved to be another spectacular triumph. He worked with lights and visual effects and repeated his Palladium success, 'Ol' Man River', during which he imitated Nat 'King' Cole, Fats Domino and Louis Armstrong. Here was an act that had form, pacing and professionalism, asserted the *NME*'s Ian Dove.[130]

Another voice commenting on his Astoria appearance felt that Brook Benton had earned the title of 'Most Underrated Singer' on the basis of his record over the past few years alone. His opening concert at the Finsbury Park Astoria last Saturday revealed that he is also one of pop music's masters of natural stagecraft. He sang magnificently, working through some of his record repertoire like 'The Boll Weevil Song', 'Fools Rush In' and 'Two Tickets To Paradise'. But the highlight was a marvellous rendition of 'Ol' Man River', in which Brook's singing ability and sense of the dramatic combined with breathtaking effect.[131] It is a pity that Brook never recorded this famous song.

The British audience has remained loyal to Brook Benton up to the present day. His 1984 UK appearances with Nancy Wilson and others[132] were received with great enthusiasm by concert-goers. Coming as they did during what was a most challenging time for the singer, the spontaneous warmth with which people made their way to the stage to shake his hand must have meant a great deal to him.

Many of Brook's original recordings have been reissued in the British Isles, for instance a double CD containing the *My Country* and *That Old Feeling* albums (2004). Mention must also be made of the museum in Brook's hometown of Camden, which has a small section dedicated to the singer that receives far more enquiries about him from the UK than anywhere else in the world.

As well as playing London and various provincial cities, Brook also guested on several TV shows, after which the tour moved on to Paris. There, at the famous Olympia, he stunned the audience with his extraordinary talent. However, he then quit the tour suddenly and flew back home to the USA: his wife was about to give birth to their fourth child and he wanted to be by her side at all costs.

After his fourth child, son Gerald, was born, Brook had to return to touring once again. As ever, he was on the road here, there and everywhere, and could seen and heard on the stages of all the big and important cities across the USA. At the start of 1963, he played San Diego and the Palladium in Los Angeles as part of a West Coast tour. On 4 December, he returned to the latter. The *California Eagle*

---

[130] *New Musical Express*, UK, 25 October 1963.
[131] Unknown source, 26 October 1963.
[132] See also page 140.

Brook onstage with unknown white lady, Ella Fitzgerald and Joe Williams.

published a brief report and was unstinting in its praise. The fabulous Brook Benton opened last night at Basin Street West for a limited stay only. Though it had been a long wait, it was well worth it. His rich voice and presentation reflects why this songster is one of the truly greats of the nation today.[133]

Interestingly, *K-E-Y Magazine* ranked Brook Benton as one of the big names in jazz.[134] Now, Brook was no jazz singer, but who in reality is exclusively so? All the big singers on the popular music scene who are classified as jazz have time and again worked with material which in essence has nothing to do with jazz. Fundamentally, it comes down not so much as to the *what* as to the *how*. If one takes the basic elements which are indispensable for that which we call jazz, namely a feel for swing, blues and spontaneity, creativity and the ability to improvise, one can or must absolutely attest to jazz elements in Benton's singing. This predisposition to jazz which is constantly evident in his vocal art is something which Brook never overemphasized or developed. In any event, this tendency and his vocal ability could have made him a jazz singer.

---

[133] *California Eagle*, 5 December 1963.
[134] *K-E-Y Magazine*, 5-12 December 1963.

Brook duets with his friend Roy Hamilton.

Brook Benton could also have been successful as an opera singer. According to his nephew, Brook Grant, who was in close contact with the singer during his final years, it is a skill Brook privately pursued, though he never seriously considered going in that direction professionally.

The concert at Basin Street West must have been quite an event, as the newspaper published a picture which shows Cassius Clay enjoying Brook Benton's show along with Ish Evans, the owner of

Basin Street West. In addition to the former heavyweight champion, Brook had invited more than 50 leading radio deejays to the club.[135]

Having already left the USA earlier in the year to appear in the Bahamas and in Surinam[136], Brook flew from San Francisco to Australia on 26 March 1964 for a two-week stint at the Chevron-Hilton Hotel in Sydney. After that, he travelled to Manila in the Philippines and then on Alaska, before returning home to New York in mid-May.[137] In July, he appeared at the Club Harlem in Atlantic City[138], and in December he played both the Mid-South Coliseum in Memphis[139] and the Back Bay Theatre in Boston[140]. These were just a few of his significant ports of call during 1964. Brook was in good company on his stage appearances. When the Palladium Club in Atlanta opened its doors in July 1965, its inaugural show featured Brook, Cannonball Adderley & His Orchestra and LaVern Baker.[141]

Let us now jump ahead to another memorable live appearance. On 12 August 1966, Brook played the Blue Room of the Roosevelt Hotel in New Orleans. He was the first black entertainer to be permitted to headline there.

According to one report of the event, it was a successful and very promising debut. Brook was flown in at short notice after Al Martino, who had been booked to appear, cancelled due to a broken toe. He didn't get to the Roosevelt Hotel until 5.30 p.m., where he only managed a brief rehearsal with the Leon Kellner Orchestra before taking the stage at 10.30 p.m. The *States-Item* reported that it was 'probably the greatest takeover ever of its kind'. Nobody noticed that the rehearsal time had been so short. Al Martino was forgotten, wherever he was in the deep canyons of New York, because Brook Benton swung. He held the crowd in the palms of his big hands. He ranged from the classic popular stuff to country & western with the ease that marks a great performer. For variety, he threw in a gaggle of impersonations – Louis Armstrong, Fats Domino, Walter Brennan and Nat 'King' Cole. These were very well done and well received. Many have labelled Benton a 'second Nat Cole', a flattering compliment any entertainer would welcome, but there's much more here than an imitation. He has a style all his own with a range that can take on any of the standards, as well as the newer, wailing-type songs. His accompanist, Clifton Smalls, gave him piano support that was just about halfway between Nashville and New York. When Benton jokingly

[135] *Eagle Rock Sentinel*, 12 December 1963.
[136] *Norfolk, V-A. Journal and Guide*, 4 April 1964.
[137] *St. Louis Argus*, 3 April 1964.
[138] *New York Courier*, 11 July 1964.
[139] *New York Courier*, 26 December 1964.
[140] *Record American*, Boston, 26 December 1964.
[141] Herman Mason, *Images of America* (Arcadia Publishing, Mount Pleasant, SC) 1965.

said, 'I'm just surprised to be here,' many in the audience agreed with him, but added, 'Thank you, it's our pleasure.' Brook Benton's show ran until 31 August.[142]

At this juncture, Cliff Smalls needs to be dealt with in a little bit more detail, as he was an important part of Brook's backing band for seven years. Born in Charleston in 1918, he had started out as a trombone player and pianist, playing with Billy Eckstine and Earl Bostic until the early '50s. Later on, he played alto and baritone sax with several different R&B groups. As a pianist, he accompanied artists like Clyde McPhatter, Ella Fitzgerald, Brook Benton and the Miracles.

After years in the business and countless live performances, Brook was able to fulfil another of his wishes. Years earlier, he had thought that only an appearance at the Copacabana could elevate an entertainer to the level of a true star. On 23 June 1966, he headlined at the Copacabana with Hank Bradford as support act. It must have been a moving moment for the singer to stand as a celebrated and recognized artist on the stage of the place where he had once worked as a busboy, and to be able to wear the so-called 'Copa bonnet', described in the Copacabana's PR folder as the 'Night Club Academy Award' or 'Laurel Wreath of Stardom'.

The reviews that Brook received testify once again to the high quality of his performance. *Billboard* reported that 'Brook Benton has a smooth ballad flair that makes his act at the Copacabana, where he opened last Thursday (23 June), a comfortable affair. He establishes a casual mood right at the start and sustains it through a delightful 55-minute run. Benton is a "good music" singer, who can also attract teenage interests. His current Victor single, "Break Her Heart", is an example of his across-the-board potential. Especially effective is a workover of one of his gold-disc winners, "Boll Weevil", which gets an added fillip from Benton's impersonations of Louis Armstrong, Nat "King" Cole, Walter Brennan and Ray Charles. Another winning segment is his country medley, which includes such standards as "I Walk The Line" and "He'll Have To Go".[143]

In the late '60s, while Brook was signed to Reprise, he played the Tachikawa NCO Club in Japan. In his column, journalist Al Ricketts describes his performance as an outstanding event. All Benton had to do the other night at Tachi was open his mouth and he drew applause. He is a swinging singer and whether he is doing 'Lover Come Back To Me', 'The More I See You', 'The Second Time Around', 'The Glory Of Love' or 'Unforgettable', he's on the right track at all times. According to Ricketts, there are few singers around capable of wrapping an entire audience around their little finger with the same flair and finesse that

---

[142] *States-Item*, 13 August 1966.
[143] *Billboard*, 2 July 1966.

Benton musters.[144]

Let us jump ahead again, this time to 1970. This was the year in which Brook enjoyed his biggest-ever international record success with Tony Joe White's 'Rainy Night In Georgia'. He was scheduled to play the Surf Club in Wildwood in the middle of August, and was described as one of the top attractions to emerge from the record world since the advent of rock. According to *Denis Grant's Shout*, he is more than a recording star: in every sense of the phrase, he is a true entertainer. Benton's versatility is unleashed as soon as he steps on the stage. He differs from the mainstream of modern singers in that he takes his audience with him – he captures them completely while on the stage – and the crowd loves every minute of it.[145]

Back in September 1963, at a party in his office on 55th Street to celebrate his 32nd birthday, Brook stated that Mother Africa was his favourite discussion topic. He said, 'I have the burning desire to go to Africa and I'm going there soon. There comes a time in everyone's life when he wants to return home. And for me there's no better time than now.'[146]

These statements were born of an emotion which Brook had carried around with him for a long time and which emerged on his birthday, when his feelings were doubtless running high. They also presented the interviewer with the critical remarks of an African American who was very conscious of his own heritage.[147]

Despite this, one has to appreciate Brook's affinity for Africa and his longing for the land of his ancestors, and take them seriously. Even so, it would be almost eight years before he could set foot on African soil and perform there as an artist.

In the autumn of 1971, Brook travelled to South Africa for a one-month tour. He and another black singer, Judy Clay, were booked by group of businessmen from East Rand for a four-week guest appearance. The orchestra leader and manager of the entire production was Fred Norman.

Benton's reception at Johannesburg's Jan Smuts Airport was so frenetic that he could hardly get out of the customs area. A huge crowd, which also included schoolchildren, turned out to welcome him. He was mobbed and jostled – everyone wanted to get his attention. Brook was reportedly so shaken that he was scarcely able to breathe in the customs hall. Finally, the singer and his entourage managed to get out of the airport and make it to their hotel unscathed. He later commented: 'It was great. I have never seen anything like it before.

---

[144] Unknown source.
[145] *Denis Grant's Shout* Vol. 9 No. 8, Week of 14-20 August 1970.
[146] Unknown source, 19 September 1963.
[147] *Amsterdam News*, 14 December 1963.

Mobbed at Johannesburg Airport, 1971.

I have been mobbed in other parts of the world, but not so much.'[148]

On the first night of his visit to South Africa, a party was held in the City Hotel in Johannesburg, where the tour retinue were staying. Of course, Brook sang that evening, and it is interesting to read how the event passed off. At first, there was strict separation according to skin colour. White guests were being served by black waiters. When Brook started to sing, an amazing change took place among everyone present. Blacks and whites mingled, were friendly with one another, and even went as far as black guests being served by whites.[149]

The situation is strongly redolent of a similar occurrence many years later when Paul Simon and his musicians and singers from the USA and Africa performed in Johannesburg. Out of what had been an explosive and dangerous atmosphere – acts of terrorism had been threatened – there developed among the concert-goers a friendly and happy togetherness. Art and music, especially when they have multicultural resonance, can be a great agent for peace.

When he was asked about apartheid in South Africa, Brook said that he was here to sing and entertain, but would not be able to do so if he were to take a stance regarding such contentious issues.[150]

---

[148] *Township Mail*, September 1971.
[149] *The Star*, Johannesburg, 15 September 1971.
[150] Ibid.

One ought not reproach Brook Benton for a lack of courage to agitate against South Africa's racial problems. Nearly 20 years before the end of apartheid, it would not have been possible for an entertainer to voice an opinion on the subject without affronting some of their public. Brook Benton's position regarding the race question is sufficiently well known. He was an intelligent, bold and energetic advocate for his race.

When Brook visited South Africa for a second time in 1982, the anti-apartheid movement had become a lot stronger, and he was blacklisted along with Ray Charles, Frank Sinatra, Rod Stewart and several other prominent artists for performing there.[151] Threatened with a worldwide boycott of his concerts and recordings, he made a solemn pledge at the end of 1983 that he would not perform in 'racist South Africa' again until majority rule was achieved.[152]

Many years after his first South African tour, Brook spoke about the song 'Lie To Me', which he had had to sing there. It was quite an old number, so he did not ordinarily include it in his repertoire. However, his black fans really wanted to hear it and vociferously demanded it time and again, which at first he could not understand. Eventually, he found out the reason, in the process discovering a different approach to the song that was revealed to him by these people. They were accustomed to being lied to and sensed this same feeling in the song 'Lie To Me', but were able to turn their negative feelings into happiness by rocking to it. This was fascinating to Brook because he had never considered anything like that before.[153]

Brook Grant explained that the reason his uncle did not want to sing this old hit any more was because he too had often been deceived and cheated during his life. 'Lie To Me' is certainly one of Brook Benton's great, timeless classics. It came out of the same Nashville session which produced the *Singing The Blues* album.

As has already been mentioned, Brook Benton visited the Caribbean numerous times, mostly the Bahamas, where he was always enthusiastically received. Reports from Nassau reflect his popularity there. After his final appearance in the Emerald Room of the Hyatt Emerald Beach Hotel, longtime fan L.O. Pfindling, Prime Minister of the Bahamas, became a new friend. Brook had played the Emerald Beach Hotel for a whole week, which was sold out up until the last day.[154]

In this show, he also performed a new song called 'Remember The Good' from his latest album, *Something For Everyone*, which

---

[151] *Black Enterprise*, December 1983.
[152] *Lakeland Ledger*, 2 January 1984.
[153] US radio network, 4-5 October 1986.
[154] Letter, MP Marketing Partners Ltd, 16 May 1973.

brought approval convincingly from the crowd. Brook, who had often played the Cat & Fiddle in Nassau, also enjoyed his return: 'It was like coming home,' he commented. 'I've always liked this place so much. It makes me feel so good to be back.'[155]

After José Feliciano had ended his 'home game' at the Royal Room of the Flamboyan Hotel on 28 April, Brook guested there from 1 till 8 May, billed as the 'Super Headliner'. The *San Juan Diary* calls him a leading exponent of blues ballads who can take on the challenges of all musical trends of his time and whose abilities as a showman put a shine on his performance.[156]

One of Brook's fans describes him not as a star, but as a galaxy that shines just as much now as it did at the start of his career. Lynn Ashby from the *Houston Chronicle* adds that Brook Benton offers a professional hour without a fuss and always entertains his listeners in the most pleasant way.[157]

Despite the great albums that Brook made with Arif Mardin for Cotillion in the late '60s and early '70s, his career as a recording artist began to stagnate, while at the same time things also became quieter for him on the big show stages. On top of that, there were financial, personal and business problems troubling the artist. For contractual reasons, he was unable to make any records for three years. A shadowy affair in which organized crime is supposed to have played a significant part – Brook refused to give in to extortion – resulted in him being charged with tax evasion. The IRS intervened, and overnight Brook and his family lost their house in St Albans and all their possessions, including irreplaceable personal items such as all the recordings Brook had of himself, his gold records, etc.

The artist's earnings were distrained, so the situation for him and his family was exceedingly precarious. We know that the records Brook Benton made during the first half of the '70s were scarcely promoted, if at all. To make ends meet, Brook had to take any gig that was offered to him. He toured around many of the smaller nightclubs in the USA, and, according to him, spent most of his time on the road in Europe.

Brook's widow recalled that he frequently visited England to appear on BBC shows. Whilst there, he also performed in Scotland and Ireland. In March and April 1976, he toured Britain with the Stylistics. The soul group from Philadelphia was at that time enjoying great success and had Brook as a special guest on their show.[158]

In Europe, Brook was amazed to discover how immensely

---

[155] *Nassau Guardian*, 12 May 1973.
[156] *San Juan Diary*, 27 April 1973.
[157] Ibid.
[158] Souvenir programme, Ember Concert Division, March-April 1976.

knowledgeable fans were about him and black music in general. Many would come up and talk to him about records he had forgotten he had recorded, and even about his personal life. Brook liked the limelight he was bathed in while in Europe and decided to bask in it for a while.[159]

During the '70s, Brook would also return to his musical roots from time to time. According to Frank Schiffman, owner of the Apollo Theater in New York, Thermon[160] T. Ruth, disc jockey, composer, singer and gospel promoter, was the initiator of the first gospel show at the Apollo. This influential protagonist of the gospel scene produced a *Gospel Caravan Show* during the '70s on which Brook Benton guested and sang 'Heaven'.[161]

To promote his 1977 album, *Makin' Love Is Good For You*, Brook undertook a big tour which took him to all big cities in the USA – among them Chicago and Los Angeles. In Los Angeles, he sang at the Dooto Music Center on 27 and 28 May 1978. Brook was the headliner, and the supporting programme included Mary Wells, the Penquin, Don Julian & The Larks, the Meadowlarks Band and Rudy Ray Moore. The concert was staged by Clarence Wiggins.

Thereafter, it wasn't always easy to find bookings for Brook, as he had problems with alcohol for a while, and also with drugs. His unstable state of health resulted in him missing rehearsals and scheduled performances. John Levy confirms that promoters turned him down because they knew about his health issues.[162]

Ruth Brown describes Brook as being on an emotional rollercoaster at this point in his life. She wasn't working with him at the time, but she too had heard that his attitude had changed. The singer

[159] David Smallwood, 'Rainy Years in America Sent Benton to Europe', unk. source, ca. 1977/78.
[160] Sometimes spelt Thurman.
[161] Thermon T. Ruth, *From the Church to the Apollo Theater* (Ruth Pubs, New York) 1995.
[162] John Levy, *Men, Women and Girl Singers: My Life As A Musician Turned Talent Manager* (Beckham Publications, Silver Spring, MD) 2000.

had reportedly become unreliable, had started drinking heavily, was taking drugs, and would not listen to anyone. It was very sad. Not having seen Brook for several years, she went to see him perform on West 57th Street and was shocked by his appearance. He was skin and bones, and, although he came over strongly enough, Brown says she sensed the changes he must have gone through from the man she had toured with, when this wonderful artist was at the top of his game. She adds that she was aware of the bitterness that existed between Brook and his old songwriting partner and recording manger, Clyde Otis, to whom he sold – some would say gave away – his publishing copyrights for $50,000. But despite everything, Brook's performance and the way he played the audience were both as strong as ever.[163] Brook himself says that these engagements in small clubs meant a great deal to him. He learned to appreciate the atmosphere there.

He had to continue performing live while he looked around for opportunities to get back into the recording business. Even the physical proximity of his audiences made it a worthwhile experience for Brook. A short video recording of a reasonably significant club appearance in Hollywood features Brook singing 'The Boll Weevil Song', 'Thank You Pretty Baby' and 'A Rainy Night In Georgia'. He is accompanied by an orchestra directed by the well-known trumpeter and bandleader Gil Askey. The recordings, which were made in 1982, reveal a singer and entertainer operating, as before, at the absolute peak of his abilities.

In the '80s, Brook Benton was also invited back to big stages time and again. In November 1983, he guested on a show called *Jazz Greats* in London and Manchester along with Rosemary Clooney, Buddy Greco, Kay Starr, Woody Herman, George Williams and others. In 1984, he returned Britain as part of a tour called *Living Legends,* which had a constantly changing bill. On 19 October, he and Nancy Wilson appeared at the Theatre Royal in Glasgow. On 21 October, he joined the Edwin Hawkins Singers and the Inspirational Choir for the *Gospel '84* show at the Wembley Conference Centre. Maureen Quinlan reports that most of the people who turned out must have come to see Brook Benton. Middle-aged fans of both sexes rushed the stage and after his performance the auditorium became rather empty.[164] On 22 October, Brook played the Bournemouth International Centre with Astrud Gilberto and Nancy Wilson. A day later, he and Nancy both guested at Sheffield City Hall, along with Teddy Wilson. This concert was broadcast live on UK TV and is documented on video. On 26 October, Brook sang at the Tunbridge Wells Assembly Hall. Elaine Delmar was the support on that occasion. On 27 October,

---

[163] Ruth Brown/Andrew Yule, ibid.
[164] *Blues & Rhythm* 5, UK, December 1984.

Brook and Nancy Wilson guested at Southport's Floral Hall. Finally, Brook and Elaine Delmar could again be heard the following day at the Hatfield Forum. On other nights, the *Living Legends* tour also included Roberta Flack, Peggy Lee, Jimmy Witherspoon, the Ramsey Lewis Trio, Gerry Mulligan, Stan Getz and Buddy Greco.

A year later, Brook appeared at the Township Auditorium in Columbia, South Carolina. There, he was awarded the Order of the Palmetto, the highest civilian honour of the state, by the Governor of South Carolina. Additionally, he was presented with the Key to the State.

In 1986, Brook once again stood on one of Chicago's big stages. In 1987, he performed at the Phelps Auditorium in his hometown of Camden. That same year he performed one last big concert in New York with the Mighty Sparrow and Ray Charles. The venue for this event was the Brooklyn Museum of Art. The three stars also toured together, taking in Florida, Los Angeles and San Francisco (to mention the most important stops) as well as Toronto, Canada.

Brook sang regularly, every few months, at Sweetwater's on West 68th and Amsterdam in New York. He managed to fill the place every time and was cheered just like in the good old days. Even Billy Eckstine, who attended one of these concerts, appeared taken with, and enthralled by his performance.

Music critic Stephen Holden wrote a review of one of these appearances for the *New York Times* which was published the following day, 28 September 1986. He describes Benton as an interesting transitional figure in the evolution of contemporary pop-soul singing, who continues to bring ballads in the same singular blend of gentility and unexpected roughness that characterized his earliest hits in the late 1950s. He croons in a sly, subdued whisper whose emotional restraint recalls the late Nat 'King' Cole, but every so often he dips and swoops into an imposing bass-baritone. Holden notes that Brook mainly sings his old hits, which, like his voice, combine an old-fashioned sense of pop decorum with cautious rock and blues elements in a manner that is unusual nowadays. The highpoints of the show were Benton's hits, 'It's Just A Matter Of Time' and 'Rainy Night In Georgia', whose sweepingly dignified melodies transcend today's mundane pop conventions.[165]

Brook made his final live appearances in early 1988, when he was invited to perform on several country music shows. Fans of this music value good singing. Of course, he was not a typical country singer with a nasal twang. Brook's singing – as ever – was bluesy and swinging, and communicated soul – even through country music. His performance aboard Opryland's *General Jackson Showboat* was

---

[165] *New York Times*, 28 September 1986.

reported to have been enthusiastically received by the audience.[166] Further appearances followed on the *Nashville Now* TV show, including one memorable occasion on 19 January 1988, when he duetted with Tony Joe White for more than five minutes on 'Rainy Night In Georgia'.[167] Given his new-found popularity in the country field, there was a clearly a hope that Brook might be able to find his way back into the charts via this route. Indeed, he had recently signed a contract to cut an album, so it seemed like it would only be a matter of time before he had another hit.[168]

Brook's daughter Vanessa told the author that her father was planning to do a song called 'You Go Around Once' on it as a duet with her. An excerpt from the lyrics will serve to express the hope he placed in the project:

> *Sometimes this old world can get you down*
> *And you feel like you've lost your best friend.*
> *A smile is just a frown turned upside down,*
> *So hold on tight and you'll soon be*
> *Back on your feet again.*

The working title of the proposed album was *After The Rain*. It was to consist predominantly of Tony Joe White compositions and Brook had already been to Louisiana to cut some demos. It would not be long before the world once again heard his inimitable way of giving vocal expression to a lyrical creation in the form of song.

Sadly, it was not to be. Brook Benton died on 9 April 1988.

---

[166] Peter Grendysa, ibid.
[167] *Wisconsin State Journal*, 19 January 1988.
[168] Grendysa, ibid.

CHAPTER 6

Style and Stagecraft of
Brook Benton the Entertainer

The form and content of Brook Benton's live performances have already been previously detailed to some extent. In order to delve deeper into Brook's stage presence and stage style, further comments about his performances are collected together and discussed below.

On stage, Brook Benton was awe-inspiring. He was tall, cut a good figure, and always took care to be well-groomed and tastefully dressed. According to a 1962 review, good looks and well-pressed suits contributed to him being able to extend his appeal beyond a limited audience.[159] That same year, the *New York Mirror* describes Brook Benton as an athletically built singer with a big smile and elegantly tailored suits.[160] Benton himself states that his new Petrocelli wardrobe strictly follows the Italian fashion line. Nothing is off the cuff.[161]

Under new management in 1963, Brook was to be repositioned. Although his wardrobe was already impeccable and of the highest quality, thousands of dollars were invested in perfectly tailored suits and accessories.

Photos of Brook Benton on stage attest to this. His widow, Mary, stated that he always had around 35 suits in his closet, and that he placed great value on smart clothing to the end. The video recording of his 1984 show in Sheffield confirms that Brook had lost none of his outer elegance. It was not the best of times for the singer, who had gone through some severe physical and psychological problems. On stage, however, he moved just as he always had done: gently, with strong expressive gestures, yet in a restrained manner and dressed in an exceptionally elegant outfit.

Brook regards himself primarily as a singer, which he confirms to the *Baltimore Afro-American* while appearing at the Royal Theater in the city. A singer should leave dancing and acrobatics to dancers and acrobats. He is accepted as a singer and that's what he does: sing. He has a soft voice, and ballads complement it. He talks softly and sings softly. According to Brook, there are a number of things which are

---

[159] Unknown source, 1962.
[160] *New York Mirror*, 5 August 1962.
[161] Unknown source, 1962.

conducive to his style. He doesn't like to be yelled at, and he thinks his audience is entitled to the same courtesy. It is also the best way to gain their attention. If someone wants to hear you, they won't tolerate a lot of noise from their neighbour who prevents them from doing so. There is also a personal enjoyment to be had in performing for a quiet audience, who applaud only when it's appropriate. Brook further points out that, when you are singing softly and the audience is listening attentively, there is a line of intimate communication, which makes for mutual enjoyment.[162]

Benton's ability to spellbind his audience with his vocal style and the way in which he interprets song lyrics is obvious. His singing stirs up feeling, captivating listeners by letting associations and memories rise up within them. It is the singer's personality as an

---

[162] *Baltimore Afro-American*, 10 July 1962.

Brook Benton in action.

interpreter which captivates, which can bring out the meaning concealed behind simple words.

Another feature of Brook Benton's qualities as an entertainer is his versatility. He feels comfortable in any setting, irrespective of whether he's playing in small or large clubs, in theatres or on other stages. This feeling permeates to the audience and a kind of dialogue ensues. The material chosen by the singer takes in his hit records, standards, spirituals and gospel songs, and Benton vocally handles each of these musical forms in a grandiose manner. Also noteworthy are his gestures and facial expressions, which are striking but not exuberant. Brook's serenity and humour round out the show. Vocal imitations of his contemporaries provide highlights.

Brook himself says that, as well as singing, he tries to entertain. He has been learning to talk to the audience to establish a friendly rapport. He is not trying to pass himself off as a comedian, but, when the audience is in the right mood, he does joke around a little. And it has paid off. Part of his routine is doing impersonations of people like Louis Armstrong, Frank Sinatra, Sammy Davis Jr, Sam Cooke, Fats Domino, Roy Hamilton and others – but this also has its dangers. One night, when he was doing his impersonations at the Apollo Theater in New York, the audience suddenly started roaring in the middle of his routine. It bothered him because it was the wrong time for them to be laughing. Then he looked around. Roy Hamilton and Sam Cooke – two of the singers he'd just impersonated – had come out from the wings

In South Africa, 1971.

and were standing there on the stage behind him! He broke up, and it took him nearly ten minutes to recover.[163]

Benton classifies himself as a singer. Not a rock'n'roll singer or a ballad singer, or a rhythm singer. Just a singer. He feels this is very helpful when he is appearing before the public, as no two audiences are alike. Sometimes he performs in front of three different kinds of audience on the same night. If he wasn't versatile with his material, and couldn't change his routine on the spur of the moment, he would be a big bomb. The same thing goes for his records: they include a little of everything. Brook believes very strongly in versatility and aspires to be a good singer of all types.[164]

Brook must have been an enthralling entertainer, as a report of his appearance at the Cat & Fiddle, Nassau on 26 June 1961 reveals. The applause for his 'Boll Weevil Song' was so loud that everyone feared the roof of the Ghana Room was going to lift off. His impersonations of Nat Cole, Sam Cooke, Jackie Wilson and Fats Domino were wildly applauded. His last number was 'I Got A Woman',

---

[163] Unknown source, ca.1961/62.
[164] Ibid.

and if it had been up to that audience, they would be listening still. His voice is soft, velvety and touching, with occasional and deliberate low-register phrases. Accompanying all this is an extremely apt use of gesture and expression. The tilt of the permed head, the sweep of manicured hands, a grimace here, a stomped foot there, the clenched fist and the paroxysm of emotion in the make-believe embrace – all these go to make Benton into the sensitive artist that he is. And that is why he had the audience, as it were, eating out of his hand.[165]

The impressive stage presence Brook displayed at the Apollo in July 1963 was similarly attested: the man with the soothing sound; a man of many talents; a show-business jack of all trades. He is definitely a master showman – his performance is always diversified and highly entertaining. Not only is he one of our finest singers, but his newly added mimicry ranks among the best, and his delightfully injected humour makes each performance a pleasure to see.[166]

In a 1963 interview with the *Defender* magazine, Brook clarifies the principles of how he sees himself as an entertainer. He invests money in himself. He puts a lot of it back into his career, because he figures that's the only way to keep his career going. When he appears at a place he's played before, he always comes back with something new – new songs, special material. That way, the people know they're not spending money to hear Brook Benton do all the same things they heard him do before. His fans are the people who support him, and he would be nowhere without them. Brook wants to show them his versatility. He is currently trying out a new French song. He has got the deep, hoarse-type voice that is right for it. He is going into up tempos and is learning that special material is a necessity now and then. Showing his versatility as good as he can do it, is his way of expressing his thanks to the fans who have supported him.[167]

And indeed, there are many instances where journalists and critics write about Brook's ability not only to sing ballads with the highest sensitivity, but also to vocally handle powerful and elegantly swinging rhythmic material.

By the age of 30, Brook had had 28 hits in succession which sold more than half a million copies, plus ten million-sellers. However, he did not want to sit back and wait for things to happen. He hadn't forgotten how hard it had been to get to the top, and he knew it would be even harder to stay there as a singer and entertainer. It was not simply a question of how he could earn more money; he was wrestling with how to attain perfection, get into the best clubs and appear in every medium where his public would be able to see his best side.

---

[165] *Nassau Guardian*, 27 June 1961.
[166] *New York Courier*, 6 July 1963.
[167] *Defender*, 25-31 May 1963.

After evaluating his performance as an entertainer so far, he wanted to make some quick changes. In future, he wanted to be seen only in the best clubs and on the best TV shows. His many one-nighters and shows in smaller clubs across the country had alerted him to him to the fact that, considering his success and the popularity of his records, he had not been correctly marketed. At the start of 1963, he appointed a new manager, a dynamic young lawyer from New York named Herbert Wright, who was National Youth Secretary of the NAACP. Wright seemed to be just the man Brook was looking for. He arrived with vigour and energy, and immediately sprang into action. Firstly, he reviewed Brook's entire stage routine with him and appointed highly respected men to write new material and modernize his repertoire. Then, Wright terminated Brook's contract with Shaw Artists and took him to Joe Glaser's Associated Booking Corporation, intending to book him into large clubs, where many people who loved his records had not yet seen him.

Success quickly followed. From the Flame Show Bar in Detroit, Brook went to New York and was engaged by a prestigious nightclub which invariably presented artists of the calibre of a Peggy Lee or a Benny Goodman, namely Basin Street East. This led to his previously mentioned memorable appearance, at which he outshone the show's headliner, trumpeter Al Hirt. Shortly after, Brook played the recently opened Small's Paradise West in Los Angeles, successfully completed a brilliant appearance on the Steve Allen TV show, then returned to the East Coast and scored a bullseye with a booking at the best club in Pittsburgh, the Holiday House.

Despite these successes, Benton and Herb Wright ended their professional partnership in December 1963. Wright was replaced by Finis Henderson, who already had greats like Sammy Davis Jr, George Kirby and Jerry Butler on his books. Henderson was also appointed President of Brook Benton Enterprises. Based in New York at 39 West 55th Street, this was a company established by Brook during his time with Herb Wright which was which was supposed to combine the recording, release and promotion of records.[168] However, this cash- and time-hungry organization was only in existence for a short while and failed to fulfil its goal of taking talented young singers and musicians to the top.

Returning to the topic of Brook Benton's style as a singer and onstage entertainer, Al Ricketts, a writer for the glossies, describes one of his shows at the Tachikawa NCO Club in Japan. Brook is referred to as a 'Reprise recording star', which means it must have taken place in 1967 or 1968. Ricketts finds that Brook is an

---

[168] *Jet*, 19 December 1963.

Brook onstage in New York with Dinah Washington, 1960.

extraordinarily good performer onstage. He talks very little, sings a lot, and comes across like a cross between Frank Sinatra and Billy Eckstine. When he sings 'That's Life', he actually sounds like Frank, whom he can impersonate to a T. Furthermore, Benton is a smooth and polished performer whose fans obviously stick with him to the very end. On this night at the Tachikawa, he only needed to open his mouth before people started applauding. The audience knew all his songs and communicated with the singer by applauding before, during and after every song. Benton is a swinging singer, and whether he sings 'Lover Come Back To Me', 'The More I See You', 'The Second Time Around', 'The Glory Of Love' or 'Unforgettable', he's always on the beam. There are few singers who could conquer their audience with such flair and finesse as Brook Benton.

The highlight of his act were his impersonations of Fats Domino, Ray Charles and Louis Armstrong during his hit, 'The Boll Weevil Song'. If one wanted to hear more, only the slightest request was necessary, and Brook would deliver a moving version of 'Ol' Man River'. All in all, it was a great show, the like of which we won't see for a very long time. Brook is a talented gentleman, who obviously enjoys stepping into the limelight in order to make a multitude of people happy. This is a man you should not miss.[169]

At the close of this chapter, Brook should be given an opportunity to have his say. In radio interviews which were broadcast in early October 1986, he goes into rather more detail about how he structures his live performances. He gladly creates medleys of several songs, but of course also performs individual songs. He enjoys imitating other singers, and has even begun to rap with his audiences. In no way does he want to bore his listeners. Brook talks about his songs to the people who come to his shows, about what they mean to him, and hopes they feel about them the same way. He thinks 'Rainy Night In Georgia' is a particularly good song to talk about. It has so many connecting points which go off in various directions. What is happening in the story of the song need not really be Georgia, it could be happening anywhere in the world; it is like the blues.[170]

By all accounts, Brook Benton remained a popular live draw throughout his career. One puzzling fact is that, towards the end of his life, he increasingly restricted himself to reproducing his old Mercury-era hits when he appeared onstage, rendering them as far as possible in contemporary arrangements, but forgoing many of his artistic qualities in the process. Whether the reason for this lies with his management at that time, or with Benton himself, remains an open question. Brook intimated to his nephew, Brook Grant, that a singer can always earn money if he has a hit.

One distinguishing characteristic of Brook Benton's music is its duality: it took its quality from old musical forms, but at the same time referenced what was to come in the future, transiting eras and styles. Brook had clearly not tired of breaking new ground – as is demonstrated by his brilliant final performances in the country music idiom. He would most definitely have surprised us with new musical material and contemporary forms of music, and his proposed *After The Rain* album – named after a Tony Joe White composition – would undoubtedly have had symbolic value. Unfortunately, in the end Brook Benton had to fall silent.

---

[169] Unknown source, ca.1967/68.
[170] US radio network, 4-5 October 1986.

CHAPTER 7

TV Shows and Film Projects

The world of film and television also had to take notice of a successful record star and respected entertainer. So it's no wonder that Brook Benton often guested on TV shows like those of Ed Sullivan, Perry Como, Dick Clark, Johnny Carson, Steve Allen, Barbara McNair and Mike Douglas. He was also a favourite guest star on local television stations, for example on KDKA-TV's *John Reed King Show* out of Pittsburgh. In actual fact, he received more offers to appear on TV than he had time for. In October 1960, when Brook had just started his journey along the road to success, he was booked onto NBC-TV's *Saturday Prom* to do two numbers, 'Kiddio' and 'Fools Rush In'.[171] On 19 November 1963, the *Washington Daily News* reported that he would be appearing live on WOOK-TV's *Teenarama*. Three days later, Brook was on the *Mike Douglas Show* when President Kennedy was assassinated. He was halfway through a duet with Roberta Sherwood when the programme was interrupted by an announcement that the President had been killed.[172]

In 1965, Brook resumed working with Clyde Otis, this time for RCA Victor, and scored a chart hit with 'Mother Nature, Father Time'. An accompanying 16mm colour film for video jukeboxes was produced by Scopitone.

In early 2000, reports emerged of a plan to compile a kind of biopic of Brook Benton from all the footage that exists of him on video, of which only a very small proportion (e.g. the 1982 Hollywood and 1984 Sheffield shows[173]) is well known and available through normal retail channels. Arguments about rights seem to have frustrated this project ever since.

The fact that Brook Benton's life and career were already the subject matter of artistic and dramatic portrayals is evidenced by two stage productions. Jackie Taylor and Jimmy Tillman wrote the pop musical *The Brook Benton Story (Just A Matter Of Time)*, which traced the late singer's life history. Another theme of the musical is the successful collaboration between Clyde Otis and his two most talented

---

[171] *Jet*, October 1960.
[172] *Akron Beacon Journal*, 23 November 1963.
[173] See pages 393 and 398.

Wednesday, December 2, 1959   *VARIETY*

Thank you..!

ED SULLIVAN

•

Third Repeat Engagement
DECEMBER 13th
ED SULLIVAN SHOW
CBS-TV

•

BROOK BENTON

Currently on a **1 NIGHT TOUR** across **AMERICA**

"IT'S JUST A MATTER OF TIME."

"ENDLESSLY"

"THANK YOU PRETTY BABY"

And the Current *HIT RECORD:*

"SO MANY WAYS"

Soon to be Released:
"THIS TIME OF THE YEAR"

stars, Brook and Dinah Washington. The production received numerous favourable reviews, as is illustrated by the following summaries.[174]

The show, which was staged at the Black Ensemble Theatre at 4520 N. Beacon, was highly recommended by the critics. Brook Benton is described as one of the pioneers in the process of achieving the high esteem which black artists were eventually accorded. However, the classification of his voice – namely that he was equipped with a Mephistophelian bass – is somewhat inaccurate. Brook was actually a baritone, but the range of his voice also allowed him to move with ease within the confines of a bass.

The Brook Benton Story was presented as part of a year-long series of events celebrating African-American artists. Co-writer Jackie Taylor had found a niche with this type of musical theatre which was highly appreciated by the public. An earlier production – a play by Taylor about Sammy Davis Jr – had been followed by a musical about Otis Redding which ran at the same time as *The Brook Benton Story*. Taylor's account of Benton's life simultaneously creates a platform for 20 of the singer's greatest hits ranging from 'The Boll Weevil Song' to 'Rainy Night In Georgia'.

Direoce Junirs, who plays Brook, receives special mention. He is tall, good-looking, blessed with a golden bass-baritone voice and is one of the best singers on the stages of Chicago. When he sings, he is a ladykiller, just like Benton was. His version of 'Rainy Night In Georgia' creates the impression that it really is raining all over the world.[175] Junirs brought the house down along with Barbara Floyd, who appeared as Dinah Washington, and Edward Wheeler, who played Clyde Otis. At the first performance, the females in the audience screamed just like fans of the Beatles had in earlier times.

Musical director Jimmy Tillman is supported by arrangers Thomas Washington (instrumentation) and George 'Paco' Patterson (vocals). With the main actors, the seven-piece band, and two veterans on backing vocals, they completely succeed in replicating the authentic Mercury crossover style. Two female dancers round things off. All in all, *The Brook Benton Story* offers a most entertaining night out at the theatre.[176]

On 12 January 2001, at the Black Spectrum Theatre in Queens, New York, the Opus Dance Theatre's production, *Rainy Night In Georgia*, celebrated the history of African-American culture through dance interpretations. The choreography was by Esther Grant-Walker

---

[174] Unknown source.

[175] Benton himself stated this to be the emotional message of the song.

[176] *Chicago Reader*, 16 May 1997; *Chicago Sun-Times*, 26 May 1997; *Chicago Weekend*, 29 May-1 June 1997; *Chicago Tribune*, 5 June 1997.

and Obedia Wright, two internationally acclaimed dancers and choreographers. The highlight was a performance of the musical legacy left behind by Brook Benton. Brook's daughter Vanessa was guest of honour and speaker at the event.

In October 2004, the Call For Peace Foundation staged a musical at the Stella Adler Theatre in Hollywood called *Queen Of The Blues*, a homage to Dinah Washington. The play, which according to writer Jerry Jones has some basis in truth, also celebrates black music icons like Brook Benton, Billie Holiday, Sarah Vaughan and Ray Charles. The box office receipts were donated to the Foundation, which promoted the cultural self-awareness, unity and security of impoverished African Americans.[177]

It is also interesting to note that one of Brook Benton's songs was used in a stage play. The 2004 Broadway revival of *A Raisin In The Sun*, Lorraine Hansberry's acclaimed 1959 drama about a struggling black family, was highlighted by his wonderful interpretation of 'Movin' Day' (Cotillion, 1970).

In 1963, Herb Wright, who was Brook's manager at the time, entered into negotiations with one of the three big US TV networks regarding a proposal for a Brook Benton television show to be launched the following year, and the company responded positively. Wright duly contacted Canadian Norman Jewison, one of the most brilliant young TV producers around at the time, to see if he would oversee the project. Jewison was keen to make the show, but a little later the TV company pulled out of the deal without specifying a reason. All they said was that they should have known a little more about Brook Benton.[178] It is conceivable that the escalating racial tensions in the USA influenced their decision. Generally speaking, in the '50s and '60s it was difficult or impossible for black artists to have their own TV show. Indeed, the first and only one to succeed was Nat 'King' Cole, who had a show in 1956. However, it only ran for half a year before being discontinued due to lack of sponsorship.

Brook Benton's relationship with the medium of film could be a chapter in itself. For years on end, plans were made to establish him in the motion picture business. For many singers, an appearance in a movie signalled a turning point, or at least gave new impetus to their career. They became known to a public who reflected more on the visual rather than the aural, and were then retroactively accepted as singers. Without wishing to diminish the vocal quality of the likes of Frank Sinatra, Dean Martin, and above all Sammy Davis Jr, it is arguable that that their second or even third careers were often sustained through the medium of film. Brook's career never got this

---

[177] *Los Angeles City Beat*, October 2004.
[178] Unknown source, late 1963.

second wind, although proposed films that were to include him were written about and discussed time and again. In the summer of 1962, the singer confided that he still did not know exactly everything he wanted to achieve in his career, but he knew what he didn't want, and that was to be an actor. He was convinced that he would never make an actor.[179]

Benton's doubts that he would be able to reach the same level as an actor as he had as a singer are understandable. He was a perfectionist and was aware of the challenges he would have to face in order to fully develop within a new artistic profession. Very soon after his first record successes, he had been asked whether he would be interested in playing the role of a black private detective in a TV series. At first, it sounded very good to him – he was quite flattered – and also the money he could have earned was attractive. But then he noticed that the role only required an actor, and that he would be given absolutely no opportunity to sing. After discussing the offer with his manager, Dave Dreyer, Brook declined. He is a professional singer, but would have been going out as an amateur actor, which wouldn't have been fair to his fans. He didn't want to exploit his success as a singer for the sake of earning a few dollars in another profession.

In fact, Brook did not even want to set foot on the Broadway stage – the big goal of every entertainer – until he felt he was ready. In conclusion, he conceded that he knew a little about acting, stage presence and that sort of thing, but certainly did not feel he could class himself as an actor. Perhaps someday, but not now.[180] However, he was soon to became indirectly involved with the film industry. His Mercury recording, 'Walk On The Wild Side', was chosen as the theme for the 1962 film of the same name. The movie was produced by Charles K. Feldman, and starred Laurence Harvey, Capucine, Jane Fonda, Ann Baxter, Barbara Stanwyck and Joanna Moore. Brook himself did not appear in it, but was nominated for an award on account of his vocal contribution. Unfortunately nothing more became of it. This is a pity, because the film received good reviews, and if Benton had made an appearance in it somewhere, somehow, it could have been the first step towards adding another facet to his artistic career. The *Brooklyn Daily* reported that his wonderful singing in *Walk On The Wild Side* had really pepped-up the proceedings at the preview of this new Columbia film, at which all the important people in show business were present.[181]

Two years later, Benton sang another title song for a film, Bacharach & David's 'A House Is Not A Home'. The picture is based

---

[179] *Sunday News*, 2 July 1962.
[180] Unknown source, 1963.
[181] *Brooklyn Daily*, 2 March 1962.

Promoting *Walk On The Wild Side* in 1962.
Left to right: Brook Benton, Dick Denham (WINX), Hal Charm (Mercury Promotion Manager), Al Jefferson (WUST) and Kay Farrell (Radio/TV columnist, *Washington Daily News*).

on a bestseller by Polly Adler and had two top-class leads in Shelley Winters and Robert Taylor. The title song, which Brook had recorded for Mercury, was also used to promote the film.[182] No wonder, for it was on its way to becoming the singer's 28th consecutive smash hit.[183]

---

[182] *Motion Picture Exhibitor*, Philadelphia, 26 August 1964.
[183] *Chicago Defender*, 5 September 1964.

As far back as 1958, a film called *Country Music Holiday* had included three of Brook's songs ('Goodbye My Darling', 'Don't Walk Away From Me' and 'Ninety-Nine Percent') on the soundtrack.

One of his biggest hits, 'Baby (You've Got What It Takes)' with Dinah Washington, has been used as incidental music in several films, notably *Two Weeks' Notice* (2002) starring Sandra Bullock and Hugh Grant, and *Hurricane* (1999) starring Denzel Washington. The latter film also included Ruth Brown's version of the Benton-Stevenson composition, 'I Don't Know'. Brook and Dinah's 'Baby' was also used as background music in *Operation Blue Sky* (1990) starring Jessica Lange and Tommy Lee Jones. Their other big hit, 'A Rockin' Good Way', was featured in *Nights In Rodanthe* (2008). Brook's Christmas song, 'This Time Of The Year', can be heard in *Untamed Heart* (1993). That same year, his famous 'Rainy Night In Georgia' rang out during the 'Every Man's Family' episode of the *In The Heat Of The Night* TV series. *When Nature Calls* (1995) includes 'The Boll Weevil Song' as background music. Brook's recording of 'It's Just A Matter Of Time' appears on the soundtrack of *Boogie Nights* (1997), while *All The Rage* aka *It's The Rage* (1999) features the Benton-Colacrai composition 'You're For Me', as performed by Clyde McPhatter. Brook can also be heard on two numbers by the Landfordaires in 2004's *The Ladykillers*: 'Trouble Of This World' and 'Troubled, Lord I'm Troubled'.

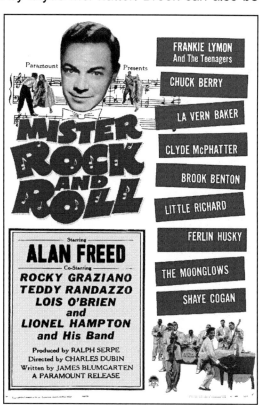

Hollywood.com lists four other movies which feature Brook Benton as singer: *Hareemu Ohgen* (1985), *Skin Deep* (1989), *Crossing The Line* (1991) and *My Son The Fanatic* (1999). His compositions are also to be found on the soundtracks of *Consenting Adults* (1992) and *All Men Are Liars* (1995).

Brook actually only appeared in one film himself, *Mister Rock And Roll* (1957), in which he sang two songs: 'Your Love Alone' was announced by Alan Freed and was then heard as background music. However, Brook was also shown miming to 'If Only I Had Known', during which he was visible for the entire performance.

In the years that followed, Benton's reservations about acting persisted, though his reluctance to enter the movie business diminished. If it didn't interfere with his singing, he could imagine having a career in acting, he said, but added that his acting ability was still an unknown quantity. According to Brook, negotiations were currently in progress to have him star in a good picture with established actors.[184] There is more to-ing and fro-ing. Brook appears to have enormous respect for the medium of film. He will not, however, throw himself headlong into the adventure of acting – that would be something he would have to prepare himself for. He has received many requests to appear on TV in straight acting roles – all of which he has turned down. After repeating his already frequently stressed reservations, Brook admits to taking acting lessons, so that if and when he becomes an actor, he will be prepared.[185] Shortly after these 1962 interviews, negotiations regarding Brook Benton's acting career appeared to be very well advanced. When it came down to it, however, the singer's reticence threw up an insurmountable barrier. The film in question was to have been shot in Paris and Algiers. However, Brook did not want to go to North Africa under any circumstances.[186]

This notwithstanding, the media of film and the musical stage both remained temptations for the singer. Dorothy Kilgallen writes in the summer of 1962 that Brook has a burning ambition to appear in a Broadway musical. While film and the musical stage are not the same thing, it is easy to imagine that the tall, handsome, well-groomed black singer would have cut a fine figure both in front of a movie camera and on a Broadway stage. As regards his live performances, all the critics describe him as an extremely talented and likeable entertainer who captivates his audiences. Time and again, Brook's personality is highlighted, the warmth and cordiality he emanates – qualities which are prerequisites for any kind of stage career.[187] However, it would appear that Brook was reflecting on his own abilities too much to be able to seize the moment and grasp the opportunity to find an even larger audience as an actor and singer.

In mid-August 1962, Brook once again confides to a reporter that he is about to start shooting a film. The shyness with which he talks about it is evidence of his uncertainty. Dino De Laurentiis, the Italian director, has offered him a big role in a film he is planning to

---

184 *Baltimore Afro-American*, 10 July 1962.
185 *Sunday Star*, 5 August 1962.
186 Unknown source.
187 *Chicago's American*, 4 August 1962.

shoot in Rome. Brook is going to play a singer, and hopes to be able to do a lot of singing in the role. He does not, however, regard himself as an actor, adding that a lot of people who *think* they are, really aren't.[188]

What an opportunity De Laurentiis could have been for Benton! An eminent producer and film-maker like him should surely have been able to entice a great singer and entertainer like Benton onto the polished floor in front of a film camera. A great chance was wasted here. At the end of the interview with the *Long Island Press*'s William Raide, Brook gets to talk about another project that is important to him, namely the plan to record an album of religious music in his own home church in Lugoff, South Carolina. His parting remark is significant: 'That's better than being a movie star.'[189] The truth of the matter was that Brook had already distanced himself from the plan to make a film with De Laurentiis. Despite this, in early 1963 there are further deliberations about a possible acting career for Brook Benton.

The singer wants to make it depend on his fan mail. If he gets enough letters encouraging him to do it, then anything is possible.[190] As regards this apparent 'one step forward, two steps back' attitude, one has to wonder whether Benton alone is to be blamed for all of this indecision. It is hard to believe that an entertainer as sure of himself onstage and in front of an audience as Brook was in the early '60s really had such great deference to acting.

In the summer of 1963, *Jet* carried a report about Brook Benton's latest film project. According to the magazine, he will be going to Hollywood in the autumn to shoot a movie that will be partially based on his life story. An independent company will produce the film. Black authors John Baldwin or John Killens will supply the script. The actresses are said to include Dorothy Dandridge and the singer Barbara McNair. Jerome Robbins will direct the film, and Benton will sing ballads and gospels in it.[191] This project was initiated by Brook's manager, Herb Wright, who asked Killens to write the script, because Baldwin was too involved with other assignments. Columbia Pictures were to release the film.

Exactly why this never came to fruition, or why Wright resigned after only managing Brook Benton for a short time, has never been established. However, it is a fact that Brook did not abandon his aspirations, for in January 1964 he unambiguously declared: 'Sure I want to be an actor... where else can I go from here?'[192] Indeed, the *Amsterdam News* reported six months later on concrete plans to shoot a film with the singer. According to the newspaper, it looks like the

---

[188] *Long Island Press*, 12 August 1962.
[189] Ibid.
[190] *Defender*, 25-31 May 1963.
[191] *Jet*, May 1963.
[192] *Journal American*, New York, 26 January 1964.

summer of 1964 will be huge for Benton. He is due to go to Hollywood in a few days' time to begin his career as an actor. In his first film, he will be seen in a lead role alongside Ann Sheridan, Peter Falk, Basil Rathbone and Frankie Fontaine. The title of the picture, which is being produced by Vaquere Productions, is *Ding Dong, The Wine's All Gone*. Benton will be playing a deaf mute. The title song will be sung by Brook Benton.[193]

In June, Brook entered into what was probably not a totally serious agreement with the well-known *Hamlet* actor, William Redfield: he would give Redfield singing lessons, and in return the actor would coach him in his role as a deaf mute.[194] By this time, Brook had finally become serious about broadening his means of artistic expression through acting. Without making a big fuss about it, he began attending the American Academy of Dramatic Arts in New York in September 1964. His teacher, Lynn Masters, had once had Marlon Brando and Sidney Poitier under her wing. Brook's explanation for taking this step is again thought-provoking. He explains to the listeners of WHBI's *Midnight Jazz Festival* that they can read in the *New Crusader* that he is a family man, and this way he can be closer to his expanding family. Of course, he does not want to give up singing.[195]

Tall and well-built, and equipped with a dominant personality, Brook is, in the opinion of various producers, definitely suitable for the film business. Naturally, he needs to learn the craft of this profession. The fact that he can sing will improve his chances of getting parts. Something which does sound strange after all that has gone before is the singer's assertion that he has always wanted to be an actor. The chance he'd had the previous year of a part in a film had been wasted. Now he will be ready for anything that comes his way.[196]

Unfortunately, a succinct announcement in the *Capital Spotlight* a couple of months earlier had already ended all speculation of a silver screen debut for Brook: 'Brook Benton... was scheduled to go before the cameras for his first movie role sometime in October, but for some reason the deal has fallen through. Some type of disagreement among the producers has caused the movie to be called off.'[197]

---

[193] *Amsterdam News*, 2 June 1964.
[194] *New York World-Telegram & Sun*, 23 June 1964.
[195] *New Crusader*, 5 December 1964.
[196] Ibid.
[197] *Capital Spotlight*, 25 September 1964.

CHAPTER 8

Brook Benton's Personality

As Brook Benton's fame and acceptance as an artist grew, so did the media interest in him. Specifically, numerous interviews with the singer appeared in print, in which he commented on ideological and social issues, and also provided an insight into how he viewed himself as a singer and entertainer. In the process, Brook revealed himself to be a reserved, level-headed, contemplative, yet humorous individual able to see through the machinations and superficialities of show business, as well as someone who gives critical consideration to fundamental social behaviours and is able to analyse them. Given his background (a childhood in a large and poor family whose members were closely bonded by love and singing and playing music together; a long road to success paved with many obstacles; and not least his life experiences as an underprivileged black in a society dominated by a white upper class, who already as a very young man had to provide for a family), Brook Benton had matured at an early age.

Just how widespread public insensitivity to the race issue continued to be, even as late as the '60s, is demonstrated by the blunt use of the word *Negro* – by both whites and blacks. There was still a long way to go before the terms *black/colored* and the present-day stock phrase, *African American*, were adopted. This, of course, does not imply that a truly harmonious climate exists between people of different skin colours in the USA, even today.

Several topics worthy of more detailed consideration may be distilled from Brook Benton's many observations: family life; social issues; racial discrimination and Civil Rights; his character, likes and interests; and of course Brook's views and self-conception regarding his life as a singer and entertainer. The commentaries which follow expand further upon these themes.

CHAPTER 9

Brook Benton the Family Man

As has already been mentioned, Brook grew up in a family of ten, who, despite having to fight daily for their survival, lived in harmony. Love for one another and trust in God formed an indestructible basis for coexistence, out of which there developed an environment of safety and security for the children. His close bond with his family home would remain with him forever. Even when he had matured into one of the greatest vocalists in America, Brook always bore in mind how much strength his mother's encouragement to go his own way and become a singer had given him. Likewise, he tried to follow his father's advice all his life: 'You're doing good. But be the same boy you were when you started.' Last but not least, the admonition from his grandmother that, whatever may happen, 'Benjamin, you be a good boy',[198] also left an enduring impression on him.

The positive attitude to life which Brook acquired from his family was essentially inextinguishable, and later helped him come through a very difficult time and try to make a fresh start. Sadly, a sudden serious illness and his unexpected early death would shatter his hopes, as well as those of the many devotees of his music and vocal art.

The value he placed upon the feeling of security within his family, and his subsequent longing for it, must especially have grown within Brook after he left Lugoff and went to New York City. His many attempts to gain a foothold as an artist and the numerous activities which secured his livelihood probably left him little time to look at girls. But in 1955 (by which time he had already made something of a name for himself as a composer), it happened: Brook met Mary Askew at a rehearsal room called Johnson Music Studio, where she worked as a secretary. He later reflected that there had been many important turning points during his life, but one of the good ones was meeting Mary, and it was to define his life from that time on.

Mary was the first girl that Brook had ever fallen in love with, and he married her shortly after they met. The couple also had children very early on: Brook Jr. arrived in 1956, Vanessa followed a year later, Roy Hamilton was born in 1959. They then waited a while for their fourth child, son Gerald, who first saw the light of day in 1963.

---

[198] *Rock & Roll Magazine*, 1959.

Brook and Mary.

Mary Benton with daughter Vanessa and youngest son Gerald, 1965.

Given his character, as Brook Benton's artistic success grew, and along with it the opportunity – and obligation – to tour, the singer was caught in an understandable dichotomy. Time and again he complained about the long absences from his family, whom he loved above anything else. Success may have brought him a nice bank account, clothes (he always possessed around 35 suits), a nice car, and many things he had always dreamed of, but it also prevented him from being with his family as often as he would have wished. Brook spent between 30 and 40 weeks on the road each year.

The singer was particularly concerned that his children should have a good and secure future, and his live appearances were of course necessary to achieve that.[199] Later, Brook once jokingly remarked that his marriage to Mary had remained intact precisely *because* of his frequent absences, as there was always a happy reunion every time he returned home.[200]

On 23 June 1962, Brook was voted Father Of The Year, an annual award presented by Lou Borders at his *Father's Day Fashion Show*.

In a profile published by *Ebony* magazine, he confesses that he has reached a point in his career where he frankly doesn't know where to turn. He doesn't want to earn more money if it means increasing the tempo of his career in return for less home life. The ideal life, as he sees it, would be to stay in New York and record, but that is not commercially practicable.[201]

Benton's plans for a career as an actor also need to be considered in this context. On WHBI's *Midnight Jazz Festival*, he explained to listeners why he had taken acting lessons: 'The reason is simple... I'm a family man and I want to be near my growing family here in St Albans. You can't take them on one-nighters.'[202]

In the autumn of 1963, Brook visited Europe. Performances in London and several British provincial cities were followed by one in Paris at the famous Olympia. As previously mentioned, following that show, Brook pulled out of the rest of the tour, which was supposed to have lasted ten weeks, in order to return to New York. In doing so, he passed up planned appearances in Munich, Rome, various Scandinavian cities and the Netherlands. He wanted to be present at the birth of his fourth child at all costs, but also hoped that the baby would be born on time, so that he would be able to appear at Basin Street West in Los Angeles at the end of November.[203]

While undertaking a three-week residency at a hotel in

---

[199] *Nite-Lifer Magazine*, April 1960.
[200] *Ebony*, April 1978.
[201] *Ebony*, May 1963.
[202] *New Crusader*, 5 December 1964.
[203] *New York Courier*, 23 November 1963.

Brook Benton, proud father of Vanessa, Brook Jr and Roy.

Melbourne in 1964, Brook confided to an Australian reporter that, as always, he was missing his wife and four children back home in New York. He had already called them four times since arriving. His biggest regret about his chosen profession was having to be a father to his children over the telephone. He said he normally only speaks to his wife when he calls, but occasionally one of the boys or his daughter needs a word of advice or encouragement.[204]

---

[204] Australian newspaper, name and date unknown.

Brook says goodbye to his children before going on tour.

Without the loving understanding and unconditional support of his wife Mary, the singer and entertainer would not have been able to cope with the difficult balancing act between the demands of show business, and those he placed upon himself as father of the family.

Brook also never forgot the family from which he came: his father and mother, to whom he owed so much. He bought his parents a comfortable apartment in New York and installed them in it after he

Arriving at the airport after a European tour.

had reached – as he termed it – the sub-zenith of his career.[205]

In 1960, Benton bought his parents a beautiful car, which he delivered to them personally. 'Oh boy, you should've seen my father', said Brook. 'Just dazed. Finally, he blurted out: "Is this really mine?"' Then Brook gave him the keys.[206]

---

[205] *Pittsburgh Courier*, 31 October 1959.
[206] *New York Daily Mirror*, 8 January 1960.

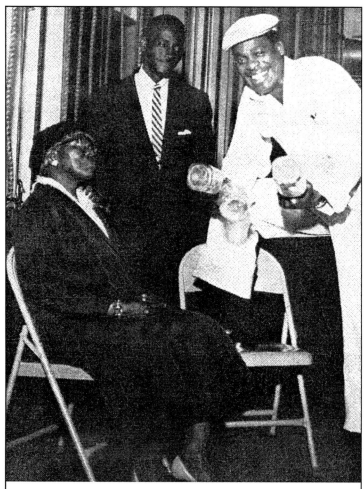

THE SWINGIN' MR. "B"
POSES AS A MILKMAN
TO AMUSE HIS SO VERY
PROUD MOTHER AND DAD.

Brook's generosity was not limited to his family. For instance, he gave a car to the guitarist Billy Johnson – his onetime musical director and one of his closest early-'60s collaborators – at a birthday party at his home in St Albans. Brook Benton's superb people skills will be described in a separate chapter.

The singer's close bond with his family is corroborated by his sisters, his brother and, of course, his daughter Vanessa, as well as his nephew Brook Grant, upon whom he had a great influence. His sister Ruth said she misses her brother terribly, as he was the one who held the various far-flung members of the Benton/Peay clan together.

Meeting up as a family on various holidays during the year, especially at Christmas, was always down to Brook's initiative.

Asked about her childhood, the thing Vanessa recalls first and foremost are the happy moments connected with the return of her father after a long absence. She describes him as a humorous, kind-hearted man who could never refuse one of his children's wishes. If he didn't want to agree to one of his sons' requests, they knew exactly what to do: their sister would be put forward as supplicant in the knowledge that, in all probability, they would achieve their goal.

The singer's widow, Mary Benton, made a touching statement regarding Brook and his family during an interview she granted to the author of this biography. She and Brook had experienced some wonderful times together. The financial crash, the loss of the beautiful home in which the family had settled and the resulting social irritations, Brook's health problems and much more besides had never been a reason for them to split up. The beauty in their relationship prevailed over everything, and Mary affirmed that all her memories were good ones.

Mary Benton died in 2010.

CHAPTER 10

Brook Benton's Social Commitment

Brook Benton's background, education and long, hard road to recognition as an artist moulded his social outlook. Sympathy and the espousal of causes for disadvantaged members of society were characteristic of the singer. From the time he first stood as a star in the limelight, he was able to audibly express his social outlook, as well as demonstrating it practically through various activities. One special concern of his were young people's problems and hardships. Brook had never finished high school because he'd had to work from a young age to help secure his family's livelihood.

In 1961, the city of New York initiated a 'Stay-in-School' programme. It had been recognized that something needed to be done about the high drop-out rate in high schools, and Brook was willing to take part in a campaign which spelt out to parents, students and the public at large the importance of education for the future of New York. On 27 August 1961, Brook, Teddy Randazzo and Neil Sedaka participated in a show at the Coliseum intended to decrease the drop-out rate in the city's high schools. He received a thank you letter from New York's mayor at the time, Robert F. Wagner, who also expressed the hope that Brook would participate in the programme again the following year (see next page).

Benton's empathy for young people was also reflected in public statements in which he came to their defence. In particular, he spoke out against generalizations that had nothing good to say about them. Teenagers have been taking the blame, he felt, for everything from the international situation to crime. The vast majority of youngsters are good citizens. Unfortunately, the delinquents are the only ones people read about, and they are few in number. It's always the bad apple that gets talked about, not the barrel of good ones. He added that, on tour, he meets a great many teenagers, most of whom are polite.[207]

In 1963, Brook took some time out from his career to launch an organization which became known as DDO: Don't Drop Out. He hoped to encourage teenagers not to quit school. He planned to visit schools across the whole country, along with other well-known celebrities, to

---

[207] *Sunday Star*, 5 August 1962.

CITY OF NEW YORK
OFFICE OF THE MAYOR
NEW YORK 7. N.Y.

Mr. Brook Benton
c/o Dave Dryer
345 West 58th Street
New York, New York

Dear Mr. Benton:

It gives me great pleasure to present you with the enclosed
Honor Citation in recognition for your enthusiastic cooperation
in support of New York City's 1961 "Stay-in-School" program.

Your participation with the City's communications media in
stressing the importance of completing a high school education
to students, their parents, teachers, counselors and the general public, was a vital factor in the success of our campaign
to reduce high school "drop-outs," which is so important to
our City's further growth and well-being.

To this award, may I add my personal thanks and deep appre-
ciation. I know I can count on your continued support in this
program in the coming year.

Sincerely,

Robert F. Wagner
MAYOR

speak to students.[208] It is not self-evident that stars will participate in activities relating to young people.

On 4 September 1965, Bedford-Stuyvesant Youth In Action held an *Olympic Games*. Brook also attended this event, seeking direct contact with the kids. Mrs Ruth A. Logan, the association's Director of Public Relations, wrote a letter to Brook on 13 September 1965, in

---

[208] Unknown source.

BEDFORD-STUYVESANT YOUTH IN ACTION, Inc.

1273 FULTON STREET

BROOKLYN, N.Y. 11216

STERLING 3-7600

September 13, 1965

MRS. DOROTHY ORR
EXECUTIVE DIRECTOR

BOARD OF DIRECTORS

WILLIAM M. CHISHOLM, ESQ.
CHAIRMAN

HARDY R. FRANKLIN
SECRETARY

MRS. SYLVIA SHAPIRO
TREASURER

ARTHUR BRAMWELL
GARVEY E. CLARKE
MRS. ALMIRA COURSEY
REV. WILLIAM J. CULLEN
MRS. GWENDOLYN DEKALB
DENIS A. DRYDEN
THOMAS R. FORTUNE
DR. HARRY D. GIDEONSE
DR. CECIL C. GLOSTER
RICHARD T. GREENE
LOUIS HERNANDEZ
MRS. BERNICE E. JOHNSON
REV. WILLIAM A. JONES
JOHN OLIVER KILLENS
REV. H. CARL MCCALL
HON. FRANKLIN W. MORTON, JR.
SYDNEY S. MOSHETTE, JR.
DR. ROBERT PALMER
MRS. ANNE W. PINKSTON
JOHN L. PROCOPE, JR.
MRS. ELSIE RICHARDSON
RUSSELL N. SERVICE
MRS. A. D. SMITH
HERBERT VON KING
DR. GARDNER C. TAYLOR
WILLIAM C. THOMPSON
OLIVER D. WALCOTT

CONSULTANT
DR. CLARENCE SENIOR

Mr. Brook Benton
175-37 Murdock
St. Albans, New York

Dear Mr. Benton:

We cannot thank you enough for taking the time to attend our Olympic Games on Saturday, September 4, 1965. Your presence gave the youngsters a sense of importance and a feeling that people outside of their own community really cared.

A copy of one of the photographs taken on Saturday is enclosed. A release has been sent to the Amsterdam News and Courier.

I hope I have the pleasure of meeting you again soon.

Sincerely,

Ruth A. Logan (Mrs.)
Director, Public Relations

RAL/gw
cc: Mrs. Orr
Mr. Hepburn

which she warmly thanked him for his visit (above). His presence had conveyed to the young people the feeling that they were being taken seriously, and that folks from outside their own community also cared about them.

There are also other examples which can be cited from the multitude of benefit events Brook Benton supported. At the beginning of January 1962, WWRL distributed more than 1,500 baskets of food, toys and clothing to the needy. This was the climax to a month-long

Brook presents a prize at the Youth In Action *Olympic Games*, 1965.

fund-raiser by the radio station. On 20 December, nearly 400 people had crammed their way into the St Nicholas Arena, at the intersection of 66th Street and Columbus Avenue in New York, to celebrate an 'all-star entertainment' which brought Count Basie, Brook Benton, Damita Jo, Ben E. King, Bobby Lewis, Maxine Brown and many others to the stage. All the proceeds of the event went towards the WWRL

Christmas Fund.[209]

In February 1963, the Delta Sigma Sorority, an association of former students, called upon their 700-plus members to support one of the biggest and most thrilling occasions in the history of their organization: on Sunday, 17 February, the Sorority would be presenting the fabulous Brook Benton in concert at the Hollywood Palladium. Nearly 3,000 visitors, members and friends of Delta Sigma were expected. Fresh from celebrating its 50th anniversary, the local chapter had selected the golden voice of Brook Benton to launch its 1963 fund-raiser. It was hoped that the cabaret concert would fill its coffers, so that it could carry on funding local and national community services.[210] Brook was honoured to be able to support such fund-raising events.

The Christmas celebration at the Junior Blind of America institute in California must have been particularly touching for the singer and the other celebrity participants. Two events had been planned: one on Friday evening for the older children, and the other on Saturday afternoon for the younger ones. They were organized under the auspices of the Foundation for the Junior Blind and were supported by the Publicists' Association of Hollywood. It was an exciting and beautiful experience for the blind children. The face of every kid reportedly sparkled with joy. They moved about freely, and squealed with delight when the names of the entertaining guests were announced. They sang along with Mimi Dillard and Jayne Mansfield. They roared applause for Brook Benton, who was the first guest to appear. The children squealed with delight when his name was announced and crowded around the stage. Brook was visibly surprised to discover that these kids were well-adjusted, happy, eager, interested, inquisitive, smart, ambitious, optimistic youngsters.[211]

Brook Benton's social involvement also extended to church projects. His attitude is understandable given his upbringing in a religious family home, his gratitude to his hometown church and choir, and his strong faith. On 29 February 1964, the Carter Community AME Church in New York burned down. Rev J.C. Carter did everything he could to rebuild it bigger and better than before. He managed to constantly increase the membership of the reconstruction committee. By April that year, the membership consisted not only of the faithful poor, but also of well-to-do citizens. Naturally, Brook Benton was among them.[212]

In April 1965, he was a guest at a reception at the Bethany

---

[209] Unknown source, 4 January 1962.
[210] *California Eagle*, 7 February l963.
[211] *California Sentinel*, 26 December 1963.
[212] *Amsterdam News*, 11 April 1964.

Methodist Church in St John's Place. There he autographed copies of his spirituals album, *If You Believe*. The proceeds from sales of the record went to the church.[213]

On 9 July 1974, Brook visited Reality House in New York. Amongst other things, this church facility ran drug rehabilitation programmes. As a very prominent and active church member, Brook declared that he was willing to campaign for this organization because he was brought up in the church, and wanted to help young people – and what better way to do it than through the church. 'If the people here are sincere, I think it's the best thing that has ever happened,' he added.[214]

Time and again Brook participated in charity events for the NAACP (National Association for the Advancement of Colored People) in New York, as well as in other cities. In September 1966, while appearing at the New York Hilton on behalf of the NAACP on what was billed as 'The Show of Shows', he was presented with an award for his selfless contributions to the Association. The other star guests that evening were Nina Simone and Carmen McRae.[215]

From 1963 onwards, Brook Benton's identity as an artist was characterized by persistent but restrained advocacy on behalf of his race. Quiet and reflective by nature, he stayed true to type when it came to the question of Civil Rights. During a residency in Detroit in 1963-64, he gave a benefit concert in aid of Civil Rights in the South. In 1970, he was voted Entertainer of the Year by NAACP delegates on account of his public support for the rights of blacks in the USA.[216]

The front page of the Brooklyn *Amsterdam News* of 17 July 1971 carries a picture of Brook and Dr Gerald Deas from the Department of Medicine at the Jamaica Hospital, New York. Brook is studying a song written by Dr Deas, 'A Black Child Can't Smile'. It is about a youngster who is suffering from sickle cell anaemia, and is, as far as we know, the first pop song ever with illness as its theme. Proceeds from the record, which was released on Cotillion, were donated by Brook to the Foundation for Research and Education in Sickle Cell Disease.[217] Showing an interest in the socially-deprived, and in many ways disenfranchised members of American society was for Brook Benton (and Gerald Deas) also strongly linked with a commitment to Civil Rights. It is no coincidence that the person in the song who is suffering from this disease is a black child, who in all probability has great difficulty in obtaining help to ease their suffering.

---

[213] *New York World-Telegram*, 24 April 1965. The *New York Courier* also reported this on 15 May.
[214] Official Reality House newsletter, July 1974.
[215] *New York Courier*, 17 September 1966.
[216] *The Voice*, 4 December 1970.
[217] *Amsterdam News*, 17 July 1971.

POPULAR ARTIST—Delta Sorority members and the general chairman of the Brook Benton cabaret concert set at the Hollywood Palladium Sunday, Feb. 17, look over one of the many popular Brook Denton albums. From the left they are: Delene Harvey, Evelyn Dixon, Estella "Betty" Lee, general show chairman, Dr. Geraldine P. Woods, first national vice president, and Ethel Maddox.

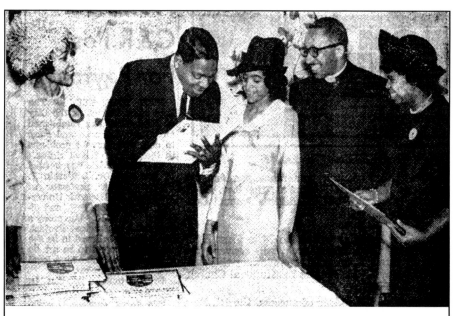

AIDS CHURCH—Record star Brook Benton was a special guest Sunday at Brooklyn's Bethany Methodist Church, where he autographed copies of his Mercury spiritual album, "If You Believe," with all the proceeds being donated to the church. He autographs a copy for Mrs. Barbara Dyce, while (left to right) Mrs. Myrtle Whitmore, the Rev. Melvin G. Williams, pastor, and Miss Beverly Dabney look on.

Brook also cut another song by Dr Deas for Cotillion, 'Soul Santa'. This song also plays subtly, cautiously and a little ironically with Civil Rights issues – issues of equality of race and colour. Two brief excerpts will serve to illustrate this:

> *Since nobody's seen Santa on Christmas*
> *When he steals down the chimney with care,*
> *Wouldn't it be so revealing*
> *Oh, if Santa had black, kinky hair?...*
>
> *Now Santa is a fine soul brother,*
> *He loves all his fellow men.*
> *He'll do anything for you,*
> *At least, he'll do what he can.*
> *Now, no matter what he looks like*
> *And no matter what you've been told,*
> *There's one thing about old Santa:*
> *The man's got soul, he's got soul, he's got soul...*

In an interview with the author of this essay, Dr Gerald Deas confirmed the correctness of these interpretations of both 'A Black Child Can't Smile' and 'Soul Santa'.

CHAPTER 11

Brook Benton and Civil Rights

As an African American from the South, Brook Benton was only too aware of his position in society. His early years in New York, and his hard struggle for recognition and success probably deepened this awareness still further. The social conditions which lay behind his musical development and life as an artist were revealed by well-disposed or fascinated critics some time after Brook had already achieved huge success and astounded the then-rock'n'roll-dominated popular music world with his polished ballad style.

Born in staid Camden in South Carolina, the home of fox hunts and a white society that lived in luxury, Brook fought the handicap of race and made his mark in the music field with an innate sense of tone and timing, born of the perhaps tormented soul of the debased and downtrodden South Carolina and Dixie Negro.[218]

The social status of African Americans at that time, and for a long time afterwards, is demonstrated by the uninhibited use of the word *Negro* to describe them. Indeed, blacks themselves also used this term. However, their self-esteem had developed far enough for the word *Negro* to have become obsolete as a description of race.

For the black population of America, the road from the 1964 *Civil Rights Act* to genuine, true equality was a long one. It must be acknowledged, however, that many prejudices have not yet been eliminated, and that racial inequality and injustice continue to cause turmoil. As for the term *Negro*, Dr Martin Luther King's speech in Washington, DC on 28 August 1963 points the way. It finishes: 'When we allow freedom to ring, when we let it ring from every village and every hamlet, from every state and every city, we will be able to speed up that day when all of God's children, black men and white men, Jews and Gentiles, Protestants and Catholics, will be able to join hands and sing in the words of the old Negro spiritual: "Free at last! Free at last! Thank God Almighty, we are free at last!"'

On 19 October 1959, Brook was booked as one of the attractions at a rock'n'roll dance show in Columbia, South Carolina. A local newspaper indignantly reported a statement the singer had made while he was there: 'A Lugoff Negro who has hit the big-time recording

---

[218] *Pittsburgh Courier*, 31 October 1959.

market in New York Saturday night recommended that the Southern Negro "live where he wants". Asked if he recommended that the average Southern Negro head north, Benton paused, stammered a minute and declared, "It's up to the individual."[219]

Evidently, at this point in time Brook was not yet free and confident enough to counter this awkward and too general a question with the necessary quick-wittedness and take it *ad absurdum*. The tense relationship between blacks and whites was at that time almost exclusively a problem specific to the USA. In post-World War II Europe race was barely an issue, and great entertainers were celebrated regardless of the colour of their skin. One only needs to think of Louis Armstrong's, Ella Fitzgerald's, Sarah Vaughan's, Nat 'King' Cole's, Sammy Davis Jr's, or even Brook Benton's triumphant appearances in London and Paris in 1963. The contact with cultures and societies outside the USA may have had an effect on the self-confidence of black artists and emboldened them to stand up for the rights of their race.

In the spring of 1960, Brook was invited to an autograph party at a Woolworth's store in Detroit. Immediately before, he had appeared at the Flame Show Bar, where he was told about the endeavours of students from the South to secure integrated seating arrangements at five-and-dime store restaurants in the South: they had organized sit-down strikes and placed pickets outside Woolworths and Kresge stores in Detroit, Lansing, and Ann Arbor. When he heard about the student action, Brook said he would be the last to pull the rug out from under the feet of black and white students with such good intentions, explaining: 'I look at myself every day in the mirror and I'm not getting any whiter. Anyway, I had to turn down the appearance, not because I'm a Negro, but because I'm for what is right.'[220] Morris and Sally Wasserman, owners of the Flame Show Bar, also agreed that Brook had made the right decision.[221]

In the South especially, people like Brook Benton were made to feel the stigma of their skin colour. However, the singer came up with an antidote: namely, not to perform at venues where audiences were segregated. On a tour of the South in 1962, his managers had agreed an itinerary of double shows. Brook didn't know that all the first shows were intended for white patrons, and all the second shows for blacks. He was disappointed that he had been deceived, and made sure that nothing like that would ever happen again. As far as he was concerned, there are only audiences – not 'white' or 'colored'. Any other way, they would just have to count him out.[222]

---

[219] *The State: Carolina's Progressive Newspaper*, 19 October 1959.
[220] Unknown source, February/March 1960.
[221] Ibid.
[222] *Baltimore Afro-American*, 10 July 1962.

For Brook, one of the most important successes in the struggle for equality of the races must have been the admission of black student Harvey Gantt to Clemson University. Clemson lies not far from Brook's hometown, and Gantt was the first black person to be enrolled there. Coincidentally, Brook was to have been the first black artist ever to perform on the Clemson college campus. However, due to an ear injury he had recently sustained after being attacked in a nightclub in St Louis, he was unable to claim this honour. His place was taken by Dakota Staton, with whom he switched appearance times. After his performance, the Dean of Clemson University invited him and his crew to spend the night on campus. Brook reported that the faculty, as well as the students, accorded him every courtesy. During a long talk with Harvey Gantt, the artist learned that many students had made friends with the young black man. Harvey felt that he was becoming increasingly accepted, in that he was now regarded as just another a 'campus Joe' and was respected for his abilities.[223] The high regard in which Gantt was held by his fellow students echoes the dream which Dr Martin Luther King so vividly expressed in his famous speech on 28 August 1963: 'I have a dream that my four little children will one day live in a nation where they will not be judged by the color of their skin, but by the content of their character.'

This dream was not to be fulfilled for a long time, and African-American exponents, artists and politicians alike, were time and again confronted by racial issues.

Benton spoke candidly on the subject in an interview with Morton Cooper. The conversation took place in August 1963 during a break between his first and second shows at Basin Street East. From the outset, the journalist stresses Brook's seriousness in his article. Contrary to the image one has of him as a constantly laughing, pleasant, young and simple man, he shows himself to be no simpleton. At present, Benton himself is not totally clear about his position. In truth, no black artist knows that. Despite his incredible success, he is painfully aware that his sole remit is simply to sing as best as he possibly can. However, he also carries an additional responsibility not to attract criticism for doing something onstage out of a natural, personal impulse that would in no way be a problem if he were a white singer. Brook regards his own behaviour as restrained. He doesn't whip his audiences into a frenzy; neither does he drive them into such raptures that they want to tear off his clothes. What he really wants to do, is to go down amongst the crowd to greet them and shake their hands. But if he did that, he would be strongly criticized. Of course, the word *Negro* is not mentioned, but he feels the message is: 'Step back,

---

[223] *Philadelphia Independent*, 9 March 1963.

man, keep a respectful distance.'[224] Later on, in Europe – and especially in the UK – Brook was able to enjoy the crucial contact he longed to have with his audiences. At the start of his career, it had been mainly teenagers and only a very few adults who had hung around the stage entrance or outside the building. In Europe, however, it was adults who stood in lines at the stage door like the teenagers had in America. These people had been fans for 20 years. They stood outside but didn't actually want any autographs; they just wanted to meet him. They reminded him of things that he no longer thought about any more. They knew his whole life story and talked to him about it in the most pleasant of ways. It was an uplifting feeling for the singer, because the more interest the public showed in him, the more interested he was in them. These experiences released some really good feelings within Brook.[225]

Let us return to the interview with Morton Cooper. Brook cites the entertainer Robert Goulet, who leaves the stage and meets his public as if it were his absolute right and is never criticized by anyone for it. It is Brook's conviction that all kinds of tensions – not just those between black entertainers and a few white nightclub owners – have built up across the USA, and will remain until such time as equal rights become a fact once and for all. Before we get to that stage, these tensions will affect everyone.

In the statements which follow, Benton goes out on a limb to such an extent that they demand to be quoted verbatim: 'We're waking up. We are tired of being pushed around. What are we – dogs? The man tells you: "Here's a uniform. Take thirteen weeks of basic training and then go to fight for your country!" So you fight and you get out, and you can't even vote for a president, or a governor, or a city councilman, or whoever... We're thinking: *Here I was, ready to die, and for what? I come back and get kicked in the pants all over again.* We're thinking: *I'm gonna die some day, but first let me* live *for a while. Let me understand what living is like. Let me get some of the best of life!* We've been through a hell of a lot, and we're tired of being shoved around.'

Brook is convinced there will be bloodshed. He doubts that he himself would be a good peace-marcher. 'I'm not a non-violent Negro,' he explains. 'If a dog, or an Alabama or Mississippi cop comes on me, I'm gonna have something to protect myself with. I am sure I wouldn't last long, so I'm not the type of guy to march. If I'm gonna go downtown to try to speak to the officials to explain the rights of my people, and they have dogs there – well, it's hard to fight off a dog with

---

[224] *Defender*, 25-31 May 1963.
[225] US radio network, 4-5 October 1986.

bare hands. So I figure I'm probably gonna have to get me a gun, or a knife, or a few bombs... These Negroes in Alabama have right on their side. Nothing they're doing is wrong; they're simply marching to demand what's been due to them for years. Their parents and grandparents and great-grandparents helped to build up that part of the country, but what did they get out of it? They worked and they died. And today their children are saying: "We haven't lived, or seen anything either." They're not citizens, no matter what it says in the book. They're not free, they're slaves – they're in something even worse than slavery. The word goes: "Look, Charlie, you can go around back and eat, but when you get the food, it's gonna be poisoned"... When a man knows he may die, you'd be surprised how many people he's ready to carry out with him!... There's the biggest problem: not "Is that guy with the club or the dogs my enemy?" – certainly he is, no two ways about it! – but "Can I be sure the man who calls himself my friend *really* is my friend?" The hardest nut to crack is finding out who's true and who's false. If you're my friend and, at the crucial moment I find out you've just been pretending, I'll blow you up as quick as the out-and-out enemy. Quicker probably.'

In Brook's view, racial tensions also exist in the big Northern cities, only they are more subtle. 'New York is like every other big city. When you are a big-name Negro, you are respected because of that name and you also get applauded. But if you don't have that name, you'll have to work hard to get it, if you want to get ahead. Every night you have to go out and perform better than you did the night before.'

Brook concedes that he loves New York and that it has become home for him and his family. They have a pleasant home on Long Island where he can also relax. He then talks about old friends of his who came with him from the South, but who didn't have the same luck as he did, and have no chance of a getting good education or other basic rights to which all Americans are entitled. They thought they would have every opportunity here, but all they found was poverty – the kind of poverty that is mainly found among blacks.

Brook reckons the dollar counts for more in New York than anywhere else. And, of course, a Negro can get gas here too. He clarifies this not immediately understandable reference as follows: 'Along about the time the Alabama marching began, my brother and I were in the car about 20 miles from our home in South Carolina. The guy at the gas station wouldn't wait on us. He wouldn't even let us use the men's room. He said, "I ain't got nothin' for you," and he ran back into the station. That wasn't in 1933. That happened in 1963. Yeah, there's one thing about New York. I can buy gas here.'[226]

---

[226] *Defender*, ibid.

In this interview, Brook laid himself wide open. For many, the singer's statements might have provided them with ammunition with which to attack him. In reality, Brook was in no way militant; rather, he was restrained and balanced. We must permit a person affected by, or suffering injustice – even if they are an artist in the public eye – to be impassioned about social abuses, and also to use a form of words that expresses what they feel in unambiguous terms. Brook never called for violence; on the contrary, he personally preferred to use other means to support his race. His background had not made it easy for him to advance in show business, but he was always proud of his race. He also appreciated his white audience and their opinion of him. In Melbourne, Benton commented that it wasn't easy to get over some of the things that people say about you. But it also made him proud, and was rewarding for him, when he heard people inside and outside showbiz say they never would have imagined a Negro doing so well.[227]

Shortly before the interview with Morton Cooper, Brook had made a change in his management. Herb Wright, his new manager, wanted to place a different emphasis on certain aspects of his personal and artistic persona. A key aspect of the image that the singer would henceforth project in public was 'Brook Benton the moderate, yet strong personality with a firm determination to play his part in the struggle for Civil Rights'.

A little over two months later, in early August 1963, shortly before the march to Washington led by Martin Luther King, Edward Weiland from the *Long Island Press* newspaper visited Brook at his Long Island home to interview him. At the beginning of his article, the journalist descriptively and reflectively attempts to get close to the mental condition of the singer, who is troubled by the oppression of his race. Now that he is standing before him, all of the questions Weiland had planned to ask Brook about his career have become unimportant. It's not easy to watch a man cry. But it's even worse to see a man's eyes grow narrow and his hands double up into tight fists and his body tremble with anger as he talks about the injustices heaped upon his people. You watch his eyes as he talks and you can feel the tears which burn inside him, but somehow refuse to flow.

This portrayal of the artist's emotional state and its effect on the interviewer seem possibly over-emphasized. There is little reason, however, to dismiss them as an exaggeration. Edward Weiland is a white man, not superficial, but possessed of deeper feelings, who is trying to get inside the psyche of a black artist so that he can think and feel like him.

But he can't, for one simple reason: the aforementioned artist is

---

[227] Unknown source, Melbourne, Australia, 1962.

black, and he is white. A white man could never really know what it means to be Brook Benton, or any other of the millions of blacks who feel the same pain as him. Weiland reflects briefly on the fact that he has met a man who is just 31 years old and has only enjoyed star status for a relatively short time, but is nevertheless incredibly profound and sensitive. He listens to Brook talking about the unrest in the South, where he was born and raised, and sees how the artist's entire body starts to tremble. He asks Brook how he feels when he reads about all the incidents down there, and Brook answers: 'How can I tell you how I feel? I can't put it in words. I just feel…sick. Yeah, sick is the only word for it.'

The journalist asks yet another question, enquiring why Brook had not joined other black leaders who had marched with their brothers from the South and had taken part in sit-ins, where they were beaten and humiliated. And Brook reiterates in quiet, dignified words, essentially the same thing he told *Defender* reporter Morton Cooper back in May: he only has one life, and does not intend to sacrifice it to a dog, or a white man with a club. But he doesn't have the courage to remain passive, either; neither is he non-violent. He would hit back. But he will support his brothers in other ways, by working and standing up for them in every way imaginable. He will donate money and hold fund-raising events. But he will not submit to the humiliations that his people are being subjected to by the white man.

Brook recalls the first indignity he ever suffered at the hands of a white man. It was an insignificant matter, but to a sensitive twelve-year-old Negro boy growing up in South Carolina, it cut deep. He had gone to a grocery store to buy a soda. He opened the ice box and just happened to pull out a Coke. He wasn't bothered what drink he bought, it just happened to be a Coke, and he was thirsty. The white store owner ordered young Benjamin to put the Coke back in the refrigerator and get himself an orange soda instead. Brook didn't really know what it was all about until the next time he went in and the shop owner told him that all white boys drink Coke, but black boys drink orange soda. Brook finally understood why the matter was handled the way it was: the store could only get a limited amount of Coca-Cola, and the owner was saving the Cokes for the white kids.

There were many other incidents in Brook Benton's life which made him painfully conscious of his skin colour. However, this one stuck in his mind more than most, as it was the first time he had suffered hurt in that regard. However, Weiland discovers that Brook's childhood in the South was not unhappy. The singer elaborates, noting that sometimes it's good to feel sad, because when you're sad, you can look forward to being happy. When you're happy, you have to worry about staying that way. He himself cannot put into words the

Brook with South African singers after one of the shows in Johannesburg, 1971.

sadness that so often surrounds him, so it comes out through his singing.[228]

On the cover of his *Born To Sing The Blues* album, Benton writes: 'I'm at my happiest when I'm... singing the blues – the tales of gloom, dejection, romantic uncertainty, or whatever the despondency of the moment may be. It's the stories that smack of emotion that make me feel a sense of personal identity.' Behind these words is a sensitive, open soul, who takes the ups and downs which are imposed upon him by external circumstances and translates them in an artistic way. It is a well known fact that sadness and pain in particular are catalysts for artistic creativity and expression. Of course, Brook Benton cannot be limited to that. He was not a depressive person; he liked to laugh, and is described as an entertainer with a sense of humour. Sadness, pain and occasionally despair are to be found in many of his song performances.

Finally, Brook tells the journalist that it was his childhood dream to one day be able to sing for all people – not just for blacks, but for everyone. The conversation between Weiland and Benton ends with a question regarding Brook's children, who are growing up

---

[228] *Long Island Press*, 4 August 1963.

in affluence and without any material concerns, never suspecting that they might also one day experience contempt on account of the colour of their skin. If it ever came to it, what would Brook tell his enquiring children? The singer reveals that he will cross that bridge when he comes to it.[229]

In 1971, Brook accepted a month-long engagement in South Africa, a country criticized worldwide for its policy of apartheid. As regards the race issue, he cannot be spared the charge of being inconsistent in this instance. Benton's refusal in South Africa to take a stand on social issues on the grounds that his job was to sing and entertain was not sufficiently convincing to completely absolve him from accusations of opportunism in this matter. Equally, there are no grounds to pillory the singer and to describe him as a traitor to his race. As a matter of fact, in 1987, Brook, along with many of his fellow artists, signed a manifesto refusing to perform in South Africa as long as apartheid continued to exist.[230]

The moderate way in which Brook stood up for his people is also evident in some songs which he sang with the intention of pointing out social abuses and articulating the rights of his race. Two recordings which can be included under this heading, 'A Black Child Can't Smile' and 'Soul Santa', have already been mentioned. An earlier song which fits into this category is 'I'm A Man', recorded for Mercury in 1964 and released that year on a Warner Bros. compilation, *The Stars Salute Dr Martin Luther King*. Written by Neil Diamond, it is a very beautiful, subdued, yet powerful song, though it can sound cluttered to some listeners on account of the style of its arrangement and Benton's vocal performance. Perhaps a better musical solution could have been found than the sweet pizzicato passage which surfaces midway, but the emphasis on stringed instruments is rooted in the tastes of the times and in the development of accompanying orchestras for black vocalists since the '50s.

Content-wise, the song is virtually a summary of the problems Brook touched upon in both of the interviews above, as is demonstrated by the following extracts:

> *I'm a man*
> *And I just want to live like one.*
> *Why must I fight for what I've won?*
> *I'm so weary*
> *And it's more than I can stand...*

---

[229] Ibid.
[230] See also page 137.

I want to hold my head up high.
I'm flesh and blood and I've got pride.
Can't they see it?
Will they ever understand?...

How do I hide the tears...
When I go to tell my son...
The things he heard, they're no more than lies,
He's as good as anyone...

I'm a man
And soon the day's gonna come
When I'll be free...

Then I'll stand tall
And be seen for what I am:
I'm a man...

Brook sings the serious lyrics beautifully and varies the refrain, which establishes and adds weight to the song's message, with feeling, power and assurance. The fact that he finishes off the repetition of the refrain in the hope-filled final stanza with a vocal *tour de force* that almost stretches his voice to the limit in the higher register should not be dismissed as overblown; rather, it should be regarded as an optimistic affirmation of a better future for his people. Furthermore, a singer should be able to display his or her vocal range when the material allows it. This song was justifiably included in the Dr Martin Luther King anthology.

Another song which must be added to Brook Benton's contribution to reducing the tensions between blacks and whites is 'Oh Lord, Why Lord', which appeared on Cotillion in 1969. The title places it somewhere close to the genre of spirituals. The vocative and exclamatory nature of the composition gives the work its hymn-like tone. The title of the song doubles as the refrain, which is repeated at the end of the narrative part of each verse. The repetition of the line *'Oh Lord, why Lord'* gives the singer the chance to show off his technique of varying the refrain. None of the repetitions sounds the same, and therefore the refrain does not wear itself out, but fulfils its purpose of memorably intensifying the mood, message and emotional demands of the composition. In this song too, Brook portrays himself as someone seeking help, a supplicant. With devotion and humility, but also self-confidence, the singer, speaking on behalf of his race, sets out his requests. Once again we encounter the same thematic content which Brook clearly articulated on many occasions:

> *Why... the color of my skin*
> *Is said to be an awful sin...*
>
> *I've got to live and live...*
> *And give much more than I can give...*
>
> *Tell me why, Lord...*
> *Why this long and bitter strife*
> *Must go on for equal rights...*
> *Why can't there be some harmony*
> *Instead of constant agony...*
>
> *I feel the weight of everlasting hate*
> *And I live with hope*
> *And just a little faith, Lord...*
>
> *I ask no special kindness*
> *I ask not for a crown*
> *I only ask for some justice*
> *To restore what's right from wrong...*
>
> *I don't ask for a kingdom to rule, Lord*
> *Justice...*

There isn't a single aggressive line in this beautiful song, only questions, requests and legitimate wishes. Its theme reflects Benton's own concerns, and he stands heart and soul behind his performance.

Brook does not seek to create a dramatic contrast between highs and lows; instead, his voice sublimely, quietly and powerfully conveys the subject matter, rising in response to each aggression. His vocal mastery turns this song, which could have lost its emotional tension due to its extensive, none-too-varied instrumental intermezzi, into a gem of popular music.

Another song which fits under this heading is 1970's 'I've Gotta Be Me', also recorded for Cotillion. Fundamentally, this song should not be regarded as a manifesto of a minority rights group in the USA. Many singers have appropriated this song and given it the tone and bearing of a self-assertive statement. The version which Sammy Davis Jr cut for Reprise conveys something of the questioning flavour of this composition. However, the artist's certainty that he will be able to find himself can already be established from the very first refrain. Davis's measured and slightly reserved, but forcefully deployed voice makes that clear. This impression is further reinforced by the powerful orchestration which underpins the song.

Benton's version presents itself completely differently. The song, into which other artists often inject pride and loud self-confidence, is initially a request he isn't sure will be fulfilled, which he performs with an insistent but soft, often sustained, head voice. Brook's gripping interpretations of passages like:

> *Lord, you know,*
> *I wanna live, not nearly survive.*
> *And I can't give up this dream*
> *That keeps me alive…*
>
> *I can't be right for somebody else*
> *If I'm not right for me...*
>
> *I've got to be free,*
> *I've got to be free…*

place this beautiful song firmly within the theme we have just discussed. His singing floats constantly between fear, hope, and the confidence of finding a way in the end. The complexity of the interpretation can be attributed to the way in which Benton uses his voice. He handles the text softly and in a reserved manner, deliberately dropping his voice when singing the word 'me' (alluding to the innermost depths of the lyrical 'I', with which the narrator must connect in order to find himself), then working up to a powerful chest voice at the end, articulating the reassuring certainty that he has – or will – become whole. Benton not only narrates; he also emphasizes the dramatic highlights. He varies the continuous rhythm through the faster or slower phrasing of certain passages, and he also varies the tone colour of his voice. Where should one place a song such as this, in which the verses quoted above are interpreted and performed in such a subtle way, if not within the wider framework of African-American struggle for social recognition and equality? The optimism and determination which the singer is able to express in the final lines are highly poignant:

> *Daring to try, do it or die,*
> *I've gotta be me!*

At this juncture, another of Brook Benton's songs needs to be discussed, namely 'Born Under A Bad Sign', which again was recorded for Cotillion. Its theme is the underprivileged individual. Inadequate education, poverty and the struggle to survive, the main motifs of the song, do not necessarily have to apply to the black population of the USA. However, Benton's view that poverty and its consequences predominantly affect America's blacks allows us to confidently assign 'Born Under A Bad Sign' to his artistic involvement with Civil Rights.

After a dramatically emphasized introduction featuring saxophone, bass, drums and organ, Benton begins to sing. The lyrics are neither pleading nor demanding; instead, he accusingly depicts (in his rendition) the bitter fate of one of society's disadvantaged. The beat of the song is hard, and the sound of the brass section unfolds directly and aggressively. Brook also sings harder here than on many of his other songs, but softens the syncopated beat by means of swinging passages. Again, two lines of the refrain, which are rendered by the singer in a variety of ways, act as the focal point of the song:

> *If it wasn't for bad luck,*
> *I wouldn't have no luck at all.*
> *I wouldn't have any luck at all.*

The final repetition of the last line of the refrain is superb. Brook again changes the wording ever so slightly, this time to:

> *I wouldn't have me no kind of luck at all.*

The words, which Brook speaks rather than sings in a very swinging way, almost anticipating the rap style of the future[231], are almost

---

[231] Brook comes closest to this later rhythmic recitative form on the 1976 Olde World recording, 'Bayou Babe'.

exclusively monosyllabic. He renders the extreme swing solo before the drums join in to bring the musical intention to a climax. Brook sings the last word, *all*, in a deep voice, stretching it out as if to consolidate the painful and irrefutable truth of his statement.

A moving and conciliatory statement by Benton closes this chapter. In a 1986 radio interview, Brook references his hit, 'Revenge', which he recorded for Mercury in 1961: 'I was really seeking revenge in my head at that time. I don't say that I was acting, trying to find revenge in reality, physically. But thinking-wise, yeah, in a lot of ways during those days. But I find that I began, as I grew older, to substitute my thinking of revenge... use love instead of revenge.'[232]

---

[232] US radio network, 4-5 October 1986.

CHAPTER 12

Brook Benton's
Character, Likes and Interests

The descriptions of Brook Benton's childhood, his views on family and family life, his social perspective, and his attitude to Civil Rights reveal a lot about the character of the artist. In this chapter, further aspects of Brook Benton's character are examined in detail, in order to round out his personality as a whole.

One particular character trait is reflected in many of the interviews that Brook gave to newspapers, magazines and radio stations: his modesty. It was not an act, but a fact, and a part of his inner being. This is confirmed not only by members of his family, but also by many people from his private and artistic milieus. Brook Benton's modesty should be understood in the sense of the original meaning of the word, namely knowing what prevents smugness and hubris from emerging, and results in propriety and moderate personal behaviour. The humble circumstances of the family in which he grew up, and that loving togetherness, left their mark on the singer's character. The advice given to him by his grandmother on her death bed, to always be a good boy, and his father's entreaty to stay the way he was and never to forget where he came from, even after he became successful, have already been mentioned and also apply here.

In a newspaper interview published shortly after the million-selling 'It's Just A Matter Of Time' and the follow-up smashes 'Endlessly' and 'Thank You Pretty Baby' had graced the charts, Brook explained that, when things were not going so well for him, he had always managed to get by with what he had. Success had not changed him. Although he was living more lavishly than before, basically none of that had influenced the way he thought about things. He had a pretty happy personality and the most important thing for him was being able to sing.[233]

Brook also recommended self-restraint and modesty to younger artists as a way of getting into a possible career. To start with, they should all invest a little, but not in the big business sense. He would much rather make sure he had a roof over his head than buy a flashy

---

[233] Unknown source, 1959.

car.[234]

At that time, the singer stood at the very beginning of his success, the continued existence and future development of which were not necessarily predictable, and it could be thought that Brook's reserve was deliberate. But if we move on a few years – the period up to 1965 can be called his 'golden years', as one success followed another – Brook's statements, his behaviour and his attitude don't change. He remains a calm, modest person, albeit one who is always

---

[234] *Pittsburgh Courier*, 31 October 1959.

concerned with his external appearance, yet is always moderate and reserved in the things he says and does. In April 1960, Benton's success curve wasn't flat, but was continuing to rise sharply. According to *Nite-Lifer Magazine*, despite all his success, Brook was still the same modest and serious-minded individual as ever, enjoying a laugh and bubbling with personality.[235]

In March 1960, Brook made his West Coast debut. He opened with a ten-day guest appearance at the Cloister Club on Sunset Strip. He interrupted his residency at the Cloister for one day and switched to the Beverly Hilton, to help the 100% Wrong Club honour a group of old stars, among them the incomparable Joe Louis, who was described as the Athlete of the Century. Robert Silvester, columnist for the *Los Angeles Sentinel*, visited Brook in his dressing room between shows and found enthusiastic and warm words for the singer. Brook revealed himself to be a gentleman who had truly proved himself worthy of all the praise showered upon him in every respect. His handshake had been firm and warm. He had been patient and friendly, flashing his pearl-white teeth when he smiled. He was a good listener, and had even agreed to suggestions for improvement made by his aides for next show. There was no hint of arrogance to be detected. And with a modesty that had appeared as genuine as a Government debenture bond, he said he was still only on his way to the top. One could never learn everything one needed to know about this business. But he was trying.[236]

In December 1963 Allan McMillan wrote: 'I am very fond of Brook Benton and he is a good example of a "real pro" inasmuch as he has never changed since he became a big star. He's the same small-town boy as he was when he was making 50 bucks a week. A few other stars who wear the armour of stardom so gallantly are Lena Horne, Sammy Davis Jr, Ella Fitzgerald, Duke Ellington, Henry Fonda, Joan Crawford, Louis Armstrong, Peggy Lee, Edward G. Robinson, Bing Crosby, John Wayne and Tallullah Bankhead.'[237]

Brook's modesty was also evident in his collaboration with Dinah Washington. In the previously mentioned 1984 radio interview, he explained how this musical cooperation had come about. Both he and Dinah had been asked if they would agree to work on a joint musical project. Brook's answer is characteristic. Although he was already a well-known and successful record star, he remained reserved and modest. Of course he would agree to the plan to do an album of duets with Dinah. It would be a pleasure, exciting, and an honour.

---

[235] *Nite-Lifer Magazine*, April 1960.
[236] *Los Angeles Sentinel*, 31 March 1960.
[237] Allan McMillan, 'On Broadway', *New York Courier*, December 1963.

Brook was never arrogant and willingly welcomed any advice relating to the presentation of his shows. In particular, he owed a lot to one showbiz legend, Moms Mabley. When he appeared at the Howard Theatre in Washington, she came to his dressing room and told him what he could do better on stage. Although he did not do so immediately, Brook heeded Mabley's suggestions and noted from the audience's reaction that her tips were correct. In particular, she taught Brook how to handle different types of audience, namely black audiences and white audiences, as well as mixed ones. In 1963, at the height of his career, Brook admitted frankly that he did not know where he would be today without the help Moms Mabley had given him.[238]

Much earlier, while he was still making his way, Brook saw that money changed anything and everything. However, he always knew and felt that money cannot ruin too much if a one is happy with one's family and with oneself. Material success made him grateful, but it could not change how he thought and felt.[239] Similar statements may also be read in the *New York Citizen-Call* of 2 December 1960. Gratitude is an essential quality of Brook Benton's character traits. The feelings of gratitude that the singer felt towards the church and choir in his hometown grew into a desire to record an album of spirituals with the latter. Unfortunately, this never happened. However, he never broke his ties to his hometown in South Carolina.

In a lengthy statement, Brook expresses his thanks to the many people who supported him on his journey to the top. Under the heading 'This I Remember', the *Hit Parader* of September-October 1962 quotes the artist's heartfelt words, which express his deep feelings of gratitude in a beautiful way: 'Yes... I remember so many things. The sacrifices my parents made for me. The years of struggling, the hopes and dreams I had when I was a nobody. I also remember my first meeting with Dave Dreyer, the songwriter, who became my manager and friend... I remember the days when success was far away. These are the memories that are important to a man. They keep him humble and level-headed. My wife Mary and I often talk of the old days. When I met her, there weren't five people in New York who knew my name... Mary and I hope to be able to make our children know that the privileges that they have were hard-earned.

'I'm not the only one who has made it the hard way... I'm not a champion of the underdog. I've been extremely fortunate in having a friend like Dave Dreyer, fortunate in having parents who wanted me to make something of myself, and fortunate in being able to use the talent that God gave me.' There is not even the slightest hint of vanity or arrogance discernible anywhere in Benton's words. Modesty, gratitude

---

[238] *Defender*, 25-31 May 1963.
[239] *New York World Telegram & Sun*, 29 July 1960.

and an ability to reflect are the criteria which shape his attitude to life, even now he has risen to become a star.

A short time before, in August 1962, Brook had confided to journalist Neal Ashby that it is just as hard to stay on top as to get there. Despite his million-sellers, and despite his appearances on the *Ed Sullivan Show* and in leading nightclubs across the country, plus a successful tour of South America and the Caribbean, he doesn't feel like he's on top yet. He will only be there once he has played the Copacabana, performed a concert at Carnegie Hall, and appeared in the capital cities of Europe. However, Brook does not spin his thoughts of success out into dizzy heights, but remains focused on the essentials. His striving to reach the top is only important with regard to his financial security and his family. It should never go so far that one can't survive coming down. After all, he was without money for a long time, and it could be that the same thing will happen again. Inner peace is the most important thing to him.[240]

Brook knows that he is successful today, and he enjoys the luxury of success. But he is also aware that that bubble could burst, and he is not at all afraid of that possibility: 'I am not overwhelmed by all this... but I am grateful to God for it. If it's my fate to be rich, I'll be rich. If it's my fate to be poor, I'll be poor.'[241]

Of course, it was easy for Brook to talk about the possibility of poverty at a time when he was a successful singer and entertainer, for the reality of such a thing seemed far away. But the time would come when fate would treat him less kindly and would lead him mentally, physically and financially to the edge of a precipice. Perhaps his faith in God was too strong, his outlook being shaped almost by a kind of fatalism. Conversely, Brook's spiritual disposition, his interest in different religions, and also the exercises he practised involving human energy pathways, reiki for instance, could have prevented his ultimate demise. It is therefore particularly tragic that a serious illness, most likely an infectious meningitis, ended his life just before an eagerly anticipated comeback.

Ruth Brown, a long-time contemporary of Brook's who often toured with him, remembers their association with fondness: 'I met Brook Benton... in Beefsteak Charlie's, a bar between Broadway and 8th Avenue, where musicians and actors met each other... Brook was sitting with Clyde Otis, a large, overwhelming bear of a man; they were sipping their drinks. I was assigned to the program of the James Moody Band and the Shirelles on Brook's tour, and we began discussing how things at Atlantic were going. When I told him things weren't all going so well, Brook said, "Why don't I take you with me, so

---

240 *New York Daily Mirror*, 5 August 1962.
241 *Long Island Press*, 4 August 1963.

you can meet my manager? Maybe you and he could negotiate a contract with Mercury.".... Brook was true to his word, because through him I was introduced to Shelby Singleton, who produced two of my albums, *Along Comes Ruth* and *Gospel Time*, for Mercury's parent company, Philips. *Along Comes Ruth* is one of my most favorite records of all time, which includes a couple of numbers written by Brook.'[242] She adds: 'Brook was a good person and it's a terrible shame that he ended up yet another who died far too soon.'[243]

Andy Bey, who was part of the supporting programme on Brook's shows at the New York Apollo and at the Regal in Washington in 1960, made a noteworthy comment about Benton's personality shortly before a show at Porgy & Bess in Vienna in March 2005: 'Brook was a wonderful entertainer and beyond that a warm-hearted, helpful and humble individual, who unfortunately passed much too soon.'[244]

One final insight regarding Brook's natural restraint and modesty still needs to be added. In 1977, he began his comeback attempt with the album *Makin' Love Is Good For You*. Asked whether he would be bothered if he were relegated to being an opening act, he leant back with a laugh: 'No, not at all. There were many times before when the people that opened for me were better than I was. No, I'll just be out there, trying to do my best.'[245]

It comes as no surprise that, as a man who awoke such great public interest, Brook Benton would be asked about his interests and hobbies by reporters. The artist enumerated several favourite pastimes which he pursued when time permitted. Having been raised in a rural area in the South, Brook preferred outdoor activities. He liked horse riding, he played baseball with kids in his neighbourhood, and he loved fishing and hunting.

For Brook, hunting was not necessarily about killing animals; rather, it was the freedom of being out in the open and being able to move around that was the attraction. On one occasion, he spent an entire day wandering through fields and meadows with his companions without shooting a single rabbit. But he didn't care. Brook always greatly enjoyed whatever he did.[246]

Brook had a similar, but very interesting experience while fishing. During an engagement at the Cat & Fiddle in Nassau, he took some time out to go deep-sea fishing and almost ended up with a record catch. He hooked a huge fish, but after a tug-of-war that lasted one hour and fifteen minutes, it eventually broke free. From the pull,

---

[242] Ruth Brown/Andrew Yule, ibid.
[243] Ibid.
[244] Author's interview with the singer.
[245] *Soul* 10, 3 July 1978.
[246] *Columbia Features* 114, 1962.

the captain estimated that it must have weighed at least 200 pounds. Brook's biggest regret was that he didn't manage to catch sight of his adversary even once.[247]

　　Brook had an extensive collection of guns, which included a

---

[247]　*Nassau Guardian*, 28 June 1961.

Winchester M1 Carbine. The jewel of the collection, however, was an old Buntline Special. He was also a 'quick draw' enthusiast. His predilection for being able to pull out a pistol as quickly as possible from its holster may sound like a peculiar hobby, but it was an interest that Brook shared with a number of other artists. Sammy Davis Jr was reportedly the quickest draw of them all.[248]

Two other hobby horses of Brook's are worthy of note: his passion for film and photography, and his great expertise in six-pocket pool. Some of the top players around were amazed at his skill with the cue.[249]

Brook also talked about one hobby that was especially dear to his heart, which was staying in touch with fans and friends from all over the world. It was astonishing to him, a boy from South Carolina, to have followers in countries like Great Britain, Ireland, Japan, in Scandinavia, Honolulu, in the Panama Canal Zone, and elsewhere.[250] However, his endeavours to stay in close contact with his fans should not necessarily be considered a hobby *per se*; it should actually be an important concern of every artist to create and cultivate such relationships.

Among all of Brook's interests, religion and esotericism rated especially highly. The singer came from a very religious family. Both his father and mother were devout, and all their children acquired the same faith along the way. All of his surviving siblings are practising Christians, and Brook himself was a religious person. Additionally, he was very interested in spiritual and even esoteric matters. In an interview for Dick Clark's radio show, *Rock, Roll & Remember*, Brook spoke quite openly about his belief in transcendental powers. While he was caught up in brooding about his current lack of success, a new vista suddenly opened up to him: he asked himself who was keeping him alive when he was asleep, making sure his heart kept beating and blood kept flowing through his veins, and arrived at the realization that there must be a greater power than himself. If this power was working inside him, then he should start to invoke it, and to understand exactly what this force is.[251]

According to his daughter Vanessa, Brook read a great deal about these subjects. Besides Christianity, his interest also extended to other religions like Islam, as well as Far Eastern doctrines of salvation. Furthermore, he occupied himself with Christian and Jewish mysticism. A selection of the books that Brook grappled with will serve to substantiate this: *Yoga* (J.F.C. Fuller), *Science Of Breath* (Yogi

---

248 *Sunday News*, 2 July 1962.
249 *Nassau Guardian*, ibid.
250 *Columbia Features*, ibid.
251 1969 interview, *Dick Clark's Rock, Roll & Remember*, broadcast 2-3 April 1988.

Ramacharaka), *The Holy Koran*, *The Urantia Book*, *The Scofield Bible*, *The King James Bible*, *The Power of Psalms*, *Back To Eden* (Jethro Kloss), *The Lost Books Of The Bible*, *The Bhagavad-Ghita*, *Pray And Grow Rich* (Catherine Ponder), *Think And Grow Rich* (Napoleon Hill), *Mind Your Body* (E.H. Shattock), *The Amazing Laws Of Cosmic Mind Power* (Joseph Murphy), *Mysticism: The Journey Within* (Robert Chaney), *The Secret Doctrine Of The Rosicrucians* (Magus Incognito), *Mystic Christianity* (Yogi Ramacharaka), *The Spirit Of The Upanishads* (Yogi Ramacharaka), *The Known And Unknown Life Of Jesus, The Christ* (Jane Aikman Welch), *Reincarnation And The Law Of Karma* (William Walker Atkinson), *Mental Therapeutics* (Theron Q. Dumont), *Fundamentals Of Yoga* (Rammurti S. Mishra) and *The Kabbalah*.

As has already been mentioned, Brook felt indebted throughout his life to the church community of his hometown of Lugoff. It was little wonder therefore that he also dedicated a short period of it to the church. Brook fell ill after a performance in late 1980, and Rev. Julius C. Carter from the Carter Community AME Church in Jamaica, New York visited him in hospital and encouraged him to enter the service of the church. He explained to *Amsterdam News* reporter Ernie Johnston Jr. how Rev. Carter came to the hospital and told him that God wanted him to work for Him. At first, Brook did not want to hear that, but following an out-of-body experience, he changed his attitude. After it was over, he felt at peace, and when he saw the light of day, he had completely changed. He felt better, and his thinking had altered.

Rev. Carter informed Brook that God wanted to take him into His service and that he had to experience pain in order to be ready. So, the singer said, he began to study, to pray, and to speak with God. He fell to his knees and thanked God. He felt good about being in the situation he was now in.

For a while, Brook preached and sang at Rev. Carter's church every Sunday afternoon and each weekday evening in what was billed an 'Old Fashion Revival'.[252] Tape recordings of these sermons still exist and are in the possession of Brook Benton's family.

As well as religion, it was esoteric subjects – for example questions about the flow of energy within the human body – which attracted the singer's interest. He occupied himself with the theory and practice of reiki and was also able to obtain a basic master's degree in the art. Alongside that came yoga exercises, which Brook carried out in order to maintain and improve his ability to concentrate. His declining mental and physical state of health in the final years of his life were probably another reason why he involved himself so extensively with such matters. These interests and exercises surely also

---

[252] *Amsterdam News*, 29 November 1980.

contributed to him being able to preserve his great artistic potential and capital – his wonderful voice – until the very end. The religious, spiritual and esoteric way in which Brook viewed and lived his life in his final years undoubtedly stabilized his psyche, and he was able to re-establish himself as a singer and artist. On the other hand, his attitude also contributed to his early death. His family doctor, Dr Gerald Deas, reported that, when he fell ill, Brook only allowed himself to be treated with natural or homeopathic remedies. Although he was suffering from from diabetes, he reportedly refused to take insulin, thereby weakening his system. It is therefore understandable how a dangerous infection like meningitis could have led to the speedy death he experienced. Brook passed away on 9 April 1988, within three days of being committed to hospital by Dr Deas.

His daughter Vanessa sees her father's spirituality as the main reason for his early death: his spirituality had brought him to the realization that it was time for him to depart.

Brook Grant recalls that his uncle especially treasured *The Urantia Book*. A cosmology compiled from the most diverse sources, it deals with the beginning of the world, the evolution of nature and man, and a range of religious issues. Much in the book is speculation and scientifically untenable (for instance the firm assumption that there are twelve planets, and much more besides), however it can enhance the reader's flow of associations and stimulate them into reflecting and meditating – which is what made it attractive to someone like Brook Benton.

Grant also reports that, during the last year of his life, his uncle had frequently spoken about dying. According to him, Brook knew that his death was imminent, and because of this had made what might be described as farewell visits to many of his friends. He was obviously not in the best of health, but according to Grant, had no problems with legal or illegal drugs. He enjoyed his life, was always ready to have a good time and liked a good laugh, just like he always had done.

Towards the end of his career and his life, Brook Benton must have felt undervalued, exploited and even betrayed. Speculative thought patterns, esotericism and spirituality were able to help him cope with his situation and get back on his feet. We know that he stood at the dawn of a new beginning, that his vocal qualities were still at their peak, and that, as before, there was or would be an audience waiting for him. His early death made a big comeback impossible and constituted an irreplaceable, painful loss both for his family, relatives and friends, and for lovers of his singing style.

CHAPTER 13

Brook Benton's Legacy

During his most successful years as a singer, Brook Benton was known and in demand all over the world. That is a simple fact best evidenced by the accompanying worldwide release of his recordings: in addition to the USA, his music was issued in South America, Europe, Asia, Africa and Australia. His records were available not only in Western Europe, but also in the former East Europe and the Soviet Union. That Britain, the Netherlands, Germany and the Scandinavian countries led the way is understandable – but there were also Benton fans in southern European countries.

Robert Pruter, author of the liner notes in the 1994 expanded reissue of *The Two Of Us* album, describes Brook Benton as a largely forgotten entertainer, which is a statement one could simply accept without challenging. However, there are still many music lovers to whom Brook Benton means something, who treasure his music, and who receive any new Benton material they discover with enthusiasm. It is a fact that many of Benton's most beautiful recordings have not remained unknown or concealed from a truly interested listenership. For several years now, this extraordinary singer has enjoyed something of a revival. Dozens of reissues of his greatest hits and anthologies, some of which are bootlegs or second-rate recordings, are currently to be found on the market (see *Discography*). Alongside the well-known Mercury and Rhino reissues, a release in the *Millennium Masters* series and others, some expanded versions of original albums have also been released: *Brook Benton At His Best* (the old Epic LP plus two bonus tracks); *The Essential Vik and RCA Recordings*; *The Two Of Us*; *This Is Brook Benton* (RCA LP *That Old Feeling* plus eight bonus tracks); and the '2-on-1' CDs, *My Country/ That Old Feeling* and *Today/Home Style*. All of these bear witness to the fact that, even many years after the singer's death, there are still people around who treasure Brook Benton and his music.

Today appeared on a Japanese CD in February 2007, while Rhino also released a new CD, *The Platinum Collection*, an anthology of the singer's Cotillion recordings, in the same year. In his *Reviews of CDs, Blu Rays, DVDs, LPs, Record Label Discographies* blogspot, Mark Barry writes: 'Having had a chart hit with his superbly soulful version of Tony Joe White's "Rainy Night In Georgia", it's not surprising that he covered three more of his tunes – "For Le Ann", "Aspen Colorado" and "Willie And Laura Mae Jones". The "Rainy Night" soundalike, "For Le Ann" features Cissy Houston on almost-operatic vocals, while the mellow and liquid style of "Aspen Colorado" suited Benton's style so well. A real gem here, however, is the wonderful self-penned "Let Me Fix It", a slinky and sexy soul song, which features the Dixie Flyers on horns and keyboards and Cissy Houston on witty duet vocals... It sent many soul fans back into second-hand record shops in London trying to find his LPs. Although it doesn't state "remastered" anywhere... the sound is wonderful throughout – a little bit hissy in a few places – but nothing that would detract. What's needed of course is a Brook Benton Rhino Handmade limited edition box set covering all five of his [Cotillion] albums, the 7" singles and hopefully even some tasty unreleased stuff (there's bound to be some and I'll bet it's good too). Whether that's commercially viable or not is another matter... A voice and a talent you need to rediscover – highly recommended.'[263]

In 2011, the UK-based Jasmine label reissued five of Brook's Mercury albums (*It's Just A Matter Of Time*, *Endlessly*, *Songs I Love To Sing*, *The Two Of Us* with Dinah Washington, and *Golden Hits*) as a 2-CD set titled *The Silky Smooth Tones of Brook Benton*. In 2013, they issued a second 2-CD, *Let Me Sing And I'm Happy*. This contains four albums (*I Love You In So Many Ways*, *The Boll Weevil Song*, *There Goes That Song Again* and *Singing The Blues*) plus bonus singles cuts. Also in 2013, *There Goes That Song Again/Singing The Blues* were issued in the UK by Sepia on a '2-on-1' CD with bonus tracks. The *Home Style* album was also recently released in Japan. Many of Brook's albums are now also available as MP3 downloads, including *It's Just A Matter Of Time*, *Endlessly*, *Songs I Love To Sing*, *The Boll Weevil Song*, *If You Believe*, *There Goes That Song Again* and *Singing The Blues*.

So what reissues are still needed in order to do justice to Brook Benton's legacy? Definitely the great Mercury albums, *Best Ballads Of Broadway*, *On The Countryside*, *Born To Sing The Blues* and *This Bitter Earth*.

While visiting a well-known New York music store which also has a large department that stocks old and new vinyl records, the author discovered that people come month after month to enquire about Brook Benton material. However, most of the interest is centred on the old Mercury LPs containing the singer's hits. On the one hand, that is gratifying; but on the other, it demonstrates that only a few Brook Benton fans are familiar with the extent of this singer's oeuvre.

---

[263] Markattheflicks.blogspot.co.uk, 26 April 2009.

Naturally, the music industry focused its PR on his most successful period, thereby influencing the public but also limiting their perspective as regards Brook Benton's artistic legacy. For Benton's fans, and for many devotees of high-quality popular vocal artistry, the reissues of his albums from the Mercury period and beyond could lead to a new view of his complete output and a deeper understanding of his work. Benton's huge, but up until now largely unacknowledged importance to American popular music, lies not only in his work as an interpreter of other people's songs, but also in no lesser part in his work as a composer and co-writer of songs. Many popular singers – male and female – have sung and interpreted his compositions, committed them to disc, and enjoyed success with them.

In doing so, they have further extended Brook Benton's musical legacy. There are over 40 cover versions of 'A Lover's Question' alone, and countless recordings of Brook's big hits – 'It's Just A Matter Of Time', 'Endlessly', 'Baby (You've Got What It Takes)' and others – by a wide variety of artists. In the mid-'80s, RCA country star Charley Pride recorded what is arguably his most interesting project to date: a tribute album to Brook Benton. Sadly, the record was not released, as Pride moved to 16th Avenue Records, who preferred new material.[264]

So what is it that remains immortal for the lovers and connoisseurs of Brook Benton's music, and what is it that connects them with Brook Benton the man?

The answer is: a magnificent singer, who, blessed with a unique voice, left behind an abundance of great vocal art; a wonderful, sensitive entertainer, who could be taken seriously as an artist, citizen and family man; and an individual impressive in his sincerity, modesty and humility.

On 16 July 2008, soul singer Percy Sledge did a show in Vienna. At the press conference afterwards, Hans Maitner asked him about Brook Benton. The immense reverence with which Sledge spoke about Brook, his vocal style and his humanity, was astonishing. He especially stressed the encouragement he had received from him as a young singer.

On 7 July 2013, Randy Crawford appeared at the Konzerthaus in Vienna as part of the annual jazz festival. In the course of her career the singer had come into contact with the music and singing style of Brook Benton, whom she most definitely appreciated. Back in 1978, she had recorded two songs written by Brook and Clyde Otis: 'Someone To Believe In' and the famous 'Endlessly'. Both were released on the *Raw Silk* LP[265]. And, of course, she could not overlook Tony Joe White's 'Rainy Night In Georgia'. This song, which was so

---

[264] Charley Pride biography, theiceberg.com.
[265] Warner Bros. BSK-3283, 1978.

memorably interpreted by Brook Benton, can be found on her *Secret Combination* album[266].

As her performance in Vienna was approaching its climax, Randy shouted to the audience, 'Are you ready for "Rainy Night In Georgia"?' The crowd erupted with cries of approbation and huge applause. She sang the song, whose ending again drew thunderous applause. In the midst of this ovation, Randy paid homage to Brook Benton, whom she described as an extraordinary singer responsible not only for the best-ever version of 'Rainy Night In Georgia', but also for many other wonderful songs. She then performed delicate and elegantly swinging *a capella* versions of both of the hits Brook recorded with Dinah Washington, 'A Rockin' Good Way' and 'Baby (You've Got What It Takes)'.

One day in New York, the author of this essay about Brook Benton was admiring a painted mural in an underpass in the Jamaica district of Queens which depicted a group of significant musicians, singers and entertainers, all of whom were former Queens residents. From left to right there was Tommy 'Hurricane' Jackson, Roy Campanella, Jackie Robinson, William 'Count' Basie, Billie Holiday, Illinois Jacquet, Ella Fitzgerald, Lena Horne, Brook Benton, Milt 'Judge' Hinton, John Coltrane, Thomas 'Fats' Waller and James Brown. A friendly African American struck up a conversation and appeared visibly proud of his erstwhile famous fellow citizens. When asked about Brook Benton, who was in the middle of the group, he mused: 'God called him so he could lead the heavenly choirs.'

The New York music critic Izzy Rowe wrote that only a few singers and entertainers will become a part of our musical legacy. Brook Benton, she felt, would be one of them, because he created a style which had a lasting effect over narrow musical borders. His singing will remain public property, like that of Sammy Davis Jr, Nat 'King' Cole or Lena Horne.[267] To echo the words of Dick Kleiner: 'He has a rich, soft voice and a way of using it that makes a sound like a breeze through a field of cello strings.'[268]

---

[266] Warner Bros. BSK-3541, 1981.
[267] *Pittsburgh Courier*, date unknown.
[268] *World Telegram*, 22 October 1959.

A Service of Memory

1931

for

1988

Brother Brook Benton

Tuesday, April 12, 1988
7:00 P.M.

Carter Community A.M.E. Church
112-25 167TH STREET • JAMAICA, NEW YORK 11433

Rev. Larry E. Dixon, *Officiating*

Order of Worship

THE ORGAN PRELUDE . . . . Bro. Vester Sims

THE PROCESSIONAL . . . . The Family

THE PRAYER OF CONSOLATION . . . . Pastor Dixon

THE HYMN OF COMFORT #189 . . . "When Peace Like A River"

FROM THE COMFORTING WORD

      The Old Testament . . . . Job 14: 1-14
      The New Testament . . . . John 14: 1-14

THE CHORAL WORSHIP . . . . The Choir
                                   "If God Is Dead"

THE REFLECTIONS . . . . Mrs. Coreania H. Carter
                                 Rev. Carl Baldwin

THE CHORAL WORSHIP . . . . The Choir
                        "The Lord Is My Light"

"I REMEMBER BROOK" . . . . Bro. Stanley Bernstein
                      Sis. Sylvia Branchcomb
                                  Rev. Prindle

THE CHORAL WORSHIP . . . . The Choir
                           "Precious Lord"

THE VIEWING

Obituary

His Life
"His Theme was Love"

Brook Benton, born in Lugoff, South Carolina on September 19, 1931 and began life as Benjamin Peay, the son of Mattie and the late Willie Peay. During his years in Lugoff, Ben sang with his family, The Peay Gospel Singers, under the direction of his father the choir director of Ephesus Methodist Church. Leaving Lugoff as a teenager, he traveled to New York, joined The Bill Lankford Quartet and completed High School. "I thought New York City was a land of opportunity. It is, but you've got to know how to go about getting it."

Seeking an opportunity, Brook practically wore grooves in the sidewalks, trudging to music publishers' offices to demonstrate his songs and voice.

"Every place I went, the answer was, "No." I worked at odd jobs to support myself and visited the publishers before and after work. About one day a week, I'd skip work and go see publishers. I lost quite a few jobs that way. I was a milkman, a chauffeur, a presser; I worked in a grocery store; I pushed a truck in the garment center... you name it, I did it."

Most people forget that Brook started out in show business as a song-writer. "Looking Back," "Nothing in the World" are two of his songs recorded by Nat (King) Cole. Clyde McPhatter recorded, "A Lovers Question", and Roy Hamilton recorded "In A Dream, Everything." He composed over three hundred publishable songs, a major part of them with the collaboration of Clyde Otis, who suggested Brook as a singer to his recording studio.

"When I showed him (Clyde) some of my poems that I thought would make good songs, he laughed at me. He said they were amateurish and he thought it was funny the way I drummed my fingers to keep time. Later, he called me and apologized and we began writing songs together."

His many unselfish efforts in behalf of charity, youth and race relations are legendary. Homespun, devoted to his family and friends, Brook wore his crown of stardom as he formerly wore his milkman's cap.

On April 9, 1988, our beloved balladeer, Ben, took his last curtain call at Mary Immaculate Hospital. A great performer, a wonderful person, fate could not have bestowed this crown of stardom on a more deserving person. He leaves to mourn his passing his mother; Mattie Peay, his devoted wife; Mary, three sons; Brook Jr., Roy and Gerald, a daughter; Vanessa, 4 grand children, six sisters; Willie Lee, Bertha, Ruth, Lillian, Dorothy and Helen, a brother; George Richard a host of nieces, nephews, relatives, friends and fans.

"If You Think God Is Dead"

I look at the sea......and I realize
No man can drain it.
I hear that wild wind blow......and I realize
No man can tame it.
I see the clouds hanging over my head
Lord, you know no man can pull them down.
But if you think God is dead......just look around
There must be a rainbow's end......but wait now
No one can find it.
We've all got to die someday, but no man can time it.
Who else can make the moon and the sunshine
over every city and every town.
But if you think my god is dead......just look around.
If you think God is dead you better look around.
Look at the trees......and look at the sea
surely you can feel the breeze......
And if you can't see God in all these things,
then you havent looked around.
You see, God is not dead.
If you don't want to see him......
You won't see him.
But if you want to see him......just look around.
If you think God is dead......people you
should look around.

Brook Benton

Done in Love by the Family

Acknowledgement

The family gratefully acknowledges all the visits, calls, cards
flowers and kindness expressed in their moment of sorrow.
May God Bless each of you.

The physical remains of Bro. Brook will be bourne to his hometown
of Lugoff, South Carolina, there to be laid to rest among his kin until
the Trumpet Call of God on that Great Gettin Up Morning.

Brook Benton's gravestone, Unity Family Life Center Cemetery, Camden, SC.
His date of birth is incorrectly shown as 17 September 1932 instead of 19 September 1931.

Part II

DISCOGRAPHY

Hans Maitner

Recording Sessions 1949-88

ABBREVIATIONS

alto-fl	alto flute	F-hrn	French horn
arr	arranger	g	guitar
as	alto saxophone	hca	harmonica
b	double bass	kbd	keyboard
backg vo	background vocals	ldr	leader
bar	baritone saxophone	org	organ
bg	bass guitar	p	piano
bgo	bongos	perc	percussion
bj	banjo	sax	saxophone
bsn	bassoon	tb	trombone
b-tb	bass trombone	tp	trumpet
cond	conductor	ts	tenor saxophone
contr	contractor	vib	vibes
d	drums	vla	viola
el-p	electric piano	vn	violin
f	flute	vo	vocal
fh	flugelhorn		

SYMBOLS

Acetate	=	○
78 rpm single	=	●
45 rpm single	=	◉
12" single	=	□
EP (extended play)	=	◪
LP (long play)	=	■
Cassette tape	=	📼
CD album	=	◎
Download	=	↓

Brook Benton recorded many songs more than once.
①, ②, ③, etc after a title indicates the version.

COUNTRY OF ORIGIN

All releases are US, except where indicated as follows:

(G)	Germany
(NL)	Netherlands
(SA)	South Africa
(UK)	United Kingdom

BILL LANDFORD & THE LANDFORDAIRES
(BILL LANDFORD FOUR on JEMF-108)
Bill Landford (vo, g), Benjamin Peay (vo) and two unknown singers; unknown org on -1.
New York City   **15 December 1949**

CO 42502-1	**Trouble Of This World** *(Unknown)*	◎ Columbia Gospel Spirit CK-47333
CO 42503	**Touch Me, Jesus** *(Lucie Campbell)*	● Columbia 30186 ◎ Columbia COL-487504-2
CO 42504	**Run On For A Long Time** *(Trad.)*	● Columbia 30203 ◎ Columbia COL-487504-2
CO 42505	**You Ain't Got Faith** **(Till You Got Religion)** ① -1 *(Will Price)*	● Columbia 30186 ■ JEMF JEMF-108 ◎ Columbia COL-487504-2
CO 42508	**Lord I've Tried** *(Unknown)*	◎ Columbia COL-487504-2
CO 42509	**Troubled, Lord I'm Troubled** *(Bill Landford)*	● Columbia 30203 ◎ Columbia COL-487504-2

BILL LANDFORD QUARTET
Bill Landford (vo (lead on -1), g), Benjamin Peay (vo (lead on -2)) and two unknown singers with Chet Atkins (g), Ernie Newton (b) and John Gordy (org).
Nashville, Tennessee   **19 May 1953**

E3-VB-0644 E3-VW-0644	**Jesus Lover Of My Soul** -1 *(Charles Wesley-Joseph Holbrook)*	● RCA Victor 20-5351 ❍ RCA Victor 47-5351
E3-VB-0645 E3-VW-0645	**The Devil Is A Real Bright Boy** -2 *(Bill Landford)*	● RCA Victor 20-5351 ❍ RCA Victor 47-5351
E3-VB-0646	**I Heard Zion Moan**	RCA, unissued
E3-VB-0647 E3-VW-0647	**I Dreamed Of A City Called Heaven** ① -2 *(Trad.)*	● RCA Victor 20-5459 ❍ RCA Victor 47-5459
E3-VB-0648 E3-VW-0648	**You Ain't Got Faith** ② -1 *(Will Price)*	● RCA Victor 20-5459 ❍ RCA Victor 47-5459
E3-VB-0649	**I Heard The Preaching Of The Elders**	RCA, unissued
E3-VB-0650	**Made Up In My Mind**	RCA, unissued
E3-VB-0651	**Goin' Home**	RCA, unissued

THE SANDMEN
Adriel McDonald (bass vo) [former member of the Ink Spots and group founder], Benjamin Peay (lead vo), Furman Haynes (baritone vo), Walter Springer (tenor vo) with unknown studio orchestra under direction of Quincy Jones.
New York City   **14 December 1954**

CO 52772 ZSP-34985	**When I Grow Too Old To Dream** ① *(Sigmund Romberg-Oscar Hammerstein II)*	● OKeh 7052 ❍ OKeh 4-7052

CO 52773	**Somebody To Love**	● OKeh 7052
ZSP-34986	*(Bill Cook)*	◐ OKeh 4-7052
		■ Epic EG-37649

CO 52774	**I Could Have Told You** ①	OKeh, unissued
	(Arthur Williams-Carl Sigman)	

CHUCK WILLIS & THE SANDMEN
Chuck Willis (lead vo), Adriel McDonald (bass vo), Benjamin Peay (vo), Furman Haynes (baritone vo) and Walter Springer (second tenor vo) with the Freddie Jackson Orchestra: Freddie Jackson (ts), unknown (tp, sax, p, g, b, d).
New York City   **17 December 1954**

CO 52796-1E	**Lawdy Miss Mary**	● OKeh 7051
	(Chuck Willis)	◐ OKeh 4-7051
		■ Epic LN-3425[1]

LINCOLN CHASE & THE SANDMEN
Lincoln Chase (lead vo), Adriel McDonald (bass vo), Benjamin Peay (vo), Furman Haynes (baritone vo) and Walter Springer (second tenor vo) with unknown studio orchestra under direction of Ray Ellis.
New York City   **4 February 1955**

CO 52939	**That's All I Need**	● Columbia 40475
ZSP-35629	*(Lincoln Chase)*	◐ Columbia 4-40475

CO 52940	**I'm Sure**	Columbia, unissued
	(Lincoln Chase)	

CO 52941	**The Message**	● Columbia 40475
ZSP-35630	*(Lincoln Chase)*	◐ Columbia 4-40475

CO 52942	**The Things That Money Can't Buy**	Columbia, unissued
	(Lincoln Chase)	

CHUCK WILLIS & THE SANDMEN
Chuck Willis (lead vo), Adriel McDonald (b vo), Benjamin Peay (vo), Furman Haynes (baritone vo) and Walter Springer (second tenor vo) with unknown studio orchestra under direction of Quincy Jones.
New York City   **21 April 1955**

CO 53231-1H	**I Can Tell**	● OKeh 7055
	(Chuck Willis)	◐ OKeh 4-7055
		■ Epic LN-3425[1]

BROOK BENTON & THE SANDMEN
Brook Benton (lead vo), Adriel McDonald (bass vo), Furman Haynes (baritone vo) and Walter Springer (tenor vo) with orchestra under direction of Quincy Jones: Joe Marshall (d), Milt Hinton (b), Mickey Baker (g), Ernest Hayes (p), Jerome Richardson (as), Sam Taylor (ts), Bud Johnson (ts) and Jimmy Cleveland (tb).
New York City   **26 May 1955**

CO 53417	**Ooh**	● OKeh 7058
ZSP-36401	*(Ollie Jones)*	◐ OKeh 4-7058

---

[1]   *Chuck Willis Wails The Blues* (1958).

CO 53418	**I Was Fool Enough To Love You**	OKeh, unissued
	(Reuben Fisher)	

BROOK BENTON
Brook Benton (vo) with unknown studio orchestra under direction of Quincy Jones.
New York City   **2 June 1955**

CO 53437	**The Kentuckian Song**	● OKeh 7058
ZSP-36400	*(Irving Gordon)*	◐ OKeh 4-7058
		■ Epic LN-3573,
		Harmony HL-7346/HS-11146

CO 53438	**Can I Help It**	■ Epic LN-3573,
	(Brook Benton)	Harmony HL-7346/HS-11146

BROOK BENTON
Brook Benton (vo) with unknown studio orchestra (p, g, b, d, vn) and chorus; King Curtis (ts) on -1.
Mercury Sound Studio, New York City   **August 1955**

11971	**Hold My Hand** ①	Mercury, unissued
	(Brook Benton-Clyde Otis-Dave Dreyer)	

11972	**It's Just A Matter Of Time** ①	● Mercury 71394
	(Brook Benton-Belford Hendricks-	◐ Mercury 71394X45
	Clyde Otis)	◨ Mercury EP-1-3394, EP-1-4033
		■ Mercury MG-20421/SR-60077,
		MG-20607/SR-60607
	With disc jockey announcement	■ Increase INCM-1959

11973	**Hurtin' Inside** -1	● Mercury 71394
	(Cirino Colacrai-Teddy Randazzo-	◐ Mercury 71394X45
	Clyde Otis-Brook Benton)	◨ Mercury EP-1-3394
		■ Mercury MG-20607/SR-60607

11974	**I Want You Forever** ①	Mercury, unissued
	(Brook Benton-Clyde Otis-Luchi De Jesus)	

11979	**Tell Me The Truth**	Mercury, unissued
	(Brook Benton-Clyde Otis-Jimmy Williams)	

BROOK BENTON
Brook Benton (vo) with unknown studio orchestra under direction of Ray Ellis.
New York City   **21 November 1955**

CO 54179	**Bring Me Love**	● OKeh 7065
ZSP-37553	*(Nye Edwards-Teacho Wiltshire)*	◐ OKeh 4-7065
		■ Epic LN-3573,
		Harmony HL-7346/HS-11146

CO 54180	**Some Of My Best Friends**	● OKeh 7065
ZSP-37552	*(Sammy Gallop-Philip Springer)*	◐ OKeh 4-7065
		■ Epic LN-3573

CO 54181	**Rock'n'Roll That Rhythm**	■ Epic LN-3573,
	(All Nite Long) *(Eddie Curtis)*	Harmony HL-7346/HS-11146

CO 54182	**Partners For Life**	■ Epic LN-3573,
	(Ruth Kardon-Hal Gordon)	Harmony HL-7346/HS-11146

BROOK BENTON

Brook Benton (vo) with unknown studio orchestra under direction of Ray Ellis.
Mercury Sound Studio, New York City   **April 1956**

12634	**Endlessly** ①	● Mercury 71443
	(Clyde Otis-Brook Benton)	◖ Mercury 71443X45/SS-10005
		◻ Mercury EP-1-3394, EP-1-4031
		■ Mercury MG-20464/SR-60146,
		MG-20607/SR-60607

12635	**So Close** ①	● Mercury 71443
	(Brook Benton-Luther Dixon-Clyde Otis)	◖ Mercury 71443X45/SS-10005
		■ Mercury MG-20565/SR-60225,
		Mercury MG-20607/SR-60607

12636	**So Many Ways** ①	◖ Mercury 71512X45/SS-10019
	(Bobby Stevenson)	◻ Mercury EP-1-3394, EP-1-4033
		■ Mercury MG-20565/SR-60225,
		Mercury MG-20607/SR-60607

12637	**How Many Times**	◖ Mercury 71558X45
	(Brook Benton-Vin Corso)	■ Mercury MG-20607/SR-60607

BROOK BENTON

Brook Benton (vo) with unknown studio orchestra under direction of Leroy Kirkland.
New York City   **24 April 1956**

CO 55867	**Anything For You**	■ Epic LN-3573,
	(Brook Benton)	Harmony HL-7346/HS-11146

CO 55868	**Love Made Me Your Fool**	● Epic 9177
JZSP-38879	*(Otis Blackwell-Alan Freed)*	◖ Epic 5-9177
		■ Epic LN-3573

CO 55869	**Give Me A Sign**	● Epic 9177
JZSP-38880	*(Brook Benton)*	◖ Epic 5-9177
		■ Epic LN-3573,
		Harmony HL-7346/HS-11146

CO 55870	**Tell Me**	■ Epic LN-3573
	(Brook Benton)	

BROOK BENTON

Brook Benton (vo) with unknown studio orchestra under direction of Leroy Kirkland.
New York City   **December 1956**

CO 57016-1C	**All My Love Belongs To You**	● Epic 9199
JZSP-39722	*(Leroy Kirkland-Rose Marie McCoy)*	◖ Epic 5-9199
		■ Harmony HL-7346/HS-11146

CO 57017	**You Should Have Told Me**	■ Epic LN-3575,
	(Leroy Kirkland-Kelly Owens-Rose Marie McCoy)	Harmony HL-7346/HS-11146

CO 57018-1C   **The Wall**   ● Epic 9199
JZSP-39721   *(Ormay Diamond-Cliff Owens-Dave Dreyer)*   ○ Epic 5-9199
                                                                ■ Epic LN-3573,
                                                                   Harmony HL-7346/HS-11146

BROOK BENTON

Brook Benton (vo) on all tracks, kazoo on -1; unknown group (b, g, d) on all tracks; unknown mixed vo group on -2; unknown male vo group on -3; unknown female vo group on -4; unknown p on -5; unknown sax on -6.
Unknown location   **1956**

The following are 28 demo recordings produced by Clyde Otis:

A Lover's Question ① -3   ■ Trip TLP-8026,
(Brook Benton-Jimmy Williams)   DJM *(UK)* DJML-073

Ain't It Good -1, -2, -5   ■ Trip TLP-8026,
(Brook Benton-Clyde Otis)   DJM *(UK)* DJML-073

Come Back My Love -4, -5   ■ Trip TLP-8026
(Roy Hamilton-Clyde Otis)

Come Let's Go -3, -5   ■ Trip TLP-8026,
(Brook Benton-Clyde Otis-Bill Henry)   DJM *(UK)* DJML-073

Completely -3   ■ Trip TLP-8026
(Belford Hendricks-Clyde Otis)

Devoted ① -3   ■ Trip TLP-8026,
(Bill Henry-Belford Hendricks-Clyde Otis)   DJM *(UK)* DJML-073

Doggone Baby, Doggone -3, -5   ■ Trip TLP-8026,
(Clyde Otis-Brook Benton)   DJM *(UK)* DJML-073

Don't Walk Away From Me -4, -5 ■ Trip TLP-8026
(Brook Benton-Clyde Otis)

Everything Will Be Alright -3   ■ Trip TLP-8026,
(Brook Benton-Clyde Otis)   DJM *(UK)* DJML-073

I'll Meet You After Church   ■ Trip TLP-8026
Next Sunday -3
(Brook Benton-Clyde Otis)

I'll Never Stop Trying -3, -5   ■ Trip TLP-8026,
(Brook Benton-Clyde Otis)   DJM *(UK)* DJML-073

I'll Stop Anything I'm Doing -3, -6 ■ Trip TLP-8026,
(Brook Benton-Clyde Otis)   DJM *(UK)* DJML-073

Keep Me In Mind -3   ■ Trip TLP-8026,
(Vin Corso-Clyde Otis)   DJM *(UK)* DJML-073

Looking Back ① -3, -5   ■ Trip TLP-8026,
(Brook Benton-Clyde Otis-Belford   DJM *(UK)* DJML-073
 Hendricks)

Mark My Word -3   ■ Trip TLP-8026
(Brook Benton-Clyde Otis)

May I? ① -3, -5   ■ Trip TLP-8026
(Brook Benton-Clyde Otis-Luchi De Jesus)

My Love Will Last -3   ■ Trip TLP-8026,
(Johnny Brandon-Jimmy Williams)   DJM *(UK)* DJML-073

Next Stop Paradise -3   ■ Trip TLP-8026,
(Dave Dreyer-Clyde Otis-Oramay   DJM *(UK)* DJML-073
Diamond)

Ninety-Nine Percent -3   ■ Trip TLP-8026,
(Clyde Otis-Brook Benton)   DJM *(UK)* DJML-073

Nothing In The World ① -3, -5   ■ Trip TLP-8026,
(Brook Benton-Clyde Otis-Belford   DJM *(UK)* DJML-073
Hendricks)

One Love Too Many -3   ■ Trip TLP-8026,
(Brook Benton-Clyde Otis)   DJM *(UK)* DJML-073

The Rest Of The Way -3, -5   ■ Trip TLP-8026
(Belford Hendricks-Clyde Otis)

This Bitter Earth ① -2, -5   ■ Trip TLP-8026
(Clyde Otis)

Walking Together -3, -5   ■ Trip TLP-8026,
(Brook Benton-Clyde Otis)   DJM *(UK)* DJML-073

What A Kiss Won't Do -3, -5   ■ Trip TLP-8026,
(Brook Benton-Clyde Otis)   DJM *(UK)* DJML-073

You Can't Get Away From Me -3   ■ Trip TLP-8026,
(Clyde Otis-Brook Benton)   DJM *(UK)* DJML-073

You're For Me ① -3, -5   ■ Trip TLP-8026,
(Brook Benton-Cirino Colacrai)   DJM *(UK)* DJML-073

You're Movin' Me -3, -5   ■ Trip TLP-8026,
(Brook Benton-Clyde Otis)   DJM *(UK)* DJML-073

BROOK BENTON
Brook Benton (vo) with unknown studio band (b, d, p, g) and chorus.
Unknown location   **1956**

A New Love   ■ Crown CLP-5402/CST-402,
(Jimmy Williams)   La Brea L-/LS-8021,
    Coronet CX-/CXS-198,
    Strand SL-/SLS-1121,
    SL-/SLS-1129

Don't Put It Off   ■ Demand DMSLP-090
(Jimmy Williams)

Dreams, Oh Dreams   ■ Crown CLP-5402/CST-402,
(Jimmy Williams)   La Brea L-/LS-8021,
    Coronet CX-/CXS-198,
    Strand SL-/SLS-1121

The Girl I Love
■ Crown CLP-5402/CST-402,
La Brea L-/LS-8021,
Coronet CX-/CXS-198,
Strand SL-/SLS-1121

Just Tell Me When
(Jimmy Williams)
■ Crown CLP-5350/CST-350,
La Brea L-/LS-8021,
Coronet CX-/CXS-210,
Strand SL-/SLS-1124

Love's That Way
(Jimmy Williams)
■ Crown CLP-5350/CST-350,
La Brea L-/LS-8021,
Coronet CX-/CXS-210,
CX-/CXS-260,
Strand SL-/SLS-1124

No One (Love) Like Her Love
[No Love Like Her Love*]
(Jimmy Williams)
■ Crown CLP-5350/CST-350,
La Brea L-/LS-8021*,
Coronet CX-/CXS-198*,
Strand SL-/SLS-1121*

Steppin' Out Tonight
(Billy Williams-Joseph Smalls)
■ Crown CLP-5350/CST-350,
La Brea L-/LS-8021,
Coronet CX-/CXS-210,
Strand SL-/SLS-1124

Won't Cha Gone
[What'cha Gone*]
[Won't Cha Love]**
(Jimmy Williams)
■ Crown CLP-5350/CST-350,
La Brea L-/LS-8021*,
Coronet CX-/CXS-210**,
Strand SL-/SLS-1124

BROOK BENTON
Brook Benton (vo), Abie Baker (b), Kenny Burrell (g), Panama Francis (d), Ernie Hayes (p) and
Heywood Henry (bar). Chorus: Orville Brooks, Joseph Smalls, Abel De Costa and Maretha Stewart.
New York City   **5 June 1957**

H4PB-4481-15 **If Only I Had Known**
             (Clyde Otis-Brook Benton)
○ RCA Victor 47-7489
◘ Vik EXA-301
■ RCA Camden CAL-564

BROOK BENTON
Brook Benton (vo), Abie Baker (b), Kenny Burrell (g) and Panama Francis (d) with unknown chorus.
New York City   **6 June 1957**

H4PB-3956-2 **Come On, Be Nice**
H4PW-3956-2 *(Clyde Otis-Brook Benton)*
● Vik X-0285
○ Vik 4X-0285

H4PB-3957-2 **I Wanna Do Everything For You**
H4PW-3957-2 *(Clyde Otis-Brook Benton)*
● Vik X-0285
○ Vik 4X-0285
■ RCA Camden CAL-564

H4PB-4511-18 **Your Love Alone**
             (Billy Myles)
◘ Vik EXA-300
■ RCA Camden CAL-564

221

MICKEY & SYLVIA

Mickey Baker (vo, g) and Sylvia Vanderpool (vo, g) with Brook Benton (whistling), Everett Barksdale (g), Abie Baker (b), King Curtis (ts), Heywood Henry (bar), Ernie Hayes (p), Panama Francis (d). Produced by Bob Rolontz.

RCA Studio A, New York City   **12 July 1957**

H4PB-4590-7	**I Gotta Be Home By Ten**	◉ Bear Family *(G)* BCD-15438[2]
	(America Trophy)	

BROOK BENTON

Brook Benton (vo), Billy Mure (ldr), Ernie Hayes (p), Lloyd Trotman (b), Al Caiola (g), Allen Hanlon (g), Panama Francis (d) and Jerome Richardson (sax on -1) with unknown chorus.

New York City   **14 November 1957**

H4PB-7836-5	**Only Your Love**	○ RCA Victor 47-7489
	(Jimmy Williams)	■ RCA Camden CAL-564
H4PB-7837-11	**Devoted** ②	● Vik X-0311
H4PW-7837-11	*(Bill Henry-Belford Hendricks-Clyde Otis)*	◐ Vik 4X-0311
		■ RCA Camden CAL-564
H4PB-7838-3	**You're For Me** ② -1	■ RCA Camden CAL-564
	(Brook Benton-Cirino Colacrai)	
H4PB-7839-2	**A Million Miles From Nowhere**	● Vik X-0311
H4PW-7839-2	*(Daryl Petty)*	◐ Vik 4X-0311
		■ RCA Camden CAL-564

BROOK BENTON

Brook Benton (vo), Leroy Kirkland (ldr), Alberto Sacaras (f), George Berg (bsn), George Auld (ts), Kenny Burrell (g), Everett Barksdale (g), Lloyd Trotman (b), Ernie Hayes (p), Joe Marshall (d) and Willie Rodrigues (d). Chorus: Lillian Clark (cond), Miriam Workman, Elise Bretton, Jerry Duane, Jerry Packer and Keith Booth.

New York City   **31 March 1958**

J4PB-2505-6	**Sentimental Daddy-O**	◉ Taragon TARCD-1082
	(Rose Marie McCoy-Leroy Kirkland)	
J4PB-2506-5	**A Door That Is Open**	■ RCA Camden CAL-564
	(Jimmy Williams-Johnny Brandon)	
J4PB-2507-2	**Crinoline Skirt**	● Vik X-0325
J4PW-2507-2	*(Rose Marie McCoy-Leroy Kirkland)*	◐ Vik 4X-0325
J4PB-2508-2	**Because You Love Me**	● Vik X-0325
J4PW-2508-2	*(Clyde Otis-Brook Benton)*	◐ Vik 4X-0325

BROOK BENTON

Brook Benton (vo) with unknown studio band (b, bj, d, g); unknown chorus on -1.

New York City   **8 July 1958**

J4PW-5359	**I'm Coming Back To You**	◐ Vik 4X-0336
	(Clyde Otis-Brook Benton)	■ RCA Camden CAL-564

---

[2] 2-CD *Love Is Strange* (1990).

| J4PW-5360 | **Crazy In Love With You** -1
 (Clyde Otis-Brook Benton) | ⦿ Vik 4X-0336
 ■ RCA Camden CAL-564 |

BROOK BENTON
Brook Benton (vo) with unknown studio orchestra and chorus under direction of Hal Mooney.
Mercury Sound Studio, New York City   **1959**

18111	**I'm In The Mood For Love** *(Jimmy McHugh-Dorothy Fields)*	■ Mercury MG-20421/SR-60077
18112	**I Can't Begin To Tell You** *(Mack Gordon-James Monaco)*	■ Mercury MG-20421/SR-60077
18142	**When I Fall In Love** *(Eddie Heyman-Victor Young)*	■ Mercury MG-20421/SR-60077
18143	**The Nearness Of You** *(Hoagy Carmichael-Ned Washington)*	■ Mercury MG-20421/SR-60077
18144	**Hold Me, Thrill Me, Kiss Me** *(Harry Nobel)*	■ Mercury MG-20421/SR-60077
18145	**But Beautiful** *(Johnny Burke-Jimmy Van Heusen)*	■ Mercury MG-20421/SR-60077
18146	**I Could Have Told You** ② *(Arthur Williams-Carl Sigman)*	■ Mercury MG-20421/SR-60077
18147	**The More I See You** *(Mack Gordon-Harry Warren)*	■ Mercury MG-20421/SR-60077
18148	**Tell Me Your Dream** *(Al Brown-Charles Daniels-Seymour Rice)*	■ Mercury MG-20421/SR-60077
18149	**Love Me Or Leave Me** *(Walter Donaldson-Gus Kahn)*	■ Mercury MG-20421/SR-60077
18150	**I'll String Along With You** *(Al Dubin-Harry Warren)*	■ Mercury MG-20421/SR-60077

BROOK BENTON
Brook Benton (vo) with unknown p.
Mercury Sound Studio, New York City   **June 1959**

| 18695 | **With All Of My Heart**
 (Brook Benton-Chris Towns) | ⦿ Mercury 71478X45/SS-10012
 ■ Mercury MG-20607/SR-60607 |

Add unknown studio orchestra and chorus under direction of Belford Hendricks:

| 18696 | **I Want You Forever** ②
 (Brook Benton-Clyde Otis-Luchi De Jesus) | ⦿ Mercury 71512X45/SS-10019
 ■ Mercury MG-21008/SR-61008
 (unissued test pressing) |
| 18697 | **The Same One** ①
 (Brook Benton-Clyde Otis) | ⦿ Mercury 71652X45/SS-10037
 ◘ Mercury EP-1-4033
 ■ Mercury MG-20607/SR-60607 |

18698	**Nothing In The World (Could Make Me Love You More Than I Do)** ② *(Brook Benton-Clyde Otis-Belford Hendricks)*	◉ Mercury 71554X45
18699	**This Time Of The Year** ① *(Cliff Owens-Jesse Hollis)*	◉ Mercury 71554X45, 71558X45, 71730, 72214 ■ Mercury Galaxy MGD-/SRD-21
18700	**Hold My Hand** ② *(Brook Benton-Clyde Otis-Dave Dreyer)*	Mercury, rejected
18701	**Someone To Believe In** ① *(Clyde Otis-Brook Benton-Bobby Stevenson)*	◎ Verve 526467-2

BROOK BENTON

Brook Benton (vo) with unknown studio orchestra and chorus under direction of Fred Norman.
Fine Recording Studios, New York City   **June 1959**

18702	**May I Never Love Again** *(Juck Erickson-Sano Marco)*	■ Mercury MG-20464/SR-60146
18703	**You'll Never Know** *(Mack Gordon-Harry Warren)*	■ Mercury MG-20464/SR-60146
18704	**People Will Say We're In Love** *(Richard Rodgers-Oscar Hammerstein II)*	■ Mercury MG-20464/SR-60146
18705	**Time After Time** *(Sammy Cahn-Jule Styne)*	■ Mercury MG-20464/SR-60146
18706	**Because Of You** *(Arthur Hammerstein-Dudley Wilkinson)*	■ Mercury MG-20464/SR-60146
18707	**A Lovely Way To Spend An Evening** *(Harold Adamson-Jimmy McHugh)*	■ Mercury MG-20464/SR-60146
18708	**Around The World** *(Victor Young-Stella Unger-Harold Adamson)*	■ Mercury MG-20464/SR-60146
18709	**Blue Skies** *(Irving Berlin)*	■ Mercury MG-20464/SR-60146
18710	**The Things I Love** *(Harold Barlow-Lew Harris-Tchaikovsky)*	■ Mercury MG-20464/SR-60146
18711	**More Than You Know** *(Edward Eliscu-Billy Rose-Vincent Youmans)*	■ Mercury MG-20464/SR-60146
18712	**(It's No) Sin** *(Chester Shull-George Hoven)*	■ Mercury MG-20464/SR-60146

BROOK BENTON

Brook Benton (vo) with unknown studio orchestra and chorus under direction of Belford Hendricks.
Mercury Sound Studio, New York City   **June 1959**

18713	**Thank You Pretty Baby** ①	O Mercury 71478X45/SS-10012
	(Brook Benton-Clyde Otis)	◻ Mercury EP-1-4031
		◼ Mercury MG-20607/SR-60607

18714	**Someday You'll Want Me To Want You**	O Mercury 71722
	(Jimmy Hodges)	

DINAH WASHINGTON & BROOK BENTON

Dinah Washington & Brook Benton (vo duet) with unknown studio orchestra and chorus under direction of Belford Hendricks.
Fine Recording Studios, New York City   **1959**

18863	**Baby (You've Got What It Takes)** ①	O Mercury 71565X45/SS-10025
	(Clyde Otis-Murray Stein)	◻ Mercury EP-1-4028
		◼ Mercury MG-20588/SR-60244
	With disc jockey announcement	◼ Increase INCM-1960

BROOK BENTON & DINAH WASHINGTON

Brook Benton & Dinah Washington (vo duet) with unknown studio orchestra and chorus under direction of Belford Hendricks.
Fine Recording Studios, New York City   **1959**

18864	**I Do**	O Mercury 71565X45/SS10025
	(Ben Raleigh-Don Wolf)	◻ Mercury EP-1-4028
		◼ Mercury MG-20588/SR-60244

BROOK BENTON

Brook Benton (vo) with unknown studio orchestra and chorus under direction of Belford Hendricks.
Mercury Sound Studio, New York City   **1959**

19208	**Someone To Believe In** ②	◼ Mercury MG-20588/SR-60244
	(Clyde Otis-Brook Benton-Bobby Stevenson)	

BROOK BENTON

Brook Benton (vo) with unknown studio orchestra and chorus under direction of Belford Hendricks; without chorus on -1.
Fine Recording Studios, New York City   **December 1959**

19547	**May I** ②	◼ Mercury MG-20565/SR-60225
	(Brook Benton-Clyde Otis-Luchi De Jesus)	

19548	**In A Dream**	◼ Mercury MG-20565/SR-60225
	(Brook Benton-Clyde Otis-Cirino Colacrai)	

19549	**This Bitter Earth** ②	◼ Mercury MG-20934/SR-60934
	(Clyde Otis)	

19550	**Fools Rush In**	O Mercury 71722
	(Where Angels Fear To Tread) ① -1	◼ Mercury MG-20602/SR-60602,
	(Johnny Mercer-Rube Bloom)	MG-20774/SR-60774

BROOK BENTON

Brook Benton (vo) with unknown studio orchestra and chorus under direction of Fred Norman.
Fine Recording Studios, New York City   **December 1959**

19551	**Because Of Everything** *(Clyde Otis-Belford Hendricks)*	■ Mercury MG-20588/SR-60244
19552	**Tell Me Now Or Never** *(Roy Hamilton-Brook Benton-Clyde Otis)*	■ Mercury MG-20565/SR-60225
19553	**Never A Greater Need** *(Clyde Otis)*	■ Mercury MG-20565/SR-60225
19554	**Hither And Thither And Yon** *(Aaron Schroeder-Wally Gold)*	◉ Mercury 71566X45/SS-10030 ◘ Mercury EP-1-4033 ■ Mercury MG-20607/SR-60607
19555	**The Ties That Bind** ① *(Vin Corso-Clyde Otis)*	◉ Mercury 71566X45/SS-10030 ◘ Mercury EP-1-4031 ■ Mercury MG-20607/SR-60607

BROOK BENTON

Brook Benton (vo) with unknown studio orchestra and chorus under direction of Belford Hendricks.
Fine Recording Studios, New York City   **December 1959**

19556	**Never Like This** *(Bobby Stevenson)*	■ Mercury MG-20565/SR-60225, Mercury MG-21008/SR-61008 *(unissued test pressing)*
19557	**One By One** *(Brook Benton-Vin Corso)*	■ Mercury MG-20565/SR-60225
19558	**Everything** *(Clyde Otis-Brook Benton)*	■ Mercury MG-20565/SR-60225
19559	**Someone To Watch Over Me** *(George & Ira Gershwin)*	■ Mercury MG-20565/SR-60225
19560	**Think Twice** ① *(Joe Shapiro-Jimmy Williams-Clyde Otis)*	◉ Mercury 71774 ■ Mercury MG-20774/SR-60774
19561	**If You But Knew** *(Brook Benton-Teddy Randazzo)*	■ Mercury MG-20565/SR-60225
19562	**The Same One** ② *(Brook Benton-Clyde Otis)*	Mercury, rejected
19563	**Nothing In The World (Could Make Me Love You More Than I Do)** ③ *(Brook Benton-Clyde Otis-Belford Hendricks)*	■ Mercury MG-21008/SR-61008 *(unissued test pressing)*
19564	**Hold My Hand** ③ *(Brook Benton-Clyde Otis-Dave Dreyer)*	■ Mercury MG-20565/SR-60225

BROOK BENTON
Brook Benton (vo) with unknown studio orchestra and chorus under direction of Fred Norman.
Mercury Sound Studio, New York City   **April 1960**

19848	**Not One Step Behind**	■ Mercury MG-20588/SR-60244
	(Brook Benton-Chris Towns)	
19849	**It's Too Late To Turn Back Now** ①	Mercury, unissued
	(Clyde Otis)	

BROOK BENTON
Brook Benton (vo) with unknown studio orchestra and chorus under direction of Belford Hendricks.
Fine Recording Studios, New York City   **April 1960**

19855	**Kiddio** ①	◉ Mercury 71652X45/SS-10037
	(Clyde Otis-Brook Benton)	◲ Mercury EP-1-4031
		■ Mercury MG-20607/SR-60607

DINAH WASHINGTON & BROOK BENTON
Dinah Washington & Brook Benton (vo duet) with unknown studio orchestra and chorus under direction of Belford Hendricks.
Fine Recording Studios, New York City   **April 1960**

19856	**A Rockin' Good Way**	◉ Mercury 71629X45/SS-10032
	(To Mess Around And Fall In Love) ①	◲ Mercury EP-1-4028
	(Brook Benton-Clyde Otis- Luchi De Jesus)	■ Mercury MG-20588/SR-60244

BROOK BENTON & DINAH WASHINGTON
Brook Benton & Dinah Washington (vo duet) with unknown studio orchestra under direction of Belford Hendricks.
Fine Recording Studios, New York City   **April 1960**

19857	**I Believe**	◉ Mercury 71629X45/SS-10032
	(Ervin Drake-Jimmy Shirl-Irvin Graham-	◲ Mercury EP-1-4028
	Al Stillman)	■ Mercury MG-20588/SR-60244

BROOK BENTON
Brook Benton (vo) with unknown studio orchestra and chorus under direction of Belford Hendricks.
Mercury Sound Studio, New York City   **1960**

19903	**Call Me**	■ Mercury MG-20588/SR-60244
	(Clyde Otis-Belford Hendricks)	
19904	**God Bless The Child** ①	Mercury, unissued
	(Billie Holiday-Arthur Herzog)	
19905	**That's The Beginning Of The End**	Mercury, unissued

BROOK BENTON
Brook Benton (whistling on -1, vo) with unknown studio orchestra under direction of Belford Hendricks.
New York City   **1960**

| 20400 | **They Can't Take That Away From Me** ① | Mercury, rejected |
| | *(George & Ira Gershwin)* | |

| 20401 | **I Don't Know Enough About You**
 (Peggy Lee-Dave Barbour) | ■ Mercury MG-20602/SR-60602 |

20401   **I Don't Know Enough About You**
 (Peggy Lee-Dave Barbour)   ■ Mercury MG-20602/SR-60602

20402   **Baby Won't You Please Come Home**
 (Charles Warfield-Clarence Williams)   ■ Mercury MG-20602/SR-60602

20403   **Moonlight in Vermont** -1
 (John Blackburn-Karl Suessdorf)   ■ Mercury MG-20602/SR-60602

20404   **I'll Be Around**
 (Alec Wilder)   ■ Mercury MG-20602/SR-60602

20405   **Your Eyes**
 (Clyde Otis-Bert Robinson)   ◉ Mercury 71820

    With announcement   ◉ USAF Program No.167 *(radio)*

20406   **If You Are But A Dream** ①
 (Moe Jaffe-Jack Fulton-Nat Bonx)   Mercury, rejected

20407   **It's Been A Long, Long Time** ①
 (Jule Styne-Sammy Cahn)   Mercury, rejected

20408   **Oh! What It Seemed To Be** ①
 (Bennie Benjamin-Frankie Carle-George Weiss)   Mercury, rejected

20409   **Lover Come Back To Me** ①
 (Sigmund Romberg-Oscar Hammerstein II)   Mercury, rejected

20410   **Why Try To Change Me Now** ①
 (Joseph McCarthy Jr.-Cy Coleman)   Mercury, rejected

20411   **September Song**
 (Maxwell Anderson-Kurt Weill)   ■ Mercury MG-20602/SR-60602

20412   **It's Been A Long, Long Time** ②
 (Jule Styne-Sammy Cahn)   ■ Mercury MG-20602/SR-60602

20413   **Oh! What It Seemed To Be** ②
 (Bennie Benjamin-Frankie Carle-George Weiss)   ■ Mercury MG-20602/SR-60602

20414   **Lover Come Back To Me** ②
 (Sigmund Romberg-Oscar Hammerstein II)   ■ Mercury MG-20602/SR-60602

20415   **Why Try To Change Me Now** ②
 (Joseph McCarthy Jr.-Cy Coleman)   ■ Mercury MG-20602/SR-60602

20416   **They Can't Take That Away From Me** ②
 (George & Ira Gershwin)   ■ Mercury MG-20602/SR-60602

20421   **If You Are But A Dream** ②
 (Moe Jaffe-Jack Fulton-Nat Bonx)   ■ Mercury MG-20602/SR-60602

20422   **For My Baby** ①
 (Clyde Otis-Brook Benton)   ◉ Mercury 71774
 ■ Mercury MG-21008/SR-61008
 (unissued test pressing)

BROOK BENTON
Brook Benton (vo) with unknown studio orchestra and chorus under direction of Belford Hendricks.
New York City   **1960**

20423	**Merry Christmas, Happy New Year** *(Vin Corso-Clyde Otis)*	● Mercury 71730
20424	**The Boll Weevil Song** ① *(Brook Benton-Clyde Otis)*	Mercury, unissued

BROOK BENTON
Brook Benton (vo) with unknown studio combo (d, b, p, perc) and chorus under direction of Malcolm Dodds (arr, cond).
Fine Recording Studios, New York City   **1961**

20744	**Shadrack** ① *(Robert MacGimsey)*	● Mercury 71912 ■ Mercury MG-20619/SR-60619, MG-20774/SR-60774, Star GELP-5355
20745	**Going Home** *(Dvorak/Adapt. Brook Benton-Malcolm Dodds)*	■ Mercury MG-20619/SR-60619, Star GELP-5355
20746	**Go Tell It On The Mountain** *(Trad.)*	■ Mercury MG-20619/SR-60619
20747	**He'll Understand And Say Well Done** *(Trad.)*	■ Mercury MG-20619/SR-60619 Star GELP-5355
20748	**Only Believe** *(Trad.)*	■ Mercury MG-20619/SR-60619 Star GELP-5355
20749	**Everytime I Feel The Spirit** *(Trad.)*	Mercury, unissued
20750	**The Lost Penny** *(J.T. Adams)*	● Mercury 71912 ■ Mercury MG-20619/SR-60619, Star GELP-5355
20751	**Remember Me (He Will Remember Me)** *(Trad.)*	■ Mercury MG-20619/SR-60619 Star GELP-5355
20752	**Just A Closer Walk With Thee** *(Trad.)*	■ Mercury MG-20619/SR-60619 Star GELP-5355
20753	**Deep River** *(Trad.)*	■ Mercury MG-20619/SR-60619 Star GELP-5355
20754	**Steal Away** *(Trad.)*	■ Mercury MG-20619/SR-60619 Star GELP-5355
20755	**A City Called Heaven** *(Hugo Frey)*	Mercury, unissued

ERNESTINE ANDERSON
Ernestine Anderson (vo) with Brook Benton (finger-snapping), unknown studio orchestra and chorus under direction of Fred Norman.
New York City   **1961**

20767	**A Lover's Question** ②	● Mercury 71772
	(Brook Benton-Jimmy Williams)	

BROOK BENTON
Brook Benton (vo) with unknown studio orchestra and chorus under direction of Belford Hendricks and Luchi De Jesus. Backing vocals by Mike Stewart Singers on -1.
New York City   **1961**

20776	**It's Just A House Without You** ①	● Mercury 71859
	(Teddy Randazzo-Cirino Colacrai-Brook Benton-Clyde Otis)	■ Mercury MG-20774/SR-60774
20777	**Fantastic Things**	Mercury, unissued
20778	**If You Have No Real Objections**	■ Mercury MG-21008/SR-61008
	(Brook Benton-Clyde Otis)	*(unissued test pressing)*
20779	**That's All I'm Living For**	Mercury, unissued
	(Brook Benton-Vin Corso)	
20780	**Come Back My Love**	Mercury, unissued
20781	**It's Too Late To Turn Back Now** ②	■ Mercury MG-20934/SR-60934
	(Clyde Otis)	
20788	**The Boll Weevil Song** ② -1	● Mercury 71820
	(Brook Benton-Clyde Otis)	◘ Mercury EP-1-4046
		■ Mercury MG-20641/SR-60641, MG-20774/SR-60774, Wing MGW-12314/SRW-16314

BROOK BENTON
Brook Benton (vo, whistling on -1) with unknown studio orchestra and chorus under direction of Stan Applebaum.
New York City   **6 and 7 July 1961**

21028	**Johnny-O**	■ Mercury MG-20641/SR-60641,
	(Brook Benton)	Wing MGW-12314/SRW-16314
21029	**Honey Babe**	◘ Mercury EP-1-4046
	(Dave Dreyer)	■ Mercury MG-20641/SR-60641, Wing MGW-12314/SRW-16314
21030	**Frankie And Johnny** ①	● Mercury 71859
	(Trad.)	■ Mercury MG-20641/SR-60641, MG-20774/SR-60774, Wing MGW-12314/SRW-16314
21031	**A Worried Man**	■ Mercury MG-20641/SR-60641
	(Brook Benton)	

21032	**Child Of The Engineer** *(Brook Benton)*	◱ Mercury EP-1-4046 ■ Mercury MG-20641/SR-60641, Wing MGW-12314/SRW-16314
21033	**Careless Love** *(Spencer Williams-W.C. Handy)*	■ Mercury MG-20641/SR-60641, Wing MGW-12314/SRW-16314
21034	**My Last Dollar** *(Brook Benton)*	■ Mercury MG-20641/SR-60641, Wing MGW-12314/SRW-16314
21035	**The Intoxicated Rat** *(Brook Benton)*	◱ Mercury EP-1-4046 ■ Mercury MG-20641/SR-60641, Wing MGW-12314/SRW-16314
21036	**Key To The Highway -1** *(Charles Segar-Big Bill Broonzy)*	■ Mercury MG-20641/SR-60641, Wing MGW-12314/SRW-16314
21037	**Four Thousand Years Ago** *(Brook Benton)*	■ Mercury MG-20641/SR-60641
21038	**It's My Lazy Day** *(Smiley Burnette)*	■ Mercury MG-20641/SR-60641, Wing MGW-12314/SRW-16314

BROOK BENTON

Brook Benton (vo) with unknown studio orchestra and chorus under direction of Stan Applebaum.
New York City   **November 1961**

22086	**Revenge** ① *(Brook Benton-Oliver Hall-Marnie Ewald)*	◉ Mercury 71903 ■ Mercury MG-20774/SR-60774
22087	**Really, Really** *(Brook Benton-Oliver Hall-Marnie Ewald)*	◉ Mercury 71903
22088	**Walk On The Wild Side** *(Mack David-Elmer Bernstein)* [Theme from the Columbia Motion Picture *Walk On The Wild Side* (1962)]	◉ Mercury 71925 ■ Mercury MG-20774/SR-60774, MG-20810/SR-60810
22089	**Somewhere In The Used To Be** *(Mack David-Elmer Bernstein)*	◉ Mercury 71925

BROOK BENTON

Brook Benton (vo) with unknown studio orchestra, chorus on -1, under direction of Quincy Jones.
Fine Recording Studios, New York City   **February 1962**

23958	**I Didn't Know What Time It Was** *(Lorenz Hart-Richard Rodgers)*	■ Mercury MG-20673/SR-60673
23959	**When I Grow Too Old To Dream** ② *(Sigmund Romberg-Oscar Hammerstein II)*	■ Mercury MG-20673/SR-60673
23960	**I Love Paris** *(Cole Porter)*	■ Mercury MG-20673/SR-60673
23961	**All Of Me** *(Seymour Simons-Gerald Marks)*	■ Mercury MG-20673/SR-60673

23962	**I Don't Know Why (I Just Do)** -1 *(Roy Turk-Fred Ahlert)*	■ Mercury MG-20673/SR-60673
23963	**Tenderly** *(Jack Lawrence-Walter Gross)*	Mercury, unissued
23964	**My Foolish Heart** ① *(Victor Young-Ned Washington)*	Mercury, unissued
23966	**Breezin' Along With The Breeze** *(Haven Gillespie-Seymour Simons- Richard Whiting)*	■ Mercury MG-20673/SR-60673
23967	**There Goes That Song Again** *(Sammy Cahn-Jule Styne)*	■ Mercury MG-20673/SR-60673
23968	**After You've Gone** *(Henry Creamer-Turner Layton)*	■ Mercury MG-20673/SR-60673
23969	**I'll Get By (As Long As I Have You)** *(Fred Ahlert-Roy Turk)*	■ Mercury MG-20673/SR-60673

BROOK BENTON

Brook Benton (vo) with unknown studio orchestra and chorus under direction of Malcolm Dodds.
New York City   **5 March 1962**

24186	**Hit Record** *(Sibelius Williams)*	◉ Mercury 71962 ■ Mercury MG-20774/SR-60774
	Hit Record [alt. take] *(Sibelius Williams)*	◎ Sepia *(UK)* 1235
24187	**Thanks To The Fool** *(Bennie Benjamin-Sol Marcus)*	◉ Mercury 71962
24312	**Two Tickets To Paradise** *(Brook Benton-Malcolm Dodds)*	◉ Mercury 72009 *(not released)*, 72177
24313	**Our Hearts Knew** ① *(Brook Benton)*	■ Mercury MG-21008/SR-61008 *(unissued test pressing)*

BROOK BENTON

Brook Benton (vo) with unknown studio orchestra under direction of Quincy Jones.
Fine Recording Studios, New York City   **7 March 1962**

24318	**Trouble In Mind** *(Richard Jones)*	■ Mercury MG-20673/SR-60673
24319	**Blues In The Night** *(Johnny Mercer-Harold Arlen)*	■ Mercury MG-20673/SR-60673
24320	**Let Me Sing And I'm Happy** *(Irving Berlin)*	■ Mercury MG-20673/SR-60673
	It's All Right	◉ Mercury 72009 *(not released)*

BROOK BENTON

Brook Benton (vo, whistling on -1) with unknown studio orchestra and backg vo by the Merry Melody Singers under direction of Jerry Kennedy.

Bradley's Studio, Nashville   **16 July 1962**

25263	**Lie To Me** ① *(Margie Singleton-Brook Benton)*	● Mercury 72024 ■ Mercury MG-20740/SR-60740, MG-20774/SR-60774
25264	**My True Confession** ① *(Ray Stevens-Margie Singleton)*	● Mercury 72135 ■ Mercury MG-20740/SR-60740
25265	**Still Waters Run Deep** *(Bob Perper-Paul Gasper)*	● Mercury 72055 ■ Mercury MG-20774/SR-60774
25266	**Hotel Happiness** ① *(Leon Carr-Earl Shuman)*	● Mercury 72055 ■ Mercury MG-20774/SR-60774
25267	**Tender Years** *(Darrell Edwards)*	● Mercury 72135
25268	**Everytime I'm Kissin' You** *(Carl Belew-Faron Young)*	■ Mercury MG-20918/SR-60918,
25269	**With The Touch Of Your Hand** *(Margie Singleton-Jerry Kennedy)*	● Mercury 72024
25270	**I Got What I Wanted** ① *(Brook Benton-Margie Singleton)*	● Mercury 72099 ■ Mercury MG-20740/SR-60740
25271	**Send For Me** *(Ollie Jones)*	■ Mercury MG-20740/SR-60740
25272	**Looking Back** ② *(Brook Benton-Clyde Otis-Belford Hendricks)*	■ Mercury MG-20740/SR-60740
25273	**Pledging My Love** *(Don Robey-Fats Washington)*	■ Mercury MG-20740/SR-60740
25274	**Take Good Care Of Her** ① *(Arthur Kent-Ed Warren)*	■ Mercury MG-20740/SR-60740
25275	**Will You Love Me Tomorrow** *(Carole King-Gerald Goffin)*	■ Mercury MG-20740/SR-60740
25276	**I Need You So**	Mercury, unissued
25277	**Chains Of Love** ① *(A. Nugetre)*	■ Mercury MG-20740/SR-60740
25278	**Tomorrow Night** *(Lonnie Johnson)*	■ Mercury MG-20740/SR-60740
25279	**Got You On My Mind** *(Joe Thomas-Howard Biggs)*	■ Mercury MG-20740/SR-60740
25280	**Valley Of Tears** ① -1 *(Antoine Domino-Dave Bartholomew)*	■ Mercury MG-20740/SR-60740

| 25281 | **Please Send Me Someone To Love** ① *(Percy Mayfield)* | Mercury, unissued |

BROOK BENTON
Brook Benton (vo) with unknown others.
Live on *Tonight Show starring Johnny Carson* (NBC-TV), New York   30 November 1962

| | **Chariot Wheels** *(Brook Benton)* | O Rockhill Recording, no number *(10" 33⅓ single-sided acetate)* |

BROOK BENTON
Brook Benton (vo) with the Joel Herron Orchestra and announcer Del Sharbutt.
Unknown location   1963

	Boll Weevil Song ③ *(Brook Benton-Clyde Otis)*	■ Treasury Department, US Savings Bonds Division No.832 *(radio)*
	Hotel Happiness ② *(Leon Carr-Earl Shuman)*	■ Treasury Department, US Savings Bonds Division No.832 *(radio)*
	Take Good Care Of Her ② *(Arthur Kent-Ed Warren)*	■ Treasury Department, US Savings Bonds Division No.832 *(radio)*

BROOK BENTON
Brook Benton (vo) with unknown studio orchestra and chorus under direction of Bill Justis.
Nashville, Tennessee   21 January 1963

27006	**Dearer Than Life** *(Ed Warren-Arthur Kent)*	◉ Mercury 72099 ■ Mercury MG-21008/SR-61008 *(unissued test pressing)*
27007	**These Hands**	Mercury, unissued
27008	**My Foolish Heart** ② *(Victor Young-Ned Washington)*	Mercury, rejected
27009	**I'll Always Be In Love With You** *(Herman Ruby-Bud Green-Sam Stept)*	Mercury, rejected

BROOK BENTON
Brook Benton (vo) with unknown studio orchestra and chorus under direction of Bill Justis and Ray Ellis.
Nashville, Tennessee   19 July 1963

1-29148	**Crack Up Time**	Mercury, unissued
1-29149	**Another Cup Of Coffee** *(Earl Shuman-Leon Carr)*	Mercury, unissued
(1-31190)	**Another Cup Of Coffee** *(Earl Shuman-Leon Carr)* [Edited version of above]	◉ Mercury 72266
2-29150	**I'll Always Love You**	■ Mercury MG-21008/SR-61008 *(unissued test pressing)*

1-29151	**Don't Hate Me (For Loving You)** *(Bennie Benjamin-Sol Marcus)*	◉ Mercury 72177
1-29152	**A Man Of Steel**	Mercury, unissued

BROOK BENTON
Brook Benton (vo) with unknown studio orchestra and chorus, Luchi De Jesus (arr, cond).
New York City   **19 August 1963**

2-29210	**Once Upon A Time** *(Lee Adams-Charles Strouse)*	■ Mercury MG-20830/SR-60830
2-29211	**As Long As She Needs Me** *(Lionel Bart)*	■ Mercury MG-20830/SR-60830
2-29212	**Till There Was You** *(Meredith Wilson)*	■ Mercury MG-20830/SR-60830
2-29213	**I'll Know** *(Frank Loesser)*	■ Mercury MG-20830/SR-60830

BROOK BENTON
Brook Benton (vo) with unknown studio orchestra and chorus, Luchi De Jesus (arr, cond).
New York City   **22 August 1963**

2-29217	**I've Never Been In Love Before** *(Frank Loesser)*	■ Mercury MG-20830/SR-60830
2-29218	**Soon** *(George & Ira Gershwin)*	■ Mercury MG-20830/SR-60830
2-29219	**If Ever I Would Leave You** *(Alan Lerner-Fred Loewe)*	■ Mercury MG-20830/SR-60830
2-29220	**Love Look Away** *(Richard Rodgers-Oscar Hammerstein II)*	■ Mercury MG-20830/SR-60830
2-29221	**Make Someone Happy** *(Betty Comden-Adolph Green-Jule Styne)*	■ Mercury MG-20830/SR-60830
2-29222	**Long Before I Knew You** *(Betty Comden-Adolph Green-Jule Styne)*	■ Mercury MG-20830/SR-60830
2-29223	**The Sweetest Sounds** *(Richard Rodgers)*	■ Mercury MG-20830/SR-60830
2-29224	**Hello Young Lovers** *(Richard Rodgers-Oscar Hammerstein II)*	■ Mercury MG-20830/SR-60830
2-29225	**You're All I Want For Always**	Mercury, unissued

BROOK BENTON
Brook Benton (vo) with unknown studio orchestra and chorus, Luchi De Jesus (arr, cond).
New York City   **August, 1963**

29310	**You're All I Want For Christmas** ① *(Bennie Benjamin-Sol Marcus)* [1 voice]	Mercury, unissued

29311   **You're All I Want For Christmas** ①   ■ Mercury MG-21008/SR-61008
                 (Bennie Benjamin-Sol Marcus) [2 voices]   *(unissued test pressing)*

1-29312   **You're All I Want For Christmas** ②   ◉ Mercury 72214
                 (Bennie Benjamin-Sol Marcus) [1 voice]   ■ Mercury Galaxy MGD-/SRD-21

29313   **You're All I Want For Christmas** ②   Mercury, unissued
                 (Bennie Benjamin-Sol Marcus) [2 voices]

BROOK BENTON & DAMITA JO

Brook Benton & Damita Jo DuBlanc (vo duet) with unknown studio orchestra and chorus, Luchi De Jesus (arr, cond).

Unknown location   **19 September 1963**

1-29340   **Yaba-Daba-Do**   ◉ Mercury 72196
                 (Bennie Benjamin-Sol Marcus)   *(promo only - withdrawn)*
                                              ■ Demand *(NL)* DMSLP-090
                                              [bootleg]

1-29341   **Stop Foolin'**   ◉ Mercury 72207
                 (Brook Benton)

1-29342   **Almost Persuaded**   ◉ Mercury 72196
                 (Dan Penn-Donnie Fritts)   *(promo only - withdrawn)*

1-29343   **Baby, You've Got It Made**   ◉ Mercury 72207
                 (Bennie Benjamin-Sol Marcus)

BROOK BENTON

Brook Benton (vo) with unknown studio orchestra, chorus on -1, Luchi De Jesus (arr, cond).

A&R Studios, New York City   **27 and 28 November 1963**

2-29491   **Born To Sing The Blues**   ■ Mercury MG-20886/SR-60886
                 (Lenny Adelson-Imogen Carpenter)

2-29492   **Since I Met You Baby** -1   ■ Mercury MG-20886/SR-60886
                 (Ivory Joe Hunter)

2-29493   **God Bless The Child** ② -1   ■ Mercury MG-20886/SR-60886
                 (Billie Holiday-Arthur Herzog)

2-29494   **I'll Never Be Free**   ■ Mercury MG-20886/SR-60886
                 (Bennie Benjamin-George Weiss)

2-29495   **Why Don't You Write Me** -1   ■ Mercury MG-20886/SR-60886
                 (Laura Hollins)

2-29496   **I Worry 'Bout You** -1   ■ Mercury MG-20886/SR-60886
                 (Harry Link-Fred Hildebrand-Vera
                  Michelena)

2-29497   **Every Goodbye Ain't Gone** -1   ■ Mercury MG-20886/SR-60886
                 (Norman Mapp)

2-29498   **The Sun's Gonna Shine In My Door** -1   ■ Mercury MG-20886/SR-60886
                 (Big Bill Broonzy)

| 2-29499 | **Nobody Knows**
(And Nobody Seems To Care) -1
(Irving Berlin) | ■ Mercury MG-20886/SR-60886 |

BROOK BENTON
Brook Benton (vo) with unknown studio orchestra and chorus, Luchi De Jesus (arr, cond).
New York City   **2 December 1963**

1-30800	**Going, Going, Gone** *(Emil Anton-Alan Thomas)*	◉ Mercury 72230 ■ Mercury MG-20918/SR-60918
1-30801	**After Midnight** **(That's When I Miss You The Most)** *(Margie Singleton-Jerry Kennedy)*	◉ Mercury 72230 ■ Mercury MG-20886/SR-60886
2-30802	**Daddy Knows** *(Norman Mapp)*	■ Mercury MG-20886/SR-60886
2-30803	**So Little Time** *(Wilhelmina Clayton)*	■ Mercury MG-20886/SR-60886

BROOK BENTON
Brook Benton (vo) with unknown others.
Unknown location   **1964?**

| | **Singing Bug** [0:51]
(Brook Benton-Clyde Otis)
[Fast version of 'The Boll Weevil Song'] | ■ Mars Broadcasting CP-1103 *(radio)* |

BROOK BENTON
Brook Benton (vo) with unknown studio orchestra and chorus, Luchi De Jesus (arr, cond).
Unknown location   **1964**

2-31049	**I'll Step Aside** *(Johnny Bond)*	■ Mercury MG-20918/SR-60918
2-31050	**I Walk The Line** ① *(Johnny Cash)*	■ Pickwick SPC-3217
2-31051	**I Don't Hurt Anymore** *(Don Robertson-Jack Rollins)*	■ Mercury MG-20918/SR-60918
2-31052	**I'm Throwing Rice** **(At The Girl That I Love)** *(Steve Nelson-Ed Nelson)*	■ Mercury MG-20918/SR-60918
2-31056	**Just Call Me Lonesome** *(Rex Griffin)*	■ Mercury MG-20918/SR-60918
2-31065	**My Shoes Keep Walking Back To You** *(Lee Ross-Bob Wills)*	■ Mercury MG-20918/SR-60918
2-31066	**Letters Have No Arms** *(Arbie Gibson-Ernest Tubb)*	■ Mercury MG-20918/SR-60918
2-31067	**All Over Again** *(Johnny Cash)*	■ Mercury MG-20918/SR-60918

2-31070	**Faded Love** (Bob Wills-John Wills)	■ Mercury MG-20918/SR-60918
2-31071	**I'd Trade All Of My Tomorrows (For Just One Yesterday)** (Jenny Lou Carson)	■ Mercury MG-20918/SR-60918
2-31072	**Don't Rob Another Man's Castle** (Jenny Lou Carson)	■ Mercury MG-20918/SR-60918
2-31073	**Unclaimed Heart**	Mercury, unissued

BROOK BENTON

Brook Benton (vo) with unknown studio orchestra and chorus under direction of Belford Hendricks.
Unknown location   **1964**

| 1-31191 | **Too Late To Turn Back Now** ③ (Clyde Otis) | ◉ Mercury 72266 |

BROOK BENTON

Brook Benton (vo) with unknown studio orchestra and chorus under direction of Alan Lorber.
Nashville, Tennessee   **May 1964**

1-32147	**On My Word** ①	■ Mercury MG-21008/SR-61008 (unissued test pressing)
1-32148	**Come On Back** (Bobby Stevenson-June Cordae)	◉ Mercury 72303
1-32149	**I'm A Man** (Neil Diamond)	Mercury, unissued
	I'm A Man [alt. take, mono] (Neil Diamond)	■ Warner Bros. W-1591[3]
	I'm A Man [different alt. take, stereo] (Neil Diamond)	■ Warner Bros. WS-1591[3]
1-32150	**Where There's A Will (There's A Way)** ① (Brook Benton)	Mercury, unissued
1-32182	**On My Word** ②	Mercury unissued
1-32183	**A House Is Not A Home** (Burt Bacharach-Hal David) [Title song from the Joseph E. Levine movie production, *A House Is Not A Home*]	◉ Mercury 72303
1-32184	**Buttermilk Sky**	Mercury, unissued
1-32185	**The Next Time I Fall In Love**	Mercury, unissued

---

[3] *The Stars Salute Dr. Martin Luther King* (1964).

BROOK BENTON

Brook Benton (vo) with unknown studio orchestra, chorus except on -1, Luchi De Jesus (arr, cond).
Unknown location   **August 1964**

1-33806	**Do It Right -1** *(Rudy Clark)*	◉ Mercury 72365 ■ Mercury MG-20934/SR-60934
1-33807	**Please, Please Make It Easy** *(Rose Marie McCoy-Ken Williams)*	◉ Mercury 72365 ■ Mercury MG-20934/SR-60934
1-33808	**What Else Do You Want From Me** *(Jimmy Williams-Larry Harrison)*	■ Mercury MG-20934/SR-60934
1-33809	**There's No Fool Like An Old Fool** *(Van McCoy)*	■ Mercury MG-20934/SR-60934
1-33825	**Learning To Love Again** *(Paul Vance-Eddie Snyder)*	■ Mercury MG-20934/SR-60934
1-33826	**Lumberjack** *(Charles Arrington)*	◉ Mercury 72333 ■ Mercury MG-20934/SR-60934
1-33827	**What Is A Woman Without A Man** *(Brook Benton)*	■ Mercury MG-20934/SR-60934
1-33828	**Fine Brown Frame** *(Geadalope Cartiero-J. Mayo Williams)*	■ Mercury MG-20934/SR-60934
1-33829	**I Had It** *(Jimmy Williams-Larry Harrison)*	■ Mercury MG-20934/SR-60934
1-33830	**Don't Do What I Did (Do What I Say)** *(Bennie Benjamin-Sol Marcus)*	◉ Mercury 72333 ■ Mercury MG-20934/SR-60934

BROOK BENTON

Brook Benton (vo) with unknown studio orchestra and chorus under direction of Fred Norman.
Unknown location   **January 1965**

1-34820	**The Special Years** *(Martha Sharp)*	◉ Mercury 72398 ■ Mercury MG-21008/SR-61008 *(unissued test pressing)*
1-34821	**One Day I'll Dry Your Tears** *(Brook Benton-Ed Townsend)*	Mercury, unissued
1-34822	**Where There's A Will (There's A Way)** ②	◉ Mercury 72398
	(Brook Benton)	
1-34823	**One More Time**	Mercury, unissued
1-34856	**A Lifetime Lease On Your Heart** *(Larry Harrison-Jimmy Williams)*	■ Mercury MG-21008/SR-61008 *(unissued test pressing)*
1-34857	**My Only Year Book**	Mercury, unissued
1-34858	**A Million Miles**	Mercury, unissued
1-34960	**My One And Only Year Book**	Mercury, unissued

BROOK BENTON
Brook Benton (vo) with unknown studio orchestra, chorus on -1, under direction of Teacho Wiltshire.
Unknown location   **May 1965**

1-36087	**I Will Warm Your Heart** [long version]	Mercury, unissued
1-36088	**Love Me Now** -1 *(Brook Benton-Ed Townsend)*	◐ Mercury 72446
1-36089	**A Sleepin' At The Foot Of The Bed** *(Eugene Wilson-Luther Patrick)*	◐ Mercury 72446
1-36090	**I Will Warm Your Heart** [short version]	Mercury, unissued

BROOK BENTON
Brook Benton (vo) with unknown others.
Unknown location   **August 1965**

1-36780	**Chains Of Love** ② *(A. Nugetre)*	Mercury, unissued
1-36781	**Valley Of Tears** ② *(Antoine Domino-Dave Bartholomew)*	Mercury, unissued

BROOK BENTON
Brook Benton (vo) with orchestra: Clifton Smalls (ldr, p), A.J. Johnson (cond), Daniel B. Bank (bar), O.L. Jackson, M.D. Liston, James Cleveland, William Butler (tb), E.E. Young (g), J. Richardson, Ernest Royal, Joseph D. Newman, Tosha Samaroff (tp), Ernest Royal (as), Sylvan Shulman, Harold Furmansky, Mac Ceppos, Arthur H. Bogin, Milton Lomask, Harry Katzman, Collymore Winston, Max Pollikoff (vn), Alfred V. Brown, Maurice P. Bialkin (vla), Seldon Powell (cello), Alva L. McCain (sax), Charles Persip (d), Milton J. Hinton, Robert G. Bushnell (b). Chorus: James Robert Sands, Jerome Graff, Eugene Thamon, Elise Bretton, Laura Leslie and Lois Winter.
RCA Studio A, New York City   **8 September 1965**

SPA1-7220	**More Time To Be With You** ① *(Bob Hilliard-Burt Bacharach)*	RCA, unissued
SPA1-7221	**You're Mine (And I Love You)** ① *(Bobby Stevenson)*	RCA, unissued

BROOK BENTON
Brook Benton (vo) with orchestra arranged and conducted by Ray Ellis: Everett Barksdale (bg), James Johnson (d), Milton J. Hinton (b), Willard Suyker, John Pizzarelli (g), George Devens (perc), Paul Griffin (p), Kermit Moore, Charles McCracken (cello), Alfred V. Brown, Archie Levin (vla), Gene Orloff, Leo Kruczek, Paul Winter, Aaron Rosand, Emanuel Green, Raoul Poliakin, Julius Schachter, David Nadien (vn). Chorus: Stephen Steck Jr, Jerome Graff, Rudy Williams, Lillian Clark, Elise Bretton, June Magruder and Lois Winter.
RCA Studio A, New York City   **15 September 1965**

SPA1-7219 SPKM-7219	**Mother Nature, Father Time** *(Brook Benton-Clyde Otis)*	◐ RCA Victor 47-8693 ■ RCA Victor LPM-/LSP-3526
SPA1-7222	**Boy, I Wish I Was In Your Place** *(Clyde Otis-Bobby Stevenson)*	■ RCA Victor LPM-/LSP-3526
SPA1-7231	**More Time To Be With You** ② *(Bob Hilliard-Burt Bacharach)*	■ RCA Victor LPM-/LSP-3526, RCA Camden CAS-2431

SPA1-7232	**You're Mine (And I Love You)** ②	○ RCA Victor 47-8693
SPKM-7232	*(Bobby Stevenson)*	■ RCA Victor LPM-/LSP-3526

BROOK BENTON

Brook Benton (vo, whistling on-1) with orchestra arranged and conducted by Ray Ellis: Everett Barksdale, Don Arnone, John Pizzarelli (g), Paul L. Griffin (p), Leon Cohen (f), Joseph Grimaldi, Jerome Richardson (sax), James L. Johnson (tb), Milton J. Hinton (b), James Osie Johnson (d), George Devens (perc), Gene Orloff, Charles Libove, Julius Schachter, Max Pollikoff, Emanuel Green, Tosha Samaroff, Sylvan Shulman, David Nadien, Theodore Israel, Richard Selwart Clarke (vn), Charles P. McCracken, Maurice P. Bialkin (cello). Chorus: Stephen Steck, Jerome Graff, Eugene Thamon, Lillian Clark, Elise Bretton, Miriam Workman and Lois Winter.
RCA Studio A, New York City   **28 September 1965**

SPA1-7234	**While There's Life (There's Still Hope)**	○ RCA Victor 47-8768
SPKM-7234	*(David Parker-Clyde Otis)*	■ RCA Victor LPM-/LSP-3526
SPA1-7235	**The Song I Heard Last Night (Play It Again)** -1 *(James Shaw-Clyde Otis)*	■ RCA Victor LPM-/LSP-3526
SPA1-7236	**Since You've Been Gone** *(Robert Williams-Luchi De Jesus)*	■ RCA Victor LPM-/LSP-3526, RCA Camden CAS-2431
SPA1-7237	**Moon River** *(Henry Mancini-Johnny Mercer)*	■ RCA Victor LPM-/LSP-3514, RCA Camden CAS-2431

BROOK BENTON

Brook Benton (vo) with orchestra arranged and conducted by Ray Ellis: Everett Barksdale (bg), George Devens (perc), Paul L. Griffin (p), James Osie Johnson (d), Willard Suyker, Don L. Arnone (g), Milton J. Hinton (b), Leon Cohen, Romeo Penque (f), Jerome Richardson (sax), J.J. Johnson (tb), George Ricci, Charles McCracken (cello), Gene Orloff, Tosha Samaroff, Raoul Poliakin, Julius Schachter, Leo Kahn, Emanuel Green, David Nadien (vn), Alfred Brown, Harold Coletta, Sylvan Shulman (vla). Chorus: Stephen Steck, Jerome Graff, Eugene Thamon, Lillian Clark, Elise Bretton, Miriam Workman and Lois Winter.
RCA Studio A, New York City   **30 September 1965**

SPA1-7238	**Life Is Too Short (For Me To Stop Loving You Now)** *(Alicia Evelyn-Brook Benton-Charles Singleton)*	■ RCA Victor LPM-/LSP-3526
SPA1-7239	**I Wanna Be With You (Everywhere You Go)** *(Brook Benton-Clyde Otis)*	■ RCA Victor LPM-/LSP-3526, RCA Camden CAS-2431
SPA1-7240	**You're So Wonderful** *(Bobby Stevenson-June Cordae)*	■ RCA Victor LPM-/LSP-3526, RCA Camden CAS-2431
SPA1-7241	**It's A Crime** *(Bobby Stevenson-June Cordae)*	■ RCA Victor LPM-/LSP-3526, RCA Camden CAS-2431
SPA1-7244	**Foolish Enough To Try** *(Brook Benton-Sidney Wyche)*	■ RCA Victor LPM-/LSP-3526, RCA Camden CAS-2431

BROOK BENTON

Brook Benton (vo) with orchestra arranged and conducted by Glenn Osser: Abe Osser (ldr), Everett Barksdale (bg), James Osie Johnson (d), George Duvivier (b), Al Casamenti (g), Paul L. Griffin (p), Gloria Agostini (harp), James Buffington, Joseph Singer (fh), George Ricci, Harvey Shapiro (cello), Harold Coletta, Emanuel Vardi, George Brown, Isador Zir (vla), Raoul Poliakin, Gene Orloff, Leo Kahn, George Ockner, Max Pollikoff, Ralph Silverman, Leo Kruczek, Paul Gershman, Emanuel Green, Tosha Samaroff, Sol Shapiro, Max Cahn (vn).

RCA Studio A, New York City   **2 October 1965**

SPA1-7245	**Call Me Irresponsible** *(Sammy Cahn-Jimmy Van Heusen)*	■ RCA Victor LPM-/LSP-3514
SPA1-7246	**Hey There** *(Richard Adler-Jerry Ross)*	■ RCA Victor LPM-/LSP-3514, RCA Camden CAS-2431
SPA1-7247	**A Nightingale Sang In Berkeley Square** ① *(Eric Maschwitz-Manning Sherwin)*	■ RCA Victor LPM-/LSP-3514
SPA1-7248	**Love Is A Many-Splendored Thing** *(Paul Webster-Sammy Fain)*	■ RCA Victor LPM-/LSP-3514, RCA Camden CAS-2431

BROOK BENTON

Brook Benton (vo) with orchestra arranged and conducted by Glenn Osser: Abe Osser (ldr), Everett Barksdale, Don Arnone (g), Paul L. Griffin (p), George Duvivier (b), Tony Miranda (F-hrn), Robert Maxwell (harp), Joseph Grimaldi, Philip L. Bodner (sax), Jerome Richardson, Romeo Penque (f), James Osie Johnson (d), George Ockner, Leo Kruczek, Arnold Eidus, Tosha Samaroff, Julius Schachter, Raoul Poliakin, Leo Kahn, Emanuel Green, David Nadien, Gene Orloff (vn), David Hankovitz, Emanuel Vardi, Alfred Brown, Harold Coletta (vla), George Ricci, Charles McCracken (cello).

RCA Studio A, New York City   **6 October 1965**

SPA1-7251	**Once In Love With Amy** *(Frank Loesser)*	■ RCA Victor LPM-/LSP-3514
SPA1-7252-2	**Try A Little Tenderness** *(Harry Woods-Jimmy Campbell-Reg Connelli)*	■ RCA Victor LPM-/LSP-3514
SPA1-7253	**More** *(Norman Newell-Riziero Ortolani-Nino Oliviero)*	■ RCA APL1-1044
SPA1-7254-2	**Hawaiian Wedding Song** *(Charles King-Al Hoffman-Dick Manning)*	■ RCA APL1-1044
SPA1-7255-1	**The Second Time Around** *(Sammy Cahn-Jimmy Van Heusen)*	■ RCA Victor LPM-/LSP-3514

BROOK BENTON
Brook Benton (vo) with orchestra arranged and conducted by Glenn Osser: Abe Osser (ldr), Everett Barksdale, Al Casamenti (g), Paul L. Griffin (p), George Duvivier (b), James Osie Johnson (d), Gloria Agostini (harp), George Ockner, David Nadien, Arnold Eidus, Gene Orloff, Paul Gershman, Leo Kruczek, Max Pollikoff, Raoul Poliakin, Charles Libove, Ralph Silverman, Tosha Samaroff, Max Cahn, Sol Shapiro, Bernard Eichen, Leo Kahn, Emanuel Green, Murray Sandry (vn), Harold Coletta, George Brown, Alfred V. Brown (vla), George Ricci, Charles McCracken, Peter Makas, Harvey Shapiro (cello).

RCA Studio A, New York City   **7 October 1965**

SPA1-7256-3	**My Darling, My Darling** *(Frank Loesser)*	■ RCA Victor LPM-/LSP-3514
SPA1-7257-3	**That Old Feeling** *(Lew Brown-Sammy Fain)*	■ RCA Victor LPM-/LSP-3514
SPA1-7258-1	**Blue Moon** *(Richard Rodgers-Lorenz Hart)*	■ RCA Victor LPM-/LSP-3514, RCA Camden CAS-2431
SPA1-7259-5	**Peg O' My Heart** *(Alfred Bryan-Fred Fisher)*	■ RCA Victor LPM-/LSP-3514

BROOK BENTON
Brook Benton (vo) with unknown p.

Unknown location   **ca. 1965**

	A Sailor Boy's Love Song ① [demo] *(Brook Benton)*	O Circle 7-3718 / J-20009 United Recording Laboratories *(10" 33⅓ single-sided acetate)*

BROOK BENTON
Brook Benton (vo) with orchestra arranged and conducted by Ray Ellis: Everett Barksdale, Vincent Bell, Sebastian Mure (g), Douglas Allan (perc), Robert Donaldson (d), Paul Griffin (p), George Duvivier (b), Richard Hixson (b-tb), Urbie Green, Dominick Gravine (tb), Gene Orloff, Emanuel Green, Max Cahn, Julius Schachter, Leo Kahn, Frederick Buldrini, Sol Shapiro, Paul Winter, Bernard Eichen, Aaron Rosand (vn), Harold R. Coletta, Richard Dickler (vla), Peter Makas, Maurice Bialkin (cello). Chorus: Arne Markussen, Jerome Graff, Eugene Thamon, Lillian Clark, Elise Bretton, Miriam Workman and Lois Winter.

RCA Studio A, New York City   **27 December 1965**

SPA1-8915 SPKM-8915	**A Sailor Boy's Love Song** ② *(Brook Benton)*	● RCA Victor 47-8830
SPA1-8916 SPKM-8916	**Only A Girl Like You** *(Clyde Otis-Frank Augustas)*	● RCA Victor 47-8768
SPA1-8917	**My Son, I Wish You Everything** *(Clyde Otis-Lou Stallman)*	RCA, unissued

BROOK BENTON

Brook Benton (vo) with orchestra conducted by David Gates: Benjamin Barrett (contr), Anita Kerr (arr), Pete Jolly (p), Morty Corb (b), William Pitman, Barney Kessel, Alton Henrickson (g), Earl Palmer (d, perc), Julius Wechter (perc), Robert Barene, Henry L. Roth, Lou Klass, James Getzoff, Paul Shure, Marvin Limonick, Ralph Schaeffer, Arnold Belnick (vn), Alvin Dinkin, Joseph Di Fiore (vla), Ralph Kramer, Frederick Seykora (cello), William Hinshaw, Richard Perissi, Henry Sigismonti (F-hrn). Chorus: Anita Kerr, Randall Shepard, Betty J. Baker and Allan Capps.

RCA Studio A, Hollywood, California   **15 January 1966**

TPA3-0023	**Funny How Time Slips Away** *(Willie Nelson)*	■ RCA Victor LPM-/LSP-3590
TPA3-0024	**I Really Don't Want To Know** *(Don Robertson-Howard Barnes)*	■ RCA Victor LPM-/LSP-3590
TPA3-0025	**He'll Have To Go** *(Joe & Audrey Allison)*	■ RCA Victor LPM-/LSP-3590
TPA3-0026	**Gone** *(Smokey Rogers)*	■ RCA Victor LPM-/LSP-3590

BROOK BENTON

Brook Benton (vo) with orchestra conducted by Pete King: C. Dudley King (ldr), Benjamin Barrett (contr), Anita Kerr (arr), Pete Jolly (p), Morty Corb (b), Barney Kessel, Joseph Gibbons, William Pitman (g), Earl Palmer (d, perc), Julius Wechter (perc), Joseph DiFiore, Paul Robyn (vla), Frederick Seykora, Edgar Lustgarten (cello), Paul Shure, Alex Murray, Robert Barene, Henry L. Roth, Lou Klass, Marvin Limonick, Arnold Belnick, Ralph Schaeffer (vn). Chorus: Anita Kerr, Randall Shepard, Betty J. Baker and Allan Capps.

RCA Studio A, Hollywood, California   **17 January 1966**

TPA3-0027	**I Walk The Line** ② *(Johnny Cash)*	■ RCA Victor LPM-/LSP-3590
TPA3-0028	**Please Help Me, I'm Falling** *(Don Robertson-Hal Blair)*	■ RCA Victor LPM-/LSP-3590
TPA3-0029	**Any Time** *(Herbert 'Happy' Lawson)*	■ RCA Victor LPM-/LSP-3590
TPA3-0030	**Walking The Floor Over You** *(Ernest Tubb)*	■ RCA Victor LPM-/LSP-3590

BROOK BENTON

Brook Benton (vo) with orchestra conducted by David Gates: Benjamin Barrett (contr), Anita Kerr (arr), Pete Jolly (p), William Pitman, Barney Kessel, Joseph Gibbons (g) Earl Palmer (d, perc), Julius Wechter (perc), Morty Corb (b), Joseph DiFiore, Alvin Dinkin (vla), Frederick Seykora, Edgar Lustgarten (cello), Henry Sigismonti, William Hinshaw, Richard Perissi (F-hrn), James Getzoff, Arnold Belnick, Ralph Schaeffer, Lou Klass, Henry L. Roth, Robert Barene, Marvin Limonick, Paul Shure (vn). Chorus: Anita Kerr, Randall Shepard, Betty J. Baker and Allan Capps.

RCA Studio A, Hollywood, California   **18 January 1966**

TPA3-0031	**He's Got You** *(Hank Cochran)*	■ RCA Victor LPM-/LSP-3590
TPA3-0032	**Hello Walls** *(Willie Nelson)*	■ RCA Victor LPM-/LSP-3590

TPA3-0033   **Cold, Cold Heart**   ■ RCA Victor LPM-/LSP-3590
                (Hank Williams)

TPA3-0034   **Have I Told You Lately That I Love You?** ■ RCA Victor LPM-/LSP-3590
                (Scott Wiseman)

BROOK BENTON

Brook Benton (vo) with orchestra arranged and conducted by Ray Ellis: Everett Barksdale (g), Herbert Lovelle (d), Milton Hinton (b), Douglas Allan (perc), George Butcher (p), John Pizzarelli, Willard Suyker (g), Chauncey Welsch, Dominick J. Gravine, Urbie Green (tb), Leonard Goines, Ernest Royal (tp), George Ricci, Peter Makas (cello), Harold Coletta, Alfred V. Brown (vla), Gene Orloff, Aaron Rosand, Raoul Poliakin, Leo Kahn, Frederick Buldrini, Matthew Raimondi, Julius Schachter, Sylvan Shulman (vn). Chorus: Stephen Steck Jr, Jerome Graff, Eugene Thamon, Lillian Clark, Elise Bretton, Peggy Powers and Lois Winter.
RCA Studio A, New York City   **24 March 1966**

TPA1-3373-6   **Impossible, Incredible, But True**   ■ RCA APL1-1044
                 (Bobby Stevenson-June Cordae)

TPA1-3374-11 **Too Much Good Lovin' (No Good For Me)** ❍ RCA Victor 47-8830
TPKM-3374-11 *(Bobby Stevenson-June Cordae)*

TPA1-3375-8   **Where Does A Man Go To Cry** ①   RCA, unissued
                 (Clyde Otis-Naverro Artis)

TPA1-3376-16 **The Roach Song** ①   RCA, unissued
                 (Clyde Otis-Freddie Briggs-Johnny
                   Northern)

BROOK BENTON

Brook Benton (vo) with orchestra arranged and conducted by Ray Ellis: Everett Barksdale (g, contr), James H. Mitchell (g), George Duvivier (b), Grady B. Tate (d), George Butcher (p), Charles Leighton (hca), Urbie Green (tb), Eddie Bert (b-tb), Joseph B. Wilder, James Nottingham, Irvin Markowitz (tp), Gene Orloff, George Ockner, Louis Stone, Frederick Buldrini, Raoul Poliakin, Emanuel Green, John Pintavalle, Sol Shapiro, Louis Haber, Irvin Spice, Max Pollikoff, Aaron Rosand (vn), Alfred V. Brown, Harold R. Coletta (vla), Charles P. McCracken, George Ricci (cello). Chorus: Lois Winter, Gretchen Rhoads, Elise Bretton, Lillian Clark, Stephen Steck Jr., Jerome Graff and Rudy Williams.
RCA Studio A, New York City   **3 June 1966**

TPA1-5026   **When We Were (Friends)**   RCA, unissued
                 (Denny Randell- Sandy Linzer)

TPA1-5027   **Keep Your Cotton Pickin' Hands**   RCA, unissued
                 Off My Gin ①
                 (Bobby Stevenson-June Corday)

TPA1-5028   **Break Her Heart** ①   RCA, unissued
                 (Lou Stallman-Clyde Otis)

TPA1-5052   **Break Her Heart** ②   ❍ RCA Victor 47-8879
TPKM-5052   *(Lou Stallman-Clyde Otis)*

TPA1-5062   **In The Evening By The Moonlight**   ❍ RCA Victor 47-8879
TPKM-5062   *(adapted by Brook Benton-Clyde Otis-*
                 Frank Augustas)

BROOK BENTON

Brook Benton (vo) with orchestra arranged and conducted by Ray Ellis: Everett Barksdale (bg), George Butcher (p, arr), Milton J. Hinton (b), Herbert E. Lovelle (d), Don Arnone, Ralph A. Casale (g), Bert Keyes (p), Arthur Marotti (vib, bgo), Wayne J. Andre, Dominick J. Gravine, Chauncey Welsch (tb), Archie Levin, Harold R. Coletta (vla), Maurice P. Bialkin, Charles P. McCracken (cello), George Ockner, George Ockner, Julius Schachter, Raoul Poliakin, Emanuel Green, Matthew Raimondi, Frederick Buldrini, Leo Kahn, Ray Free (vn). Chorus: Lois Winter, Peggy Powers, Elise Bretton, Louise Stuart Davis, Stephen Steck Jr., Jerome Graff and Eugene Thamon.

RCA Studio A, New York City   **8 July 1966**

TPKM-5186-9	**Where Does A Man Go To Cry** ② *(Clyde Otis-Naverro Artis)*	● RCA Victor 47-8944
TPKM-5187-1	**So True in Life – So True In Love** *(Bert Keyes-Charles Singleton)*	● RCA Victor 47-8995
TPKM-5188	**Keep Your Cotton Pickin' Hands** **Off My Gin** ② *(Bobby Stevenson-June Cordae)*	RCA, rejected

BROOK BENTON

Brook Benton (vo) with orchestra arranged and conducted by Billy May: John Audino, Ray Triscari, Uan Rasey, Pete Candoli (tp), Tommy Pederson, Joe Howard, Lew McCreary, Robert Knight (tb), Willie Schwarts, Willie Smith (as), Justin Gordon, Harry Klee (ts), Robert Hardaway (bar), Michael Melvoin (p), John Collins, Mundell Lowe (g), Chuck Berghofer (b), Hal Blaine (d) and Larry Bunker (perc).

RCA Studio A, Hollywood, California   **5 August 1966**

TPA3-4691-14	**I'm Beginning To See The Light** *(Harry James-Duke Ellington-Johnny Hodges-Don George)*	■ RCA *(UK)* SF-7859 *(factory sample - unissued)*
TPA3-4692-12	**It's Been A Long, Long Time** ③ *(Sammy Kahn-Julie Styne)*	■ RCA *(UK)* SF-7859 *(factory sample - unissued)*
TPA3-4693-4	**There Goes My Heart** *(Benny Davis-Abner Silver)*	■ RCA *(UK)* SF-7859 *(factory sample - unissued)*
	There Goes My Heart [alt. take] *(Benny Davis-Abner Silver)*	■ RCA-APL 1-1044
TPA3-4694-2	**Makin' Whoopee** *(Gus Kahn-Walter Donaldson)*	■ RCA *(UK)* SF-7859 *(factory sample - unissued)*

BROOK BENTON

Brook Benton (vo) with orchestra arranged and conducted by Billy May: John Audino, Ray Triscari, Uan Rasey, Don Fagerquist (tp), Tommy Pederson, Joe Howard, Lew McCreary, William Schaefer (tb), Willie Schwarts, Willie Smith (as), Justin Gordon, Harry Klee (ts), Robert Hardaway (bar), Michael Melvoin (p), John Collins, Mundell Lowe (g), Chuck Berghofer (b), Hal Blaine (d) and Larry Bunker (perc).

RCA Studio A, Hollywood, California   **8 August 1966**

TPA3-4695-3	**Lover Come Back To Me** ③ *(Sigmund Romberg-Oscar Hammerstein II)*	■ RCA *(UK)* SF-7859 *(factory sample - unissued)*
TPA3-4696-6	**There, I've Said It Again** *(Dave Mann-Redd Evans)*	■ RCA *(UK)* SF-7859 *(factory sample - unissued)*

	There, I've Said It Again [alt. take] *(Dave Mann-Redd Evans)*	■ RCA APL1-1044
TPA3-4697-6	**Sweet Georgia Brown** *(Ben Bernie-Maceo Pinkard-Ken Casey)*	■ RCA *(UK)* SF-7859 *(factory sample - unissued)*
	Sweet Georgia Brown [alt. take] *(Ben Bernie-Maceo Pinkard-Ken Casey)*	◎ Curb D2-77445
TPA3-4698-6	**Unforgettable** *(Irving Gordon)*	■ RCA *(UK)* SF-7859 *(factory sample - unissued)*
	Unforgettable [alt. take] *(Irving Gordon)*	■ RCA APL1-1044

BROOK BENTON

Brook Benton (vo) with orchestra arranged and conducted by Rene Hall: Michel Rubini (p), Charles E. Norris, Louis Morell, Carol Kaye (g), Ray Pohlman, George Callender (b), Nick Pelico (perc), Hal Blaine (d), Jelse Ehrlich, Harry Hyams (cello), Sidney Sharp, Leonard Malarsky, Israel Baker, Ralph Schaeffer, Tilor Zelig, Emmet Sargeant, Harry Bluestone, William Kurasch and Bernard Kundell (vn).

RCA Studio A, Hollywood, California   **8 August 1966**

TPA3-4707 TPKM-4707	**The Roach Song** ② *(Clyde Otis-Freddie Briggs-Johnny Northern)*	◉ RCA Victor 47-8944
TPA3-4708	**Keep Your Cotton Pickin' Hands Off My Gin** ③ *(Bobby Stevenson-June Cordae)*	RCA, unissued
TPA3-4709 TPKM-4709	**Wake Up** *(Clyde Otis-Brook Benton)*	◉ RCA Victor 47-9096

BROOK BENTON

Brook Benton (vo) with orchestra arranged and conducted by Billy May: John Audino, Ray Triscari. Uan Rasey, Don Fagerquist (tp), Tommy Pederson, Joe Howard, Lew McCreary, William Schaefer (tb), Willie Schwarts, Willie Smith (as), Justin Gordon, Harry Klee, Robert Hardaway (ts), Michael Melvoin (p, org), Charles Berghofer (b), Hal Blaine (d), Mundell Lowe and Larry Bunker (g).

RCA Studio A, Hollywood, California   **9 August 1966**

TPA3-4699-7	**Just As Much As Ever** *(Charles Singleton-Larry Coleman)*	■ RCA *(UK)* SF-7859 *(factory sample - unissued)*
	Just As Much As Ever [alt. take] *(Charles Singleton-Larry Coleman)*	■ RCA APL1-1044
TPA3-4700-5	**Sentimental Journey** *(Bud Green-Les Brown-Benjamin Homer)*	■ RCA *(UK)* SF-7859 *(factory sample - unissued)*
TPA3-4701-7	**Beyond The Sea (La Mer)** *(Jack Lawrence-Charles Trenet)*	■ RCA *(UK)* SF-7859 *(factory sample - unissued)*
	Beyond The Sea (La Mer) [alt. take] *(Jack Lawrence-Charles Trenet)*	◎ Curb D2-77445
TPA3-4702-9	**I Only Have Eyes For You** *(Harry Warren-Al Dubin)*	■ RCA *(UK)* SF-7859 *(factory sample - unissued)*

I Only Have Eyes For You [alt. take]　　■ RCA APL1-1044
(Harry Warren-Al Dubin)

BROOK BENTON

Brook Benton (vo) with orchestra arranged and conducted by Fred Norman: Everett Barksdale (g), Bernard Purdie (d), Bert Keyes (p, a), Robert Bushness (b), James Sedlar, Myron D. Shain (tp), Heywood Henry (bar), Richard J. Harris (tb), Betty Glamann (harp), Joseph Benjamin (b, vla), Ted Sommer (perc), Archie Levin, David Mankovitz (vla), Peter Makas, Maurice P. Bialkin (cello), Leo Kahn, Frederick Buldrini, Ray Free, Louis Gabowitz, Harry Cykman, Jack Zayde, Charles Libove, Bernard Eichen (vn). Chorus: Lois Winter, Peggy Powers, Maretha Stewart, Elise Bretton, Stephen Steck Jr, Jerome L. Graff, Bob Mitchell and Eugene Thamon.
RCA Studio A, New York City　　　　　　　　　　　　　　**28 September 1966**

TPA1-7579 TPKM-7579	**Our First Christmas Together** *(Charles Singleton-Bert Keyes)*	● RCA Victor 47-9031
TPA1-7580 TPKM-7580	**Silent Night** *(Franz Gruber-Joseph Mohr)*	● RCA Victor 47-9031
TPA1-7581	**I Wish An Old Fashioned Christmas** **To You** *(Alicia Evelyn)*	RCA, unissued
TPA1-7582 TPKM-7582	**If You Only Knew** *(Teddy Randazzo-Brook Benton)*	● RCA Victor 47-8995

BROOK BENTON

Brook Benton (vo -1) with orchestra arranged and conducted by Bert DeCoteaux: Everett Barksdale (g, contr), Wallace Richardson, Eric Gale (g), Joseph Macho Jr. (b), Paul L. Griffin (p), Bernard Purdie (d), Eddie Bert (b-tb), Ernest Royal, Joseph B. Wilder (tp), Buddy Lucas (bar), Douglas Allan (vib), Jerome Richardson (f), Aaron Rosand, Harry Cykman, Frederick Buldrini, Avram Weiss, Jack Zayde, Emanuel Green (vn). Chorus: on -2: Lesley Miller, Melba Mourman, Doris Troy, Helena Walquen, Gregory Carroll, James Jones, Alex Bradford, Agness Wallace, Ella Mitchell, Alberta Bradford, Willie J. McPhatter and Robert Pinkstone.
Webster Hall Studios, New York City　　　　　　　　　　　**3 January 1967**

UPA1-3601	**Don't Look For Me** -1, -2 *(John Carter-Bobby Bradford)*	RCA, unissued
UPA1-3602	**Goodnight My Love, Pleasant Dreams** *(George Motola-John Marascalco)* -1	■ RCA APL1-1044
UPA1-3603	**Bump With A Boom** -1, -2 *(Lincoln Chase)*	RCA, unissued
UPA1-3604	**All My Love Belongs To You** [instr] *(Henry Glover-Sally Nix)*	■ RCA APL1-1044
UPKM-3604	**All My Love Belongs To You** [vocal] -1 *(Henry Glover-Sally Nix)*	● RCA Victor 47-9096

BROOK BENTON

Brook Benton (vo) with orchestra arranged and conducted by Luchi De Jesus: Everett Barksdale (contr), George Butcher (p), Robert Donaldson (d), Sal DiTroia, Carl Lynch (g), Lloyd Buchanan (b), Lou Nazzaro (perc), Donald Corrado (F-hrn), Robert Alexander, Frank Saracco (tb). Chorus: Valerie Simpson, Lesley Miller and Eileen Gilbert.

Webster Hall Studios, New York City   **20 January 1967**

UPA1-3687	**Keep The Faith, Baby**	◉ RCA Victor 47-9105
UPKM-3687	*(Luchi De Jesus-Mayme Watts-Lila Lerner)*	
UPA1-3688	**Going To Soulsville**	◉ RCA Victor 47-9105
UPKM-3688	*(Brook Benton)*	

BROOK BENTON

Brook Benton (vo) with unknown studio orchestra arranged and conducted by Billy Strange on -1 and Belford Hendricks on -2, all other songs arranged by Ernie Freeman; unknown chorus on -3.

New York City   **1967**

K6099	**Laura (What's He Got That I Ain't Got)**	◐ Reprise 0611
	(Leon Ashley-Margie Singleton) -1, -3	■ Reprise R-/RS-6268
K6100	**You're The Reason I'm Living** -1, -3	◐ Reprise 0611
	(Bobby Darin)	■ Reprise R-/RS-6268
K6119	**The Glory Of Love** -3	◐ Reprise 0649
	(Billy Hill)	■ Reprise R-/RS-6268
K6175	**Weakness In A Man** -1	◐ Reprise 0649
	(Jerry Chesnut)	
	Here We Go Again -1, -3	■ Reprise R-/RS-6268
	(Red Steagall-Don Lanier)	
	Medley:	
	I Left My Heart In San Francisco	■ Reprise R-/RS-6268
	(George Cory-Douglass Cross) **– San Francisco (Be Sure To Wear Some Flowers In Your Hair)** *(John Phillips)*	
	Lingering On -3	■ Reprise R-/RS-6268
	(Scott English-Stanley Gelber-James Last)	
	Ode To Billie Joe	■ Reprise R-/RS-6268
	(Bobbie Gentry)	
	Stick-To-It-Ivity -3	■ Reprise R-/RS-6268
	(Baker Knight)	
	(There Was A) Tall Oak Tree -3	■ Reprise R-/RS-6268
	(Dorsey Burnette)	
	This Is Worth Fighting For -3	■ Reprise R-/RS-6268
	(Edgar DeLange-Sam Stept)	

BROOK BENTON
Brook Benton (vo) with unknown studio orchestra arranged and conducted by Belford Hendricks.
New York City   **1968**

| L5356 | **Lonely Street**
*(Kenny Sowder-Carl Belew-
W.S. Stevenson)* | ⊙ Reprise 0676 |
| L5357 | **Instead (Of Loving You)**
(Williams-Barton) | ⊙ Reprise 0676 |

BROOK BENTON
Brook Benton (vo) with unknown studio orchestra arranged and conducted by Jerry Leiber and Mike Stoller.
Atlantic Studios, New York City   **5 August 1968**

| CO-14977 | **Do Your Own Thing**
(Jerry Leiber-Mike Stoller) | ⊙ Atlantic test pressing, no number,
Cotillion 45-44007
■ Cotillion SD-9002 |
| CO-14978 | **I Just Don't Know What To Do**
With Myself
(Burt Bacharach-Hal David) | ⊙ Cotillion 45-44007
■ Cotillion SD-9002 |

BROOK BENTON
Brook Benton (vo) with unknown studio orchestra arranged by Arif Mardin; backg vo by the Sweet Inspirations.
Fame Studios, Muscle Shoals, Alabama   **18 February 1969**

CO-16331	**I Still Believe In Rainbows**	Cotillion, unissued
CO-16332	**Destination Heartbreak** *(Doc Pomus-George Fischoff)*	■ Cotillion SD-9002
CO-16333	**Woman Without Love** *(Jerry Chesnut)*	⊙ Cotillion 45-44034 ■ Cotillion SD-9002
CO-16334	**She Knows What To Do For Me** *(Malcolm Rebennack-Jessie Hill)*	⊙ Cotillion 45-44031 ■ Cotillion SD-9002
CO-16335	**Touch 'Em With Love** *(John Hurley-Ronnie Wilkins)*	⊙ Cotillion 45-44031 ■ Cotillion SD-9002
CO-16336	**Nothing Can Take The Place Of You** *(Patrick Robinson-Toussaint McCall)*	⊙ Cotillion 45-44034 ■ Cotillion SD-9002

BROOK BENTON
Brook Benton (vo) with unknown studio orchestra arranged and conducted by Hutch Davie.
A&R Studios, New York City   **11 March 1969**

| CO-16513 | **With Pen In Hand**
(Bobby Goldsboro) | ■ Cotillion SD-9002 |
| CO-16514 | **Oh Lord, Why Lord**
(Phil Trim) | ■ Cotillion SD-9002 |

CO-16515	**Set Me Free** *(Claude Putnam)*	■ Cotillion SD-9002
CO-16516	**Hiding Behind The Shadow Of A Dream** *(Myrna March-Richie Grasso)*	■ Cotillion SD-9002
CO-16517	**What A Wonderful World** *(George Weiss-George Douglas)*	Cotillion, unissued
CO-16518	**Gee, You Look So Pretty**	Cotillion, unissued
CO-16519	**Break Out** *(Gary Illingworth-Myrna March)*	■ Cotillion SD-9002

BROOK BENTON

Brook Benton (vo), Arif Mardin (arr) with Cold Grits: Bill Carter (org), Dave Crawford (p), Cornell Dupree and Jimmy O'Rourke (g), Harold Cowart (b) and Tubby Ziegler (d).
Overdubbed at Atlantic Recording Studios, New York City: Sweet Inspirations (backg vo), vocal obbligatos by Cissy Houston.
Criteria Studios, Miami, Florida   **5 November 1969**

CO-18059	**The Lonely One**	Cotillion, unissued
CO-18060	**Life Has Its Little Ups And Downs** *(Margaret Ann Rich)*	■ Cotillion SD-9018
CO-18061	**Rainy Night In Georgia** ① [3:51] *(Tony Joe White)* [See also CO-18173]	■ Cotillion SD-9018
CO-18062	**My Way** [5:33] *(Paul Anka-Jacques Revaux-Claude François)* [See also CO-18794 to CO-18796]	■ Cotillion SD-9018
CO-18063	**Can't Take My Eyes Off You** ① *(Bob Crewe-Bob Gaudio)*	■ Cotillion SD-9018
CO-18064	**We're Gonna Make It** *(Gene Barge- Billy Davis-Carl Smith-Raynard Miner)*	■ Cotillion SD-9018
CO-18065	**I've Gotta Be Me** *(Walter Marks)*	◉ Cotillion 45-44078 ■ Cotillion SD-9018
CO-18066	**Baby** *(Brook Benton)*	■ Cotillion SD-9018
CO-18067	**Desertion** *(Dorian Burton-Herman Kelly)*	■ Cotillion SD-9018
CO-18068	**A Little Bit Of Soap** [3:56] *(Bert Russell-Robert Mellin)* [See also CO-18795]	■ Cotillion SD-9018
CO-18069	**Where Do I Go From Here?** *(Brook Benton-James Shaw)*	◉ Cotillion 45-44057 ■ Cotillion SD-9018

CO-18173   **Rainy Night In Georgia** ① [3:29]   ● Cotillion 45-44057
                     (Tony Joe White)
                     [Edited version of CO-18061]

BROOK BENTON WITH THE DIXIE FLYERS

Brook Benton (vo, whistling on -1), Arif Mardin (arr, cond) with the Dixie Flyers: Jim Dickinson (g, kbds), Charlie Freeman (ldr, g), Mike Utley (el-p, org), Tommy McClure (b) and Sammy Creason (d, perc).
Overdubbed at Atlantic Recording Studios, New York City: Joe Newman (tp), Benny Powell (tb), George Dorsey (as), King Curtis (ts), Pepper Adams (bar) and Stu Scharf (12-string guitar) on -1. String section under direction of Gene Orloff. Sweet Inspirations (backg vo), vocal obbligatos by Cissy Houston.
Criteria Studios, Miami, Florida   **3 March 1970**

CO-18725   **Don't It Make You Want To Go Home** -1   ● Cotillion 45-44078
                     [Don't It Make You Wanta Go Home*]   ■ Cotillion SD-9028*
                     (Joe South)

CO-18726   **Aspen Colorado**   ■ Cotillion SD-9028
                     (Tony Joe White)

CO-18727   **Willie And Laura Mae Jones**   ■ Cotillion SD-9028
                     (Tony Joe White)

                     Willie And Laura Mae Jones [alt. take]   ◎ Rhino DBK-506
                     (Tony Joe White)

CO-18728   **Old Man Willis**   Cotillion, unissued
                     (Tony Joe White)

CO-18729   **It's All In The Game**   ■ Cotillion SD-9028
                     (Carl Sigman-Charles Dawes)

                     It's All In The Game [alt. take]   ◎ Rhino DBK-506
                     (Carl Sigman-Charles Dawes)

CO-18730   **Don't Think Twice, It's All Right**   ■ Cotillion SD-9028
                     (Bob Dylan)

BROOK BENTON WITH THE DIXIE FLYERS

Brook Benton (vo, whistling on -1), Arif Mardin (arr, cond) with the Dixie Flyers: Jim Dickinson (g, kbds), Charlie Freeman (ldr, g), Mike Utley (el-p, org), Tommy McClure (b) and Sammy Creason (d, perc).
Overdubbed at Atlantic Recording Studios, New York City: Joe Newman (tp), Benny Powell (tb), George Dorsey (as), King Curtis (ts), Pepper Adams (bar) and Stu Scharf (12-string guitar) on -1. String section under direction of Gene Orloff. Sweet Inspirations (backg vo), vocal obbligatos by Cissy Houston.
Criteria Studios, Miami, Florida   **5 March 1970**

CO-18731   **Are You Sincere**   ■ Cotillion SD-9028
                     (Wayne Walker)

CO-18732   **For Le Ann**   ■ Cotillion SD-9028
                     (Tony Joe White)

CO-18733   **Born Under A Bad Sign**   ■ Cotillion SD-9028
                     (Booker T. Jones-William Bell)

CO-18734	**Whoever Finds This I Love You** *(Mac Davis)*	○ Cotillion 45-44110 ■ Cotillion SD-9028
	Whoever Finds This I Love You [alt. take] *(Mac Davis)*	◉ Rhino DBK-506
CO-18735	**Before You See A Big Man Cry**	Cotillion, unissued
CO-18736	**Let Me Fix It** *(Brook Benton)*	○ Cotillion 45-44093 ■ Cotillion SD-9028

BROOK BENTON (with COLD GRITS)

CO-18794	**My Way** [4:08] *(Paul Anka-Jacques Revaux-Claude François)* [Edited version of CO-18062]	○ Cotillion 45-44072
CO-18795	**A Little Bit Of Soap** [3:25] *(Bert Russell-Robert Mellin)* [Edited version of CO-18068]	○ Cotillion 45-44072
CO-18796	**My Way** [3:34, mono] *(Paul Anka-Jacques Revaux-Claude François)* [Edited version of CO-18062]	○ Cotillion 45-44072 *(promo)*
ST-CO-18796	**My Way** [3:34, stereo] *(Paul Anka-Jacques Revaux-Claude François)* [Edited version of CO-18062]	○ Cotillion 45-44072 *(promo)*

BROOK BENTON WITH THE DIXIE FLYERS

Brook Benton (vo), Arif Mardin (arr, cond) with the Dixie Flyers: Mike Utley (p, org), Cornell Dupree, Charlie Freeman (g), Tommy McClure (b) and Sammy Creason (d). Memphis Horns: Wayne Jackson (tp) and Andrew Love (ts) on -1. Chuck Rainey (b) replaces McClure on -2. Sweet Inspirations (backg vo).

Criteria Studios, Miami, Florida   **22 September 1970**

CO-20152	**Shoes** *(Don Covay-George Soule)*	○ Cotillion 45-44093 ■ Cotillion SD-9050
CO-20153	**Heaven Help Us All** *(Ron Miller)*	○ Cotillion 45-44110 ■ Cotillion SD-058
CO-20154	**The Way I Love You**	Cotillion, unissued
CO-20155	**I'll Paint You A Song**	Cotillion, unissued
CO-20156	**Please Send Me Someone To Love** ② -1 *(Percy Mayfield)*	○ Cotillion 45-44130 ■ Cotillion SD-9050
CO-20157	**Poor Make Believer** -2 *(James Lately-Homer Banks-Don Davis)*	○ Cotillion 45-44152 ■ Cotillion SD-9050
CO-20158	**When The Light Goes On Again**	Cotillion, unissued
CO-20159	**She Even Woke Me Up To Say Goodbye** *(Mickey Newbury-Doug Gilmore)*	○ Cotillion 45-44130 ■ Cotillion SD-9050

BROOK BENTON
Brook Benton (vo) with unknown studio orchestra and chorus arranged and conducted by Arif Mardin.
Atlantic Studios, New York City   **8 October 1970**

CO-20311	**Soul Santa**	● Cotillion 45-44141
	(Gerald Deas-Brook Benton)	◉ Atlantic 782316-2

BROOK BENTON
Brook Benton (vo) with Dave Crawford (el-p, org), Cornell Dupree (g), Chuck Rainey (b), Ray
Lucas (d) and Romeo Penque (f) on -1. Sweet Inspirations (backg vo), Cissy Houston (vo) on -1.
Atlantic Studios, New York City   **14 and 15 December 1970**

CO-20839	**Willoughby Grove** -1	■ Cotillion SD-9050
	(Bobby Scott-Danny Meehan)	
CO-20840	**Movin' Day**	● Cotillion 45-44152
	(Spencer Michlin-John Murtaugh)	■ Cotillion SD-9050
CO-20841	**I'm Comin' Home**	Cotillion, unissued
CO-20842	**Feelin' Good**	Cotillion, unissued

BROOK BENTON
Brook Benton (vo) with Dave Crawford (el-p, org), Cornell Dupree (g), Chuck Rainey (b) and Ray
Lucas (d). Memphis Horns: Wayne Jackson (tp) and Andrew Love (ts) on -1. Sweet Inspirations
(backg vo).
Atlantic Studios, New York City   **18 December 1970**

CO-20854	**If You Think God Is Dead** ①	Cotillion, unissued
	(Brook Benton)	
CO-20855	**Till I Can't Take It No More** ①	Cotillion, unissued
CO-20856	**Country Comfort** -1	■ Cotillion SD-9050
	(Elton John-Bernie Taupin-Dick James)	

BROOK BENTON
Brook Benton (vo) with Dave Crawford (el-p, org), Cornell Dupree (g), Chuck Rainey (b) and Ray
Lucas (d). Memphis Horns: Wayne Jackson (tp) and Andrew Love (ts) on -1. Sweet Inspirations
(backg vo).
Atlantic Studios, New York City   **17 December 1970**

CO-20857	**Till I Can't Take It No More** ②	Cotillion, unissued
CO-20858	**Sidewalks Of Chicago**	Cotillion, unissued
	(Dave Kirby)	
(CO-21268)	**Sidewalks Of Chicago**	■ Cotillion SD-9050
	(Dave Kirby)	
	[Edited version of above]	
CO-20859	**Our Hearts Knew** ②	Cotillion, unissued
	(Brook Benton)	
CO-20860	**Doing The Best I Can**	■ Cotillion SD-058
	(Trad.)	
CO-20861	**Jam Tune**	Cotillion, unissued

BROOK BENTON

Brook Benton (vo) with Dave Crawford (kbds), Cornell Dupree (g), Chuck Rainey (b) and Ray Lucas (d). Cissy Houston, Myrna Smith, Sylvia Shemwell, Judy Clay, Deidre Tuck, Sammy Turner, J.R. Bailey, Ronald Bright, Myrna Summers & The Interdenominational Singers (backg vo).

Atlantic Studios, New York City   **22 December 1970**

CO-20894   **Precious Lord**   ■ Cotillion SD-058
                  (Thomas A. Dorsey)

CO-20895   **Take A Look At Your Hands** [4:14]   ■ Cotillion SD-058
                  (Ralph McDonald-William Salter)
                  [*See also* CO-22007]

BROOK BENTON

Brook Benton (vo, whistling on -1) with Dave Crawford (kbds), Cornell Dupree (g), Chuck Rainey (b) and Ray Lucas (d). Cissy Houston, Myrna Smith, Sylvia Shemwell, Judy Clay, Deidre Tuck, Sammy Turner, J.R. Bailey, Ronald Bright, Myrna Summers & The Interdenominational Singers (backg vo).

Atlantic Studios, New York City   **21 December 1970**

CO-20896   **Going Home In His Name**   ■ Cotillion SD-058
                  (Ellis Johnson)

CO-20897   **I Dreamed Of A City Called Heaven** ②   ■ Cotillion SD-058
                  (Trad.)

CO-20898   **Let Us All Get Together With The Lord**   ◉ Cotillion 45-44141
                  (Moe Jaffe-Bickley Reichner)   ■ Cotillion SD-058

CO-20899   **If You Think God Is Dead** ② [4:42]   ■ Cotillion SD-058
                  (Brook Benton)
                  [*See also* CO-22008]

CO-20900   **Oh Happy Day** -1   ■ Cotillion SD-058
                  (Edwin Hawkins)

BROOK BENTON

Brook Benton (vo) with Dave Crawford (p), Cornell Dupree (g), Chuck Rainey (b) and Bernard Purdie (d). Sweet Inspirations (backg vo).

Atlantic Studios, New York City   **3 May 1971**

CO-22007   **Take A Look At Your Hands** [3:09]   ◉ Cotillion 45-44119
                  (Ralph McDonald-William Salter)
                  [Edited version of CO-20895]

CO-22008   **If You Think God Is Dead** ② [4:42]   ◉ Cotillion 45-44119, 45-44138
                  (Brook Benton)
                  [Identical to CO-20899]

CO-22011   **A Black Child Can't Smile**   ◉ Cotillion 45-44138
                  (Gerald Deas)

CO-22012   **Big Mable Murphy**   ■ Cotillion SD-9050
                  (Dallas Frazier)

CO-22013   **He Gives Us All His Love**   Cotillion, unissued

BROOK BENTON
Brook Benton (vo) with Dave Crawford (p), Cornell Dupree (g), Chuck Rainey (b), Bernard Purdie (d) and Neal Rosengarden (tp). Sweet Inspirations (backg vo).
Atlantic Studios, New York City   **4 May 1971**

CO-22020	**Save The Last Dance For Me** *(Doc Pomus-Mort Shuman)*	■ Cotillion SD-9050
CO-22021	**Be My Friend**	Cotillion, rejected

BROOK BENTON
Brook Benton (vo) with unknown studio orchestra. Produced for the Miller Beer-Brewing Company of Milwaukee, Wisconsin by Billy Davis and McCann-Erickson.
Unknown location   **1971**

	All Vocal Jingle (Straight Jingle) *(Bill Backer & McCann-Erickson)*	◻ Miller High Life GA-621 *(promo)* ▣ Miller C-7925 *(promo)*
	City People	▣ Miller C-7925 *(promo)*
	5 O'Clock World	▣ Miller C-7925 *(promo)*
	Heading Home	▣ Miller C-7925 *(promo)*
	Orange Candles	◻ Miller High Life GA-621 *(promo)* ▣ Miller C-7925 *(promo)*

BROOK BENTON
Brook Benton (vo) with unknown studio orchestra arranged and conducted by Bergen White on -1, Billy Arnell on -2.
Mayfair Studios, New York City   **2 May 1972**

72 NY 889	**If You Got The Time** -1 **[If You've Got The Time*]** *(Bill Backer)*	◉ MGM K-14440 ■ MGM SE-4874*
72 NY 890	**You Take Me Home Honey** -2 *(Sandy Theoret-Bill Backer)*	◉ MGM K-14440 ■ MGM SE-4874

BROOK BENTON
Brook Benton (vo) with unknown studio orchestra arranged and conducted by Riley Hampton on -1, Fred Norman on -2.
Mayfair Studios, New York City   **November 1972**

72 NY 934	**Sweet Memories** -1 *(Mickey Newbury)*	■ MGM SE-4874
72 NY 935	*Medley:* **For The Good Times** *(Kris Kristofferson)* – **It's Just A Matter Of Time** ② *(Brook Benton-Belford Hendricks-Clyde Otis)* -1	■ MGM SE-4874
72 NY 936	**Alone** -2 *(Francis Lai)*	■ MGM SE-4874
72 NY 937	**In Your World** -1 *(Sandy Theoret)*	■ MGM SE-4874

72 NY 938	**For All We Know** -1 *(James Griffin-Fred Karlin-Robb Royer)*	■ MGM SE-4874
72 NY 939	**I've Been To Town** -1 *(Rod McKuen)*	■ MGM SE-4874
72 NY 940	**Send Back My Heart** -2 *(Brook Benton)*	■ MGM SE-4874
72 NY 941	**Remember The Good** -1 *(Mickey Newbury)*	■ MGM SE-4874

BROOK BENTON

Brook Benton (vo) with unknown studio orchestra; unknown chorus on -1.
New York City   **1973**

	Lay Lady Lay [5:22] -1 *(Bob Dylan)*	■ All Platinum AP-3021
BRS-810-A	**Lay Lady Lay** [Edited version, 3:21] -1 *(Bob Dylan)*	○ Brut BR-810 ■ All Platinum AP-3021
BRS-810-B	**A Touch Of Class** *(George Barrie-Sammy Cahn)*	○ Brut BR-810 ■ All Platinum AP-3021

BROOK BENTON

Brook Benton (vo) with unknown studio orchestra.
New York City   **1974**

BRS-816-A	**South Carolina** *(Wayne Bickerton-Tony Waddington)*	○ Brut BR-816 ■ All Platinum AP-3021
BRS-816-B	**All That Love Went To Waste** *(George Barrie-Sammy Cahn)*	○ Brut BR-816 ■ All Platinum AP-3021
	Jealous Guy *(John Lennon)*	■ All Platinum AP-3021
	On Your Side Of The Bed *(Brook Benton)*	■ All Platinum AP-3021
	Sister And Brother *(Brook Benton)*	■ All Platinum AP-3021
	The Night Has Many Eyes *(Brook Benton)*	■ All Platinum AP-3021
	When Summer Turns To Fall *(Brook Benton)*	■ All Platinum AP-3021

BROOK BENTON

Brook Benton (vo) with unknown studio orchestra arranged and conducted by James Allen Smith.
Unknown location   **November 1974**

| SS-01590 | **I Keep Thinking To Myself** ①
(Clyde Otis) | ○ Stax STN-0231
■ Bulldog *(UK)* BDL-2039 |

SS-01591	**The Winds Of Change** *(Clyde Otis-Herman Kelly)*	◐ Stax STN-0231
	These Arms You Pushed Away *(Becki Bluefield)*	◉ Tring International *(UK)* GRF-164
	You've Never Been This Far *(Conway Twitty)*	◉ Tring International *(UK)* GRF-164

BROOK BENTON

Brook Benton (vo) with unknown studio orchestra
Unknown location   **ca. 1974**

	Try To Win A Friend (When It's Over) *(Larry Gatlin)*	■ Army Reserve Program No.248 *(radio)*

BROOK BENTON

Brook Benton (vo) with E. Royal, J. Grimes, A. Stewart (tp), D. Harris, F. Zito, D. Griffin (tb), J. Buffington, A. Richmond (F-hrn), S. Powell, G. Marge, H. Henry, L. Scott, B. Greene (woodwinds), M. Ross (hca), B. Randle, B. Cuomo (kbds), W. Morris (g), J. Williams (b), C. Oliver (d), C. Derry (congas) and the Irving Spice Strings (vn). Tommy Keith, Harry Ray, Walter Morris and Al Goodman (backg vo).
All Platinum Studios, Englewood, New Jersey   **1975**

AP-276-NO	**Can't Take My Eyes Off Of You** ② *(Bob Crewe-Bob Gaudio)*	◐ All Platinum AP-2364 ■ All Platinum AP-3015, All Platinum *(UK)* 9109 303
AP-277-NO	**Weekend With Feathers** *(Bennie Benjamin-Sol Marcus)*	◐ All-Platinum AP-2364 ■ All Platinum AP-3015, All Platinum *(UK)* 9109 303
	All In Love Is Fair *(Stevie Wonder)*	■ All Platinum AP-3015, All Platinum *(UK)* 9109 303
	I Had To Learn (The Hard Way) *(Sammy Lowe-Betty Lowe)*	■ All Platinum AP-3015, All Platinum *(UK)* 9109 303
	It Started All Over Again *(Albert Goodman-Harry Ray-Walter Morris)*	■ All Platinum AP-3015, All Platinum *(UK)* 9109 303
	Mr. Bartender *(Sylvia Robinson-Bernadette Randle- Michael Burton)*	◐ All Platinum *(UK)* 6146 311 ■ All Platinum *(UK)* 9109 303
	My Funny Valentine *(Richard Rodgers-Lorenz Hart)*	◐ All Platinum *(UK)* 6146 315 ■ All Platinum AP-3015, All Platinum *(UK)* 9109 303
	Nightingale In Berkeley Square ② **[A Nightingale Sang In Berkeley Square*]** *(Eric Maschwitz-Manning Sherwin)*	■ All Platinum AP-3015, All Platinum *(UK)* 9109 303*
	Now Is The Time *(Sammy Lowe-Betty Lowe)*	■ All Platinum AP-3015, All Platinum *(UK)* 9109 303

Taxi	◉ All Platinum *(UK)* 6146 311	
(Sylvia Robinson-Michael Burton)	■ All Platinum *(UK)* 9109 303	
You Were Gone	◉ All Platinum *(UK)* 6146 315	
(Albert Goodman-Harry Ray-Walter Morris)	■ All Platinum AP-3015,	
	All Platinum *(UK)* 9109 303	

BROOK BENTON

Brook Benton (vo) with unknown studio orchestra; unknown chorus on all tracks except on -1.
Odo and Opal Studios, New York City **1976**

The following were remakes produced for a US and UK TV-promoted album:

SMX-02078	**It's Just A Matter Of Time** ③	◉ Musicor Startime MU-1961
	(Brook Benton-Belford Hendricks-	■ TVP TVP-1008,
	Clyde Otis)	Musicor MUX-4603
SMX-02079	**So Close** ②	◉ Musicor Startime MU-1961
	(Brook Benton-Luther Dixon-Clyde Otis)	■ TVP TVP-1008,
		Musicor MUX-4603
SMX-02080	**So Many Ways** ②	◉ Musicor Startime MU-1962
	(Bobby Stevenson)	■ TVP TVP-1008,
		Musicor MUX-4603
SMX-02081	**Thank You Pretty Baby** ② -1	◉ Musicor Startime MU-1962
	(Brook Benton-Clyde Otis)	■ TVP TVP-1008,
		Musicor MUX-4603
SMX-02082	**The Boll Weevil Song** ④	◉ Musicor Startime MU-1963
	(Brook Benton-Clyde Otis)	■ TVP TVP-1008,
		Musicor MUX-4603
SMX-02083	**Frankie And Johnny** ②	◉ Musicor Startime MU-1963
	(Trad.)	■ TVP TVP-1008,
		Musicor MUX-4603
SMX-02084	**Kiddio** ②	◉ Musicor Startime MU-1964
	(Clyde Otis-Brook Benton)	■ TVP TVP-1008,
		Musicor MUX-4603
SMX-02085	**The Same One** ③	◉ Musicor Startime MU-1964
	(Brook Benton-Clyde Otis)	■ TVP TVP-1008,
		Musicor MUX-4603
SMX-02086	**Rainy Night In Georgia** ② -1	◉ Musicor Startime MU-1965
	(Tony Joe White)	■ TVP TVP-1008,
		Musicor MUX-4603
SMX-02087	**Hotel Happiness** ③	◉ Musicor Startime MU-1965
	(Leon Carr-Earl Shuman)	■ TVP TVP-1008,
		Musicor MUX-4603
	Fools Rush In ②	■ TVP TVP-1008,
	(Johnny Mercer-Rube Bloom)	Musicor MUX-4603
	For My Baby ②	■ TVP TVP-1008,
	(Clyde Otis-Brook Benton)	Musicor MUX-4603

I Got What I Wanted ② *(Brook Benton-Margie Singleton)*	■ TVP TVP-1008, Musicor MUX-4603
It's Just A House Without You ② *(Teddy Randazzo-Cirino Colacrai-* *Brook Benton-Clyde Otis)*	■ TVP TVP-1008, Musicor MUX-4603
Lie To Me ② *(Margie Singleton-Brook Benton)*	■ TVP TVP-1008, Musicor MUX-4603
My True Confession ② *(Ray Stevens-Margie Singleton)*	■ TVP TVP-1008, Musicor MUX-4603
Revenge ② *(Brook Benton-Oliver Hall-Marnie Ewald)*	■ TVP TVP-1008, Musicor MUX-4603
Shadrack ② *(Robert MacGimsey)*	■ TVP TVP-1008, Musicor MUX-4603
Think Twice ② *(Joe Shapiro-Jimmy Williams-Clyde Otis)*	■ TVP TVP-1008, Musicor MUX-4603
The Ties That Bind ② *(Vin Corso-Clyde Otis)*	■ TVP TVP-1008, Musicor MUX-4603

BROOK BENTON

Brook Benton (vo) with unknown studio orchestra; vocal arrangements by Tasha Thomas.
Bell Sound Studios and Media Sound Studios, New York City   **1977**

OWD 001 AS	**Makin' Love Is Good For You** [5:23] *(Tony Joe White)* [See also OWR 1100 SA]	□ Olde World OWD-001
OWD 001 BS	**Endlessly** ② *(Clyde Otis-Brook Benton)*	□ Olde World OWD-001 ■ Olde World OWR-7700
	Endlessly ② [alt. vocal] *(Clyde Otis-Brook Benton)*	■ Bulldog *(UK)* BDL-2039
OWR 1100 SA	**Makin' Love Is Good For You** [3:33] *(Tony Joe White)* [Edited version of OWD 001 AS]	◉ Olde World OWR-1100 ■ Olde World OWR-7700
	Makin' Love Is Good For You [3:33] *(Tony Joe White)* [alt. vocal]	■ Pickwick SPC-3693, Bulldog *(UK)* BDL-2039
OWR 1100 SB	**Better Times** *(Clyde Otis-Duncan Cleary-Bob* *Schaffner-Bob Both)*	◉ Olde World OWR-1100 ■ Olde World OWR-7700
	Better Times [alt. vocal] *(Clyde Otis-Duncan Cleary-Bob* *Schaffner-Bob Both)*	■ Bulldog *(UK)* BDL-2039
OWR 1107 AS	**Soft** *(Clyde Otis-Herman Kelley)*	◉ Olde World OWR-1107
	Soft [alt. vocal] *(Clyde Otis-Herman Kelley)*	■ Bulldog *(UK)* BDL-2039, Sounds of Florida SOF-5001

| OWR 1107 BS | **Glow Love** | ◉ Olde World OWR-1107 |

Glow Love
(Clyde Otis-Herman Kelley)
[From the motion picture, *The Big Score*]

OWR 1107 BS **Glow Love** [alt. vocal]   ■ Sounds of Florida SOF-5001
(Clyde Otis-Herman Kelley)

A Lover's Question ③   ■ Olde World OWR-7700
(Brook Benton-Jimmy Williams)

A Lover's Question ③ [alt. vocal]   ■ Pickwick SPC-3693,
(Brook Benton-Jimmy Williams)   Bulldog *(UK)* BDL-2039

A Tribute To 'Mama'   ■ Pickwick SPC-3693,
(Clyde Otis-Duncan Cleary)   Bulldog *(UK)* BDL-2039

Bayou Babe   ◉ Sounds of Florida SOF-206
(Clyde Otis-Duncan Cleary)   *(promo only)*
     ■ Pickwick SPC-3693,
     Bulldog *(UK)* BDL-2039,
     Sounds of Florida SOF-5001

I Keep Thinking To Myself ②   ■ Olde World OWR-7700,
(Clyde Otis)

I Keep Thinking To Myself ② [alt. vocal]   ■ Pickwick SPC-3693,
(Clyde Otis)   Bulldog *(UK)* BDL-2039,
     Sounds of Florida SOF-5001

I Love Her   ■ Olde World OWR-7700
(Clyde Otis-James Smith)

I Love Her [alt. vocal]   ■ Pickwick SPC-3693,
(Clyde Otis-James Smith)   Bulldog *(UK)* BDL-2039,
     Sounds of Florida SOF-5001
     ◎ Tring International *(UK)* GRF-164

Let Me In Your World   ■ Bulldog *(UK)* BDL-2039
(Clyde Otis-Herman Kelley)

Let The Sun Come Out   ■ Olde World OWR-7700
(Clyde Otis-Duncan Cleary)

Let The Sun Come Out [alt. vocal]   ■ Bulldog *(UK)* BDL-2039,
(Clyde Otis-Duncan Cleary)   Sounds of Florida SOF-5001

Lord You Know How Men Are   ■ Olde World OWR-7700
(Clyde Otis)

Lord You Know How Men Are [alt. vocal]   ■ Bulldog *(UK)* BDL-2039
(Clyde Otis)

Love Is Best Of All   ■ Bulldog *(UK)* BDL-2039,
(Andy Feiger-Bernice Ross)   Sounds of Florida SOF-5001

Old Fashioned Strut   ■ Bulldog *(UK)* BDL-2039,
(Irving Berlin)   Spinna *(SA)* SPIN(V)-3330

Sunshine
(Clyde Otis-Herman Kelley)
■ Pickwick SPC-3693,
Bulldog *(UK)* BDL-2039,
Sounds of Florida SOF-5001

There's Still A Little Love Left In Me
(Clyde Otis-Herman Kelley-Frank Green)
■ Olde World OWR-7700

There's Still A Little Love Left In Me
[alt. vocal]
(Clyde Otis-Herman Kelley-Frank Green)
■ Pickwick SPC-3693,
Bulldog *(UK)* BDL-2039

Til' I Can't Take It Anymore
(Clyde Otis-Ulysses Burton)
■ Olde World OWR-7700

Till I Can't Take It Anymore [alt. vocal]
(Clyde Otis-Ulysses Burton)
■ Bulldog *(UK)* BDL-2039

**Trust Me To Do What You Want Me To
(And I'll Do It)** *(Clyde Otis-James Smith)*
■ Pickwick SPC-3693,
Bulldog *(UK)* BDL-2039

We Need What We Need
(Clyde Otis-Herman Kelley)
■ Bulldog *(UK)* BDL-2039,
Sounds of Florida SOF-5001

**You're Pulling Me Down
[Pulling Me Down*]**
(Clyde Otis-Duncan Cleary)
◎ Sounds of Florida SOF-206
(promo only)
■ Bulldog *(UK)* BDL-2039*,
Sounds of Florida SOF-5001

BROOK BENTON

Brook Benton (vo) with unknown studio orchestra. Produced by Jimmy Nebb.
Unknown location, South Carolina   **1979**

79 NP 4434	**I Cried For You** [6:31] *(Arthur Freed-Gus Arnheim-Abe Lyman)*	☐ Polydor PRO-108 *(promo)*
79 NP 4434 S CA 400 AS	**I Cried For You** [4:22] *(Arthur Freed-Gus Arnheim-Abe Lyman)* [Edited version of 79 NP 4434]	◎ Polydor PD-2015, Catawba CA-400
79 NP 4435 S	**Love Me A Little** *(Art Crafer-Jimmy Nebb)*	◎ Polydor PD-2015
CA 400 BS	**Jet** *(Harry Revel-Bennie Benjamin-George Weiss)*	◎ Catawba CA-400

BROOK BENTON

Brook Benton (vo) with unknown studio orchestra; unknown chorus on all tracks except on -1.
Unknown location   **1982**

The following were remakes produced for a Dutch TV-promoted album:

A Rainy Night In Georgia ③ -1
(Tony Joe White)
■ Arrival *(NL)* AN-8141

**A Rockin' Good Way
(To Mess Around And Fall In Love)** ②
(Brook Benton-Clyde Otis- Luchi De Jesus)
■ Arrival *(NL)* AN-8141

Baby (You've Got What It Takes) ②
(Clyde Otis-Murray Stein)
■ Arrival *(NL)* AN-8141

The Boll Weevil Song ⑤
(Brook Benton-Clyde Otis)
■ Arrival *(NL)* AN-8141

Endlessly ③
(Clyde Otis-Brook Benton)
■ Arrival *(NL)* AN-8141

Hotel Happiness ④
(Leon Carr-Earl Shuman)
■ Arrival *(NL)* AN-8141

It's Just A Matter Of Time ④
(Brook Benton-Belford Hendricks-
Clyde Otis)
■ Arrival *(NL)* AN-8141

Kiddio ③
(Clyde Otis-Brook Benton)
■ Arrival *(NL)* AN-8141

Lie To Me ③
(Margie Singleton-Brook Benton)
■ Arrival *(NL)* AN-8141

Revenge ③
(Brook Benton-Oliver Hall-Marnie Ewald)
■ Arrival *(NL)* AN-8141

The Same One ④
(Brook Benton-Clyde Otis)
■ Arrival *(NL)* AN-8141

So Many Ways ③
(Bobby Stevenson)
■ Arrival *(NL)* AN-8141

Thank You Pretty Baby ③ -1
(Brook Benton-Clyde Otis)
■ Arrival *(NL)* AN-8141

Think Twice ③
(Joe Shapiro-Jimmy Williams-Clyde Otis)
■ Arrival *(NL)* AN-8141

BROOK BENTON

Brook Benton (vo, whistling on -1) with Jim Brock (d, perc), Doug Hawthorne (b), Duke Hall (kbds), Andre Ferreri, Ron Henderson, John Sharpe (g) and Tony Hayes (bar). Horn section: Jon Thornton, Ray L. Alexander, Mike Balogh, M.J. Kincaid, Ron Anderson, Nat Speir Jr and Phil Thompson. String section: Scott Rice, Martha Geissler, Bob Ennis and Elda Franklin, Aleo Sica, Lisa Spring, Dennis Spring, Beth Seivers, Linda Scott and Shari Link. Background vocals: Reese Culbreeth, David Floyd, Nell Abraham, Michael Federal, Robert L. Hall, Sonya R. Lee, Pernier Lee Jr, Ron Henderson, Thomas Moore's Children's Chorus, Glenda Cook's Children's Chorus.
Arthur Smith Studios, Charlotte, North Carolina   **14 October 1983**

Beautiful Memories
(Freddy Weller-Mike Stewart-Danny Jones)
■ HMC HM-830724,
HMC Radio RS1/RS2 *(radio LP)*

Blue Decorations
(Jerry Gillespie)
● HMC 830724
■ HMC HM-830724,
HMC Radio RS1/RS2 *(radio LP)*

Child
(Dobie Gray-Bud Reneau-Wray Chafin)
● HMC 830724
■ HMC HM-830724,
HMC Radio RS1/RS2 *(radio LP)*

Christmas Makes The Town	■ HMC HM-830724,
(Such A Happy Place) *(Duke Hall)*	HMC Radio RS1/RS2 *(radio LP)*
Decorate The Night	■ HMC HM-830724,
(Dobie Gray-Bud Reneau-Wray Chafin)	HMC Radio RS1/RS2 *(radio LP)*
I Wish Everyday Could Be Like	■ HMC HM-830724,
Christmas	HMC Radio RS1/RS2 *(radio LP)*
(David Erwin-Jim Carter)	
I've Got The Christmas Spirit	■ HMC HM-830724,
(Susan Collins-Michael Barbiero-Jimmy	HMC Radio RS1/RS2 *(radio LP)*
Maelen-Paul Shaffer)	
Merry Christmas All	■ HMC HM-830724,
(Andy Kozak-Vincent Montana)	HMC Radio RS1/RS2 *(radio LP)*
This Time Of Year ② -1	■ HMC HM-830724,
[This Time Of The Year*]	HMC Radio RS1/RS2 *(radio LP)**
(Cliff Owens-Jesse Hollis)	
When A Child Is Born	■ HMC HM-830724,
(Fred Jay-Zacar)	HMC Radio RS1/RS2 *(radio LP)*

BROOK BENTON
Brook Benton (vo) with unknown studio orchestra on -1.
Probably Arthur Smith Studios, Charlotte, North Carolina   **Prob. 14 October 1983**

Brook's Christmas Impressions -1	■ HMC Radio RS1/RS2 *(radio LP)*
Merry, Merry Christmas from	■ HMC Radio RS1/RS2 *(radio LP)*
Brook Benton [spoken message]	

BROOK BENTON
Brook Benton (vo)
Overdubbed at Screen Door Music, Buda, Texas on 7 and 8 October 2011: Kevin McKinney (guitars), George Reiff (b), Jamie Oldaker (d), Bukka Allen (o on -1, p on -2), Brian Standefer (cello on -2), Gina Holton and Karla Manzur (backg vo).
Inergi Studios, Houston, Texas   **July 1984**

God Is About To Do -1	⬇ Tate Music Group
(Morris Chapman)	
It Was Time -2	⬇ Tate Music Group
(Barry Mann-Cynthia Weil)	

BROOK BENTON
Brook Benton (vo) with Bo Thorpe and His Orchestra: Paul Butcher (tp), Cole Burgess (ts), Phil Rugh (p) and unknown others.
Live at the Omni International Hotel, Atlanta, Georgia   **31 December 1984**

Rainy Night In Georgia ④	■ Hindsight HSR-231[4]
(Tony Joe White)	

---

[4] Various Artists LP, *Bo Thorpe 'Live At The Omni – December 31, 1984'* (1986).

TONY JOE WHITE & BROOK BENTON

Tony Joe White (vo, gtr), Brook Benton (vo) with the *Nashville Now* studio band.

Live on *Nashville Now* (TNN), Nashville, Tennessee   **19 January 1988**

Rainy Night In Georgia ⑤
(Tony Joe White)

◉ *Swampfox In The Country*
[Bootleg, no label or number]

OKeh 7052 (1955)

OKeh 7055 (1955)

OKeh 7058 (1955)

Epic 9199 (1957)

Vik X-0311 (1957)

Mercury 71394 (1958)

US Releases

78s

BILL LANDFORD & THE LANDFORDAIRES

Columbia 30186	Touch Me, Jesus / You Ain't Got Faith (Till You Got Religion)	1/1950
Columbia 30203	Run On For A Long Time / Troubled, Lord I'm Troubled	10/1950

BILL LANDFORD QUARTET

RCA Victor 20-5351	Jesus Lover Of My Soul / The Devil Is A Real Bright Boy	6/1953
RCA Victor 20-5459	I Dreamed Of A City Called Heaven / You Ain't Got Faith	10/1953

CHUCK WILLIS & THE SANDMEN

OKeh 7051	Lawdy Miss Mary *(reverse without the Sandmen)*	2/1955

LINCOLN CHASE & THE SANDMEN

Columbia 40475	That's All I Need / The Message	3/1955

THE SANDMEN

OKeh 7052	When I Grow Too Old To Dream / Somebody To Love	4/1955

CHUCK WILLIS & THE SANDMEN

OKeh 7055	I Can Tell *(reverse without the Sandmen)*	5/1955

BROOK BENTON & THE SANDMEN*
BROOK BENTON**

OKeh 7058	Ooh* / The Kentuckian Song**	8/1955

BROOK BENTON

OKeh 7065	Bring Me Love / Some Of My Best Friends	1/1956
Epic 9177	Love Made Me Your Fool / Give Me A Sign	8/1956
Epic 9199	All My Love Belongs To You / The Wall	2/1957
Vik X-0285 [RCA]	Come On, Be Nice / I Wanna Do Everything For You	7/1957
Vik X-0311 [RCA]	Devoted / A Million Miles From Nowhere	12/1957
Vik X-0325 [RCA]	Crinoline Skirt / Because You Love Me	4/1958
Mercury 71394	It's Just A Matter Of Time / Hurtin' Inside	1/1959
Mercury 71443	Endlessly / So Close	3/1959

45s

BILL LANDFORD QUARTET

RCA Victor 47-5351	Jesus Lover Of My Soul / The Devil Is A Real Bright Boy	6/1953
RCA Victor 47-5459	I Dreamed Of A City Called Heaven / You Ain't Got Faith	10/1953

CHUCK WILLIS & THE SANDMEN

OKeh 4-7051	Lawdy Miss Mary *(reverse without the Sandmen)*	2/1955

LINCOLN CHASE & THE SANDMEN

Columbia 4-40475	That's All I Need / The Message	3/1955

THE SANDMEN

OKeh 4-7052	When I Grow Too Old To Dream / Somebody To Love	4/1955

CHUCK WILLIS & THE SANDMEN

OKeh 4-7055	I Can Tell *(reverse without the Sandmen)*	5/1955

BROOK BENTON & THE SANDMEN*
BROOK BENTON**

OKeh 4-7058	Ooh* / The Kentuckian Song**	8/1955

BROOK BENTON

OKeh 4-7065	Bring Me Love / Some Of My Best Friends	1/1956
Epic 5-9177	Love Made Me Your Fool / Give Me A Sign	8/1956
Epic 5-9199	All My Love Belongs To You / The Wall	2/1957
Vik 4X-0285 [RCA]	I Wanna Do Everything For You / Come On, Be Nice	7/1957
Vik 4X-0311 [RCA]	A Million Miles From Nowhere / Devoted	12/1957
Vik 4X-0325 [RCA]	Crinoline Skirt / Because You Love Me	4/1958
Vik 4X-0336 [RCA]	Crazy In Love With You / I'm Coming Back To You	8/1958
Mercury 71394X45	It's Just A Matter Of Time / Hurtin' Inside	1/1959
Mercury 71443X45	Endlessly / So Close	3/1959
	(also stereo SS-10005X45)	
RCA Victor 47-7489	Only Your Love / If Only I Had Known	3/1959
Mercury 71478X45	Thank You Pretty Baby / With All Of My Heart	7/1959
	(also stereo SS-10012X45)	
Mercury 71512X45	So Many Ways / I Want You Forever	9/1959
	(also stereo SS-10019X45)	
Mercury 71554X45	Nothing In The World / This Time Of The Year	12/1959
Mercury 71558X45	This Time Of The Year / How Many Times	12/1959

DINAH WASHINGTON & BROOK BENTON*
BROOK BENTON & DINAH WASHINGTON**

Mercury 71565X45	Baby (You've Got What It Takes)* / I Do**	1/1960
	(also stereo SS-10025X45)	

BROOK BENTON

Mercury 71566X45	The Ties That Bind / Hither And Thither And Yon	1/1960
	(also stereo SS-10030X45)	

DINAH WASHINGTON & BROOK BENTON*
BROOK BENTON & DINAH WASHINGTON**

Mercury 71629X45	A Rockin' Good Way (To Mess Around And Fall In Love)* / I Believe**	5/1960
	(also stereo SS-10032X45)	

BROOK BENTON

Mercury 71652X45	Kiddio / The Same One	7/1960
	(also stereo SS-10037X45)	
Mercury 71722	Fools Rush In / Someday You'll Want Me To Want You	10/1960
Mercury 71730	Merry Christmas, Happy New Year / This Time Of The Year	11/1960

ERNESTINE ANDERSON

Mercury 71772	A Lover's Question *(reverse without Brook Benton)*	1/1961

BROOK BENTON

Mercury 71774	Think Twice / For My Baby	1/1961
Mercury 71820	The Boll Weevil Song / Your Eyes	4/1961
Mercury 71859	Frankie And Johnny / It's Just A House Without You	8/1961
Mercury 71903	Revenge / Really, Really	10/1961
Mercury 71912	Shadrack / The Lost Penny	12/1961
Mercury 71925	Walk On The Wild Side / Somewhere In The Used To Be	1/1962
Mercury 71962	Hit Record / Thanks To The Fool	4/1962
Mercury 72009	Two Tickets To Paradise / It's Alright *(not released)*	
Mercury 72024	Lie To Me / With The Touch Of Your Hand	7/1962
Mercury 72055	Hotel Happiness / Still Waters Run Deep	11/1962
Mercury 72099	I Got What I Wanted / Dearer Than Life	2/1963
Mercury 72135	My True Confession / Tender Years	5/1963
Mercury 72177	Two Tickets To Paradise / Don't Hate Me (For Loving You)	8/1963

RCA Victor 47-5351 (1953, promo)

Columbia 4-40475 (1955)

OKeh 4-7058 (1955, promo)

Mercury 71443X45 (1959)

Mercury 71565X45 (1960)

Mercury SS-10032X45 (1960)

269

Mercury 72196 (1963, promo - withdrawn)

Mercury 72207 (1963)

RCA Victor 47-8830 (1966)

RCA Victor 47-9096 (1967, promo)

Reprise 0611 (1967)

Cotillion 44007 (1968, promo)

BROOK BENTON & DAMITA JO

Mercury 72196	Yaba-Daba-Do / Almost Persuaded *(promo only - withdrawn)*	1963
Mercury 72207	Baby, You've Got It Made / Stop Foolin'	12/1963

BROOK BENTON

Mercury 72214	You're All I Want For Christmas / This Time Of The Year	11/1963
Mercury 72230	Going, Going, Gone / After Midnight	12/1963
Mercury 72266	Too Late To Turn Back Now / Another Cup Of Coffee	3/1964
Mercury 72303	A House Is Not A Home / Come On Back	7/1964
Mercury 72333	Lumberjack / Don't Do What I Did (Do What I Say)	9/1964
Mercury 72365	Do It Right / Please, Please Make It Easy	11/1964
Mercury 72398	The Special Years / Where There's A Will (There's A Way)	2/1965
Mercury 72446	Love Me Now / A Sleepin' At The Foot Of The Bed	6/1965
RCA Victor 47-8693	Mother Nature, Father Time / You're Mine (And I Love You)	10/1965
RCA Victor 47-8768	While There's Life (There's Still Hope) / Only A Girl Like You	2/1966
RCA Victor 47-8830	Too Much Good Lovin' / A Sailor Boy's Love Song	5/1966
RCA Victor 47-8879	Break Her Heart / In The Evening By The Moonlight	6/1966
RCA Victor 47-8944	Where Does A Man Go To Cry / The Roach Song	9/1966
RCA Victor 47-8995	So True In Life – So True In Love / If You Only Knew	10/1966
RCA Victor 47-9031	Our First Christmas Together / Silent Night	11/1966
RCA Victor 47-9096	Wake Up / All My Love Belongs To You	1/1967
RCA Victor 47-9105	Keep The Faith, Baby / Going To Soulsville	1/1967
Reprise 0611	Laura (What's He Got That I Ain't Got) / You're The Reason I'm Living	7/1967
Reprise 0649	The Glory Of Love / Weakness In A Man	12/1967
Reprise 0676	Instead (Of Loving You) / Lonely Street	3/1968
Atlantic, no cat no	Do Your Own Thing *(single-sided test pressing)*	9/1968
Cotillion 45-44007	Do Your Own Thing / I Just Don't Know What To Do With Myself	9/1968
Cotillion 45-44031	She Knows What To Do For Me / Touch 'Em With Love	4/1969
Cotillion 45-44034	Nothing Can Take The Place Of You / Woman Without Love	5/1969

BROOK BENTON (with COLD GRITS)

Cotillion 45-44057	Rainy Night In Georgia / Where Do I Go From Here?	12/1969
Cotillion 45-44072	My Way [4:08] / A Little Bit Of Soap	4/1970
Cotillion 45-44072	My Way (Edited Version) [3:34] *(mono/stereo promo)*	4/1970

BROOK BENTON WITH THE DIXIE FLYERS*
BROOK BENTON (with COLD GRITS)**

Cotillion 45-44078	Don't It Make You Want To Go Home* / I've Gotta Be Me**	7/1970

BROOK BENTON WITH THE DIXIE FLYERS

Cotillion 45-44093	Shoes / Let Me Fix It	11/1970
Cotillion 45-44110	Whoever Finds This I Love You / Heaven Help Us All	4/1971

BROOK BENTON

Cotillion 45-44119	Take A Look At Your Hands / If You Think God Is Dead	5/1971

BROOK BENTON WITH THE DIXIE FLYERS

Cotillion 45-44130	Please Send Me Someone To Love / She Even Woke Me Up To Say Goodbye	8/1971

BROOK BENTON

Cotillion 45-44138	A Black Child Can't Smile / If You Think God Is Dead	11/1971
Cotillion 45-44141	Soul Santa / Let Us All Get Together With The Lord	12/1971

BROOK BENTON*
BROOK BENTON WITH THE DIXIE FLYERS**

Cotillion 45-44152	Movin' Day* / Poor Make Believer**	5/1972
MGM K-14440	If You Got The Time / You Take Me Home, Honey	9/1972
Brut BR-810	Lay Lady Lay / A Touch Of Class	1973

Brut BR-816	South Carolina / All That Love Went To Waste	1973
Stax STN-0231	I Keep Thinking To Myself / The Winds Of Change	11/1974
All Platinum AP-2364	Weekend With Feathers / Can't Take My Eyes Off Of You	10/1976
Musicor Startime MU-1961	It's Just A Matter Of Time / So Close [TVP recordings]	1977
Musicor Startime MU-1962	So Many Ways / Thank You Pretty Baby [TVP recordings]	1977
Musicor Startime MU-1963	The Boll Weevil Song / Frankie And Johnny [TVP recordings]	1977
Musicor Startime MU-1964	Kiddio / The Same One [TVP recordings]	1977
Musicor Startime MU-1965	Rainy Night In Georgia / Hotel Happiness [TVP recordings]	1977
Olde World OWR-1100	Makin' Love Is Good For You / Better Times	1977
Olde World OWR-1107	Soft / Glow Love	1978
Polydor PD-2015	I Cried For You / Love Me A Little	1979
Catawba CA-400	I Cried For You / Jet [Polydor recordings]	1982
HMC 830724	Blue Decorations / Child *(blue vinyl)*	1983
Sounds of Florida SOF-206	You're Pulling Me Down / Bayou Babe *(promo only)*	1984

Reissue 45s

BROOK BENTON

Mercury Celebrity Series C-30079	It's Just A Matter Of Time / Hurtin' Inside	1971
Mercury Celebrity Series C-30088	Endlessly / So Many Ways	1971

DINAH WASHINGTON & BROOK BENTON

Mercury Celebrity Series C-30090	Baby (You've Got What It Takes) / A Rockin' Good Way (To Mess Around And Fall In Love)	1971

BROOK BENTON

Mercury Celebrity Series C-30101	This Time Of The Year / Merry Christmas, Happy New Year	1972
Mercury Celebrity Series C-30119	Think Twice / Kiddio	1972
Mercury Celebrity Series C-30123	Walk On The Wild Side / Hotel Happiness	1972
Mercury Celebrity Series C-30133	Someday You'll Want Me To Want You / Fools Rush In	1972
Confidence SC-69	Lay Lady Lay / South Carolina [Brut recordings]	1974

BROOK BENTON (with COLD GRITS)*
BROOK BENTON**

Atlantic Oldies Series OS-13107	Rainy Night In Georgia* / Nothing Can Take The Place Of You** [Cotillion recordings]	1975

BROOK BENTON*
DINAH WASHINGTON & BROOK BENTON**

Million Seller 310	The Boll Weevil Song* / Baby (You've Got What It Takes)** [Mercury recordings]	1981?

BROOK BENTON

Mercury Timepieces 812 065-7	Endlessly / Fools Rush In	1983
Gusto GT4-2244	So Many Ways / Thank You Pretty Baby [TVP recordings]	1983
Gusto GT4-2245	The Boll Weevil Song / Frankie And Johnny [TVP recordings]	1984

Cotillion 45-44078 (1970)

MGM K-14440 (1972)

Brut BR-810 (1973)

Brut BR-816 (1973)

Stax STN-0231 (1974, promo)

All Platinum AP-2364 (1976)

Olde World OWR-1100 (1977)

Polydor PRO-108 (1979, 12" promo)

Catawba CA-400 (1982)

HMC 830724 (1983, blue vinyl)

Mercury C-30119 (1972, reissue)

Confidence SC-69 (1974, reissue)

274

DINAH WASHINGTON & BROOK BENTON

Mercury Timepieces
  812 997-7
	Baby (You've Got What It Takes) /
	  A Rockin' Good Way (To Mess Around And Fall In Love)
		1984

BROOK BENTON

Collectables COL-4219	Kiddio / Endlessly [Mercury recordings]	1986
Collectables COL-4220	It's Just A Matter Of Time [Mercury recording] *(Reverse is 'Never Gonna Give You Up' by Jerry Butler)*	1986

DINAH WASHINGTON & BROOK BENTON

Collectables COL-4264	Baby (You've Got What It Takes) /
	  A Rockin' Good Way (To Mess Around And Fall In Love)
	  [Mercury recordings]
		1988

BROOK BENTON

Mercury Timepieces 872 796-7	It's Just A Matter Of Time / Hurtin' Inside	1989
Mercury Timepieces 872 798-7	Endlessly / So Many Ways	1989
Ripete 4004	Can't Take My Eyes Off You [All Platinum recording] *(Reverse is 'A Dollar Down' by Louis Jordan)*	1989

BROOK BENTON

Collectables COL-4343	Think Twice [Mercury recording] *(Reverse is 'A Natural Man' by Lou Rawls)*	1992
Collectables COL-4366	Boll Weevil Song / Hotel Happiness [Mercury recordings]	1993

10" Acetates

BROOK BENTON

Rockhill Recording, no number	Chariot Wheels *(single-sided 33⅓ rpm acetate)*	1962

Circle 7-3718 / J-20009
  [United Recording
  Laboratories]
	A Sailor Boy's Love Song *(single-sided 33⅓ rpm acetate)*	1965

12" Singles

BROOK BENTON

Olde World OWD-001	Makin' Love Is Good For You [5:23] / Endlessly	1977
Polydor PRO-108	I Cried For You [6:31] *(promo, same both sides - stereo/stereo)*	1979

EPs

BROOK BENTON
Mercury EP-1-3394   ***Brook Benton***   1959
It's Just A Matter Of Time / Hurtin' Inside / Endlessly / So Many
Ways

DINAH WASHINGTON & BROOK BENTON
Mercury EP-1-4028   ***The Two Of Us***   1960
Baby (You've Got What It Takes) / I Do / A Rockin' Good Way
(To Mess Around And Fall In Love) / I Believe

BROOK BENTON
Mercury EP-1-4031   ***Golden Hits (Volume 1)***   1962
Endlessly / Thank You Pretty Baby / The Ties That Bind / Kiddio

Mercury EP-1-4033   ***It's Just A Matter Of Time***   1962
So Many Ways / The Same One / Hither And Thither And Yon /
It's Just A Matter Of Time

Mercury EP-1-4046   ***The Boll Weevil Song***   1962
Honey Babe / Child Of The Engineer / The Intoxicated Rat / The
Boll Weevil Song

VARIOUS ARTISTS
Vik EXA-300 [RCA]   ***Mister Rock And Roll (Scene 1)***   1957
Your Love Alone
Other tracks by Teddy Randazzo.

Vik EXA-301 [RCA]   ***Mister Rock And Roll (Scene 2)***   1957
If Only I Had Known
Other tracks by Teddy Randazzo.

Miller High Life GA-621   ***If you've got the time... we've got the beer***   1970
(promo only)   Straight Jingle / Orange Candles
Other tracks by Johnny Mack and the Troggs.

EP Mercury EP-1-4028 (1960)

EP Mercury EP-1-4031 (1962)

EP Mercury EP-1-4033 (1962)

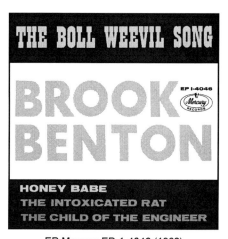

EP Mercury EP-1-4046 (1962)

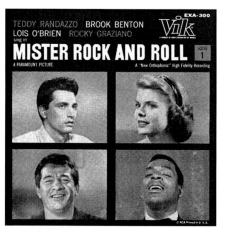

Various Artists EP Vik EXA-300 (1957)

Various Artists EP Vik EXA-301 (1957)

LPs

BROOK BENTON
Epic LN-3573   ***Brook Benton At His Best***   1959
  (mono)   The Wall / You Should Have Told Me / Rock'n'Roll That Rhythm /
                      Partners For Life / Anything For You / Love Made Me Your Fool /
                      The Kentuckian Song / Can I Help It / Bring Me Love / Some Of
                      My Best Friends / Give Me A Sign / Tell Me

Mercury   ***It's Just A Matter Of Time***   1959
MG-20421/SR-60077   The Nearness Of You / I Can't Begin To Tell You / Tell Me Your
  (mono/stereo)   Dream / I'm In The Mood For Love / But Beautiful / When I Fall In
                      Love / Hold Me, Kiss Me, Thrill Me / I'll String Along With You / The
                      More I See You / Love Me Or Leave Me / I Could Have Told You /
                      It's Just A Matter Of Time

Mercury   ***Endlessly***   1959
MG-20464/SR-60146   People Will Say We're In Love / Because Of You / More Than You
  (mono/stereo)   Know / Blue Skies/ Time After Time / A Lovely Way To Spend An
                      Evening / Endlessly / The Things I Love / (It's No) Sin / Around The
                      World / May I Never Love Again / You'll Never Know

Mercury   ***I Love You In So Many Ways***   1960
MG-20565/SR-60225   Tell Me Now Or Never / Never Like This / Hold My Hand / May I /
  (mono/stereo)   Never A Greater Need / So Many Ways / If You But Knew / One
                      By One / Someone To Watch Over Me / Everything / So Close /
                      In A Dream

DINAH WASHINGTON & BROOK BENTON
Mercury   ***The Two Of Us***   1960
MG-20588/SR-60244   Call Me / Baby (You've Got What It Takes) *(with Dinah Washington)* /
  (mono/stereo)   Not One Step Behind / A Rockin' Good Way (To Mess Around And
                      Fall In Love) *(with Dinah Washington)* / Someone To Believe In /
                      I Do *(with Dinah Washington)* / Because Of Everything / I Believe
                      (with Dinah Washington)
                      Remaining four tracks by Dinah Washington only.

BROOK BENTON
Mercury   ***Songs I Love To Sing***   1960
MG-20602/SR-60602   Moonlight In Vermont / It's Been A Long Long Time / Lover Come
  (mono/stereo)   Back To Me / If You Are But A Dream / Why Try To Change Me
                      Now / September Song / Oh! What It Seemed To Be / Baby Won't
                      You Please Come Home / They Can't Take That Away From Me /
                      I'll Be Around / I Don't Know Enough About You / Fools Rush In
                      (Where Angels Fear To Tread)

RCA Camden CAL-564   ***Brook Benton*** [compilation]   1960
  (mono)   You're For Me / Only Your Love / A Million Miles From Nowhere /
                      Devoted / Your Love Alone / I Wanna Do Everything For You /
                      A Door That Is Open / Crazy In Love With You / I'm Coming Back
                      To You / If Only I Had Known

La Brea L-/LS-8021   ***Songs From The Heart*** [compilation]   1961
  (mono/stereo)   What'cha Gone / Just Tell Me When / Love's That Way / Steppin'
                      Out Tonight / A New Love / No Love Like Her Love / The Girl I
                      Love / Dreams, Oh Dreams [Crown recordings]

Mercury MG-20607/SR-60607 *(mono/stereo)*	**Golden Hits** [compilation] It's Just A Matter Of Time / Endlessly / So Close / So Many Ways / Thank You Pretty Baby / Hurtin' Inside / Kiddio / The Same One / The Ties That Bind / Hither And Thither And Yon / How Many Times / With All Of My Heart	1961
Mercury MG-20619/SR-60619 *(mono/stereo)*	**If You Believe** Go Tell It On The Mountain / He'll Understand And Say Well Done / Just A Closer Walk With Thee / Only Believe / Remember Me / Going Home / Shadrack / Steal Away / The Lost Penny / Deep River	1961
Mercury MG-20641/SR-60641 *(mono/stereo)*	**The Boll Weevil Song and 11 Other Great Hits** [compilation] The Boll Weevil Song / Honey Babe / A Worried Man / Careless Love / My Last Dollar / A Key To The Highway / Frankie And Johnny / The Intoxicated Rat / Johnny-O / It's My Lazy Day / Child Of The Engineer / Four Thousand Years Ago	1961
Columbia Record Club No.13	**Golden Hits** [reissue] Mercury recordings.	1962

DINAH WASHINGTON & BROOK BENTON

Columbia Record Club No.17	**The Two Of Us** [reissue] Mercury recordings.	1962

BROOK BENTON

Columbia Record Club No.19	**Songs I Love To Sing** [reissue] Mercury recordings.	1962
Mercury MG-20673/SR-60673 *(mono/stereo)*	**There Goes That Song Again** When I Grow Too Old To Dream / There Goes That Song Again / All Of Me / I Love Paris / I Didn't Know What Time It Was / Trouble In My Mind / Blues In The Night / I Don't Know Why (I Just Do) / Breezin' Along With The Breeze / After You've Gone / I'll Get By / Let Me Sing And I'm Happy	1962
Mercury MG-20740/SR-60740 *(mono/stereo)*	**Singing The Blues (Lie To Me)**[5] Lie To Me / Chains Of Love / Got You On My Mind / Valley Of Tears / Take Good Care Of Her / My True Confession / I Got What I Wanted / Will You Love Me Tomorrow / Pledging My Love / Tomorrow Night / Send For Me / Looking Back	1962
Columbia Record Club No.96	**Brook Benton** [compilation] Mercury recordings.	1963
Mercury MG-20774/SR-60774 *(mono/stereo)*	**Golden Hits (Volume 2)** [compilation] Hotel Happiness / Lie To Me / Still Waters Run Deep / Fools Rush In (Where Angels Fear To Tread) / It's Just A House Without You / Shadrack / The Boll Weevil Song / Frankie And Johnny / Hit Record / Think Twice / Revenge / Walk On The Wild Side	1963
Mercury MG-20830/SR-60830 *(mono/stereo)*	**Best Ballads Of Broadway** Once Upon A Time / Make Someone Happy / I've Never Been In Love Before / Long Before I Knew You / Till There Was You / Hello, Young Lovers / As Long As She Needs Me / Soon / I'll Know / If Ever I Would Leave You / Love, Look Away / The Sweetest Sounds	1963

---

[5] A copy of SR-60740 has been discovered with the title *Lonely & Blue* instead of *Lie To Me* on the front, and with different liner notes, but otherwise identical in every respect. This rarity is not listed in any reference works. It is possible that it was an early test pressing.

Mercury MG-20886/SR-60886 *(mono/stereo)*	***Born To Sing The Blues*** Born To Sing The Blues / Daddy Knows / Why Don't You Write Me / So Little Time / Since I Met You Baby / The Sun's Gonna Shine In My Door / After Midnight / Every Goodbye Ain't Gone / I Worry 'Bout You / God Bless the Child / Nobody Knows / I'll Never Be Free	1964
Mercury MG-20918/SR-60918 *(mono/stereo)*	***On The Countryside*** Going, Going, Gone / Faded Love / I'd Trade All of My Tomorrows (For Just One Yesterday) / Don't Rob Another Man's Castle / All Over Again / Everytime I'm Kissin' You / My Shoes Keep Walking Back to You / Just Call Me Lonesome / Letters Have No Arms / I Don't Hurt Anymore / I'm Throwing Rice (At The Girl That I Love) / I'll Step Aside	1964
Mercury MG-20934/SR-60934 *(mono/stereo)*	***This Bitter Earth*** This Bitter Earth / Don't Do What I Did (Do What I Say) / Please, Please Make It Easy / There's No Fool Like An Old Fool / Fine Brown Frame / What Is A Woman Without A Man / Lumberjack / Do It Right / What Else Do You Want From Me / Learning To Love Again / I Had It / It's Too Late To Turn Back Now	1964
Star GELP-5355	***Only Believe*** [compilation] Same as 1961 LP Mercury SR-60619, *If You Believe*, except 'Go Tell It On The Mountain', 'Everytime I Feel The Spirit' and 'A City Called Heaven' omitted.	1964?
Gladwynne GL-/GLS-2016 *(mono/stereo)*	***50's Spectacular*** [compilation] Crown recordings. Same as 1961 LP La Brea L-/LS-8021, *Songs From The Heart.*	1965
Harmony [Columbia] HL-7346/HS-11146 *(mono/el. stereo)*	***The Soul Of Brook Benton*** [compilation] Bring Me Love / The Kentuckian Song / Can I Help It / Partners For Life / Rock'n'Roll That Rhythm / The Wall / All My Love Belongs To You / You Should Have Told Me / Anything For You / Give Me A Sign [Columbia/Epic recordings]	1965
Mercury MG-21008/SR-61008 *(mono/stereo)*	***The Special Years*** [unissued test pressing] The Special Years / Our Hearts Know / Never Like This / On My Word / I'll Always Love You / Dearer Than Life / I Want You Forever / Nothing In The World / For My Baby / If You Have No Real Objections / You're All I Want For Christmas / A Lifetime Lease On Your Heart	1965
RCA Victor LPM-/LSP-3526 *(mono/stereo)*	***Mother Nature, Father Time*** While There's Life (There's Still Hope) / Mother Nature, Father Time / I Wanna Be With You (Everywhere You Go) / Life Is Too Short (For Me To Stop Loving You Now) / You're So Wonderful / It's A Crime / Boy, I Wish I Was In Your Place / Since You've Been Gone / The Song I Head Last Night (Play It Again) / Foolish Enough To Try / You're Mine (And I Love You) / More Time To Be With You	1965
RCA Victor LPM-/LSP-3514 *(mono/stereo)*	***That Old Feeling*** That Old Feeling / My Darling, My Darling / A Nightingale Sang In Berkeley Square / Love Is A Many-Splendored Thing / Once In Love With Amy / Try A Little Tenderness / Hey There / Call Me Irresponsible / Peg O' My Heart / Blue Moon / The Second Time Around / Moon River	1966

RCA Victor LPM-/LSP-3590 *(mono/stereo)*	**My Country** Cold, Cold Heart / Funny How Time Slips Away / Please Help Me, I'm Falling / I Walk The Line / He's Got You / I Really Don't Want To Know / Walking The Floor Over You / Hello Walls / Gone / Any Time / He'll Have To Go / Have I Told You Lately That I Love You?	1966

Wing [Mercury]
MGW-12314 *(mono)*
SRW-16314 *(stereo)*

The Boll Weevil Song and Other Great Hits [compilation]   1966
Same as LP Mercury MG-20641/SR-60641, *The Boll Weevil
Song and 11 Other Great Hits*, except 'A Worried Man' and
'Four Thousand Years Ago' omitted.

Reprise R-/RS-6268
(mono/stereo)

Laura, what's he got that I ain't got   1967
Laura (What's He Got That I Ain't Got) / Ode To Billie Joe / Here
We Go Again / This Is Worth Fighting For / Stick-To-It-Ivity / (There
Was A) Tall Oak Tree / *Medley:* I Left My Heart In San Francisco –
San Francisco (Be Sure To Wear Some Flowers In Your Hair) /
Lingering On / The Glory Of Love / You're The Reason I'm Living

From this point all new releases were in stereo.

Cotillion SD-9002

Do Your Own Thing   1969
Touch 'Em With Love / Nothing Can Take The Place Of You /
Destination Heartbreak / Woman Without Love / Break Out /
She Knows What To Do For Me / Set Me Free / With Pen In
Hand / Hiding Behind The Shadow Of A Dream / I Just Don't
Know What To Do With Myself / Oh Lord, Why Lord / Do Your
Own Thing

Pickwick SPC-3217

As Long As She Needs Me [compilation]   1969
Mercury recordings. Includes the prev. unissued 'I Walk The Line'.

Cotillion SD-9018

Today   1970
Rainy Night In Georgia / My Way / Life Has Its Little Ups And
Downs / Can't Take My Eyes Off You / We're Gonna Make It /
A Little Bit Of Soap / Baby / Where Do I Go From Here? /
Desertion / I've Gotta Be Me

Cotillion SD-9028

Home Style   1970
Whoever Finds This I Love You / For Lee Ann / Willie And Laura
Mae Jones / It's All In The Game / Don't It Make You Wanta Go
Home / Aspen Colorado / Don't Think Twice, It's All Right / Born
Under A Bad Sign / Are You Sincere / Let Me Fix It

RCA Camden CAS-2431

I Wanna Be With You [compilation]   1970
I Wanna Be With You (Everywhere You Go) / Moon River / Foolish
Enough To Try / Hey There / Since You've Been Gone / You're So
Wonderful / Love Is A Many-Splendored Thing / More Time To Be
With You / Blue Moon / It's A Crime

Cotillion SD-058

The Gospel Truth   1971
Let Us All Get Together With The Lord / Oh Happy Day / Heaven
Help Us All / Going Home In His Name / Take A Look At Your
Hands / If You Think God Is Dead / I Dreamed Of A City Called
Heaven / Doing The Best I Can / Precious Lord

Cotillion SD-9050	***Story Teller*** Movin' Day / Willoughby Grove / Shoes / Poor Make Believer / Please Send Me Someone To Love / Big Mable Murphy / She Even Woke Me Up To Say Goodbye / Save The Last Dance For Me / Sidewalks Of Chicago / Country Comfort	1971
Trip TLP-8026 [Springboard Int'l]	***Ain't It Good*** [2-LP] Ain't It Good / One Love Too Many / Don't Walk Away From Me / You're For Me / May I? / You're Movin' Me / Nothing In The World / Devoted / Next Stop Paradise / Keep Me In Mind / I'll Never Stop Trying / Walking Together / What A Kiss Won't Do / Come Let's Go / My Love Will Last / Come Back My Love / A Lover's Question / I'll Stop Anything I'm Doing / Everything Will Be Alright / Completely / The Rest Of The Way / I'll Meet You After Church Next Sunday / This Bitter Earth / Looking Back / Mark My Word / Doggone Baby, Doggone / You Can't Get Away From Me / Ninety-Nine Percent [28 demo recordings from 1956]	1972
MGM SE-4874	***Something For Everyone*** Sweet Memories / *Medley:* For The Good Times – It's Just A Matter Of Time / You Take Me Home Honey / Alone / In Your World / For All We Know / If You've Got The Time / I've Been To Town / Send Back My Heart / Remember The Good	1973
Springboard SPX-6005	***Brook Benton*** [2-LP compilation] Nothing In The World / I'll Never Stop Trying / What A Kiss Won't Do / You're For Me / This Bitter Earth / Completely / You Can't Get Away From Me / Ninety-Nine Percent / One Love Too Many / Devoted / Come Let's Go / Next Stop Paradise / Come Back My Love / Looking Back / A Lover's Question / Doggone Baby, Doggone [16 demo recordings from 1956]	1973
RCA APL1-1044	***Sings A Love Story*** All My Love Belongs To You (Instrumental) / Hawaiian Wedding Song / More / There I've Said It Again / I Only Have Eyes For You / Impossible, Incredible, But True / Unforgettable / There Goes My Heart / Just As Much As Ever / Goodnight My Love, Pleasant Dreams	1975
All Platinum AP-3015	***This Is Brook Benton*** Can't Take My Eyes Off Of You / It Started All Over Again / Weekend With Feathers / All In Love Is Fair / Now Is The Time / My Funny Valentine / You Were Gone / Nightingale In Berkeley Square / I Had To Learn (The Hard Way)	1976
TVP TVP-1008 [Springboard Int'l.]	***The Incomparable Brook Benton*** [LP, also 2-LP] It's Just A Matter Of Time / Kiddio / The Same One / It's Just A House Without You / My True Confession / Fools Rush In / Think Twice / Hotel Happiness / Thank You Pretty Baby / The Boll Weevil Song / Rainy Night In Georgia / So Close / Frankie And Johnny / Revenge / Lie To Me / So Many Ways / I Got What I Wanted / The Ties That Bind / Shadrack / For My Baby [TVP recordings]	1976
All Platinum AP-3021	***Brook Benton*** Lay Lady Lay / All That Love Went To Waste / South Carolina / Jealous Guy / On Your Side Of The Bed / When Summer Turns To Fall / Sister And Brother / A Touch Of Class / The Night Has Many Eyes / Lay Lady Lay [Brut recordings]	1977

| Harlem Hit Parade
HHP-8005 [Pickwick] | ***His Greatest Hits*** [compilation]
Mercury recordings. | 1977 |

| Musicor MUX-4603
[Springboard Int'l.] | ***Double Gold – The Best Of Brook Benton*** [2-LP]
Same as 1976 LP TVP TVP-1008, *The Incomparable Brook Benton.*
TVP recordings. | 1977 |

| Olde World OWR-7700 | ***Makin' Love Is Good For You***
Let The Sun Come Out / Endlessly / A Lover's Question / Lord
You Know How Men Are / I Love Her / Til' I Can't Take It Anymore /
I Keep Thinking To Myself / Better Times / Makin' Love Is Good
For You / There's Still A Little Love Left In Me | 1977 |

| Up Front UPX-61001 | ***Brook Benton*** [2-LP]
28 demo recordings also on 1972 2-LP Trip TLP-8026-2. | 1977 |

| Olde World OWR-7707 | ***Hot And Sensitive*** [unissued?]
Both sides of Olde World single OWR-1107 (Glow Love / Soft)
state that they are from this LP. The album, however, remains
untraced and was most likely never released. Various Olde World
cuts which may have been intended for inclusion subsequently
appeared on the compilation LPs Pickwick SPC-3693 (1979),
Bulldog *(UK)* BDL-2039 (1983) and Sounds of Florida SOF-5001
(1984). | 1978 |

| 51 West Q-16027 | ***So Close*** [compilation]
TVP recordings. | 1979 |

| 51 West QR-16057 | ***The Pick Of Brook Benton*** [compilation]
TVP recordings. | 1979 |

| Pickwick SPC-3693 | ***Makin' Love Is Good For You*** [compilation]
Makin' Love Is Good For You / A Lover's Question / There's Still
A Little Love Left In Me / I Keep Thinking To Myself / Sunshine /
Bayou Babe / Trust Me To Do What You Want Me To Do (And I'll
Do It) / I Love Her / A Tribute To 'Mama' [Olde World recordings] | 1979 |

| Phoenix10 PHX-337 | ***The Best Of Brook Benton*** [compilation]
Same as 1976 LP TVP TVP-1008, *The Incomparable Brook Benton.*
TVP recordings. | 1981 |

| Phoenix20 P-20 609 | ***The Incomparable Brook Benton*** [2-LP compilation]
Same as 1976 LP TVP TVP-1008, *The Incomparable Brook Benton.*
TVP recordings. | 1981 |

| Audio Fidelity 20609 | ***The Incomparable Brook Benton*** [2-LP compilation]
Same as 1976 LP TVP TVP-1008, *The Incomparable Brook Benton.*
TVP recordings. | 1982 |

| HMC HM-830724 | ***Beautiful Memories Of Christmas***
Beautiful Memories / Christmas Makes The Town / Child / I Wish
Everyday Could Be Like Christmas / Merry Christmas All / Blue
Decorations / I've Got The Christmas Spirit / Decorate The Night /
This Time Of Year / When A Child Is Born | 1983 |

| Allegiance AV-5033 | ***Memories Are Made Of This*** [compilation]
Same as LP Epic LN 3573, *At His Best*, except 'The Wall' and
'The Kentuckian Song' omitted. | 1984 |

De Luxe [King] 7861	**20 Golden Pieces of Brook Benton** [compilation] Olde World and Stax recordings. Same as 1983 UK LP Bulldog BDL-2039, *20 Golden Pieces Of Brook Benton*.	1984
K-Tel 7203	**The Best of Brook Benton** [compilation]	1984
Mercury 822 321-1 M-1 [Polygram]	**It's Just A Matter Of Time – His Greatest Hits** [compilation]	1984
Sounds of Florida SOF-5001	**Soft** [compilation] Bayou Babe / I Keep Thinking To Myself / Soft / Sunshine / I Love Her / Let The Sun Come Out / You're Pulling Me Down / We Need What We Need / Love Is Best Of All / Glow Love [Olde World recordings]	1984
Sugarhill SH-9138 [All Platinum]	**This Is Brook Benton** [compilation] Same as 1976 LP All Platinum AP-3015, *This Is Brook Benton*.	1984

DINAH WASHINGTON & BROOK BENTON

Mercury 824 823-1 [Polygram]	**The Two Of Us** [reissue] Same as LP Mercury SR-60244, *The Two Of Us*.	1985

BROOK BENTON

Pair P2-18390 (PDL2-1100)	**Brook Benton's Best** [2-LP compilation] Same as 1976 LP TVP TVP-1008, *The Incomparable Brook Benton*. TVP recordings.	1985
SMI SMI-2 [Suffolk Marketing Inc.]	**The Satin Sound** [2-LP compilation] 24 Mercury plus two Cotillion recordings.	1985?
Rhino RNFP-71497	**The Brook Benton Anthology (1959-1970)** [2-LP compilation] Mercury and Cotillion recordings.	1986

VARIOUS ARTISTS

Coronet CX-/CXS-198 *(mono/stereo)*	**Brook Benton Sings** A New Love / No Love Like Her Love / The Girl I Love / Dreams, Oh Dreams *Other tracks by Charlie Francis & His Group.*	1960
Coronet CX-/CXS-210 *(mono/stereo)*	**Brook Benton Sings** Steppin' Out Tonight / Just Tell Me When / Won't Cha Love / Love's That Way *Other tracks by Charlie Francis & His Group.*	1960
Mercury MG-20493/SR-60172 *(mono/stereo)*	**14 Newies But Goodies** So Many Ways *Other tracks by the Platters, the Diamonds, Rod Bernard, Jivin'* *Gene, Phil Phillips, David Carroll, Boyd Bennett, Ralph Marterie,* *Dinah Washington, Jimmy McCracklin, Sarah Vaughan and Sil* *Austin.*	1960
Mercury MG-20511/SR-60217 *(mono/stereo)*	**Golden Goodies** It's Just A Matter Of Time / Endlessly *Other tracks by Dinah Washington, Sarah Vaughan, the Platters* *June Valli, the Diamonds, Phil Phillips and Sil Austin.*	1960

Mercury MG-20581/SR-60241 *(mono/stereo)*	**14 More Newies But Goodies** Baby (You've Got What It Takes) *(with Dinah Washington)* / It's Just A Matter Of Time *Other tracks by Johnny Preston, the Platters, Sarah Vaughan,* *Rusty Draper, Elton Anderson, Patti Page, George Jones, Jivin'* *Gene, Nick Adams, Dinah Washington, Sil Austin and Ernestine* *Anderson.*	1960
Mercury PGE-003 *(stereo)*	**General Electric Presents A Stereo Show Case Of Stars** **(Galaxy of Mercury Stars)** [stereo demonstration record] It's Just A Matter Of Time *Other tracks by Xavier Cugat, David Carroll, Herman Clebanoff,* *Hal Mooney, Richard Hayman, Frederick Fennell, the Platters,* *Damita Jo, Dinah Washington, Billy Eckstine and Eddie Howard.*	1961?
Mercury PPSD-1-12 *(stereo)*	**Mercury Sounding 1961** [stereo demonstration record] Announcer presents Brook Benton singing 'It's Just A Matter Of Time' *Other tracks by Raimundo Nuñez, Al Cohn & Zoot Sims, Jose* *Melis, the Platters, Max Roach, Quincy Jones, Xavier Cugat,* *Richard Hayman, Mike Simpson, Pete Rugolo, Frederick Fennell,* *Bastianini and the London Symphony Orchestra.*	1961
Mercury SRD-3 *(stereo)*	**A Miracle In Sound** [stereo demonstration record] Announcer presents Brook Benton singing 'The Nearness Of You' *Other tracks by David Carroll, Griff Williams, the Clebanoff* *Strings, Pete Rugolo, Patti Page, Dick Contino, Lou Stein,* *Sarah Vaughan, Ramsey Lewis and others.*	1961
Mercury MGD-/SRD-9 *(mono/stereo)*	**Galaxy Music From 16 Great Artists** It's Just A Matter Of Time *Other tracks by Xavier Cugat, the Platters, David Carroll, Damita Jo,* *the Clebanoff Strings, Dinah Washington, Quincy Jones, Billy* *Eckstine, Jose Melis, Eddy Howard, Jan August, George Jones,* *Griff Williams, Eddie Heywood and Dick Contino.*	1961
Mercury MGD-/SRD-11 *(mono/stereo)*	**Galaxy Of Golden Hits** Kiddio *Other tracks by Patti Page, Dinah Washington, the Platters, Eddy* *Howard, Richard Hayman, Frankie Laine, Sarah Vaughan, Tony* *Martin, the Diamonds, Tiny Hill and George Jones.*	1961
Mercury MGD2-/SRD2-13 *(mono/stereo)*	**Galaxy 30** [2-LP] It's Been A Long Long Time *Other tracks by Xavier Cugat, David Carroll, Patti Page, Jan* *August, Dinah Washington, Richard Hayman, the Clebanoff* *Strings, Sarah Vaughan, Jose Melis, Billy Eckstine, Dick Contino* *and Quincy Jones.*	1961
Columbia GS-9	**The Headliners (Volume 2)** Think Twice [Mercury recording] *Other tracks by the Brothers Four, the Dave Brubeck Quartet,* *Johnny Cash, the Miles Davis Quintet, Percy Faith, Lester Lanin,* *Mitch Miller & The Gang, Jerry Murad's Harmonicats, Patti Page,* *Dinah Washington and Roger Williams.*	1962

Columbia GS-11	**The Headliners (Volume 3)** Revenge [Mercury recording] *Other tracks by the the Banjo Barons, Dave Brubeck, Ray Conniff,* *Ferrante & Teicher, Jerry Murad's Harmonicats, Andre Kostelanetz,* *Steve Lawrence, Les Paul & Mary Ford, Andre Previn, Marty* *Robbins, Bobby Vee, Andy Williams and Roger Williams.*	1962
Mercury MG-20651/SR-60651 *(mono/stereo)*	**Chart Winners** The Boll Weevil Song *Other tracks by Damita Jo, the Clebanoff Strings, Abbe Lane, the* *Diamonds, George Jones, the Platters, Dinah Washington, Jose* *Melis, Leroy Van Dyke, Clyde McPhatter and Claude Gray.*	1962
Mercury MG-20687/SR-60687 *(mono/stereo)*	**Twist With The Stars** Hurtin' Inside *Other tracks by Patti Page, Quincy Jones, the Platters, Dinah* *Washington, Johnny Preston, David Carroll, Billy Eckstine,* *Richard Hayman, Clyde McPhatter, Tom & Jerry and Damita Jo.*	1962
Spectrum SDLP-191 [Pickwick Int'l]	**Hulla Baloo!** Dreams, Oh Dreams *Other tracks by Roy Orbison, Roger Miller, Bobby Freeman, Betty* *Everett, Gene Pitney, Maxine Brown, Lloyd Price, Garnet Mimms* *and the Clovers.* Same as LP Design DLP-19, *Hulla Baloo!*	1962
Almor A-106	**Stargazing** Love's That Way / The Girl I Love / Steppin' Out Tonight / Dreams, Oh Dreams *Other tracks by Chuck Jackson and Jimmy Soul.*	1963
Crown [Modern] CLP-5350/CST-350 *(mono/stereo)*	**Brook Benton and Jesse Belvin** Love's That Way / No One (Love) Like Her Love / Steppin' Out Tonight / Just Tell Me When / Won't Cha Gone (Love) *Other tracks by Jesse Belvin.*	1963
Crown [Modern] CLP-5402/CST-402 *(mono/stereo)*	**The Great Brook Benton and Jesse Belvin** The Girl I Love / A New Love / Dreams, Oh Dreams *Other tracks by Jesse Belvin.*	1963
Design [Pickwick Int'l] DLP-/SDLP-191 *(mono/stereo)*	**Hulla Baloo!** Dreams, Oh Dreams *Other tracks by Roy Orbison, Roger Miller, Bobby Freeman, Betty* *Everett, Gene Pitney, Maxine Brown, Lloyd Price, Garnet Mimms* *and the Clovers.* Same as LP Spectrum SDLP-191, *Hulla Baloo!*	1963
Design [Pickwick Int'l] DLP-/SDLP-192 *(mono/stereo)*	**Joe Tex – Brook Benton – Marvin Davis** A New Love Like Her Love / The Girl I Love / Dreams, Oh Dreams *Other tracks by Joe Tex and Marvin Davis.*	1963
Mercury MG-20810/SR-60810 *(mono/stereo)*	**Hit Motion Picture Themes** Walk On The Wild Side *Other tracks by David Carroll, Dick Contino, Xavier Cugat, Caesar* *Giovannini, Billy Eckstine, Shirley Horn, Carl Stevens and the* *Clebanoff Strings.*	1963

Mercury MG-20813/SR-60813 *(mono/stereo)*	***Irving Berlin Songs*** Let Me Sing And I'm Happy *Other tracks by Richard Hayman, Dinah Washington, the* *Clebanoff Strings, David Carroll, Eddie Heywood, Billy Eckstine &* *Sarah Vaughan, Vivian Blaine, Harry Simeone Chorale, Eddy* *Howard and Dick Contino.*	1963
United Artists UAL-3314	***Golden Treasure Chest*** Just Tell Me When *Other tracks by the Penguins, the Meadowlarks, the Medallions,* *Dave 'Baby' Cortez, Chuck Jackson, the Del Vikings, Neil Sedaka,* *Joe Houston, Jimmy Soul, the Tokens and the Hollywood Argyles.*	1963
Mercury MG-20826/SR-60826 *(mono/stereo)*	***Original Golden Hits Of The Great Blues Singers*** Kiddio *Other tracks by Clyde McPhatter, Buster Brown, Lee Dorsey,* *Chuck Jackson, Frankie Lymon, Ray Charles, Chuck Willis,* *Lightnin' Hopkins, Ivory Joe Hunter, Billy Bland and Elmore James.*	1964
Mercury Galaxy Series MGD-/SRD-21 *(mono/stereo)*	***Christmas In The Air – On The Air*** You're All I Want For Christmas / This Time Of The Year *Other tracks by Johnny Mathis, the Harry Simeone Chorale, Ray* *Stevens, the Mitchell Trio and the Platters.*	1964
Mercury Original Golden Hits MGH-25002/SRH-65002 *(mono/stereo)*	***Original Golden Hits Of The Great Blues Singers (Volume 2)*** Lie To Me *Other tracks by Chuck Jackson, Lightnin' Hopkins, Bobby Bland,* *Little Junior Parker, Lowell Fulson, Howlin' Wolf, Gene Allison,* *Roscoe Gordon, Clyde McPhatter, Muddy Waters and Johnny* *Adams.*	1964
Mercury Original Golden Hits MGH-25008/SRH-65008 *(mono/stereo)*	***Original Golden Town And Country Hits (Volume 1)*** The Boll Weevil Song *Other tracks by Jerry Wallace, Patti Page, Claude Gray, Jerry* *Fuller, Rex Allen, Tom & Jerry, Patsy Cline, Rusty Draper, Ned* *Miller, Faron Young and Leroy Van Dyke.*	1964
Palace M-815	***Brook Benton – Sweet And Sour Sounds*** Just Tell Me When / Steppin' Out Tonight *Other tracks by the Bruce Darrel Jazz Orchestra.*	1964?
RCA Victor PRM-161	***12 Great Guys on RCA Victor*** *(promo only)* A Million Miles From Nowhere *Other tracks by Mario Lanza, John Gary, Eddie Fisher, Peter* *Nero and others.*	1964
Spin-O-Rama S-142 [Premier]	***50's All Star Golden Oldies*** Love's That Way *Other tracks by Faye Adams, the Nutmegs, the Isley Brothers, the* *Chiffons, Chuck Jackson, Dave 'Baby' Cortez, Jo Ann Campbell,* *the Del Vikings and the Bobbettes.*	1964?
Warner Bros. W-/WS-1591 *(mono/stereo)*	***The Stars Salute Dr. Martin Luther King*** I'm A Man [different takes used on mono and stereo versions] *Other tracks by Louis Armstrong, Count Basie, Harry Belafonte,* *Nat 'King' Cole, Sammy Davis Jr, Lena Horne, Della Reese, Joe* *Williams and Nancy Wilson.*	1964

Coronet CX-/CXS-260 *(mono/stereo)*	**Kings And Queens** Love's That Way *Other tracks by Ray Charles, Lena Horne, Chuck Jackson, Little* *Richard, Jimmy Soul & The Belmonts, Maxine Brown.*	1965
Grand Prix K-/KS-429 *(mono/stereo)*	**Don Covay & Brook Benton** Steppin' Out Tonight / Just Tell Me When / Won't Cha (Love) Gone / A New Love / No One (Love) Like Her Love / The Girl I Love / Dreams, Oh Dreams / Love's That Way *Other tracks by Don Covay.*	1965
Strand SL-/SLS-1121 *(mono/stereo)*	**The Dynamic Brook Benton Sings (Volume 1)** A New Love / No Love Like Her Love / The Girl I Love / Dreams, Oh Dreams *Other tracks by Jackie Jocko.*	1965
Strand SL-/SLS-1124 *(mono/stereo)*	**The Dynamic Brook Benton Sings (Volume 2)** Won't Cha Gone / Just Tell Me When / Love's That Way / Steppin' Out Tonight *Other tracks by Jackie Jocko.*	1965
Strand SL-/SLS-1129 *(mono/stereo)*	**Golden Oldies (Volume 1)** A New Love *Other tracks by the Harptones, the Angels, the Cashmeres,* *Dave 'Baby' Cortez, the Fireflies, Larry Hall, the Fiestas, Chris* *Columbo and Gary Criss.*	1965
Wyncote W-/SW-9095 [Cameo-Parkway] *(mono/stereo)*	**All The Hits With All The Stars (Volume 5)** Loves That Way / Dreams, Oh Dreams / The Girl I Love *Other tracks by Lloyd Price, Chuck Jackson and Betty Everett.*	1965
Custom CM-2038	**Dance Party** Love's That Way *Other tracks by Trini Lopez, Johnny Rivers, Ray Charles, Neil* *Sedaka, the Dave Clark Five, Steve Alaimo, Jerry Cole, Little* *Richard and Ritchie Valens.*	1966
Wyncote W-/SW-9113 [Cameo-Parkway] *(mono/stereo)*	**All The Hits With All The Stars (Volume 6)** Just Tell Me When *Other tracks by Ray Charles, Jimmy Dean, Maynard Ferguson,* *John Gary, Merv Griffin, Teddy Wilson and Frankie Laine.*	1966
Mercury SR-61189 *(stereo)*	**Golden Era Of Dance & Songs (Volume 2)** It's Just A Matter Of Time *Other tracks by Dusty Springfield, Dinah Washington, Eddy* *Howard, Robert Maxwell, Frankie Laine, Sarah Vaughan, Patti* *Page, Billy Eckstine and Teresa Brewer.* Half of 2-LP Mercury SRM2-601 (see below).	1968?
Palace PST-773 *(stereo)*	**Brook Benton Sings Blues Favorites** Same tracks as LP Palace M-815, different cover.	1967?
Premier PM-/PS-9022 *(mono/stereo)*	**Starring Lou Rawls with Special Guest Stars** Won't Cha Love / Love's That Way / Just Tell Me When / Dreams, Oh Dreams *Other tracks by Lou Rawls and Joe Tex.* Same as UK LP Deacon DEA-1022ST, *Brook Benton Sings.*	1967?

Mercury SRM2-601	**Golden Era of Dance & Songs – 22 All Time Golden Hits** [2-LP]	1968

It's Just A Matter Of Time
Other tracks by Dusty Springfield, Dinah Washington, Teresa Brewer, Sarah Vaughan, Vic Damone, the Harmonicats, Frankie Laine, Eddy Howard. Lesley Gore, David Carroll, Patti Page, Dick Contino, Robert Maxwell, Georgia Gibbs, Billy Eckstine, Richard Hayman and Bobby Hebb.

Atlantic SD-8274	**The Super Hits (Volume 5)**	1970

Rainy Night In Georgia
Other tracks by R.B. Greaves, Aretha Franklin, Tyrone Davis, Lulu, Wilson Pickett, Crosby, Stills, Nash & Young, Blues Image, Led Zeppelin, Thunderclap Newman, the Rascals and Nazz.

Cotillion SD-CTNSM1	**Cotillion Sales Meeting – Winter 1970** (promo)	1970

A Little Bit Of Soap
Other tracks by Ronnie Hawkins, Troyka, Freddie King, Lord Sutch, Quill, the Memphis Horns, Blackwell and Sweet Stavin' Chain.

Gallery DEA-1022ST	**Starring Lou Rawls with Special Guest Stars**	1970

Won't Cha Love / Love's That Way / Just Tell Me When / Dreams, Oh Dreams
Other tracks by Lou Rawls and Joe Tex.
Same as LP Premier PS-9022, *Starring Lou Rawls with Special Guest Stars.*

Increase INCM-2004 [Chess]	**Cruisin' 1959**	1970

It's Just A Matter Of Time [with disc jockey announcement]
Other tracks by the Olympics, Big Jay McNeely, the Skyliners, Chuck Berry, Dinah Washington, Bo Diddley, the Crests, Lloyd Price, Phil Phillips, the Flamingos and Wilbert Harrison.

Increase INCM-2005 [Chess]	**Cruisin' 1960**	1970

Baby (You've Got What It Takes) *(with Dinah Washington)* [with disc jockey announcement]
Other tracks by Joe Jones, Little Anthony & The Imperials, Jack Scott, Hank Ballard & The Midnighters, the Tempos, the Hollywood Argyles, Maurice Williams & The Zodiacs, Johnny Preston, Toni Fisher, Duane Eddy and Buster Brown.

Musicor MDS-1026 [Springboard Int'l]	**The Great Stars Of Song**	1970

Only Your Love / Dreams, Oh Dreams
Other tracks by Jerry Butler, Gene Pitney, Al Martino and Lou Rawls.

Musicor MDS-1039 [Springboard Int'l]	**Soul Explosion**	1970

Brook Benton – one song, no details
Other tracks by Little Anthony & The Imperials, Sam Cooke, Inez Foxx, Joe Tex, Ray Charles, Lou Rawls, the Toys, Jerry Butler, Dinah Washington, Frankie Lymon, Jimmy Soul, Maxine Brown and Tommy Edwards.

Musicor MDS-1047 [Springboard Int'l]	**Getting Together With The Jackson 5**	1970

Just Tell Me When
Other tracks by the Platters, the Jackson 5, Inez & Charlie Foxx, Jerry Butler, Frankie Lymon and Tommy Hunt.

Cotillion Religious Series SD-052	**Heavenly Stars** Heaven Help Us All *Other tracks by the Sweet Inspirations, Myrna Summers & The Interdenomonational Singers, Roberta Flack, Solomon Burke, Aretha Franklin, Wilson Pickett and Marion Williams.*	1971
Atlantic SD2-500	**Heavy Soul** Shoes *Other tracks by King Floyd, Little Esther, Jackie Moore, Wilson Pickett, Aretha Franklin, Garland Green, Tyrone Davis, King Curtis and others.*	1972
Atlantic SD2-504	**The Soul Years 1948-1973** Rainy Night In Georgia *Other tracks by various Atlantic soul stars.*	1972
Atlantic PR-170	**Whatever's Fair! Atlantic Soul Explosion '72** [2-LP] *(promo)* Poor Make Believer *Other tracks by Aretha Franklin, Wilson Pickett, King Curtis, the Persuaders, Betty Wright, Howard Tate, the Patterson Singers, Donny Hathaway, Tami Lynn, Richard Evans, David Newman, Isaac Hayes, Rahsaan Roland Kirk, Yusef Lateef and Les McCann.*	1972
Columbia Musical Treasury P2S-5606	**More Of The 50's Greatest Love Songs** [2-LP] All My Love *Other tracks by Doris Day, Les Brown, Percy Faith, Dinah Shore and others.*	1972
Columbia Musical Treasury P2S-5708	**The Fabulous Years:** **50 Fabulous Hits of the Fabulous 50's**[6] [2-LP] It's Just A Matter Of Time *Other tracks by Mitch Miller, Teresa Brewer, Rosemary Clooney, Frankie Laine, Dinah Shore, Mary Martin, Tony Bennett, Johnny Mathis, Don Cherry, Dinah Washington, Johnnie Ray, Doris Day, Patti Page, Connie Francis and others.*	1972
Trolley Car Record & Filmworks TC-5004 [Columbia Special Products]	**Brothers In Song – 16 Original Hits** No Love Like Her Love / Just Tell Me When [Crown recordings] *Other tracks by the Isley Brothers, Chuck Berry, Lloyd Price, Jimi Hendrix, Jerry Butler, Ray Charles and Chuck Jackson.*	1972?
Warner Special Products SP-2000	**Black Gold: 24 Carats** [2-LP] Rainy Night In Georgia *Other tracks by Aretha Franklin, Roberta Flack, Otis Redding, the Drifters, Ben E. King and others (24 tracks).*	1973
Candlelite Music CMI-3266	**Country Music Cavalcade: Nashville Scrapbook** For The Good Times / It's Just A Matter Of Time [MGM recordings] *Other tracks by Ricky Nelson, Conway Twitty, Roy Orbison, Connie Francis, Tommy Edwards, the Ink Spots, Hank Williams Jr, Jimmy Jones and Joey Heatherton.*	1977
Mistletoe MLP-1209 [Springboard Int'l]	**The Best Of Christmas** This Time Of The Year / You're All I Want For Christmas [Mercury recordings] *Other tracks by Liberace, Bobby Helms, Gene Autry and the Harry Simeone Chorale.*	1977

---

[6] Despite the title, the album only includes 30 songs.

Mistletoe MLP-1213 [Springboard Int'l]	**Soulful Christmas** This Time Of The Year / You're All I Want For Christmas [Mercury recordings] *Other tracks by Jerry Butler, Charles Brown, Patti La Belle and Sonny Til & Orioles.*	1977
Mistletoe MLP-1235 [Springboard Int'l]	**Merry Christmas** You're All I Want For Christmas [Mercury recording] *Other tracks by Rosemary Clooney, Enzo Stuarti, Bobby Helms, Gene Autry, Liberace, the Midnight Strings, Billy Vaughn and the 50 Guitars of Tommy Garrett.* Same as LP Holiday HDY-1944, *Merry Christmas.*	1978
H-Teller House TS-79-463	**Soul Train Special** Kiddio / My Love Will Last / May I *Other tracks by Melba Moore, Dionne Warwick and Ray Charles.*	1979
Laurie LES-4020	**Great Love Songs Of The 50's And 60's** It's Just A Matter Of Time *Other tracks by Dion & The Belmonts, the Platters, Gene Pitney, Dionne Warwick and the Passions.*	1979
Laurie LES-4023	**Collector's Records of the 50's and 60's (Volume 7)** It's Just A Matter Of Time [re-recording] *Other tracks by the Shirelles, the Passions, the Mystics, Bill Haley & His Comets, Carlo, Dion, Dionne Warwick, Gene Pitney, the Chiffons, Ernie Maresca, Bobby Goldsboro, Boots Walker and Dean & Jean.*	1979
Old Gold 5005	**Jerry Blavat Remembers The Fabulous Fifties (Volume 5)** It's Just A Matter Of Time *Other tracks by the Platters, Conway Twitty, Frankie Lymon, the Crests, the Diamonds, Jerry Lee Lewis, the Danleers, the Crew Cuts, Big Bopper, Dinah Washington, Ritchie Valens, the Five Satins and Bobby Day*	198?
JEMF JEMF-108 [John Edwards Memorial Foundation]	**Jubilee To Gospel** You Ain't Got Faith *(Bill Landford Four)* *Other tracks by Wings Over Jordan, the Wiseman Sextet, the Jubilee Singers, the Virginia Female Singers, the Birmingham Jubilee Singers, the Cornfed Four, the Golden Gate Quertet, the Norfolk Jazz Quartet, the Famous Blue Jays Of Alabama, the Dunham Jubilee Singers, the Heavenly Gospel Singers, the Georgia Peach, the Selah Jubilee Singers, the Alphabetical Four and the Fairfield Four.*	1980
Holiday HDY-1944	**Merry Christmas** You're All I Want For Christmas *Other tracks by Rosemary Clooney, Enzo Stuarti, Bobby Helms, Gene Autry, Liberace, the Midnight Strings, Billy Vaughn, and the 50 Guitars of Tommy Garrett.* Same as LP Mistletoe MLP-1235, *Merry Christmas.*	1981
Laurie LES-4035	**Oldies But Goodies from Radio Stations (Volume 1)** [2-LP] It's Just A Matter Of Time [re-recording] *Other tracks by the Shirelles, the Capris, Del Shannon, Dionne Warwick, B.J. Thomas, the Isley Brothers, Bill Haley & His Comets, Chuck Jackson, Ernie Maresca, Gene Pitney, the Skyliners, Dion & The Belmonts, the Chiffons, Dean & Jean, the Five Discs, Jimmy Curtiss, Dion, Bernadette Carroll and Carlo.*	1981

Epic EG-37649	**OKeh Rhythm & Blues** Somebody To Love *(The Sandmen)* *Other tracks by Smiley Lewis, Chuck Willis, Big Maybelle Smith,* *Screamin' Jay Hawkins, Titus Turner, Larry Darnell, the Ravens,* *Johnnie Ray, the Marquees, Billy Stewart, the Schoolboys, the* *Treniers, Paul Gayten, Little Joe & The Thrillers, Doc Bagby,* *Red Saunders, Little Richard and the Sheppards.*	1982
Era BU-4430	**Moments To Remember** It's Just A Matter Of Time *Other tracks by the Four Lads, Patti Page, the Gaylords, the* *Four Aces and others.*	1982
Warner Lambert BU-5290	**Solid Gold From Listerine** Rainy Night In Georgia *Other tracks by Percy Sledge, Mel Carter, the 5th Dimension,* *Shirley & Company, Shalamar, A Taste Of Harmony, the Delfonics,* *Gladys Knight & The Pips, the Four Tops, the Cornelius Brothers* *and Tavares.*	1984
Hindsight HSR-231	**Bo Thorpe 'Live At The Omni – December 31, 1984'** Rainy Night In Georgia *Other tracks by Bo Thorpe & His Orchestra, Jean Dennis, the* *4 Lads and the Generation Singers.*	1986
Rhino R1-70645	**Billboard Top R&B Hits – 1959** It's Just A Matter Of Time *Other tracks by Fats Domino, LaVern Baker, Jackie Wilson,* *James Brown, Lloyd Price, Phil Philips, Dee Clark, the Falcons* *and the Coasters.*	1989
Rhino R1-70646	**Billboard Top R&B Hits – 1960** Kiddio / Baby (You've Got What It Takes) *(with Dinah* *Washington)* / A Rockin' Good Way (To Mess Around And Fall In Love) *(with Dinah Washington)* *Other tracks by Jerry Butler, Jackie Wilson, Buster Brown, Bobby* *Marchan, Barrett Strong, Marv Johnson and Fats Domino.*	1989

Dinah Washington LPs featuring Brook Benton tracks

Mercury MG-20769/SR-60769 *(mono/stereo)*	**Dinah Washington – This Is My Story (Volume 2)** Baby (You've Got What It Takes) *(with Dinah Washington)*	1963
Mercury MG-20789/SR-60789 *(mono/stereo)*	**Dinah Washington – Golden Hits (Volume 2)** Baby (You've Got What It Takes) *(with Dinah Washington)*	1963
Mercury MGP2-103/SRP2-603 *(mono/stereo)*	**Dinah Washington – This Is My Story** [2-LP] Compilation of LP MG-20765/SR-60765 + MG-20769/SR-60769. Baby (You've Got What It Takes) *(with Dinah Washington)*	1963
Wing SRW-16414	**The Unforgettable Dinah Washington** Baby (You've Got What It Takes) *(with Dinah Washington)*	1970

Selected CDs

Taragon TARCD-1082 (2001)

Mercury 836755-2 (1989)

BROOK BENTON

RCA 90109 [BMG]	**16 Top Tracks** RCA recordings.	1988
Mercury 836755-2 [PolyGram]	**Forty Greatest Hits** [2-CD] Mercury recordings.	1989
RCA 9597-2-R [BMG]	**This Is Brook Benton** LP *That Old Feeling* plus eight bonus tracks	1989
Curb D2-77445	**Greatest Hits** Includes previously unissued alt. takes of 'Sweet Georgia Brown' and 'Beyond The Sea (La Mer)' [RCA recordings]	1991
Interpress CHRG-009	**Christmas Gold** HMC recordings.	1994

DINAH WASHINGTON & BROOK BENTON

Verve 526467-2 [PolyGram]	**The Two Of Us** Includes previously unissued first version of 'Someone To Believe In'.	1994

BROOK BENTON

TKO Collectors CB-017	**Red Hot And Blue** Olde World recordings.	2000
Taragon TARCD-1082 [BMG]	**The Essential Vik and RCA Victor Recordings** Includes the previously unissued 'Sentimental Daddy-O'.	2001
Verve 60415 [Universal]	**Songs I Love To Sing** Mercury recordings.	2003
RCA 625852 [BMG]	**My Country / That Old Feeling** RCA recordings.	2004

Rhino DBK-506	***Today / Home Style*** Includes previously unissued alt. takes of 'Willie & Laura Mae Jones', 'It's All In The Game' and 'Whoever Finds This I Love You'. [Cotillion recordings]	2004
United Audio Entertainment 9601-2	***I Got What I Wanted*** TVP recordings.	2004
Collector's Choice Music CCM-532 [Sony/BMG]	***Brook Benton At His Best*** OKeh and Epic recordings.	2005
Warner Platinum/Rhino 8122-79993-5	***The Platinum Collection*** Cotillion recordings.	2007

VARIOUS ARTISTS

Columbia Gospel Spirit CK-47333	***The Gospel Tradition (Volume 1: The Roots & The Branches)*** Includes the previously unissued 'Trouble Of This World' by Bill Landford & The Landfordaires [Columbia recording]	1991
Atlantic 782316-2	***Soul Christmas*** Includes 'Soul Santa'.	1994
Columbia COL-487504-2 [Sony]	***There Will Be No Sweeter Sound*** [2-CD] Includes 'Touch Me, Jesus', 'Run On For A Long Time', 'You Ain't Got Faith', 'Troubled, Lord I'm Troubled' and the previously unissued 'Lord I've Tried' by Bill Landford & The Landfordaires. [Columbia recordings]	1998

Downloads

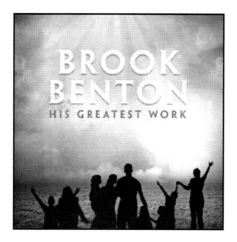

BROOK BENTON
Tate Music Group   ***His Greatest Work*** [2-track album]   2014
God Is About To Do / It Was Time
Companion release to Steve Kasmiersky's book, 'God Is About
To Do!' (Tate Publishing, Mustang, OK) 2014.

In 1983, Texan musician Steve Kasmiersky was persuaded to make a substantial investment in an interesting recording project: an album consisting of a mixture of new material and remakes by four black hit-makers of the past: Arthur Prysock, Ed Townsend, Johnny Nash and Brook Benton. Sadly, it was never completed because the producer misappropriated most of the budget, but it did provide an opportunity for Steve and Brook to meet. They quickly became firm friends, drawn together by a strong musical and spiritual bond.

In the wake of this disaster, Steve offered to produce an album for Brook. The singer duly flew down to Houston in the summer of 1984 and cut the above two songs – one religious, the other commercial – then returned to New York while Steve tried to raise money for further sessions. Time passed, until one day Steve heard on the radio that Brook had died.

Initially, he was stunned. He then got angry at God and told Him it wasn't fair. They had an album to finish, and Brook had so much more music in him. It wasn't until years later, when he was hit by a personal crisis, that Steve finally realized the importance of the gift Brook had left him. He drew great strength from the inspirational message of the song 'God Is About To Do': that you should not lose heart and give up when everything looks bleak, because *'God is about to do His greatest work in you'*. It literally saved his life and Steve decided to write a book about his experiences, to pass on this invaluable message to others.

He was also moved to release the recordings he'd made with Brook a quarter of a century earlier, but with updated backings. Brook's vocal tracks were stripped from the original master tape and overdubbed in a small studio near Austin, Texas by local musicians directed by famed Tulsa, Oklahoma drummer Jamie Oldaker (see page 264).

The story of Steve's involvement with Brook Benton and the recordings they made together is covered in much greater detail in his book. He also writes very movingly about Brook's funeral service, which he attended.

Tapes

REEL-TO-REEL TAPES (7½ ips, 4-track stereo)

BROOK BENTON

Mercury ST-60607	***Golden Hits***	1961
	Same as LP Mercury SR-60607, *Golden Hits.*	
Mercury ST-60934	***This Bitter Earth***	1964
	Same as LP Mercury SR-60934, *This Bitter Earth.*	

VARIOUS ARTISTS

Mercury ST-60687	***Twist With The Stars***	1962
	Same as LP Mercury SR-60687, *Twist With The Stars.*	
RCA Victor, unk cat no	***Old 'n' Golden Goodies (Volumes 1 & 2)***	196?
	A Million Miles From Nowhere	
	Other tracks on Volume 1 by Neil Sedaka, Don Gibson, Ray Peterson, Della Reese, the Isley Brothers, Mickey & Sylvia, Joe Valino, Floyd Robinson, Floyd Cramer, Kay Starr, Boots Brown and His Blockbusters; on Volume 2 by the Isley Brothers, Duane Eddy, Gale Garnett, Paul Anka, Peggy March, the Tokens, Dave 'Baby' Cortez, Jesse Belvin, Neil Sedaka, Skeeter Davis and Boots Randolph.	
Atlantic M-8274	***Superhits (Volume 5)***	197?
	Rainy Night in Georgia	
	Other tracks by R.B. Greaves, Aretha Franklin, Tyrone Davis, Lulu, Crosby, Stills, Nash & Young, Blues Image, Led Zeppelin, Thunderclap Newman, the Rascals and Nazz.	

REEL-TO-REEL TAPES (3¾ ips, 4-track stereo)

BROOK BENTON

Cotillion, unk cat no	***Do Your Own Thing***	1969
	Same as LP Cotillion SD-9002, *Do Your Own Thing.*	
Cotillion 94332	***Story Teller***	1971
	Same as LP Cotillion SD-9050, *Story Teller.*	

VARIOUS ARTISTS

Mercury/Philips W-9

American Airlines Astrovision Program No.9: Jazz & Popular 1965
('Enjoy This Glittering Galaxy of 65 All-Star Performances –
3 Hour Program')
There's No Fool Like An Old Fool / This Bitter Earth
Other tracks by Dinah Washington, Original Cast, Johnny Mathis,
the Bitter End Singers, the Mitchell Trio, the Robert Farnon Orch,
Shirley Bassey, the Smothers Brothers, Roger Miller, the Woody
Herman Band, Teresa Brewer, the Serendipity Singers, Sarah
Vaughan, Horst Jankowski, Julie Rogers, Oscar Peterson &
Clark Terry, Sue Raney, Harry Secombe, the Swingle Singers
and Quincy Jones.

Mercury MEF-601

Golden Era of Dance & Songs – 22 All Time Golden Hits [2-LP]   1968
Same as 1968 2-LP Mercury SRM2-601

CASSETTE TAPES

BROOK BENTON

MGM, unk cat no	***Something For Everyone*** Same as LP MGM SE-4874, *Something For Everyone*	1973
Mercury 822 321-4 M-1	***It's Just A Matter Of Time – His Greatest Hits*** No details.	1984

DINAH WASHINGTON & BROOK BENTON

Mercury 824 823-4	***The Two Of Us*** Same as LP Mercury SR 60244, *The Two Of Us.*	198?

BROOK BENTON

RCA 9597-R	***This Is Brook Benton*** 20 RCA titles from 1965-66.	1989

VARIOUS ARTISTS

Increase INCR-2004 [Chess]	***Cruisin' 1959*** Same as LP Increase INCM-2004, *Cruisin' 1959.*	1970
Increase INCR-2005 [Chess]	***Cruisin' 1960*** Same as LP Increase INCM-2005, *Cruisin' 1960.*	1970
Mercury MC4-61087	***Original Oldies (Volume 4) – Rhythm & Blues*** Kiddio *Other tracks by unknown artists.*	197?
Miller Beer C-7925	***High Life*** All Vocal Jingle (Straight Jingle) / City People / Orange Candles / Heading Home / 5 O'Clock World *Other tracks by the Troggs and Johnny Mack.*	1971
Mistletoe, unk cat no	***The Best Of Christmas*** Same as LP Mistletoe MLP-1209, *The Best Of Christmas.*	1977
Mistletoe, unk cat no	***Soulful Christmas*** Same as LP Mistletoe MLP-1213, *Soulful Christmas.*	1977
Richmond 2228	***The Best Of Easy Listening*** No details.	1996

Warner Special Products	***Nutty Novelty Records of the 60's***	199?
4568	The Boll Weevil Song	
	Other tracks by unknown artists.	

8-TRACK CARTRIDGES (in label order)

These cartridges were produced between 1965 and 1979 for use in the American Auto-Player. Cartridge size was approx 5¼ x 4 inches. Tape width was ¼ inch.

BROOK BENTON

Capitol, unk cat no	***Brook Benton (Volume 2)***	196?

Hotel Happiness / Lie To Me / Still Waters Run Deep / Fools Rush In (Where Angels Fear To Tread) / It's Just A House Without You / Shadrack / The Boll Weevil Song / Frankie And Johnny / Hit Record / Think Twice / Revenge / Walk On The Wild Side

Capitol, unk cat no	***Brook Benton's Golden Hits***	196?

How Many Times / So Many Ways / The Same One / Kiddio / With All My Heart / Hurtin' Inside / Hither And Thither And Yon / Thank You Pretty Baby / Endlessly / It's Just A Matter Of Time / So Close / The Ties That Bind

Cotillion TP-9018	***Today***	197?

Rainy Night In Georgia / Desertion / We're Gonna Make It / A Little Bit Of Soap / Life Has Its Little Ups And Downs / Can't Take My Eyes Off You / My Way / Baby / Where Do I Go From Here? / I've Gotta Be Me

Cotillion, unk cat no	***Story Teller***	1971

Movin' Day / Sidewalks Of Chicago / She Even Woke Me Up To Say Goodbye / Willoughby Grove / Big Mable Murphy / Shoes / Poor Make Believer / Save The Last Dance For Me / Please Send Me Someone To Love / Country Comfort

51 West QA-16027	***So Close***	197?

So Close / The Same One / Think Twice / Frankie And Johnny / For My Baby / Revenge / The Ties That Bind / I Got What I Wanted / Lie To Me / So Many Ways

TVP, unk cat no [Springboard Int'l.]	***The Incomparable Brook Benton (20 of His Biggest Hits)***	1976

It's Just A Matter Of Time / Kiddio / It's Just A House Without You / My True Confession / Frankie And Johnny / Fools Rush In / Think Twice / Hotel Happiness / Thank You Pretty Baby / The Boll Weevil Song / Rainy Night In Georgia / So Close / Revenge / Lie To Me / The Same One / So Many Ways / I Got What I Wanted / The Ties That Bind / Shadrack / For My Baby [TVP recordings]

Musicor Double Gold, unk cat no	***The Best Of Brook Benton –*** *** Newly Recorded For Your Listening Pleasure***	1977

It's Just A Matter Of Time / Kiddio / The Same One / My True Confession / Fools Rush In / Think Twice / Hotel Happiness / Thank You Pretty Baby / The Boll Weevil Song / Rainy Night In Georgia / So Close / Frankie And Johnny / Revenge / Lie To Me / So Many Ways / I Got What I Wanted / The Ties That Bind / Shadrack / For My Baby / It's Just A House Without You [TVP recordings]

Olde World, unk cat no	***Makin' Love Is Good For You***	1977

Makin' Love Is Good For You / I Love Her / A Lover's Question / Til' I Can't Take It Anymore / I Keep Thinking To Myself / Better Times / Let The Sun Come Out / A Lover's Question / Lord You Know How Men Are / Endlessly / Makin' Love Is Good For You / There's Still A Little Love Left In Me

Unk label + cat no	**Brook Benton Sings** No Love Like Her Love / Love's That Way / Dreams, Oh Dreams / Won't Cha Love / The Girl I Love / Steppin' Out Tonight / A New Love / Just Tell Me When	197?
Up-Front 8T-UPX-61001	**Brook Benton** 16 demo recordings also on LP Up-Front UPX-61001 and 2-LP Trip TLP-8026-2.	197?

VARIOUS ARTISTS

Altone 512.0303	**Sweet And Sour Sounds** No Love Like Her Love / The Girl I Love / Steppin' Out Tonight / Just Tell Me When *Other tracks by Bruce Darrel.*	196?
RCA Victor P8S-116	**Lotsa Soul!** You're Mine (And I Love You) / More Time To Be With You / Mother Nature, Father Time *Other tracks by Kenny Carter, Joe Williams, Sam Cooke.*	196?
Vogue V8-103	**Brook Benton and Jessie Belvin** The Girl I Love / Dreams, Oh Dreams / A New Love *Other tracks by Jessie Belvin.*	196?
Warner Special Products, unk cat no	**Black Gold** Rainy Night In Georgia *Other tracks by Aretha Franklin, Percy Sledge, Joe Tex,* *Jackie Moore, Booker T. & The MGs, R.B. Greaves, Otis* *Redding, King Curtis, Roberta Flack & Donny Hathaway,* *Clarence Carter, Manu Dibango, Betty Wright, Ben. E. King,* *the Drifters, Carla Thomas, Sam & Dave, the Persuaders,* *King Floyd, the Spinners, the Beginning Of The End and* *Wilson Pickett.*	196?

Jukebox Records

Cover of Mercury Compact 33 set SB-SR-60774 and label of record C-7094 (1963).

7" 33⅓ rpm LONG-PLAY SINGLES
These were sets of five discs featuring songs from one album.

BROOK BENTON

Mercury Compact 33	***Songs I Love To Sing* (Pop Pre-Pak SB-SR-60602)**	
C-7010 *(stereo)*	Moonlight In Vermont / It's Been A Long, Long Time	1960
C-7011 *(stereo)*	Lover Come Back To Me / Why Try To Change Me Now?	1960
C-7012 *(stereo)*	September Song / Oh! What It Seemed To Be	1960
C-7013 *(stereo)*	They Can't Take That Away From Me /	1960
	Baby Won't You Please Come Home	
C-7014 *(stereo)*	I Don't Know Enough About You / I'll Be Around	1960
Mercury Compact 33	***There Goes That Song Again* (Pop Pre-Pak SB-SR-60673)**	
C-7070 *(stereo)*	When I Grow Too Old To Dream / There Goes That Song Again	1962
C-7071 *(stereo)*	I Love Paris / All Of Me	1962
C-7072 *(stereo)*	I Didn't Know What Time It Was / Blues In The Night	1962
C-7073 *(stereo)*	I Don't Know Why (I Just Do) / Breezin' Along With The Breeze	1962
C-7074 *(stereo)*	After You've Gone / I'll Get By (As Long As I Have You)	1962
Mercury Compact 33	***Golden Hits (Volume 2)* (Pop Pre-Pak SB-SR 60774)**	
C-7090 *(stereo)*	Lie To Me / Hotel Happiness	1963
C-7091 *(stereo)*	Fools Rush In / Still Waters Run Deep	1963
C-7092 *(stereo)*	Shadrack / Hit Record	1963
C-7093 *(stereo)*	The Boll Weevil Song / Frankie And Johnny	1963
C-7094 *(stereo)*	Revenge / Walk On The Wild Side	1963

7" 33⅓ rpm 'LITTLE LPs'
These were long-playing 6-track EPs specially made for jukeboxes.

BROOK BENTON

Mercury Compact 6	***Six Unabridged Selections***	11/1961
MG-200-C *(mono)*	Endlessly / So Many Ways / Kiddio / The Boll Weevil Song /	
	Frankie And Johnny / It's Just A House Without You	
Mercury Compact 6	***Six Unabridged Selections***	1962
SR-600-C *(stereo)*	Same tracks as MG-200-C.	

Mercury Compact 6 MG-211-C *(mono)* SR-611-C *(stereo)*	**There Goes That Song Again** I Didn't Know What Time It Was / When I Grow Too Old To Dream / I Don't Know Why (I Just Do) / There Goes That Song Again / After You've Gone / Blues In The Night	1962
Mercury Compact 6 MG-632-C *(mono)* SR-632-C *(stereo)*	**Golden Hits (Volume 2)** Think Twice / It's Just A House Without You / The Boll Weevil Song / Revenge / Walk On The Wild Side / Hotel Happiness	1963
Mercury Compact 6 MG-243-C *(mono)* SR-643-C *(stereo)*	**On The Countryside** Everytime I'm Kissin' You / I'll Step Aside / I Don't Hurt Anymore / My Shoes Keep Walking Back To You / Faded Love / Don't Rob Another Man's Castle	1964
Cotillion SD-7-9018 *(stereo)*	**Brook Benton (LLP #108)** Life Has Its Little Ups And Downs / My Way [Promo edit] / Can't Take My Eyes Off You / We're Gonna Make It / I've Gotta Be Me	5/1970

VARIOUS ARTISTS

Mercury Compact 6 MG 646-C *(mono)* SR-646-C *(stereo)*	**Golden Goodies** It's Just A Matter Of Time *Other tracks by Dinah Washington, Sarah Vaughan, Phil Phillips and the Platters.*	1964

Radio Spots and Transcription Discs

45s

USAF Program No.99	***Music In The Air***	1960

Baby (You've Got What It Takes) *(Dinah Washington & Brook Benton)* [with announcement]
Reverse is 'Beyond The Sea' by Bobby Darin.

USAF Program No.167	***Music In The Air***	1961

Your Eyes [with announcement]
Reverse is 'The Thrill Is Gone' by the Ray Conniff Singers.

EPs

Cover and Side 2 of United States Air Force RAD 71-1 (1971)

Mercury EPS-1	***Choice Selections from Long-Playing Album Releases***	1960

So Close
Other tracks by Quincy Jones, Lou Stein-John Cali, Antal Dorati, Frederick Fennell and Marcel Dupre.

The following three EPs were specially created for radio programming. Each contains four abridged selections that run for 60 seconds.

Mercury MEP-63	***Disc Jockey Sixty Second Special***	1960

It's Just A Matter Of Time
Other tracks by the Mark IV, the Diamonds and Patti Page.

Mercury MEP-70	***Disc Jockey Sixty Second Special***	1960

Endlessly
Other tracks by the Diamonds, the Mark IV and Sarah Vaughan.

Mercury MEP-74	***Disc Jockey Sixty Second Special***	1960

So Close
Other tracks by Sophie Tucker, John Cali & Lou Stein, Quincy Jones, the Modernaires and Griff Williams.

United States Air Force RAD 71-1	***Find Yourself A Star (Series #5)***	1971

Recruitment disc for the USAF featuring different music stars.
Side 2 includes 30- and 60-second spots by Brook Benton.

TNT TNT-101	**Unknown title**	1988
	There Goes That Song Again	
	Other tracks by Jimmy McCracklin and the Mills Brothers.	

12" LPs

Armed Forces Records	**Untitled**	1960
AFD-430	Kiddio	
	Other tracks by Patti Page and Dakota Staton. Reverse (AFD-429) features Tony Bennett, the Fleetwoods and J.P. Morgan.	

Armed Forces Records	**Untitled**	1960
AFD-438	Fools Rush In (Where Angels Fear To Tread)	
	Other tracks by Charles Wolcott, Glenn Osser and Nelson Riddle. Reverse (AFD-437) features the Julian 'Cannonball' Adderley Quintet, Johnny Mathis and the Browns.	

American Heart Assoc.	**ET– III**[7]	2/1961
GRC-6352A	Commentary by Brook Benton + excerpts from 'Peg O' My Heart' and 'Blue Skies'.	

AFRTS[8]	**Untitled**	1961
SSL-14006 (P-7696)	Frankie And Johnny / It's Just A House Without You	
	Other four tracks are by Ray Martin, Bud Dalshiell and the Brothers Four. Reverse (SSL-14005 (P-7695)) features Sam Cooke, Del Shannon, the Chantels and Ray Charles.	

Armed Forces Records	**Untitled**	1961
AFD-469/470	The Boll Weevil Song	
	Other tracks by the Joiner, Arkansas State College Exchange Students Marching Band, Pat Boone, Les Paul & Mary Ford, Henry Mancini, Nat 'King' Cole, Rene & Pachango Orchestra, Goofus, Los Chavales de España, the Melachrino Strings & Orchestra, Peter Nero and the Sound of Griff Williams.	

Armed Forces Records	**Untitled**	1961
AFD-481	Frankie And Johnny	
	Other tracks by the Fleetwoods, Troy Shondell, the Chantels and Lawrence Welk. Reverse (AFD-482) is Judy Garland live at Carnegie Hall.	

AFRTS	**Untitled**	1962
SSL-14799 (P-8107)	Still Waters Run Deep / Hotel Happiness	
	Other four tracks by Ray Charles and Cozy Cole. Reverse (SSL-14800 (P-8108)) features Nat 'King 'Cole, Bette Davis & Debbie Burton and Bert Kaempfert.	

AFRTS	**Untitled**	1963
SSL-15011 (P-8223)	Dearer Than Life / I Got What I Wanted	
	Other tracks by Steve Lawrence and Ray Ellis & His Orchestra. Reverse (SSL-15012 (P-8224)) features Peter, Paul & Mary, Bill Pursell, Si Zentner & His Orchestra and Tony Martin.	

---

[7] ET = Electronic Transcription.
[8] Armed Forces Radio & Televison Service.

Treasury Department No. 832 (1963)   Armed Forces Radio RL 48-4 (1964)

AFRTS RL-2-4 SSL-15304 (P-8410)	***Untitled*** The Tender Years / My True Confession *Other tracks by Andy Williams, Sarah Vaughan and Dion.* *Reverse (SSL-15303 (P-8409)) features the New Christy Minstrels,* *the Glencoves, Bob Hope and the Ray Charles Singers.*	1963
Treasury Department US Savings Bonds Division No.832 (XGPB-162)	***Del Sharbutt and Joel Herron Orchestra –*** ***'Guest Star' Brook Benton*** Interview with Brook Benton conducted by Del Sharbutt + 3 specially recorded songs: 'The Boll Weevil Song', 'Take Good Care Of Her' and 'Hotel Happiness' *Reverse (No.831 (XGPB-161)) by Connie Boswell.*	1963
United States Army XPB-1179	***Young Americans In Action*** Interview with Brook Benton conducted by Hugh Downs [2:00]. *Other tracks by Leslie Uggams, Richie Ginther, Myrna Blythe,* *Jerome Wilson, Tracey Dey, Dick York, Meredith MacRae,* *Donna Lynn and Sam Pottle.*	1963
AFRTS RL 47-4	***Top Pops No.83*** Too Late To Turn Back Now / Another Cup Of Coffee *Other tracks by Elvis Presley, Marvin Gaye, Mary Wells,* *Al Martino, Johnny Tillotson, Bobby Darin, King Curtis, the* *Rolling Stones, Trini Lopez , Kitty Wells, George Hamilton IV,* *George Jones and Melba Montgomery*	1964
AFRTS RL 48-4 (P-22560)	***Brook Benton – Greatest Hits*** Its Just A Matter Of Time / Endlessly / Thank You Pretty Baby / So Many Ways / Kiddio / The Boll Weevil Song / Hotel Happiness *Reverse (P-22559) features live performances by Johnny Mathis.*	1964
AFRTS RL 5-5	***Top Pops No.93*** A House Is Not A Home *Other tracks by Elvis Presley, Lesley Gore, Ruby & The* *Romantics, the Ventures, Eydie Gorme, the New Christy* *Minstrels, John Zacherle, Kai Winding, Nino Tempo & April* *Stevens, Ray Charles, Pat Boone, Hank Williams Jr and* *Buddy Cagle.*	1964

AFRTS RL 9-1 (1970)

Army Reserve No.248 (1976)

| AFRTS RL 16-5 | **Top Pops No.104** | 1964 |

AFRTS RL 16-5   **Top Pops No.104**   1964
Lumberjack
Other tracks by the Animals, Sandy Nelson, Burl Ives, Nancy Wilson, the Jelly Beans, Elvis Presley, Sam Cooke, Ray Charles, George Jones & Melba Montgomery, Carl Smith, Patsy Cline and Jimmy C. Newman.

Mars Broadcasting   **Contests And Promotions**   1964
CP-1103
Singing Bug [0:52]
Other tracks by the Pat Boone, Roger Williams, Bobby Rydell, Johnny Cash, Dick Clark, Timi Yuro, Jimmie Clanton, Joe Dowell, Steve Allen, Della Reese, Bob Conrad., Steve Lawrence and the Tokens.

AFRTS   **Untitled**   1966
SSL-18087 (P-9945)
The Roach Song / Where Does A Man Go To Cry
Other three tracks are selections from 'Sugar And Spice And Everything Nice' by Ami Rouselle. Reverse (SSL-18088 (P-9946)) features Carmen Cavallaro, Eddie Heywood and Lalo Schifrin.

AFRTS RL 20-7   **Untitled**   1966
SSL-18144 (P-9978)
Cold Cold Heart / Funny How Time Slips Away / Walking The Floor Over You
Other three tracks are selections by Arthur Lyman. Reverse (SSL-18143 (P-9977)) features two tracks by David Rose & His Orchestra and four tracks by the Living Strings plus Trumpet.

AFRTS RL 36-0   **Brook Benton – Today**   1970
(P-11802)
My Way / Can't Take My Eyes Off You / We're Gonna Make It / Desertion / I've Gotta Be Me [Cotillion recordings]
Reverse (P-11801) features B.B. King.

AFRTS RL 9-1   **Brook Benton – Home Style**   1970
(P-12129)
Whoever Finds This I Love You / It's All In The Game / Don't Think Twice It's All Right / Born Under A Bad Sign / Are You Sincere [Cotillion recordings]
Reverse (P-12130) features Donna Hathaway.

Merry Christmas

from

Brook Benton

and

We are proud to present the New Brook Benton Beautiful Memories of Christmas Special.

The format of this 45 minute program includes 6 income potential commercial minutes all for your use.

The annual royalty is $55. A 5 year prepaid royalty is $105. Should you have a sister station with a more appropriate format, please share this information.

To insure that you are the first station in your primary coverage area with rights to air this special, call toll free 1-800-642-2504 (Nationwide) 1-800-642-2503 (North Carolina) and we will forward your license. Exclusive rights information is available.

 Happy Holidays

United States Marine Corps, unknown no.	***Sounds of Solid Gold (Volume 15)*** Endlessly *Other tracks by the Drifters, Connie Francis, Dee Clark, Billy Grammer, Lynna Anderson, Barbra Streisand, Mary Travers and Honey Cone.*	1971
Unknown label + cat no.	***Vault of Mercury*** [60:00] Brook Benton – one song, no details *Other tracks by the Platters, the Diamonds, the Danleers, the Big Bopper, Phil Phillips, Dinah Washington, Clyde McPhatter, the Hondells, Lesley Gore, Freddie & The Dreamers, the Blues Magoos, Spanky & Our Gang, Rod Stewart and Paper Lace.*	1974
Army Reserve No.248	***William B. & Company*** ***Guest Artist: Brook Benton – Host: William B. Williams*** **(Air week: 25 January 1976)** Interview with Brook Benton + You Take Me Home [MGM] / Rainy Night in Georgia [Cotillion] / For All We Know [MGM] / Try To Win A Friend [unknown label] / Big Mable Murphy [Cotillion]. *Reverse (Program No.247, Air week 01/18/1976) features Sy Oliver.*	1976

HMC Radio RS1/RS2	***Merry Christmas from Brook Benton***	1983

(Aired on various dates in December 1983) [45:00]
Brook Benton talks about Christmas and introduces his songs.

Side 1

Announcer – (fade in) Beautiful Memories *(fade out)*	2:53
Brook Benton talks about...	0:23
Decorate The Night	3:25
Announcer with background music	2:07
This Time Of The Year *(fade out)*	2:32
Brook Benton talks about...	0:15
Child *(fade out)*	3:11
Brook Benton talks about...	0:34
Christmas Makes The Town *(fade out)*	2:38
Announcer with background music	1:01

Side 2

Brook Benton talks about...	
(fade in) Blue Decorations *(fade out)*	4:00
Brook Benton talks about... (with background music)	1:30
(fade in) Merry Christmas All *(fade out)*	2:33
Announcer with background music	2:08
Talking song – Brook's Christmas Impressions	1:05
[only issued on this LP]	
I've Got The Christmas Spirit *(fade out)*	3:50
Brook Benton talks about...	0:22
I Wish Everyday Could Be Like Christmas	2:50
Announcer with background music	1:00
Merry, Merry Christmas from Brook Benton	0:48
[spoken message, only issued on this LP]	
When A Child Is Born	3:41
Announcement – Brook Brenton information	0:30

The following LPs were produced for United Stations Programming Network:

USP, unknown cat no	***Solid Gold Scrapbook with Dick Bartley*** [5-LP]	
	Show No. 2 [of a set of five] *– **Weather Or Not*** [60:00]	1986

Brook Benton – one song, no details
Other tracks by Dee Clark, the Cascades, Jonathan Edwards, the Beatles, the Kinks, Bobby Hebb, the Carpenters, Simon & Garfunkel, the Parade, the Temptations, Stevie Wonder and Lou Christie.

USP Show No.321	***Dick Clark's Rock, Roll & Remember***	1988

(Air Date: 2-3 April 1988)
Interview with Brook Benton from 1969 + the following original recordings:
Hour 1, Side 1: Endlessly / Interview / It's Just A Matter Of Time
Other tracks by Lou Rawls, Al Green and Rita Coolidge.
Hour 1, Side 2: Interview / So Many Ways
Other tracks by the Dovells, the Drifters, Bobby Hebb, Ace and Blood, Sweat & Tears.
Hour 2, Side 1: Think Twice / Interview / Kiddio
Other tracks by Roy Hamilton, Blue Magic, the Righteous Brothers, Joe Henderson and Ray Charles.
Hour 2, Side 2: Interview / The Boll Weevil Song
Other tracks by Bread, the Mamas & Papas, the Hollies and the Zombies.

Hour 3, Side 1: Baby (You've Got What It Takes) *(with Dinah Washington)* / Interview / A Rockin' Good Way (To Mess Around & Fall In Love) *(with Dinah Washington)*
Other tracks by Andy Gibb, the Jackson 5, Brenda Lee, Michael Jackson, James & Bobby Purify, Dick & Dee Dee, and Ferrante & Teicher.
Hour 3, Side 2: Interview / Lie To Me
Other tracks by Dr. Hook, the Carpenters, Elvis Presley and the 5th Dimension.
Hour 4, Side 1: Revenge / Interview / Hotel Happiness
Other tracks by Aretha Franklin, Ike & Tina Turner, Dusty Springfield, the Four Tops and Brian Hyland.
Hour 4, Side 2: Interview / Rainy Night In Georgia
Other tracks by the Youngbloods, Gladys Knight & The Pips, the Cascades, Buddy Holly and Tommy Roe.

Unknown label + cat no	**Final Hits** [60:00]	1988

Brook Benton – one song, no details
Other tracks by the Everly Brothers, Buddy Holly, the Drifters, the Beatles, the Searchers, Creedence Clearwater Revival, Brian Hyland, Jackie Wilson, Jay & The Americans, the Righteous Brothers, the Animals, the Rascals and the Hollies.

The following LPs were produced for United Stations Radio Networks:

Unistar 1A/1B	**Solid Gold Scrapbook: A Music Menagerie**	1989

(Air Date: 6 August 1990)
Interview with Brook Benton + The Boll Weevil Song.
Other tracks by Elvis Presley, Lobo, Marvin Gaye, Jackie Wilson, Tom Jones, Harry Chapin, Fabian, the Tokens, Rubbermaid, Honey Cone, Major Lance, Smokey Robinson, the Miracles, Jefferson Airplane and America.

Unistar 2A/2B	**Solid Gold Scrapbook: A Birthday Salute**	1989

(Air Date: 19 September 1989) [59:30]
Interview with Brook Benton from 1984 + the following original Mercury and Cotillion recordings: It's Just A Matter Of Time / So Many Ways / The Ties That Bind / Kiddio / Think Twice / Baby (You've Got What It Takes) *(with Dinah Washington)* / A Rockin' Good Way (To Mess Around & Fall In Love) *(with Dinah Washington)* / Rainy Night In Georgia / Revenge / Lie To Me / The Same One / Shadrack / The Boll Weevil Song / Frankie And Johnny / Fools Rush In / Endlessly

Unistar 3A/3B	**Solid Gold Scrapbook: A Birthday Salute**	1990

(Air Date: 19 September 1990) [53:00].
Interview with Brook Benton from 1984 + the following original Mercury and Cotillion recordings: It's Just A Matter Of Time / Endlessly / Thank You Pretty Baby / So Many Ways / Baby (You've Got What It Takes) *(with Dinah Washington)* / A Rockin' Good Way (To Mess Around & Fall In Love) *(with Dinah Washington)* / Kiddio/ The Same One / Fools Rush In / Think Twice / The Boll Weevil Song / Frankie And Johnny / Lie To Me / Hotel Happiness / Rainy Night In Georgia

Unistar 5A/5B	**Solid Gold Scrapbook: April Showers** **(Air Date: 6 April 1990)** Interview with Brook Benton + Rainy Night In Georgia. *Other tracks by James Taylor, the Beatles, the Hollies, the* *Fortunes, Lou Christie, Elvis Presley, Eddie Rabbitt, Albert* *Hammond, the Cascades, the Carpenters, B.J. Thomas, Dee* *Clark, the Temptations and Creedence Clearwater Revival.*	1990

16" TRANSCRIPTION DISCS

AFRTS SSL-12023 (P-6785)	**Untitled** Thank You Pretty Baby / I Can't Begin To Tell You / Tell Me Your Dream / I'll String Along With You / The More I See You / Love Me Or Leave Me *Reverse (SSL-12024 (P-6786)) features Les Baxter.*	1959
AFRTS SSL-12216 (P-6882)	**Untitled** So Many Ways / I Want You Forever *Other tracks by the Rock-A-Teens, Chet Atkins and the Crests.* *Reverse (SSL-12215 (P-6881)) features Anita Bryant with Monty* *Kelly, Dinah Washington and Tommy Sands.*	1959

Bootlegs

CD

TONY JOE WHITE
No label or number   ***Swampfox In The Country***   1989
Compilation of Tony Joe White's appearances on the TV show
Nashville Now (TNN). Includes 'Rainy Night In Georgia' [duet with
Brook Benton recorded in January 1988].

UK Releases

78s

BROOK BENTON

Philips PB-639	Love Made Me Your Fool / Give Me A Sign	1956
RCA RCA-1044	A Million Miles From Nowhere / Devoted	2/1958
Mercury AMT-1014	It's Just A Matter Of Time / Hurtin' Inside	12/1958
Mercury AMT-1043	Endlessly / So Close	5/1959

45s

BROOK BENTON

RCA RCA-45-1044	A Million Miles From Nowhere / Devoted	2/1958
Mercury 45-AMT-1014	It's Just A Matter Of Time / Hurtin' Inside	12/1958
Mercury 45-AMT-1043	Endlessly / So Close	5/1959
Mercury 45-AMT-1061	Thank You Pretty Baby / With All Of My Heart	8/1959
Mercury 45-AMT-1068	So Many Ways / I Want You Forever	10/1959

DINAH WASHINGTON & BROOK BENTON*
BROOK BENTON & DINAH WASHINGTON**

Mercury 45-AMT-1083	Baby (You've Got What It Takes)* / I Do**	2/1960

BROOK BENTON

Mercury 45-AMT-1097	The Ties That Bind / Hither And Thither And Yon	5/1960

DINAH WASHINGTON & BROOK BENTON*
BROOK BENTON & DINAH WASHINGTON**

Mercury 45-AMT-1099	A Rockin' Good Way (To Mess Around And Fall In Love)* / I Believe**	6/1960

BROOK BENTON

Mercury 45-AMT-1109	Kiddio / The Same One	8/1960
Mercury 45-AMT-1121	Fools Rush In / Someday You'll Want Me To Want You	11/1960
Mercury 45-AMT-1134	For My Baby / Think Twice	2/1961
Mercury 45-AMT-1148	The Boll Weevil Song / Your Eyes	5/1961
Mercury 45-AMT-1157	Frankie And Johnny / It's Just A House Without You	9/1961
Mercury 45-AMT-1168	Revenge / Really, Really	1/1962
Mercury 45-AMT-1172	Walk On The Wild Side / Somewhere In The Used To Be	3/1962
Mercury 45-AMT-1178	Hit Record / Thanks To The Fool	6/1962
Mercury 45-AMT-1187	Lie To Me / With The Touch Of Your Hand	9/1962
Mercury 45-AMT-1194	Hotel Happiness / Still Waters Run Deep	12/1962
Mercury AMT-1203	I Got What I Wanted / Dearer Than Life	4/1963
Mercury AMT-1208	My True Confession / Tender Years	7/1963
Mercury AMT-1212	Two Tickets To Paradise / Don't Hate Me	10/1963

BROOK BENTON & DAMITA JO

Mercury AMT-1217	Baby You've Got It Made / Stop Foolin'	12/1963

BROOK BENTON

Mercury MF-806	Going, Going, Gone / After Midnight	2/1964
Mercury MF-822	Too Late To Turn Back Now / Another Cup Of Coffee	7/1964
Mercury MF-828	A House Is Not A Home / Come On Back	9/1964
Mercury MF-842	Do It Right / Please, Please Make It Easy	1/1965
Mercury MF-863	Love Me Now / A-Sleepin' At The Foot Of The Bed	6/1965
RCA Victor RCA-1491	Mother Nature, Father Time / You're Mine (And I Love You)	11/1965

Reprise RS-20611	Laura (What's He Got That I Ain't Got) /	1967
	You're The Reason I'm Living	
Atlantic 584 222	Do Your Own Thing /	10/1968
	I Just Don't Know What To Do With Myself	
Atlantic 584 266	Touch 'Em With Love / She Knows What To Do For Me	5/1969
Atlantic 584 267	Nothing Can Take The Place Of You / Woman Without Love	7/1969

BROOK BENTON (with COLD GRITS)

| Atlantic 584 315 | Rainy Night In Georgia / Where Do I Go From Here? | 2/1970 |

BROOK BENTON WITH THE DIXIE FLYERS*
BROOK BENTON (with COLD GRITS)**

| Atlantic 2091 028 | Don't Make You Want To Go Home* / I've Gotta Be Me** | 9/1970 |

BROOK BENTON WITH THE DIXIE FLYERS*
BROOK BENTON (with COLD GRITS)**

| Atlantic 2091 050 | Shoes* / Rainy Night In Georgia** / My Way** [3:36] | 1/1971 |

BROOK BENTON

MGM 2006 301	Sweet Memories / If You've Got The Time	7/1973
All Platinum 6146 311	Mr. Bartender / Taxi	1/1976
All Platinum 6146 315	My Funny Valentine / You Were Gone	4/1976

Reissue 45s

BROOK BENTON

| Mercury Revived 45 | Boll Weevil Song / Walk On The Wild Side | 5/1969 |
| MF-1099 | | |

DINAH WASHINGTON & BROOK BENTON*
BROOK BENTON & DINAH WASHINGTON**

| Mercury Revived 45 | A Rockin' Good Way (To Mess Around And Fall In Love)* / | 5/1969 |
| MF-1100 | I Do** | |

BROOK BENTON (with COLD GRITS)

| Atlantic K-10118 | Rainy Night In Georgia / Where Do I Go From Here? | 1972 |

BROOK BENTON (with COLD GRITS)*
BROOK BENTON WITH THE DIXIE FLYERS**

| Atlantic K-10638 | Rainy Night In Georgia* / Shoes** | 6/1975 |

DINAH WASHINGTON & BROOK BENTON*
BROOK BENTON & DINAH WASHINGTON**

| Philips 6198 160 | A Rockin' Good Way (To Mess Around And Fall In Love)* / | 7/1977 |
| | Fools Rush In** | |

Acetates

BROOK BENTON

| Emidisc | It's Just A House Without You *(single-sided acetate)* | 1961 |

Philips PB-639 (1956, promo)

Mercury 45-AMT-1014 (1958)

Mercury 45-AMT-1148 (1961, promo)

Mercury 45-AMT-1168 (1962, promo)

RCA Victor RCA-1491 (1965, promo)

RCA Victor RCA-1491 (1965)

Atlantic 584 315 (1970)

Atlantic K-10118 (1972, reissue)

MGM 2006 301 (1973)

All Platinum 6146 311 (1976)

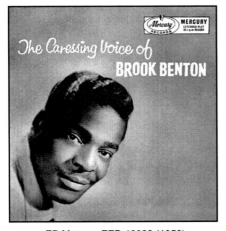

EP Mercury ZEP-10023 (1959)

EP Mercury ZEP-10046 (1960)

EP Mercury ZEP-10076 (1960)

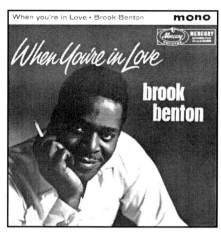

EP Mercury ZEP-10107 (1961)

EP Mercury ZEP-10120 (1961)

EP Mercury ZEP-10125 (1961)

EP Bravo! BR-376 (1963)

EP Mercury 10030 MCE (1964)

EPs

BROOK BENTON

RCA RCX-169 *(mono)*	**Brook Benton** I'm Coming Back To You / Crazy In Love With You / Crinoline Skirt / Because You Love Me	1959
Fontana TFE-17151 *(mono)*	**At His Best** The Wall / Rock'n'Roll That Rhythm (All Night Long) / Anything For You / Can I Help It	1959
Mercury ZEP-10023 *(mono)*	**The Caressing Voice Of Brook Benton** So Close / Endlessly / Hurtin' Inside / It's Just A Matter Of Time	1959
Mercury ZEP-10046 *(mono)*	**Make A Date With Brook Benton** Thank You Pretty Baby / With All Of My Heart / So Many Ways / I Want You Forever	1960
Mercury ZEP-10076 *(mono)*	**I'm In The Mood For Love** The Nearness Of You / I Can't Begin To Tell You / Tell Me Your Dream / I'm In The Mood For Love	1960
Mercury ZEP-10091 *(mono)* SEZ-19009 *(stereo)*	**When I Fall In Love** When I Fall In Love / But Beautiful / I'll String Along With You / The More I See You	1960
Mercury ZEP-10107 *(mono)* SEZ-19019 *(stereo)*	**When You're In Love** Around The World / Because Of You / A Lovely Way To Spend An Evening / Blue Skies	1961

DINAH WASHINGTON & BROOK BENTON*
BROOK BENTON & DINAH WASHINGTON**

Mercury ZEP-10120 *(mono)* SEZ-19022 *(stereo)*	**A Rocking Good Way** A Rockin' Good Way (To Mess Around And Fall In Love)* / I Do** / I Believe** / Baby (You've Got What It Takes)*	1961

BROOK BENTON

Mercury ZEP-10125 *(mono)* SEZ-19024 *(stereo)*	**So Warm** People Will Say We're In Love / More Than You Know / May I Never Love Again / You'll Never Know	1961
Mercury 10004 MCE *(mono)*	**Blues – Gospel – Spiritual** Go Tell It On The Mountain / Remember Me / Deep River / Just A Closer Walk With Thee	1961
Bravo! BR-376 *(mono)*	**Brook Benton** Steppin' Out Tonight / Just Tell Me When / Won't Cha Gone / A New Love	1963
Mercury 10030 MCE *(mono)*	**Born To Sing The Blues** Born To Sing The Blues / Since I Met You Baby / I Worry 'Bout You / I'll Never Be Free	1964
Summit LSE-2040 *(mono)*	**Brook Benton** A New Love / No Love Like Her Love / The Girl I Love / Dreams, Oh Dreams	1964
Mercury 10037 MCE *(mono)*	**I Don't Hurt Anymore** I Don't Hurt Anymore / Lie To Me / Hotel Happiness / Tomorrow Night	1966

VARIOUS ARTISTS

Mercury ZEP-10133	*Hitsville!*	1962
(mono)	Kiddio	
	Other tracks by the Crew Cuts, the Diamonds and Phil Phillips.	

LPs

BROOK BENTON

| Mercury MMC-14015 | *It's Just A Matter Of Time* | 1958 |
| (mono) | | |

| Mercury MMC-14022 | *Endlessly* | 1959 |
| (mono) | | |

| RCA Camden CDN-143 | *Brook Benton* [compilation] | 1959 |
| (mono) | | |

| Mercury MMC-14042 | *I Love You In So Many Ways* | 1960 |
| (mono) | | |

DINAH WASHINGTON & BROOK BENTON

Mercury	*The Two Of Us*	1960
MMC-14055 *(mono)*		
CMS-18037 *(stereo)*		

BROOK BENTON

Mercury	*Songs I Love To Sing*	1960
MMC-14060 *(mono)*		
CMS-18041 *(stereo)*		

Mercury	*The Boll Weevil Song and 11 Other Great Hits*	1961
MMC-14090 *(mono)*	Same as US LP Mercury MG-20641/SR-60641.	
CMS-18060 *(stereo)*		

Mercury	*There Goes That Song Again*	1961
MMC-14108 *(mono)*		
CMS-18068 *(stereo)*		

| Mercury | *Golden Hits* [UK compilation] | 1962 |
| MMC-14124 *(mono)* | It's Just A Matter Of Time / Hurtin' Inside / Endlessly / So Close / Thank You Pretty Baby / So Many Ways / Baby (You've Got What It Takes) *(with Dinah Washington)* / Shadrack / Kiddio / The Boll Weevil Song / Frankie And Johnny / Revenge / Lie To Me / Hotel Happiness | |

| Mercury 20024 MCL | *Born To Sing The Blues* | 1962 |
| (mono) | | |

| Mercury 20040 MCL | *It's Just A Matter Of Time* | 1963 |
| (mono) | | |

| Mercury 20053 MCL | *This Bitter Earth* | 1963 |
| (mono) | | |

Mercury	*Golden Hits* [US compilation]	1964
20060 MCL/SMCL		
(mono/stereo)		

DINAH WASHINGTON & BROOK BENTON

Mercury 20069 MCL *(mono)*	***The Two Of Us***	1964

BROOK BENTON

Hallmark HM-536	***The Soul Of Brook Benton*** [compilation]	1966
Mercury MG-2022	***The Boll Weevil Song and Other Great Hits*** [compilation] Same as US LP Wing MGW-12314 *(mono)*, *The Boll Weevil Song and Other Great Hits*	1966
RCA Victor RD-7797 *(mono)*	***That Old Feeling*** Same as US LP RCA Victor LSP-3514, *That Old Feeling*	1966
RCA Victor SF-7859 *(stereo)*	***Brook Benton – The Billy May Way*** [factory sample – unissued] Lover Come Back To Me / Unforgettable / There Goes My Heart / Just As Much As Ever / Beyond The Sea (La Mer) / Makin' Whoopee / There, I've Said It Again / It's Been A Long, Long Time / I Only Have Eyes For You / I'm Beginning To See The Light / Sweet Georgia Brown / Sentimental Journey	1966
Realm RM-52083	***The Soul Of Brook Benton*** [compilation]	1966
Wing WL-1153 *(mono)*	***Brook Benton*** [compilation] Same as US LP Wing MGW-12314 *(mono)*, *The Boll Weevil Song and Other Great Hits*	1966
Fontana Special SFL-13164 *(stereo)*	***Brook Benton*** [compilation] Same as US LP Wing SRW-16314 *(stereo)*, *The Boll Weevil Song and Other Great Hits*	1967
Mercury MVL-307 *(mono)*	***Best Ballads Of Broadway***	1967
Mercury MVL-308 *(mono)*	***On The Countryside***	1967

From this point all releases were in stereo.

Atlantic 588 187	***Do Your Own Thing***	1969
Fontana International SFJL-951 *(stereo)*	***My True Confession*** [compilation] Mercury recordings.	1969
Fontana International SFJL-970 *(stereo)*	***Send For Me*** [compilation] Mercury recordings.	1969
Mercury 20184 MCL/SMCL *(mono/stereo)*	***Golden Hits (Volume 2)*** [compilation]	1970
Mercury International 21051-SHWL *(stereo)*	***Songs I Love To Sing***	1970
Atlantic 2400 024	***Home Style***	1970
Atlantic 2465 004	***Today***	1970
Philips International 6336 268	***Hot Millions Of The 50's & 60's*** [compilation] 17 Mercury tracks + Rainy Night In Georgia.	1970

RCA Camden CDS-1087 *(stereo)*	*I Wanna Be With You* [compilation]	1970
Atlantic 2400 202	*Gospel Truth*	1971
Atlantic ATL-1017 (renumbered K-40302)	*Story Teller*	1971
MGM 2315 245	*Something For Everyone*	1972
RCA International INTS-1492	*That Old Feeling*	1974

All Platinum   ***Mister Bartender***   1976
9109 303 DE LUX   Mr. Bartender / Can't Take My Eyes Off Of You / It Started All Over
Again / Weekend With Feathers / All In Love Is Fair / Now Is The
Time / My Funny Valentine / You Were Gone / Taxi / A Nightingale
Sang In Berkeley Square / I Had To Learn (The Hard Way)

DJM DJML-073   ***20 Historic Demo Tracks: Looking Back***   1976
You're For Me / Doggone Baby, Doggone / Next Stop Paradise /
A Lover's Question / Keep Me In Mind / Ain't It Good / What A
Kiss Won't Do / Everything Will Be Alright / I'll Never Stop Trying /
99 Per Cent / I'll Stop Anything I'm Doing / Walking Together /
Devoted / You're Movin' Me / My Love Will Last / One Love Too
Many / Come Let's Go / Nothing In The World / Looking Back /
You Can't Get Away From Me

RCA Starcall   ***Lovin'*** [compilation]   1976
HY-1029   Same as US RCA Camden CAS-2431, *I Wanna Be With You.*

TVP TVP-1008-KO   ***The Incomparable Brook Benton***   1976
  [Springboard Int'l.]   Same as US LP TVP TVP-1008, *The Incomparable Brook Benton.*

Double Value 6612 116 ***Spotlight On Brook Benton*** [compilation]   1977
26 Mercury tracks + 2 All Platinum tracks ('Mr. Bartender' and
'All In Love Is Fair').

Warwick WW-5031   ***The Incomparable Brook Benton***   1977
Same as US LP TVP TVP-1008, *The Incomparable Brook Benton.*
TVP recordings.

RCA International   ***Sings The Standards*** [compilation]   1981
INTS-5085

Phoenix PHX-1019   ***Best Of (Volume 1)*** [compilation]   1982

Bulldog BDL-2039   ***20 Golden Pieces Of Brook Benton*** [compilation]   1983
Bayou Babe / Sunshine / Endlessly / Old Fashioned Strut / Soft /
Trust Me To Do What You Want Me To Do (And I'll Do It) / Pulling
Me Down / Makin' Love Is Good For You / Love Is Best Of All /
A Tribute To 'Mama' / Let The Sun Come Out / We Need What We
Need / Better Times / A Lover's Question / Let Me In Your World /
I Love Her / Lord You Know How Man Are / Till I Can't Take It
Anymore / I Keep Thinking To Myself / There's Still A Little Love
Left In Me [Olde World recordings]

DINAH WASHINGTON & BROOK BENTON
Mercury 6463 181   ***The Two Of Us***   1983
  [Phonogram]

BROOK BENTON

Audio Fidelity AFEMP-1024	**The Incomparable Brook Benton** [2-LP compilation] Same as US LP TVP TVP-1008, *The Incomparable Brook Benton.* TVP recordings.	1984
K-Tel GM-0208	**Endlessly** [compilation]	1984
K-Tel GM-0229	**The Best Of Brook Benton** [compilation]	1984
RCA International INT-89092	**Sings The Standards** [compilation]	1984
Timeless TIME-1	**The Best Of Brook Benton** [compilation]	1984
Castle UNLP-010	**Unforgettable** [compilation]	1986
Topline TOP-158 [Charly]	**Endlessly** [compilation]	1987
Harmony HARLP-109	**Portrait Of A Song Stylist** [compilation]	1989

VARIOUS ARTISTS

Fidelio ATL-4125	**Brook Benton Sings (Volume 1)** A New Love / No Love Like Her Love / The Girl I Love / Dreams, Oh Dreams *Other tracks by Jackie Jocko.*	1963/64
Summit ATL-4125	**Brook Benton Sings (Volume 1)** Same as LP Fidelio ATL-4125.	1965
Summit ATL-4139	**Brook Benton Sings (Volume 2)** What Cha Gone / Just Tell Me When / Love's That Way / Steppin' Out Tonight *Other tracks by Jackie Jocko.*	1965
Summit ATL-4180	**Great Stars Of Broadway** A New Love / No Love Like Her Love / The Girl I Love *Other tracks by Andre Previn, Pearl Bailey, Little Richard and Memphis Slim.*	1965
Mercury International MWL-21018	**After Midnight** It's Just A Matter Of Time *Other tracks by Sarah Vaughan, Dinah Washington, Billy Eckstine, Damita Jo and the Platters.*	1968
Crown CRS-2001	**Brook Benton Sings** A New Love / No Love Like Her Love / The Girl I Love / Dreams, Oh Dreams *Other tracks by Jackie Jocko.*	1970
Deacon DEA-1022ST [Gallery]	**Starring Lou Rawls with special Guest Stars** Love's That Way / Just Tell Me When / Won't Cha Love / Dreaming (Dreams, Oh Dreams) *Other tracks by Lou Rawls and Joe Tex.*	1970
Atlantic Gospel Series 2400 116 [Polydor]	**Super Heavenly Stars** Heaven Help Us All *(with the Dixie Flyers)* *Other tracks by Aretha Franklin, Wilson Pickett, Solomon Burke, Roberta Flack, the Sweet Inspirations, Myrna Summers & The Interdenominational Singers and Marion Williams.*	1971

Atlantic K-20025 [Kinney Music]	***It All Started Here*** Shoes *(with the Dixie Flyers)* *Other tracks by Aretha Franklin, Wilson Pickett, Clarence Carter, Sam & Dave, Roberta Flack, Donny Hathaway, the Drifters, the Beginning Of The End, King Curtis, King Floyd, Little Sister, the Persuaders, Dionne Warwick and Otis Redding.*	1972
Atlantic K-40542 [Kinney Music]	***The 2nd Rosko Show*** Rainy Night In Georgia *Other tracks by Aretha Franklin, Wilson Pickett, Bobby Newton, the Capitols, the Drifters, King Curtis, Donnie Hathaway, Percy Sledge, Cross Country, the Detroit Spinners and Otis Redding.*	1974
Atlantic K-40550 [Kinney Music]	***208 Atlantic Black Gold*** Rainy Night In Georgia *Other tracks by Arthur Conley, the Drifters, the Coasters, Wilson Pickett, Joe Tex and Percy Sledge.*	1974
Atlantic K-50164 [Kinney Music]	***Atlantic Black Gold (Volume 2)*** Shoes *(with the Dixie Flyers)* *Other tracks by the Average White Band, Jimmy Castor, Margie Joseph, Ben E. King, Aretha Franklin, Blue Magic, Dee Dee Warwick, the Drifters, Herbie Mann, Don Covay, Sister Sledge, Tony & Tyrone, Otis Redding, Tammi Lynn, Roberta Flack, Gene Page, the Detroit Spinners and Eddie Harris.*	1975
All Platinum 9299 767 [Phonogram]	***All Platinum Gold*** Mr. Bartender *Other tracks by Hank Ballard, the Rimshots, Retta Young, Timothy Wilson, the Moments, Sylvia & The Moments, Calender, Elenore Mills, Shirley & Company, Derek Martin, the Whatnauts, Sylvia and Chuck Jackson.*	1976
DJM DJD-28031 [Springboard Int'l]	***Monster Soul*** [2-LP] A Lover's Question *(demo)* *Other tracks by the Bells, Baby Washington, Dave 'Baby' Cortez, the Chantels, the Isley Brothers, Gladys Knight & The Pips, Patti Labelle & The Blue-Belles, Maxine Brown, Lee Dorsey, King Curtis, Alvin Robinson, the Dixie Cups, the Jelly Beans, Deon Jackson, Evie Sands, the Capitols, the Manhattans, Sly Stone, the Ohio Players with Gloria Barnes, the Ad Libs, the O'Jays and Donnie Elbert.*	1976
Mercury 6641 868 [Phonogram]	***Back To Back*** [2-LP] LP 9199 869, *Passing Strangers* with Sarah Vaughan & Billy Eckstine (reissue of Mercury LP 20155-MCL) + LP 9199 870 *The Two Of Us* with Dinah Washington & Brook Benton (reissue of Mercury LP 20069-MCL)	1978
Warwick WW-5047	***Black Velvet – 20 Greatest Hits*** It's Just A Matter Of Time [TVP recording] *Other tracks by Gladys Knight, Billy Ocean, Dionne Warwick, Kenny Williams, Mary Wells, Billy Paul, Johnny Nash, Jerry Butler, Nina Simone, Barry White, Deniece Williams, Harold Melvin, Dobie Gray, Jimmy Helms, Maxine Brown, Danny Williams, O.C. Smith, Madeline Bell and Lou Rawls.*	1978
Street Sounds LVBAL-1	***Love Ballads*** [14-LP] Rainy Night In Georgia *142 tracks by Otis Redding, the Moments, the Delfonics and many other (mostly soul) artists. Also issued as a 7-cassette set.*	1984

Music For Pleasure MFP-5780	**Magic Moments** That Old Feeling *Other tracks by unknown artists.*	1985
Topline TOP-149 [Charly]	**Soul Mining** Rainy Night In Georgia *Other tracks by Sam & Dave, Eddie Floyd, Clarence Carter, Rufus* *Thomas, Fontella Bass, Dobie Gray, Major Harris, the Esquires,* *Jackie Lee, the Olympics and Barbara George.*	1986

CDs

BROOK BENTON

Tring International GRF-164	**Endlessly** Includes the previously unissued Stax cuts 'You've Never Been This Far' and 'These Arms You Pushed Away', plus an alt. take of the Olde World recording 'I Love Her'.	1998
Spectrum 982 647-1 [Universal]	**For My Baby – The Brook Benton Collection**	2005
Jasmine JASCD-687	**The Silky Smooth Tones of Brook Benton** [2-CD] 54 Mercury recordings from 1959-60: five albums (*It's Just A* *Matter Of Time*, *Endlessly*, *Songs I Love To Sing*, *The Two Of Us* (with Dinah Washington*) and *Golden Hits*).	2011
Jasmine JASCD-744	**Let Me Sing And I'm Happy** [2-CD] 59 Mercury recordings from 1960-62: four albums (*I Love You In* *So Many Ways*, *The Boll Weevil Song And 11 Other Great Hits*, *There Goes That Song Again* and *Singing The Blues*) plus eleven single cuts.	2013
Sepia 1235	**There Goes That Song Again / Singing The Blues** Includes a previously unissued alt. take of 'Hit Record'.	2013
Jasmine JASCD-784	**The Early Years 1953-1959** [2-CD] 62 from OKeh, Epic, RCA Victor and Vik, plus the 1956 demo sessions.	2014

Tapes

CASSETTE TAPES

BROOK BENTON

MGM 3110 245 -ST	**Something For Everyone**	1972
RCA International INTK-5085	**Brook Benton Sings Standards**	1981
Timeless TIMC-1	**The Best Of Brook Benton**	1984
Castle UNMC-010	**Unforgettable** TVP recordings.	1986

VARIOUS ARTISTS

Mercury 7175 095 [Philips]	**Hot Millions Of The 50's & 60's**	1970

Mercury 7599 366 [Phonogram]	**Back To Back** *Passing Strangers* with Sarah Vaughan & Billy Eckstine [LP Mercury 20155-MCL] + *The Two Of Us* with Dinah Washington & Brook Benton [US LP Mercury 20069-MCL]	1978
Street Sounds ZCBAL-1	**Love Ballads** [7-CD] Rainy Night In Georgia *142 tracks by Otis Redding, the Moments, the Delfonics and many other (mostly soul) artists. Also issued as a 14-LP set.*	1984
Topline KTOP-149 [Charly]	**Soul Mining** Rainy Night In Georgia *Other tracks by Sam & Dave, Eddie Floyd, Clarence Carter, Rufus Thomas, Fontella Bass, Dobie Gray, Major Harris, the Esquires, Jackie Lee, the Olympics and Barbara George.*	1986

International Releases

In the course of our extensive research we have repeatedly come across interesting discographical discoveries which we absolutely must share with our readers. Although the information presented below is by no means exhaustive, it is a testament to the immense popularity of Brook Benton across the globe.

ANGOLA

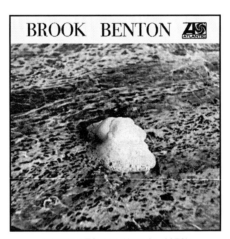

Atlantic ATS-504 (Angola, 1970)

45s

BROOK BENTON (with COLD GRITS)

Atlantic ATS-488	Rainy Night In Georgia / Where Do I Go From Here?	1969
Atlantic ATS-504	A Little Bit Of Soap / My Way *(picture sleeve)*	1970

ARGENTINA

33⅓ rpm 7" Singles

BROOK BENTON

Philips AA-128000	Por Los Barrios Bajos *(Walk On The Wild Side)* / En Alguna Parte *(Somewhere In The Used To Be)* [Mercury recordings]	1962

45s

BROOK BENTON

Interdisc S-015	Amar Es Bueno Para Ti *(Makin' Love Is Good For You)* / Definitivamente *(Endlessly)* [Olde World recordings]	1977

EPs

BROOK BENTON
Mercury EP-1-3394   ***Brook Benton***   1959
Es Solo Cuestion De Tiempo *(It's Just A Matter Of Time)* /
Dolor Profundo *(Hurtin' Inside)* / Infinitamente *(Endlessly)* /
De Tan Diferentes Maneras *(So Many Ways)*

LPs

BROOK BENTON
RCA Victor LPM-3514   ***Ese Viejo Sentimiento (That Old Feeling)***   1966
Same as US LP RCA Victor LPM-3514, *That Old Feeling.*

Atlantic 81013   ***Estilos***   197?
  [WEA]   Cotillion recordings.

VARIOUS ARTISTS
Vik LZ-1009   ***Bailando Rock Lento***   1958
De Haberlo Sebido (If Only I Had Known).
Other tracks by Elvis Presley, Floyd Cramer, the Twins, Jim &
John, Teddy Randazzo, Willie Rodriguez, Judy Faye, Varetta
Dillard, Joe Reisman, Budd Albright, Harry Balfonte, the Equadors,
the Lane Brothers, Jimmy Spellman and Reed Harper.

Vik LZ-1015   ***Yo Traigo Los Discos! Serie Popular Bailable!***   1958
Locamente Enamorado De Ti (Crazy In Love With You).
Other tracks by Del Wood, the Twins, Lalo Mantone, Elio Mauro,
Ninon Mondejar, Henri Rene and others.

Atlantic MH-504106   ***The 2nd Rosko Show***   1974
  [WEA]   Same as UK LP Atlantic K-40542, *The 2nd Rosko Show.*

AUSTRALIA

45s

BROOK BENTON

Mercury 45272	It's Just A Matter Of Time / Hurtin' Inside	1959
Mercury 45287	Endlessly / So Close	1959
Mercury 45306	Thank You Pretty Baby / With All Of My Heart	1959
Mercury 45317	So Many Ways / I Want You Forever	1959

DINAH WASHINGTON & BROOK BENTON*
BROOK BENTON & DINAH WASHINGTON**
Mercury 45331   Baby (You've Got What It Takes)* / I Do**   1960

BROOK BENTON
Mercury 45338   The Ties That Bind / Hither And Thither And Yon   1960

DINAH WASHINGTON & BROOK BENTON*
BROOK BENTON & DINAH WASHINGTON**
Mercury 45346   A Rockin' Good Way (To Mess Around And Fall In Love)* /   1960
          I Believe**

Mercury 45331 (Australia, 1960)

Mercury 45400 (Australia, 1961)

Philips BF-71 (Australia, 1963)

Atlantic AK-3752 (Australia, 1971)

EP Philips DJ-133 (Australia, 1964)

EP Mercury PRA EP-111 (Australia, 1970)

BROOK BENTON

Mercury 45354	Kiddio / The Same One	1960
Mercury 45366	Fools Rush In / Someday You'll Want Me To Want You	1960
Mercury 45376	Think Twice / For My Baby	1961
Mercury 45400	The Boll Weevil Song / Your Eyes	1961
Mercury 45420	Frankie And Johnny / It's Just A House Without You	1961
Mercury 45441	Revenge / Really, Really	1962
Mercury 45444	Shadrack / The Lost Penny	1962
Mercury 45452	Walk On The Wild Side / Somewhere In The Used To Be	1962
Mercury 45468	Hit Record / Thanks To The Fool	1962
Mercury 45481	Lie To Me / With The Touch Of Your Hand	1962
Philips BF-9	Hotel Happiness / Still Waters Run Deep [Mercury recordings]	1962
Philips BF-22	I Got What I Wanted / Dearer Than Life	1963
Philips BF-71	You're All I Want For Christmas / This Time Of The Year	1963
Philips BF-126	A House Is Not A Home / Come On Back	1964
Reprise 0611	Laura (What's He Got That I Ain't Got) /	
	You're The Reason I'm Living	1967
Reprise 0649	Weakness In A Man / The Glory Of Love	1968
Atlantic AK-2568	Do Your Own Thing / I Just Don't Know What To Do With Myself	1968

BROOK BENTON (with COLD GRITS)

Atlantic AK-3480	Rainy Night In Georgia / Where Do I Go From Here?	1970
Atlantic AK-3671	Baby / My Way	1971

BROOK BENTON WITH THE DIXIE FLYERS*
BROOK BENTON (with COLD GRITS)**

Atlantic AK-3752	Don't It Make You Want To Go Home* / I've Gotta Be Me**	1971

EPs

BROOK BENTON

Philips DJ-44	***DJ 'Rush!': Lie To Me*** (promo)	1962
	Lie To Me / My True Confession / I Got What I Wanted / Looking Back	
Philips DJ-133	***DJ 'Rush!': Born To Sing The Blues*** (promo)	1964
	Born To Sing The Blues / The Sun's Gonna Shine In My Door / I Worry 'Bout You / Never Be Free	

BROOK BENTON & DINAH WASHINGTON

Mercury PRA EP-111	***Untitled***	1970
	It's Just A Matter Of Time / Fools Rush In / A Rockin' Good Way *(with Dinah Washington)* / Baby (You've Got What It Takes)*(with Dinah Washington)*	

LPs

BROOK BENTON

Eclipse Record Club ZP-20464	***Endlessly*** Same as US LP Mercury MG-20464, *Endlessly.*	1959
Trip/Astor TLX-8026	***Ain't It Good*** Same as US 2-LP Trip TLP-8026-2, *Ain't It Good.*	1972

VARIOUS ARTISTS

J&B JB-408	***The Very Best Of Jackie Wilson & Brook Benton*** The Boll Weevil Song / Rainy Night In Georgia / It's Just A Matter Of Time / Fools Rush In / Kiddio / Lie To Me / Frankie And Johnny / Revenge / Think Twice *Other tracks by Jackie Wilson.*	1990

BELGIUM

45s

BROOK BENTON

Mercury 71.903	Revenge / Really, Really	1961
RCA 8693	You're Mine (And I Love You) / Mother Nature, Father Time	1965

BROOK BENTON (with COLD GRITS)

Atlantic BE-650192 [Barclay]	Rainy Night In Georgia / Where Do I Go From Here?	1970

BROOK BENTON

RCA Victor PB-9247	A Million Miles From Nowhere / Moon River *(promo)*	1975
RCA Victor 74 15 164	A Million Miles From Nowhere / Moon River	1975
Philips 61680291W	Endlessly / Fools Rush In [Mercury recordings]	1978

BRAZIL

33⅓ rpm 7" Singles

BROOK BENTON*
BROOK BENTON WITH THE DIXIE FLYERS**

Atco ACS-205.034	My Way* / I've Gotta Be Me**	1970

CANADA

78s

LINCOLN CHASE & THE SANDMEN

Columbia 40475	That's All I Need / The Message	1955

BROOK BENTON

Epic 9177	Give Me A Sign / Love Made Me Your Fool	1956
Epic 9199	All My Love Belongs To You / The Wall	1956
Vik X-0311	A Million Miles From Nowhere / Devoted	1957
Mercury 71394	It's Just A Matter Of Time / Hurtin' Inside	12/1958
Mercury 71443	Endlessly / So Close	3/1959
Mercury 71478	Thank You Pretty Baby / With All Of My Heart	6/1959
Mercury 71512	So Many Ways / I Want You Forever	10/1959

45s

BROOK BENTON

Mercury 71394X	It's Just A Matter Of Time / Hurtin' Inside	12/1958
Mercury 71443X	Endlessly / So Close	3/1959
Mercury 71478X	Thank You Pretty Baby / With All Of My Heart	6/1959
Mercury 71512X	So Many Ways / I Want You Forever	10/1959

DINAH WASHINGTON & BROOK BENTON*
BROOK BENTON & DINAH WASHINGTON**

Mercury 71626X	A Rockin' Good Way (To Mess Around And Fall In Love)* / I Believe**	5/1960

Mercury 71478 (Canada, 1959)

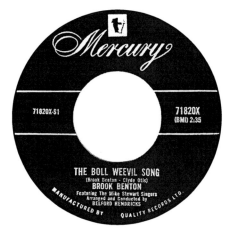

Mercury 71820X (Canada, 1961)

RCA Victor 47-8693 (Canada, 1965)

RCA Victor 47-8995 (Canada, 1966)

Reprise 0611 (Canada, 1967)

Reprise 0649 (Canada, 1967)

BROOK BENTON

Mercury 71820X	The Boll Weevil Song / Your Eyes	5/1961
Mercury 71859X	Frankie And Johnny / It's Just A House Without You	8/1961
Mercury 72024X	Lie To Me / With The Touch Of Your Hand	8/1962
RCA Victor 47-8693	Mother Nature, Father Time / You're Mine (And I Love You) (picture sleeve)	10/1965
RCA Victor 47-8768	Where There's Life (There's Still Hope) / Only A Girl Like You	2/1966
RCA Victor 47-8830	Too Much Good Lovin' / A Sailor Boy's Love Song	5/1966
RCA Victor 47-8944	Where Does A Man Go To Cry / The Roach Song	9/1966
RCA Victor 47-8995	If You Only Knew / So True In Life – So True In Love	11/1966
RCA Victor 47-9031	Silent Night / Our First Christmas Together	12/1966
RCA Victor 47-9096	Wake Up / All My Love Belongs To You	2/1967
Reprise 0611	Laura (What's He Got That I Ain't Got) / You're The Reason I'm Living	8/1967
Reprise 0649	Weakness In A Man / The Glory Of Love	12/1967

BROOK BENTON (with COLD GRITS)

Cotillion COT-44057	Rainy Night In Georgia / Where Do I Go From Here?	12/1969

BROOK BENTON WITH THE DIXIE FLYERS

Cotillion COT-44093	Whoever Finds This I Love You / Let Me Fix It	11/1970

BROOK BENTON

King K-2243	It's Just A Matter Of Time / So Close [TVP recordings]	1984
King K-2245	The Boll Weevil Song / Frankie & Johnny [TVP recordings]	1984
King K-2247	Rainy Night In Georgia / Hotel Happiness [TVP recordings]	1984

Reissue 45s

BROOK BENTON

Stardust URC-1237	The Boll Weevil Song / Hotel Happiness	19??
Underground UND-1237	The Boll Weevil Song / Hotel Happiness	19??

EPs

VARIOUS ARTISTS

Vik EXA-300	***Mister Rock And Roll (Scene 1)*** Your Love Alone *Other tracks by Teddy Randazzo.*	1957
Vik EXA-301	***Mister Rock And Roll (Scene 2)*** If Only I Had Known. *Other tracks by Teddy Randazzo.*	1957
Mercury GRS-1	***Gold Rush Sampler*** [33⅓ rpm] Endlessly *Other tracks by Tony Martin, Clyde McPhatter, Frankie Laine, Sarah Vaughan and Eddy Howard.*	1961

LPs

BROOK BENTON

Mercury MG-20934	***This Bitter Earth***	1964
Wing XW-12314 [Mercury]	***The Boll Weevil Song and Other Great Hits*** Same as US LP Wing SRW-16314 *(stereo)*, *The Boll Weevil Song and Other Great Hits*	1966

VARIOUS ARTISTS

Birchmount BM-665	***Soul Explosion***	1967
	Same as US LP Musicor MDS-1039, *Soul Explosion*.	
Masterseal MS-201	***Brook Benton Sings Blues Favorites***	196?
(33-2099)	Just Tell Me When / Steppin' Out Tonight	
	Other tracks by the Bruce Darrel Jazz Orchestra.	

CHILE

45s

BROOK BENTON

Mercury 7-14027	Es Solo Cuestion De Tiempo *(It's Just A Matter Of Time)* /	1959
	Me Duele Adentro *(Hurtin' Inside)*	
Mercury 7-14036	Para Siempre *(Endlessly)* / Tan Cerca *(So Close)*	1959
Mercury 7-14042	Gracias Preciosa *(Thank You Pretty Baby)* /	1959
	Con Todo Mi Corazón *(With All Of My Heart)*	
Mercury 7-14068	Los Tontos Se Agolpan *(Fools Rush In)* /	1960
	Algun Dia Querras Que *(Someday You'll Want Me To Want You)*	
Mercury 127 030 MCF	El Disco del Año *(Hit Record)* /	1962
	Gracias A Un Tonto *(Thanks To The Fool)*	

DENMARK

Mercury 127 077 MCF (Denmark, 1962)

Mercury 127 112 MCF (Denmark, 1963)

45s

BROOK BENTON

Mercury 71512-X-45	So Many Ways / I Want You Forever	1959
Mercury 127 030 MCF	Hit Records / Thanks To The Fool *(picture sleeve)*	1962
Mercury 127 077 MCF	Hotel Happiness / Still Waters Run Deep *(picture sleeve)*	1962
Mercury 127 112 MCF	Two Tickets To Paradise / Don't Hate Me *(picture sleeve)*	1963

EP

BROOK BENTON
Mercury 60148	***Brook Benton***	196?
	It's Just A Matter Of Time / Hurtin' Inside / Endlessly / So Close	

VARIOUS ARTISTS
RCA EPA-9526	***Mister Rock And Roll (Scene 1)***	1957
	Your Love Alone	
	Other tracks by Teddy Randazzo.	
RCA EPA-9527	***Mister Rock And Roll (Scene 2)***	1957
	If Only I Had Known	
	Other tracks by Teddy Randazzo.	
Mercury 60307	***Unknown title***	1960
	Kiddio / The Same One	
	Other tracks by Clyde McPhatter.	

FINLAND

Mercury 71394x45 (Finland, 1959)

45s

BROOK BENTON
Mercury 71394 x45	It's Just A Matter Of Time / Hurtin' Inside	1959
[R.E. Westerlund]		
Mercury 71820 x45	The Boll Weevil Song / Your Eyes	1961
[R.E. Westerlund]		

FRANCE

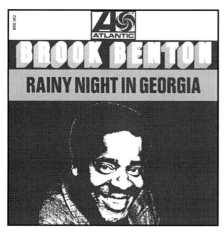

Atlantic 650 192 (France, 1969)   Atlantic 650 217 (France, 1970)

45s

BROOK BENTON

Mercury MM-10132 [Barclay]	It's Just A Matter Of Time / Endlessly	1960
Mercury MM-10147 [Barclay]	This Time Of The Year / How Many Times	1960
Mercury MM-10153 [Barclay]	The Ties That Bind / Hither And Thither And Yon	1960

DINAH WASHINGTON & BROOK BENTON*
BROOK BENTON & DINAH WASHINGTON**

Mercury MM-10154 [Barclay]	A Rockin' Good Way (To Mess Around And Fall In Love)* / I Believe**	1960

BROOK BENTON

Mercury MM-10156 [Barclay]	Fools Rush In / They Can't Take That Away From Me	1960
Reprise RV-20.150	The Glory Of Love / Weakness In A Man	1967

BROOK BENTON (with COLD GRITS)

Atlantic 650 192	Rainy Night In Georgia / Where Do I Go From Here?	1969

BROOK BENTON WITH THE DIXIE FLYERS

Atlantic 650 217	Shoes / Let Me Fix It	1970

EPs

BROOK BENTON

Mercury 14215 MEP	***Brook Benton***	1959
	It's Just A Matter Of Time / Hurtin' Inside / Endlessly / So Close	
Mercury 14219 MEP	***Brook Benton***	1960
	I Want You Forever / So Many Ways / With All My Heart / Thank You Pretty Baby	

RCA 75.602	**Brook Benton** You're For Me / Your Love Alone / I Wanna Do Everything For You / If Only I Had Known	1960
Mercury 14234 MEP	**Brook Benton** Kiddio / The Same One / The Ties That Bind / Hither And Thither And Yon	1960
Mercury 14237 MEP	**Brook Benton** Fools Rush In / Someday You'll Want Me To Want You / Baby Won't You Please Come Home / They Can't Take That Away From Me	1961
Philips 434.501 BE	**Brook Benton** Frankie And Johnny / Think Twice / For My Baby / It's Just A House Without You [Mercury recordings]	1961
Mercury 126 011 MCE	**La Rue Chaude** Walk On The Wild Side / Somewhere In The Used To Be / Shadrack / Go Tell It On The Mountain	1962
Mercury 126 032 MCE	**Spiritual** Go Tell It On The Mountain / Remember Me / Just A Closer Walk With Thee / Deep River	1962
Mercury 126 082 MCE	**4 Slow Rocks** Hotel Happiness / Lie To Me / Send For Me / Take Good Care Of Her	1962
RCA Victor 86.494 M	**Brook Benton** Mother Nature, Father Time / You're Mine / I Wanna Be With You / Boy, I Wish I Was In Your Place	1966
Reprise RVEP-60.109 (ED.6268-1) [Vogue]	**Ode To Billie Joe** Ode To Billie Joe / Laura (What's He Got That I Ain't Got) / You're The Reason I'm Living	1967

LPs

BROOK BENTON

Reprise CRV-6077 (RS.6268) [Vogue]	**Ode To Billie Joe**	1967
Philips 6336 268	**Hot Millions Of The 50's & 60's** Mercury recordings.	197?

VARIOUS ARTISTS

Atlantic 940.009 [Barclay]	**R. et B. Formidable (Volume 10)** Touch 'Em With Love *Other tracks by Tyrone Davis, Ralph 'Soul' Jackson, Sam & Dave, the Sweet Inspirations, the Noble Knights, Joe Tex, Otis Rush, Gloria Walker, Johnny Copeland, Solomon Burke and Lou Johnson.*	197?

(WEST) GERMANY

45s

BROOK BENTON

Teldec 4x0311 [Telefunken-Decca]	Devoted / A Million Miles From Nowhere	1957
Mercury R-21 151 [Electrola]	It's Just A Matter Of Time / Hurtin' Inside	1/1959
Mercury R-21 197 [Electrola]	Endlessly / So Close	3/1959
Mercury R-21 271 [Electrola]	Thank You Pretty Baby / With All Of My Heart	9/1959
Mercury R-21 339 [Electrola]	So Many Ways / I Want You Forever	12/1959

DINAH WASHINGTON & BROOK BENTON*
BROOK BENTON & DINAH WASHINGTON**

Mercury R-21 426 [Electrola]	Baby (You've Got What It Takes)* / I Do**	1/1960

BROOK BENTON

Mercury R-21 606 [Electrola]	Kiddio / The Same One	9/1960
Mercury R-21 702 [Electrola]	Fools Rush In / Somebody You'll Want Me To Want You	10/1960
RCA 47-9321	If Only I Had Known *(Reverse is 'Kiddio' by Teddy Randazzo)*	1960
Mercury R-21 893 [Electrola]	The Boll Weevil Song / Your Eyes	1/1961
Mercury R-21 902 [Electrola]	Think Twice / For My Baby	1/1961
Mercury R-21 947 [Electrola]	Frankie And Johnny / It's Just A House Without You	9/1961
Mercury R-22 028 [Electrola]	Revenge *(Reverse is 'Walk On By' by Leroy Van Dyke)*	1962
Mercury MCF 127 010	Revenge *(Reverse is 'Walk On By' by Leroy Van Dyke)*	1962
Mercury MCF 127 014	Walk On The Wild Side / Shadrack	1962
Mercury MCF 127 056	Lie To Me / With The Touch Of Your Hand	1962
Mercury MCF 127 077	Hotel Happiness / Still Waters Run Deep	1963
Mercury MCF 127 104	My True Confession / Tender Years	1963
RCA Victor 47-8693	Mother Nature, Father Time / You're Mine (And I Love You)	1966
RCA Victor TST-75302	***RCA Victor presents 16 new '66' short versions*** [promo] Includes Brook Benton's 'The Song I Heard Last Night' from LP *Mother Nature, Father Time.*	1966
RCA Victor 47-8768	While There's Life / Only A Girl Like You	1966
RCA Victor 47-8879	Break Her Heart / In The Evening By The Moonlight	1966
RCA Victor 47-8944	The Roach Song / Where Does A Man Go To Cry	1966
RCA Victor 47-15164	A Million Miles From Nowhere / Devoted	1970
Reprise RA-0611	Laura (What's He Got That I Ain't Got) / You're The Reason I'm Living	1967
Atlantic ATL.70.328	Do Your Own Thing / I Just Don't Know What To Do With Myself	11/1968
Atlantic ATL.70.376	She Knows What To Do For Me / Touch 'Em With Love	1969

BROOK BENTON (with COLD GRITS)

Atlantic ATL.70.420	Rainy Night In Georgia / Where Do I Go From Here?	1970

BROOK BENTON

Polydor 2051 214	It's Just A Matter Of Time / So Many Ways [TVP recordings]	1977

Mercury R-21 702 (West Germany, 1960)

Mercury R-22 028 (West Germany, 1962)

Mercury MCF 127 056 (West Germany, 1962)

RCA Victor 47-8693 (West Germany, 1966)

RCA Victor 47-8944 (West Germany, 1966)

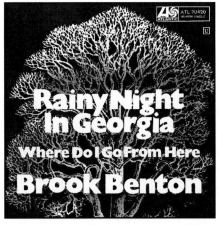

Atlantic ATL.70.420 (West Germany, 1970)

338

EPs

VARIOUS ARTISTS

Mercury R-41123 [Electrola]	***4 Hits – 4 Artists*** Endlessly *Other tracks by the Diamonds, the Platters and Rusty Draper.*	1959
RCA EPA-9526	***Mister Rock And Roll (Scene 1)*** Your Love Alone *Other tracks by Teddy Randazzo.*	1959
RCA EPA-9527	***Mister Rock And Roll (Scene 2)*** If Only I Had Known *Other tracks by Teddy Randazzo.*	1959
RCA EPA-9619	***Rockin' Party (Volume 2)*** Crazy In Love With You *Other tracks by the Crew Cuts and Don Sargent.*	1959

LPs

BROOK BENTON

RCA LSP-3514	***That Old Feeling***	1966
RCA LSP-3526	***Mother Nature, Father Time***	1966
RCA LSP-3590	***My Country***	1966
Atlantic ATL-40048	***Today***	1971
Atlantic ATL-40224	***The Gospel Truth***	1971
Atlantic STL-40314	***Story Teller***	1972
Master MA-0020983	***20 Greatest Hits*** TVP and 1950s demo recordings.	197?
Mercury 822 321-1Q	***It's Just A Matter Of Time – His Greatest Hits***	1984
Bellaphon 230-07-062	***Greatest Hits***	1985

VARIOUS ARTISTS

S&R International (Donauland-Club) 462119	***30 Years Popmusic*** The Boll Weevil Song [original Mercury version] *Other tracks by the Everly Brothers, Del Shannon, the Marcels, Bobby Vee, Gene McDaniels, Johnny Tillotson, Leroy Van Dyke, the Dave Brubeck Quartet, Helen Shapiro, the Tokens, Jimmy Dean, Eden Kane, the Highwaymen, Ben E. King and Chubby Checker.*	1961
Telefunken/ Decca / RCA / London / Warner Bros. MU-84/2	***Informations-Schallplatte: Liste Januar 1966 / II*** Preview disc containing shortened versions of 'Mother Nature, Father Time' and 'You're Mine (And I Love You)' *Other tracks by the Mamas & Papas, Nancy Sinatra, P.F. Sloan, We Five, Paul & Barry Ryan, the Knickerbockers, Leroy Van Dyke and José Feliciano.*	1/1966

Atlantic ATL-60032	**Most Beautiful Soul Ballads** [2-LP] Rainy Night In Georgia *Other tracks by Arthur Conley, Sam & Dave, Percy Sledge, Carla Thomas & Otis Redding, Clarence Carter, Don Covay, R.B. Greaves, Aretha Franklin, Solomon Burke, Otis Redding, Wilson Pickett and Joe Tex.*	1972
Midi MID-20030	**That's Soul 2** Shoes *(with the Dixie Flyers)* *Other tracks by Aretha Franklin, the Persuaders, Otis Redding, King Curtis, Clarence Carter, Wilson Pickett, Roberta Flack & Donny Hathaway, the Beginning of The End, the Drifters, Sam & Dave and King Floyd.*	1973
Midi MID-60015	**Gospel Story** [2-LP] Precious Lord *Other tracks by Sandra Williams, Myrna Summers, Mighty Clouds Of Harmony, Walter Arties, Jimmy (James) Ellis, Harmonizing Four, Alfred Bolden, Marion Williams, Little Richard and Gloria Griffin.*	1973
Arcade, unk cat no	**Soul Power** Shoes *(with the Dixie Flyers)* *Other tracks by King Curtis, Wilson Pickett, Sam & Dave, Otis Redding, Clarence Carter and Arthur Conley.*	1976
Mercury 6498 045	**Rock! Rock! Rock'n'Roll! Rhythm & Blues Party** Pledging My Love *Other tracks by Huey 'Piano' Smith, Louis Jordan, Ruth Brown, Clyde McPhatter, the Platters, Little Richard, Jerry Butler, Fats Domino and Chuck Jackson.*	1980
Atlantic 781911-1	**The Golden Age Of Black Music 1960-1970** Rainy Night In Georgia *Other tracks by Ben E. King, Percy Sledge, Aretha Franklin, Arthur Conley, Sam & Dave, Otis Redding, Clarence Carter and Tyrone Davis.*	1988
Bellaphon 250-31-022	**I Can't Stop Loving You – Oldies zum Kuscheln** Endlessly *Other tracks by Percy Sledge, Ben E. King, Alan Sorrenti, Alain Barrière, Skeeter Davis, Johnnie Ray, Lobo, Fausto Leali, Pat Boone, Don Gibson and others.*	1991

Tapes

CASSETTE TAPES

BROOK BENTON

Master MA-00920983	**20 Greatest Hits** TVP and 1950s demo recordings.	197?

VARIOUS ARTISTS

Mercury 7133 045	**Rock! Rock! Rock'n'Roll! Rhythm & Blues Party** No details.	1980

GREECE

45s

DINAH WASHINGTON & BROOK BENTON*
BROOK BENTON & DINAH WASHINGTON**
Mercury 3046   Baby, You've Got What It Takes* / I Do**   1960

BROOK BENTON
RCA Victor 47G-1164   Mother Nature, Father Time / You're Mine (And I Love You)   1965

BROOK BENTON (with COLD GRITS)*
BROOK BENTON**
Atlantic 2019.002   Rainy Night In Georgia* / Touch 'Em With Love**   1970

HONG KONG

45s

BROOK BENTON
Mercury HK-388X   Kiddio / So Many Ways   1960

INDIA

78s

BROOK BENTON
Mercury AMT.1068   So Many Ways / I Want You Forever   1959

IRAN

EPs

VARIOUS ARTISTS
4 Top EX-4008   ***West Side Story***   1962
                      Walk On The Wild Side
                      Other tracks by Elmer Bernstein.

IRELAND

RCA ERC-1044 (Ireland, 1957)

78s

BROOK BENTON

RCA ERC-1044	A Million Miles From Nowhere / Devoted	1957

ISRAEL

Mercury 45-90 (Israel, 1959)

45s

BROOK BENTON

Mercury 45-90 [Hed-Arzi]	It's Just A Matter Of Time / Hurtin' Inside	1959

LPs

VARIOUS ARTISTS

RCA Victor LPM-2740	***The Great Singles Now On LP!***	196?

A Million Miles From Nowhere
Other tracks by Neil Sedaka, Don Gibson, Dave 'Baby' Cortez, Ray Peterson, Della Reese, the Isley Brothers, Mickey & Sylvia, Joe Valino, Floyd Robinson, Floyd Cramer, Kay Starr and Boots Brown.

Mercury AN-64-29	***Galaxy***	1961

Same as US LP Mercury SRD-9, *Galaxy Music From 16 Great Artists.*

Mercury AN-64-52	***Surprise Party Sunshine***	1961

Same as US LP Mercury SRD2-13, *Galaxy 30.*

Mercury AN-64-63	***Chart Winners***	1962

Same as US LP Mercury MG-20651, *Chart Winners.*

Mercury AN-66-53	***Surprise Party With The Stars***	1962

Same as US LP Mercury MG-20687, *Twist With The Stars.*

ITALY

45s

BROOK BENTON

Mercury 127 013 MCF	Walk On The Wild Side / Somewhere In The Used To Be	1962
	(Dalla colonna sonora orig. del film 'Anime Sporche')	
Mercury 127 092 MCF	I Got What I Wanted / Dearer Than Life	1963

BROOK BENTON (with COLD GRITS)

Atlantic ATL-NP 03154	Rainy Night In Georgia / Where Do I Go From Here?	1969
Atlantic ATL-NP 03161	My Way / A Little Bit Of Soap	1970

BROOK BENTON

Polydor 2095 133	I Cried For You / Love me A Little *(picture sleeve)*	1979

EPs

BROOK BENTON

Mercury 60184	***It's Just A Matter Of Time***	196?

It's Just A Matter Of Time / Hurtin' Inside / Endlessly / So Close

Mercury 60212	***Thank You Pretty Baby***	196?

So Many Ways / Thank You Pretty Baby / With All Of My Heart / I Want You Forever

VARIOUS ARTISTS

RCA Italiana A72V-0231	***Teddy Randazzo n.1 –***	1957
	Dalla colonna sonora del film 'Mister Rock'n'Roll'	

Your Love Alone
Other tracks by Teddy Randazzo.

RCA Italiana A72V-0232   **Teddy Randazzo n.2 –**   1957
Dalla colonna sonora del film 'Mister Rock'n'Roll'
If Only I Had Known
Other tracks by Teddy Randazzo.

LPs

VARIOUS ARTISTS

Curcio GSR-13   **La Grande Storia Del Rock No.13**   1981
Love's That Way
Other tracks by Carla Thomas, the Shirelles, Lonnie Mack and Muddy Waters & Otis Spann.

Curcio GSR-43   **La Grande Storia Del Rock No.43**   1981
Revenge / The Boll Weevil Song / It's Just A Matter Of Time / Think Twice / Thank You Pretty Baby / Hotel Happiness / Rainy Night In Georgia [Arrival *(NL)* recordings]
Other tracks by Lonnie Smith.

Curcio GSR-54   **La Grande Storia Del Rock No.54** [Arrival *(NL)* recordings]   1982
A Rockin' Good Way / You've Got What It Takes / So Many Ways / The Same One / Kiddio / Lie To Me / Endlessly
Other tracks are live recordings by Bo Diddley.

Success 2141   **Soul Hits (Volume 1)**   1989
Rainy Night In Georgia / Kiddio
Other tracks by George McCrae, Ben E. King & The Drifters, Percy Sledge, Clarence Carter, the Platters, Tina Turner, Sam & Dave, Ike & Tina Turner and Gladys Knight & The Pips.

Success 2142   **Soul Hits (Volume 2)**   1989
Baby You've Got What It Takes
Other tracks by James Brown, Harold Melvin & The Blue Notes, Sam Cooke, Martha Reeves, George McCrae, Jimmy Ruffin, Sam & Dave, Eddie Floyd and Dobie Gray.

JAMAICA

45s

BROOK BENTON
Mercury 71478X45   Thank You Pretty Baby / With All Of My Heart   1959

JAPAN

45s

BROOK BENTON
Mercury MS-71 [King]   It's Just A Matter Of Time / Hurtin' Inside   1959
Mercury MS-77 [King]   Endlessly / So Close   1959
Mercury MS-84 [King]   Thank You Pretty Baby   1959
(Reverse is 'Broken Hearted Melody' by Sarah Vaughan)
Mercury MS-92 [King]   So Many Ways   1960
(Reverse is 'Unforgettable' by Dinah Washington)
Mercury MS-134 [King]   Think Twice / For My Baby   1961

DINAH WASHINGTON & BROOK BENTON*
BROOK BENTON & DINAH WASHINGTON**
Mercury MS-99 [King]   Baby (You've Got What It Takes)* / I Do**   1960

BROOK BENTON
Philips M-1018 [Mercury] Walk On The Wild Side / Somewhere In The Used To Be   1962

BROOK BENTON (with COLD GRITS)
Atlantic DT-1153   Rainy Night In Georgia / Where Do I Go From Here?   1969

LPs

DINAH WASHINGTON & BROOK BENTON
Mercury SFX-10570   **The Two Of Us**   1960
  [Phonogram]   Same as US LP Mercury SR-60244, *The Two Of Us.*

VARIOUS ARTISTS
Philips SM-7072   **Standard In Rock**   1960s
  [Mercury]   *One side each by Brook Benton and Clyde McPhatter.*

Nippon Gramophone   **Polydor / MGM / Atlantic Hits** [promo only]   1970
PR-5105   Rainy Night In Georgia
                      Other tracks by Orietta Berti, the Mike Curb Congregation,
                      John B. Sebastian (Lovin' Spoonful), Crosby, Stills, Nash &
                      Young, the Rascals and Otis Redding.

Mercury SFX-10609   **The Diamonds vs. Brook Benton – The Rock'n'Roll Collection**   19??
  [Phonogram]   **(Volume 7)**
                      It's Just A Matter Of Time / So Many Ways / Kiddio / Thank You
                      Pretty Baby / Think Twice / Baby (You've Got What It Takes) *(with*
                      Dinah Washington)

CDs

BROOK BENTON
Warner Music Japan   **Today**   2007
WPCR-25245

Warner Music Japan   **Home Style**   2013
WPCR-27696

KOREA

LPs

VARIOUS ARTISTS
Asia THL-70261   **Unknown title**   1969
                      Brook Benton – one song, no details
                      Other tracks by the Teddy Bears, Ben E. King, the Exiters, Marianne
                      Faithfull, Ral Donner, Conway Twitty, Andy Williams, Ray Charles,
                      Bobby Hebb, Brian Hyland, the McCoys and Earl Grant.

K-Tel SKPR-035   **Great Artists, Great Hits**   1991
                      Think Twice / Rainy Night In Georgia / It's Just A Matter Of
                      Time / Hotel Happiness / The Boll Weevil Song / Lie To Me /
                      Kiddio / So Many Ways
                      Other tracks by Timi Yuro.

MEXICO

45s

BROOK BENTON

Polydor 170	Llore Por Ti *(I Cried For You)* [same track both sides] *(promo)*	1980

33⅓ rpm 12" Singles

BROOK BENTON

Polydor 3020	Llore Por Ti *(I Cried For You)* [6:31 version] / Amame Un Poquito *(Love Me A Little)* [5:00 version] [Red vinyl]	1979
Polydor 2141 235	Llore Por Ti *(I Cried For You)* [6:31 version] / Amame Un Poquito *(Love Me A Little)* [5:00 version] [Some copies pressed on green or translucent yellow vinyl]	1979

EPs

VARIOUS ARTISTS

Gamma GX-07.796	***Hits & Soul*** A Mi Mañera *(My Way)* [4:10] Other tracks by Aretha Franklin, Otis Redding and Percy Sledge.	1970

LP

BROOK BENTON

Ariola ML-5066	***The Best Of Brook Benton*** TVP recordings.	1977

NETHERLANDS

45s

BROOK BENTON

Mercury 957 079 [C.N. Roodny]	Endlessly / So Close	1959
Mercury 957 168 [C.N. Roodny]	Kiddio / The Same One	1960
Mercury 127 000 MCF [Philips]	Shadrack / The Lost Penny	1961
Mercury 127 010 MCF [Philips]	Revenge *(Reverse is 'Walk On By' by Leroy Van Dyke)*	6/1962
Mercury 127 013 MCF [Philips]	Walk On The Wild Side / Somewhere In The Used To Be	1962
Mercury 127 014 MCF [Philips]	Walk On The Wild Side / Shadrack	1962
Mercury 127 030 MCF [Philips]	Hit Record / Thanks To The Fool	6/1962
Mercury 127 056 MCF [Philips]	Lie To Me / With The Touch Of Your Hand	10/1962
Mercury 127 077 MCF [Philips]	Hotel Happiness / Still Waters Run Deep	12/1962
Mercury 127 092 MCF [Philips]	I Got What I Wanted / Dearer Than Life	3/1963

Mercury 127 030 MCF (Netherlands, 1962)

Mercury 127 104 MCF (Netherlands, 1963)

Mercury 127 137 MCF (1964)

EP Mercury 126 000 MCE (1961)

Mercury 127 104 MCF [Philips]	My True Confession / Tender Years	1963
Mercury 127 112 MCF [Philips]	Two Tickets To Paradise / Don't Hate Me	1963
Mercury 127 128 MCF [Philips]	Going, Going, Gone / After Midnight	1963
Mercury 127 137 MCF [Philips]	Another Cup Of Coffee / Too Late To Turn Back Now	5/1964
Mercury 127 157 MCF [Philips]	Lumberjack / Don't Do What I Did (Do What I Say)	1964
Mercury 127 174 MCF [Philips]	Do It Right / Please, Please Make It Easy	1964
Mercury 127 205 MCF [Philips]	Love Me Now / A-Sleepin' At The Foot Of The Bed	1965

DINAH WASHINGTON & BROOK BENTON*
BROOK BENTON & DINAH WASHINGTON**

Mercury 127 444 MCF [Philips]	A Rockin' Good Way (To Mess Around And Fall In Love)* I Do**	1960

347

BROOK BENTON

Mercury Favorieten Expres 129 200 MJF [Philips]	I Got What I Wanted / Dearer Than Life	5/1963
Mercury Favorieten Expres 129 202 MJF [Philips]	Tender Years / My True Confession	8/1963
Mercury Favorieten Expres 129 205 MJF [Philips]	Two Tickets To Paradise / Don't Hate Me	1963
Mercury Favorieten Expres 129 209 MJF [Philips]	Going Going Gone / After Midnight	1964
Mercury Favorieten Expres 129 212 MJF [Philips]	Another Cup Of Coffee / Too Late to Turn Back Now	6/1964
Mercury Favorieten Expres 129 218 MJF [Philips]	A House Is Not A Home / Come On Back	1964

BROOK BENTON (with COLD GRITS)

Atlantic 44057	Rainy Night In Georgia / Where Do I Go From Here?	1970

Reissue 45s

BROOK BENTON

RCA Victor OLD-25014	A Million Miles From Nowhere / Moon River	19??

EPs

BROOK BENTON

Mercury 126 000 MCE	**Shadrack** Shadrack / I'm In The Mood For Love / Revenge / Careless Love	1961
Mercury 126 082 MCE	**4 Slow Rocks** Lie To Me / Hotel Happiness / Send For Me / Take Good Care Of Her	1962
Mercury 126 091 MCE	**Unknown title** Still Waters Run Deep / Hotel Happiness / I Got What I Wanted / Dearer Than Life	1963
Mercury 126 199 MCE	**Born To Sing The Blues** Born To Sing The Blues / Since I Met You Baby / I'll Never Be Free / I Worry 'Bout You	1964
Mercury 126 211 MCE	**I Don't Hurt Anymore** Lie To Me / Hotel Happiness / Tomorrow Night / I Don't Hurt Anymore	1965

VARIOUS ARTISTS

Mercury 126 022 MCE	**Twist With The Stars** Hurtin' Inside *Other tracks by Patti Page, Clyde McPhatter and Johnny Preston.*	1961

LPs

BROOK BENTON

Mercury 125 002 MCL *(mono)* 135 002 MCY *(stereo)*	*Songs I Love To Sing*	1960
Mercury 125 029 MCL *(mono)* 135 029 MCY *(stereo)*	*It's Just A Matter Of Time*	1960

DINAH WASHINGTON & BROOK BENTON

Mercury 125 070 MCL *(mono)* 135 070 MCY *(stereo)*	*The Two Of Us*	1960

BROOK BENTON

Mercury 125 132 MCL *(mono)* 135 132 MCY *(stereo)*	*Golden Hits*	1961
Mercury 125 202 MCL *(mono)* 135 202 MCY *(stereo)*	*Lie To Me – Brook Benton Singing The Blues*	1962
Mercury 125 303 MCL *(mono)* 135 303 MCY *(stereo)*	*Golden Hits (Volume 2)*	1963
Mercury 125 305 MCL *(mono)* 135 305 MCY *(stereo)*	*The Boll Weevil Song and 11 Other Great Hits*	1963
Mercury 125 919 MCL *(mono)* 135 919 MCY *(stereo)*	*Born To Sing The Blues*	1964
Mercury 125 936 MCL *(mono)* 135 936 MCY *(stereo)*	*On The Countryside*	1964
Mercury 125 952 MCL *(mono)* 135 952 MCY *(stereo)*	*This Bitter Earth*	1964
Philips International 856 304 YPY	*Greatest Hits* Mercury recordings.	1967

DINAH WASHINGTON & BROOK BENTON

Philips International 856 306-YPY	*The Two Of Us*	1967

BROOK BENTON

Fontana International 858 008 FPY *(stereo)*	*My True Confession* Mercury recordings.	1967
Fontana International 858 041 FPY *(stereo)*	*Send For Me* Mercury recordings.	1967

Mercury International 134 522 MFY	*It's Just A Matter Of Time*	1970
Mercury International 134 532 MFY	*Endlessly*	1970
Mercury International 134 538 MFY	*Songs I Love To Sing*	1970
Mercury International 134 619 MFY	*Portraits In Blues (Born To Sing The Blues)*	1970

DINAH WASHINGTON & BROOK BENTON

Mercury International 134 636 MFY	*The Two Of Us*	1970

BROOK BENTON

Fontana Special 6430 042	*The Best Of Brook Benton*	1972
Fontana Special 6430 057	*Songs I Love To Sing*	1972
Fontana Special 6430 058	*It's Just A Matter Of Time*	1972
Fontana Special 6430 059	*Lie To Me – Brook Benton Singing The Blues*	1972

DINAH WASHINGTON & BROOK BENTON

Fontana Special 6430 116	*Remember (The Two Of Us)*	1973
Fontana International 9279 114 ST	*The Two Of Us*	1973

BROOK BENTON

RCA International NL-43513	*Sings Standards*	1981

Arrival AN-8141 [Imperial]	*A Touch Of Brook Benton* [re-recordings of hits] Thank You Pretty Baby / Baby (You've Got What It Takes) / A Rainy Night In Georgia / Hotel Happiness / The Same One / A Rockin' Good Way (To Mess Around And Fall In Love) / Endlessly / Revenge / The Boll Weevil Song / It's Just A Matter Of Time / Kiddio / Lie To Me / Think Twice / So Many Ways	1982

DINAH WASHINGTON & BROOK BENTON

Mercury 6463 181	*Music For The Millions – The Two Of Us*	1982

VARIOUS ARTISTS

Mercury International 134 543 MFY *(stereo)*	*After Midnight* No details.	1970

CDs

BROOK BENTON

ELAP Music 50163562	***Greatest Hits*** 1982 Arrival recordings.	2001
Hallmark 709702	***It's Just A Matter Of Time*** Reissue of Brook's first Mercury album.	2010

Tapes

CASSETTE TAPES

DINAH WASHINGTON & BROOK BENTON

Mercury 7145 181	***Music For The Millions – The Two Of Us***	197?

BROOK BENTON

Arrival AN-8142 [Imperial]	***A Touch Of Brook Benton*** [re-recordings of hits] Same as LP Arrival AN-8141.	1982
Unknown label + cat no	***16 Lovin' Memories*** A Rainy Night In Georgia / Hotel Happiness / It's Just A Matter Of Time / Lie To Me / Thank You Pretty Baby / Shadrack / Fools Rush In / Keep Me In Mind / The Boll Weevil Song / Kiddio / Think Twice / Revenge / Frankie And Johnny / My True Confession / It's Just A House Without You / Ain't It Good	1989

Bootlegs

LPs

Demand DMSLP-090	***Rock And Roll That Rhythm*** RCA, Epic, Mercury and Crown recordings. Includes 'Don't Put It Off' [Crown] and 'Yaba-Daba-Do' *(with Damita Jo)* [Mercury]	198?

NEW ZEALAND

45s

BROOK BENTON

Mercury 71443	Endlessly / So Close	1959
Mercury 71478	With All Of My Heart / Thank You Pretty Baby	1959
Mercury 71512	So Many Ways / I Want You Forever	1959
Mercury S45-4330 [Pye]	It's Just A Matter Of Time / Hurtin' Inside	1959

DINAH WASHINGTON & BROOK BENTON*
BROOK BENTON & DINAH WASHINGTON**

Mercury 71565	Baby (You've Got What It Takes)* / I Do**	1960

BROOK BENTON

Mercury 71566	The Ties That Bind / Hither And Thither And Yon	1960

DINAH WASHINGTON & BROOK BENTON*
BROOK BENTON & DINAH WASHINGTON**

Mercury 71629	A Rockin' Good Way (To Mess Around And Fall In Love)* / I Believe**	1960

Mercury 71478 (New Zealand, 1959)

Mercury 71566 (New Zealand, 1960)

Mercury 71629 (New Zealand, 1960)

Reprise RO.611 (New Zealand, 1967)

BROOK BENTON

Mercury 71652	Kiddio / The Same One	1960
Mercury 71722	Fools Rush In / Someday You'll Want Me To Want You	1960
Mercury SS-10009	So Many Ways *(stereo)* / I Want You Forever *(stereo)*	1960
Mercury 71820	The Boll Weevil Song / Your Eyes	1961
Mercury 71859	Frankie And Johnny / It's Just A House Without You	1961
Mercury 71903	Revenge / Really, Really	1962
Mercury 71912	Shadrack / The Lost Penny	1962
Mercury 71925	Walk On The Wild Side / Somewhere In The Used To Be	1962
Mercury 127 030 MCF	Hit Record / Thanks To The Fool	1962
Mercury 127 062 MCF	Lie To Me / The Touch Of Your Hand	1962
Mercury 127 077 MCF	Hotel Happiness / Still Waters Run Deep	1962
Mercury 72099	Dearer Than Life / I Got What I Wanted	1963
Reprise RO.611 [HMV]	Laura (Tell Me What He's Got That I Ain't Got) / You're The Reason I'm Living	1967

BROOK BENTON WITH THE DIXIE FLYERS

Atlantic ATL-51	Shoes / Let Me Fix It	1970

NORWAY

78s

BROOK BENTON
Mercury AMT-1014   It's Just A Matter Of Time / Hurtin' Inside   1959

Mercury MNS-3051 (Norway 1959)   Philips 320 140 BF (Norway, 1962)

45s

BROOK BENTON

Mercury 45-AMT-1014	It's Just A Matter Of Time / Hurtin' Inside	1959
Mercury MNS-3051	Endlessly / So Close	1959
Mercury MNS-3055	Thank You Pretty Baby / With All Of My Heart	1959

DINAH WASHINGTON & BROOK BENTON*
BROOK BENTON & DINAH WASHINGTON**

Mercury MNS-3072	Baby (You've Got What It Takes)* / I Do**	1960

BROOK BENTON

Mercury 71652X45	Kiddio / The Same One	1960
Mercury 71774	Think Twice / For My Baby	1961
Mercury 71820	The Boll Weevil Song / Your Eyes	1961
Philips 320 102 BF	Frankie And Johnny / It's Just A House Without You	1961
Philips 320 137 BF	Revenge / Really, Really	1961
Philips 320 140 BF	Shadrack / The Lost Penny	1962
Mercury 127 013 MCF	Walk On The Wild Side / Somewhere In The Used To Be	1962
Mercury 127 030 MCF	Hit Record / Thanks To The Fool	1962
Mercury 127 077 MCF	Hotel Happiness / Still Waters Run Deep	1962
Mercury 127 082 MCF	Dearer Than Life / I Got What I Wanted *(picture sleeve)*	1963
Mercury 127 104 MCF	My True Confession / Tender Years *(picture sleeve)*	1963
Mercury 127 128 MCF	Going Going Gone / After Midnight	1964
Mercury 127 157 MCF	Lumberjack / Don't Do What I Did (Do What I Say) *(picture sleeve)*	1964

PHILIPPINES

Mercury 71629 (Philippines, 1960)   Mercury 71820 (Philippines, 1961)

78s

BROOK BENTON

Mercury 71394	It's Just A Matter Of Time / Hurtin' Inside	1959
Mercury 71443	Endlessly / So Close	1959
Mercury 71478	Thank You Pretty Baby / With All Of My Heart	1959

DINAH WASHINGTON & BROOK BENTON*
BROOK BENTON & DINAH WASHINGTON**

Mercury 71629	A Rockin' Good Way (To Mess Around And Fall In Love)* / I Believe**	1960

BROOK BENTON

Mercury 71820	The Boll Weevil Song / Your Eyes	1961

PORTUGAL

45s

BROOK BENTON (with COLD GRITS)

Atlantic N-28-89	Rainy Night In Georgia / Where Do I Go From Here?	1969

PERU

45s

BROOK BENTON

FTA GF-501 [RCA]	Hacer El Amor Es Bueno Para Ti *(Makin' Love Is Good For You)* / Interminablemente *(Endlessly)* [Olde World recordings]	1978

RUSSIA

LPs

VARIOUS ARTISTS
Champion 108   ***Anthology of American Music: Pop & Rock & Roll***   1992
So Many Ways
Other tracks by the Crests, the Platters, Little Richard, Fats Domino, Little Anthony & The Imperials, Mickey & Sylvia, the Willows, Jimmie Rodgers, the Moonglows and Duane Eddy.

SOUTH AFRICA

78s

BROOK BENTON
Mercury MER-2039   Kiddio / The Same One   1960

Mercury MRC-1013 (South Africa, 1962)

45s

BROOK BENTON

Philips SSP-979	Call Me / Because Of Everything	1960
Mercury MRC-1010	Lie To Me / The Touch Of Your Hand	1962
Mercury MRC-1013	Still Waters Run Deep / Hotel Happiness	1962
Mercury MRC-1082	This Bitter Earth / Endlessly	1964
Mercury MRC-1098	Looking Back / So Many Ways	4/1967
Reprise R21.060	Laura / You're The Reason I'm Living	1967
Reprise R21.067	The Glory Of Love / Here We Go Again	1967
Brotherhood RTS-201	Kiddio / Lie To Me [TVP recordings]	1977

LPs

BROOK BENTON
Mercury SR-9013   ***It's Just A Matter Of Time***   1961

Mercury SR-9033	*Lie To Me – Brook Benton Singing The Blues*	1962
Mercury SR-9037	*Golden Hits (Volume 2)*	1963
Mercury SR-9038	*Golden Hits*	1963
Mercury MG-2018	*A Lovely Way To Spend An Evening*	1963
Mercury MG-2028	*Born To Sing The Blues*	1964
Mercury MG-2056	*Best Ballads Of Brodway*	1967
Mercury STAR-716	*Lie To Me – Brook Benton Singing The Blues*	1968
Mercury STAR-1015	*Golden Hits*	1970
Fontana Special BP-1005	*Brook Benton (The Boll Weevil Song)* Same as UK LP Fontana Special SFL-13164, *The Boll Weevil Song and Other Great Hits.*	1970
Atlantic ATC-9186	*Nothing Can Take The Place Of You*	1970
Atlantic ATL-1016	*Home Style*	1971
Atlantic ATL-1017	*Story Teller*	1972
Atlantic ATL-1024	*Today*	1972
Atlantic ATL-4022	*The Soul Of Brook Benton*	1978
Atlantic-Cotillion ATC-9320	*The Gospel Truth* Same as US LP Cotillion SD-058, *The Gospel Truth.*	1980
Atlantic ATL-1074	*Brook Benton In South Africa*	1982
Spinna SPIN(V)-3330	*Better Times* Olde World recordings. Includes the very rare 'Old Fashioned Strut'.	1984
Mercury SUL-3015	*16 Greatest Love Songs*	1986

VARIOUS ARTISTS

Stax, unknown cat no	*Stax Is Soul* [2-LP] Brook Benton – one song, no details *Other tracks by the Staple Singers, Mel & Tim, William Bell, Albert King, the Bar Kays, Rufus Thomas and others.*	1975

Tapes

CASSETTE TAPES

BROOK BENTON

Mercury MCSTAR-716	*Lie To Me – Brook Benton Singing The Blues*	1981
Atlantic ZAT-1074	*Brook Benton In South Africa*	1982
Spinna L4-SPIN (EV)-3330	*Better Times* Olde World recordings. Includes the very rare 'Old Fashioned Strut'.	1984

SPAIN

Atlantic H-580 (Spain, 1969)

45s

BROOK BENTON (with COLD GRITS)

Atlantic H-580	Noche De Lluvia En Georgua *(Rainy Night In Georgia)* / Lo Haremos *(We're Gonna Make It)* (picture sleeve)	1969

EPs

BROOK BENTON

Mercury 126 006 MCE	***Brook Benton*** Honey Babe / Frankie And Johnny / Child Of The Engineer / The Intoxicated Rat	1962
Mercury 126 052 MCE	***Brook Benton*** When I Grow Too Old To Dream / I Love Paris / I Don't Know (I Just Do) / Blues In The Night	1962
Mercury 126 132 MCE	***Brook Benton y el Blues*** My True Confession / Send For Me / Will You Love Me Tomorrow / Got You On My Mind	1963

VARIOUS ARTISTS

Mercury MG-10.091	***Where*** Hurtin' Inside / Endlessly *Other tracks by the Platters.*	1959
Mercury MG-10.092	***Cuatro Estrellas*** So Many Ways *Other tracks by the Gaylords, David Carroll and Sarah Vaughan.*	1959
Mercury MG-10.098	***Lluvia de Estrellas*** Baby (You've Got What It Takes) *(with Dinah Washington)* *Other tracks by Sarah Vaughan and the Modernaires.*	1959
Mercury MG-10.157	***Unknown title*** Thank You Pretty Baby / Hither And Thither And Yon *Other tracks by Johnny Preston.*	1960

Mercury 126 015 MCE	***Exitos***	1962
	Walk On The Wild Side	
	Other tracks by Clyde McPhatter, Leroy Van Dyke and Claude Gray.	
Mercury 126 115 MCE	***Desfile de Exitos***	1963
	Hotel Happiness	
	Other tracks by Lesley Gore, Johnny Preston and Margie Singleton.	
El Torro ET-15.009	***Unknown title*** [33⅓ rpm]	
	I Wanna Do Everything For You / Hurtin' Inside / You're For Me.	
	Other tracks by Clyde McPhatter, the Del Vikings and the Diamonds.	

LPs

VARIOUS ARTISTS

Mercury 125 305 MCL	***Ritmo de Juventud***	1962
	Revenge / Somewhere In The Used To Be	
	Other tracks by unknown artists.	
Sarpe SGAE-GER-17	***Las Grandes Estrellas del Rock***	1982
[Iberofón]	Same as Italian LP Curcio GSR-54, *La Grande Storia del Rock*	
	No.54 (1981). Features Brook Benton and Bo Diddley.	

CDs

BROOK BENTON

El Toro ETCD-1050	***Brook Benton – The Singer***	2012
	25 Okeh, Epic, Vik and Mercury recordings 1954-61.	

VARIOUS ARTISTS

El Toro ETCD-1051	***Brook Benton – The Songwriter***	2012
	25 songs by Brook Benton, Clyde McPhatter, Ivory Joe	
	Hunter, Priscilla Bowman, Teddy Randazzo, the Five Keys,	
	Elvis Presley, Billy Barnes, Ernestine Anderson, Ruth Brown,	
	Jay B. Lloyd, the Diamonds, the Del Vikings, Wade Flemons,	
	LaVern Baker, Louis Jordan, Sonny Wilson, Johnny Oliver	
	and Bobby 'Blue' Bland.	

SWEDEN

45s

BROOK BENTON

Mercury B 45-814	It's Just A Matter Of Time / Hurtin' Inside	1959
Mercury 71962	Hit Record / Thanks To The Fool	1962
Mercury 127 056 MCF	Lie To Me / With The Touch Of Your Hand	1962

BROOK BENTON (with COLD GRITS)

Atlantic ATL 70.420	Rainy Night In Georgia / Where Do I Go From Here?	1970
[Metronome]	*(picture sleeve)*	

BROOK BENTON WITH THE DIXIE FLYERS

Atlantic ATL 70.469	Shoes / Let Me Fix It	1970
[Metronome]	*(picture sleeve)*	

Mercury B 45-814 (Sweden, 1959)   Mercury 127 056 MCF (Sweden, 1962)

EPs

BROOK BENTON
Mercury EP 60.148   ***The Caressing Voice Of Brook Benton***   1959
Endlessly / So Close / It's Just A Matter Of Time / Hurtin' Inside

TAIWAN

10" LPs

VARIOUS ARTISTS
Universal UHM No.32   ***Unknown title***   1963
Revenge
Other tracks by Dion, Fats Domino, Ferrante & Teicher, the
Shirelles, Chubby Checker, Sandra Dee, Connie Francis, the
Highwaymen and the Tokens.

Universal UHM No.57   ***Unknown title***   1964
My True Confession
Other tracks by Elvis Presley, Jan And Dean, the Surfaris,
the Orlons, Ray Stevens, Lonnie Mack, Johnny Cash, Doris
Troy, Marvin Gaye, Bobby Bare and Stevie Wonder.

Universal UHM No.213   ***Unknown title***   1969
Hotel Happiness
Other tracks by Little Eva, Elvis Presley, Marcie Blaine, the
4 Seasons, Joanie Sommers, Ned Miller, Duane Eddy, Vikki
Carr, the Cookies, the Highwaymen and Guy Mitchell.

Queen Q-NL-8524   ***Unknown title***   196?
Lie To Me
Other tracks by Brenda Lee, Les Paul & Mary Ford, Joey Dee,
Sammy Davis, Chubby Checker, the Crystals, Brian Hyland,
Rex Allen and Frank Ifield.

12" LPs

BROOK BENTON
Large World LW-434   ***Rainy Night In Georgia***   1970
                                          Same as US LP Cotillion SD-9018, *Today.*

VARIOUS ARTISTS
Mercury HS-131   ***14 More Newies But Goodies***   1960?
                                          It's Just A Matter Of Time, Baby / You Got What It Takes *(with*
                                          Dinah Washington)
                                          Other tracks by Johnny Preston, the Platters, Sarah Vaughan,
                                          Rusty Draper, Elton Anderson, George Jones, Jivin' Gene, Nick
                                          Adams, Dinah Washington, Sil Austin and Ernestine Anderson.
                                          Same as US Mercury SR-60241, *14 More Newies But Goodies*

THAILAND

45s

BROOK BENTON (with COLD GRITS)
Atlantic 44072   My Way / A Little Bit Of Soap   1970

TURKEY

45s

BROOK BENTON
Reprise 68.703   The Glory Of Love / Weakness In A Man   1967

BROOK BENTON (with COLD GRITS)
Atlantic 70502   My Way / We're Gonna Make It   1970

URUGUAY

LP

RCA Victor LPM-3514   ***Ese Viejo Sentimiento*** *(That Old Feeling)*   1965
                                          Same as US LP RCA Victor LPM-3514, *That Old Feeling.*

YUGOSLAVIA

LPs

BROOK BENTON
Radio-Televizija Beograd   ***Mister Bartender***   1976
RTB-5614   Same as UK LP All Platinum Phonogram 9109 303 DE LUX,
                                          Mister Bartender.

Radio-Televizija Beograd	**Lie To Me – Brook Benton Singing The Blues**	197?
RTB-5818	Same as US LP Mercury SR 60740, *Lie To Me – Brook Benton Singing The Blues.*	

VARIOUS ARTISTS

Atlantic	**Most Beautiful Soul Ballads** [2-LP]	1972
SUZY ATL-60032	Rainy Night In Georgia	
	Other tracks by Arthur Conley, Sam & Dave, Percy Sledge, Carla Thomas & Otis Redding, Clarence Carter, Don Covay, R.B. Greaves, Aretha Franklin, Solomon Burke, Otis Redding, Wilson Pickett and Joe Tex.	

APPENDIX I

Unissued & Rejected Titles

BILL LANDFORD QUARTET
1953
E3-VB-0646	I Heard Zion Moan	RCA, unissued
E3-VB-0649	I Heard The Preaching Of The Elders	RCA, unissued
E3-VB-0650	Made Up In My Mind	RCA, unissued
E3-VB-0651	Goin' Home	RCA, unissued

THE SANDMEN
1954
CO 52774	I Could Have Told You	OKeh, unissued

LINCOLN CHASE & THE SANDMEN
1955
CO 52940	I'm Sure	Columbia, unissued
CO 52942	The Things That Money Can't Buy	Columbia, unissued

BROOK BENTON & THE SANDMEN
1955
CO 53418	I Was Fool Enough To Love You	OKeh, unissued

BROOK BENTON
1955
11971	Hold My Hand	Mercury, unissued
11974	I Want You Forever	Mercury, unissued
11979	Tell Me The Truth	Mercury, unissued

1959
18700	Hold My Hand	Mercury, rejected
19562	The Same One	Mercury, rejected
19563	Nothing In The World	Mercury, unissued *(test pressing made)*

1960
19849	It's Too Late To Turn Back Now	Mercury, unissued
19904	God Bless The Child	Mercury, unissued
19905	That's The Beginning Of The End	Mercury, unissued
20400	They Can't Take That Away From Me	Mercury, rejected
20406	If You Are But A Dream	Mercury, rejected
20407	It's Been A Long, Long Time	Mercury, rejected
20408	Oh! What It Seemed To Be	Mercury, rejected
20409	Lover Come Back To Me	Mercury, rejected
20410	Why Try To Change Me Now?	Mercury, rejected
20424	The Boll Weevil Song	Mercury, unissued

1961

20749	Everytime I Feel The Spirit	Mercury, unissued
20755	A City Called Heaven	Mercury, unissued
20777	Fantastic Things	Mercury, unissued
20778	If You Have No Real Objections	Mercury, unissued *(test pressing made)*
20779	That's All I'm Living For	Mercury, unissued
20780	Come Back My Love	Mercury, unissued

1962

23963	Tenderly	Mercury, unissued
23964	My Foolish Heart	Mercury, unissued
24313	Our Hearts Knew	Mercury, unissued *(test pressing made)*
24321	It's All Right	Mercury 72009 *(not released)*
25276	I Need You So	Mercury, unissued
25281	Please Send Me Someone To Love	Mercury, unissued

1963

27007	These Hands	Mercury, unissued
27008	My Foolish Heart	Mercury, rejected
27009	I'll Always Be In Love With You	Mercury, rejected
1-29148	Crack Up Time	Mercury, unissued
2-29150	I'll Always Love You	Mercury, unissued *(test pressing made)*
1-29152	A Man Of Steel	Mercury, unissued
2-29225	You're All I Want For Always	Mercury, unissued
29310	You're All I Want For Christmas [1 voice]	Mercury, unissued
29311	You're All I Want For Christmas [2 voices]	Mercury, unissued *(test pressing made)*
29313	You're All I Want For Christmas [2 voices]	Mercury unissued
1-29340	Yaba-Daba-Do	Mercury 72196 *(promo only – withdrawn)*
1-29342	Almost Persuaded	Mercury 72196 *(promo only – withdrawn)*

1964

2-31073	Unclaimed Heart	Mercury, unissued
1-32147	On My Word	Mercury, unissued *(test pressing made)*
1-32149	I'm A Man	Mercury, unissued
1-32150	Where There's A Will (There's A Way)	Mercury, unissued
1-32182	On My Word	Mercury, unissued
1-32184	Buttermilk Sky	Mercury, unissued
1-32185	The Next Time I Fall In Love	Mercury, unissued

1965

1-34821	One Day I'll Dry Your Tears	Mercury, unissued
1-34823	One More Time	Mercury, unissued
1-34856	A Lifetime Lease On Your Heart	Mercury, unissued *(test pressing made)*
1-34857	My Only Year Book	Mercury, unissued
1-34858	A Million Miles	Mercury, unissued
1-34960	My One And Only Year Book	Mercury, unissued
1-36087	I Will Warm Your Heart [long version]	Mercury, unissued
1-36090	I Will Warm Your Heart [short version]	Mercury, unissued
1-36780	Chains Of Love	Mercury (remake), unissued
1-36781	Valley Of Tears	Mercury (remake), unissued
SPA1-7220	More Time To Be With You	RCA (remake), unissued
SPA1-7221	You're Mine (And I Love You)	RCA (remake), unissued
SPA1-8917	My Son, I Wish You Everything	RCA, unissued

1966

TPA1-3375-8	Where Does A Man Go To Cry	RCA (remake), unissued
TPA1-3376-16	The Roach Song	RCA (remake), unissued
TPA1-5026	When We Were Friends	RCA, unissued
TPA1-5027	Keep Your Cotton Pickin' Hands Off My Gin	RCA, unissued
TPA1-5028	Break Her Heart	RCA, unissued
TPKM-5188	Keep Your Cotton Pickin' Hands Off My Gin	RCA, rejected
TPA3-4691-14	I'm Beginning To See The Light	RCA, unissued
		(UK factory sample exists)
TPA3-4692-12	It's Been A Long, Long Time	RCA, unissued
		(UK factory sample exists)
TPA3-4693-4	There Goes My Heart	RCA, unissued
		(UK factory sample exists)
TPA3-4694-2	Makin' Whoopee	RCA, unissued
		(UK factory sample exists)
TPA3-4695-3	Lover Come Back To Me	RCA, unissued
		(UK factory sample exists)
TPA3-4696-6	There, I've Said It Again	RCA, unissued
		(UK factory sample exists)
TPA3-4697-6	Sweet Georgia Brown	RCA, unissued
		(UK factory sample exists)
TPA3-4698-6	Unforgettable	RCA, unissued
		(UK factory sample exists)
TPA3-4708	Keep Your Cotton Pickin' Hands Off My Gin	RCA, unissued
TPA3-4699-7	Just As Much As Ever	RCA, unissued
		(UK factory sample exists)
TPA3-4700-5	Sentimental Journey	RCA, unissued
		(UK factory sample exists)
TPA3-4701-7	Beyond The Sea (La Mer)	RCA, unissued
		(UK factory sample exists)
TPA3-4702-9	I Only Have Eyes For You	RCA, unissued
		(UK factory sample exists)
TPA1-7581	I Wish An Old Fashioned Christmas To You	RCA, unissued

1967

UPA1-3601	Don't Look For Me	RCA, unissued
UPA1-3603	Bump With A Boom	RCA, unissued

1969

16331	I Still Believe In Rainbows	Cotillion, unissued
16517	What A Wonderful World	Cotillion, unissued
16518	Gee, You Look So Pretty	Cotillion, unissued
18059	The Lonely One	Cotillion, unissued

1970

18728	Old Man Willis	Cotillion, unissued
18735	Before You See A Big Man Cry	Cotillion, unissued
20154	The Way I Love You	Cotillion, unissued
20155	I'll Paint You A Song	Cotillion, unissued
20158	When The Light Goes On Again	Cotillion, unissued
20841	I'm Comin' Home	Cotillion, unissued
20842	Feelin' Good	Cotillion, unissued
20854	If You Think God Is Dead	Cotillion, unissued
20855	Till I Can't Take It No More [Version 1]	Cotillion, unissued
20857	Till I Can't Take It No More [Version 2]	Cotillion, unissued
20859	Our Hearts Knew	Cotillion, unissued
20861	Jam Tune	Cotillion, unissued

1971

22013	He Gives Us All His Love	Cotillion, unissued
22021	Be My Friend	Cotillion, rejected

APPENDIX II

US Picture Sleeve Singles

1960

Mercury 71566	The Ties That Bind / Hither And Thither And Yon
Mercury 71629	A Rockin' Good Way (To Mess Around And Fall In Love) / I Believe *(both sides with Dinah Washington)*
Mercury 71652	Kiddio / The Same One
Mercury 71722	Fools Rush In / Someday You'll Want Me To Want You
Mercury 71730	This Time Of The Year / Merry Christmas, Happy New Year

1961

Mercury 71774	Think Twice / For My Baby
Mercury 71820	The Boll Weevil Song / Your Eyes
Mercury 71859	Frankie And Johnny / It's Just A House Without You
Mercury 71903	Revenge / Really, Really
Mercury 71912	Shadrack / The Lost Penny

1962

Mercury 71925	Walk On The Wild Side / Somewhere In The Used To Be *(Two different designs: one with a photo of Benton, the other with a photo of the stars who appeared in the 'Walk On The Wild Side' movie)*
Mercury 71962	Hit Record / Thanks To The Fool *(Two different designs: one with a photo of Benton wearing a tie, the other of Benton without a tie)*
Mercury 72024	Lie To Me / With The Touch Of Your Hand
Mercury 72055	Hotel Happiness / Still Waters Run Deep

1963

Mercury 72099	I Got What I Wanted / Dearer Than Life (Sweeter Than Honey)
Mercury 72135	My True Confession / Tender Years
Mercury 72177	Two Tickets To Paradise / Don't Hate Me *(Some in colour, some B&W)*
Mercury 72214	You're All I Want For Christmas / This Time Of The Year
Mercury 72230	Going, Going, Gone / After Midnight

1964

Mercury 72266	Another Cup Of Coffee / Too Late To Turn Back Now *(Two different designs: one with a photo of Benton wearing a tie, the other of Benton without a tie)*
Mercury 72303	A House Is Not A Home / Come Back
Mercury 72333	Lumberjack / Don't Do What I Did (Do What I Say)
Mercury 72365	Do It Right / Please, Please Make It Easy

1965

RCA Victor 47-8693	Mother Nature, Father Time / You're Mine (And I Love You)

1988

Mercury 812065-7	*Golden Oldies Volume 70:* Endlessly / Fools Rush In

Mercury 71629 (1960)

Mercury 71774 (1961)

Mercury 71859 (1961)

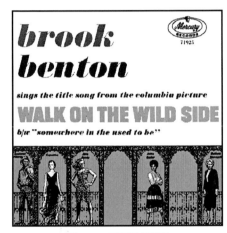

Mercury 71925 (1962)

Mercury 72055 (1962)

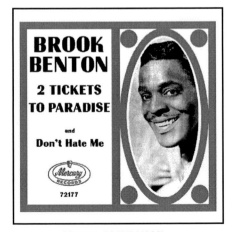

Mercury 72177 (1963)

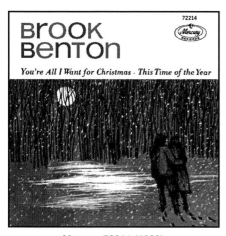

Mercury 72214 (1963)

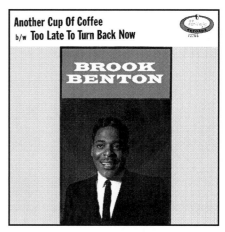

Mercury 72266 (1964)

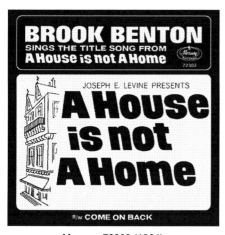

Mercury 72303 (1964)

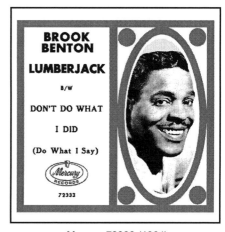

Mercury 72333 (1964)

Mercury 72365 (1964)

RCA Victor 47-8693 (1965)

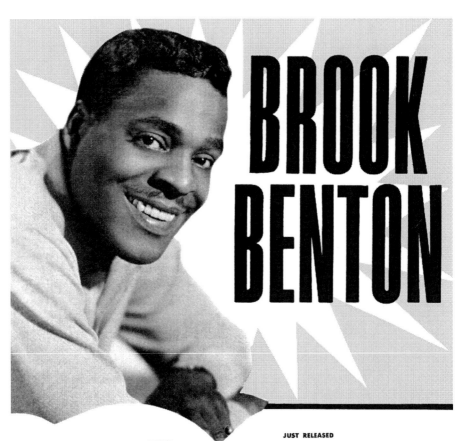

BROOK BENTON

JUST RELEASED

"LIE TO ME"

b/w

"WITH THE TOUCH OF YOUR HAND"

MERCURY 72024

Hit Album

BROOK BENTON, Quincy Jones & Orch.

MERCURY MG 20673

MERCURY hi-fidelity

APPENDIX III

Brook Benton's Hits

BILLBOARD 'HOT 100' POP SINGLES CHART

Date of chart entry	Highest position attained	Time on chart	Title	Label and catalogue number
10 Mar 1958	82	4 wks	A Million Miles From Nowhere	Vik 4X-0311
26 Jan 1959	3	18 wks	It's Just A Matter Of Time	Mercury 71394
23 Feb 1959	78	4 wks	Hurtin' Inside	Mercury 71394
20 Apr 1959	12	13 wks	Endlessly	Mercury 71443
18 May 1959	38	7 wks	So Close	
13 Jul 1959	16	14 wks	Thank You Pretty Baby	Mercury 71478
20 Jul 1959	82	1 wk	With All Of My Heart	
19 Oct 1959	6	16 wks	So Many Ways	Mercury 71512
21 Dec 1959	66	5 wks	This Time Of The Year	Mercury 71554
25 Jan 1960	5	15 wks	Baby (You've Got What It Takes) *(with Dinah Washington)*	Mercury 71565
11 Apr 1960	37	9 wks	The Ties That Bind /	Mercury 71566
18 Apr 1960	58	6 wks	Hither And Thither And Yon	
23 May 1960	7	13 wks	A Rockin' Good Way (To Mess Around And Fall In Love) *(with Dinah Washington)*	Mercury 71629
8 Aug 1960	7	17 wks	Kiddio	Mercury 71652
22 Aug 1960	16	12 wks	The Same One	
14 Nov 1960	24	10 wks	Fools Rush In	Mercury 71722
26 Dec 1960	93	1 wks	Someday You'll Want Me To Want You	
13 Feb 1961	11	12 wks	Think Twice	Mercury 71774
6 Feb 1961	28	8 wks	For My Baby	
15 May 1961	2	16 wks	The Boll Weevil Song	Mercury 71820
21 Aug 1961	20	8 wks	Frankie And Johnny	Mercury 71859
2 Oct 1961	45	5 wks	It's Just A House Without You	
20 Nov 1961	15	10 wks	Revenge	Mercury 71903

Date of chart entry	Highest position attained	Time on chart	Title	Label and catalogue number
13 Jan 1962	19	9 wks	**Shadrack**	Mercury 71912
13 Jan 1962	77	2 wks	**The Lost Penny**	
17 Feb 1962	43	7 wks	**Walk On The Wild Side**	Mercury 71925
5 May 1962	45	8 wks	**Hit Record**	Mercury 71962
25 Aug 1962	13	10 wks	**Lie To Me**	Mercury 72024
24 Nov 1962	3	12 wks	**Hotel Happiness**	Mercury 72055
8 Dec 1962	89	1 wk	**Still Waters Run Deep**	
9 Mar 1963	28	8 wks	**I Got What I Wanted**	Mercury 72099
9 Mar 1963	59	8 wks	**Dearer Than Life**	
15 Jun 1963	22	9 wks	**My True Confession**	Mercury 72135
7 Sep 1963	32	10 wks	**Two Tickets To Paradise**	Mercury 72177
25 Jan 1964	35	7 wks	**Going, Going, Gone**	Mercury 72230
9 May 1964	43	8 wks	**Too Late To Turn Back Now**	Mercury 72266
16 May 1964	47	7 wks	**Another Cup Of Coffee**	
18 Jul 1964	75	7 wks	**A House Is Not A Home**	Mercury 72303
3 Oct 1964	53	7 wks	**Lumberjack**	Mercury 72333
19 Dec 1964	67	4 wks	**Do It Right**	Mercury 72365
3 Jul 1965	100	1 wk	**Love Me Now**	Mercury 72446
13 Nov 1965	53	7 wks	**Mother Nature, Father Time**	RCA Victor 47-8693
19 Aug 1967	78	4 wks	**Laura (What's He Got That I Ain't Got)**	Reprise 0611
26 Oct 1968	99	2 wks	**Do Your Own Thing**	Cotillion 45-44007
5 Jul 1969	74	6 wks	**Nothing Can Take The Place Of You**	Cotillion 45-44034
10 Jan 1970	4	15 wks	**Rainy Night In Georgia**	Cotillion 45-44057
18 Apr 1970	72	6 wks	**My Way**	Cotillion 45-44072
30 May 1970	45	7 wks	**Don't It Make You Want To Go Home** *(with the Dixie Flyers)*	Cotillion 45-44078
26 Dec 1970	67	6 wks	**Shoes** *(with the Dixie Flyers)*	Cotillion 45-44093

Chart compiled by Billboard.
Chart information courtesy of 'Top Pop 1955-1982' by Joel Whitburn
(Record Research Inc, Menomonee Falls, WI) 1983

BILLBOARD 'BUBBLING UNDER THE HOT 100' POP SINGLES CHART

Chart commenced 1 June 1959.

Date of chart entry	Highest position attained	Time on chart	Title	Label and catalogue number
5 May 1962	106	3 wks	**Thanks To The Fool** *(flip of 'Hit Record' - see Hot 100)*	Mercury 71962
18 Aug 1962	120	1 wk	**With The Touch Of Your Hand** *(flip of 'Lie To Me' - see Hot 100)*	Mercury 72024
9 Nov 1963	108	4 wks	**Stop Foolin'** *(with Damita Jo)*	Mercury 72207
16 Nov 1963	111	4 wks	**Baby, You've Got It Made** *(with Damita Jo)*	Mercury 72207
5 Dec 1964	119	1 wk	**Please, Please Make It Easy** *(flip of 'Do It Right' - see Hot 100)*	Mercury 72365
20 Mar 1965	129	1 wk	**The Special Years**	Mercury 72398
5 Mar 1966	122	3 wks	**Only A Girl Like You**	RCA Victor 47-8768
28 May 1966	126	2 wks	**Too Much Good Lovin' (No Good For Me)**	RCA Victor 47-8830
7 Oct 1972	104	4 wks	**If You've Got The Time**	MGM K-14440

Chart compiled by Billboard.
Chart information courtesy of 'Bubbling Under The Hot 100 1959-1981' by Joel Whitburn
(Record Research Inc, Menomonee Falls, WI) 1982

BILLBOARD R&B SINGLES CHART

Top 30 'Hot R&B Singles' chart from 20 October 1958. This was increased to 40 places from 30 January 1965, 50 from 6 August 1966, and 100 from 14 July 1973.

Date of chart entry	Highest position attained	Time on chart	Title	Label and catalogue number
9 Feb 1959	1	15 wks	**It's Just A Matter Of Time**	Mercury 71394
9 Feb 1959	23	3 wks	**Hurtin' Inside**	Mercury 71394
4 May 1959	3	12 wks	**Endlessly**	Mercury 71443
4 May 1959	5	12 wks	**So Close**	Mercury 71443
20 Jul 1959	1	14 wks	**Thank You Pretty Baby**	Mercury 71478
19 Oct 1959	1	17 wks	**So Many Ways**	Mercury 71512
4 Jan 1960	12	2 wks	**This Time Of The Year**	Mercury 71554
25 Jan 1960	1	17 wks	**Baby (You've Got What It Takes)** *(with Dinah Washington)*	Mercury 71565
18 Apr 1960	15	4 wks	**The Ties That Bind**	Mercury 71566

Date of chart entry	Highest position attained	Time on chart	Title	Label and catalogue number
23 May 1960	1	13 wks	**A Rockin' Good Way (To Mess Around And Fall In Love)** *(with Dinah Washington)*	Mercury 71629
22 Aug 1960	1	14 wks	**Kiddio**	Mercury 71652
10 Oct 1960	21	1 wk	**The Same One**	
28 Nov 1960	5	10 wks	**Fools Rush In**	Mercury 71722
20 Feb 1961	2	13 wks	**For My Baby**	Mercury 71774
20 Feb 1961	6	14 wks	**Think Twice**	
29 May 1961	2	12 wks	**The Boll Weevil Song**	Mercury 71820
11 Sep 1961	14	6 wks	**Frankie And Johnny**	Mercury 71859
6 Jan 1962	12	5 wks	**Revenge**	Mercury 71903
2 Jun 1962	19	3 wks	**Hit Record**	Mercury 71962
8 Sep 1962	3	15 wks	**Lie To Me**	Mercury 72024
8 Dec 1962	2	13 wks	**Hotel Happiness**	Mercury 72055
30 Mar 1963	4	8 wks	**I Got What I Wanted**	Mercury 72099
6 Jul 1963	7	10 wks	**My True Confession**	Mercury 72135
5 Oct 1963	15	7 wks	**Two Tickets To Paradise**	Mercury 72177

No R&B charts were published between 30 November 1963 and 30 January 1965. During this period, the following records charted in the Billboard 'Hot 100' and would therefore probably also have been R&B hits: **Going, Going, Gone** [Mercury 72230], **Too Late To Turn Back Now** [Mercury 72266], **Another Cup Of Coffee** [Mercury 72266], **A House Is Not A Home** [Mercury 72303], **Lumberjack** [Mercury 72333] and **Do It Right** [Mercury 72365].

18 Dec 1965	26	5 wks	**Mother Nature, Father Time**	RCA Victor 47-8693
12 Jul 1969	11	8 wks	**Nothing Can Take The Place Of You**	Cotillion 45-44034
17 Jan 1970	1	14 wks	**Rainy Night In Georgia**	Cotillion 45-44057
25 Apr 1970	25	6 wks	**My Way**	Cotillion 45-44072
13 Jun 1970	31	4 wks	**Don't It Make You Want To Go Home** *(with the Dixie Flyers)*	Cotillion 45-44078
26 Dec 1970	18	9 wks	**Shoes** *(with the Dixie Flyers)*	Cotillion 45-44093
7 Jan 1978	49	17 wks	**Makin' Love Is Good For You**	Olde World OWR-1100

Chart compiled by Billboard.
Chart information courtesy of 'Top R&B Singles 1942-1995' by Joel Whitburn
(Record Research Inc, Menomonee Falls, WI) 1996

"Mr. Hit Maker"
BROOK BENTON

New Single Release
"DO IT RIGHT"

Current Album
"THIS BITTER EARTH"

JANUARY - MARCH
Cross Country Tour

Personal Management	Bookings:	Exclusively on
C. B. Atkins	**Associated Booking Corp.**	**MERCURY**
39 West 55th Street		**RECORDS**

BILLBOARD POP ALBUMS CHART

Chart commenced 8 January 1955 as 'Best Selling Popular Albums', fluctuating in size between 15 and 50 positions up until 9 January 1961. Between 9 January and 3 April 1961, approximately 200 albums were listed each week as 'essential inventory' without being ranked. From 3 April 1961, separate charts were published for mono and stereo albums (150 and 50 positions respectively), finally being combined into one 'Top LPs' chart on 17 August 1963.

Date of chart entry	Highest position attained	Time on chart	Title	Label and catalogue number
5 Jun 1961	82	20 wks	*Golden Hits*	Mercury MG-60607
25 Sep 1961	70	13 wks	*The Boll Weevil Song and 11 Other Great Hits*	Mercury SR-60641
17 Feb 1962	77	7 wks	*If You Believe*	Mercury SR-60619
27 Oct 1962	40	15 wks	*Singing The Blues*	Mercury SR-60740
13 Apr 1963	82	6 wks	*Golden Hits (Volume 2)*	Mercury SR-60774
28 Oct 1967	156	4 wks	*Laura, what's he got that I ain't got*	Reprise R-/RRS-6268
19 Jul 1969	189	2 wks	*Do Your Own Thing*	Cotillion SD-9002
21 Feb 1970	27	23 wks	*Today*	Cotillion SD-9018
22 Aug 1970	199	2 wks	*Home Style*	Cotillion SD-9028

Chart compiled by Billboard.
Chart information courtesy of 'Top Pop Albums 1955-1992' by Joel Whitburn
(Record Research Inc, Menomonee Falls, WI) 1993

BILLBOARD SOUL LPs CHART

Chart commenced 30 January 1965 as 'Hot R&B LPs'. Renamed 'Best Selling Soul LPs' from 23 August 1969.

Date of chart entry	Highest position attained	Time on chart	Title	Label and catalogue number
21 Feb 1970	4	21 wks	*Today*	Cotillion SD-9018

Chart compiled by Billboard.
Chart information courtesy of 'Top R&B Albums 1955-1998' by Joel Whitburn
(Record Research Inc, Menomonee Falls, WI) 1999

APPENDIX IV

Brook Benton the Composer

There are three performing rights societies in the USA, BMI, ASCAP and SESAC. Brook Benton's songs were all published by BMI-affiliated music companies. Brook is named as composer or co-composer on all the following titles on the BMI database:

Work Title	BMI Work Number
A Lover's Question – *See* Lover's Question	
A Rockin' Good Way – *See* Rockin' Good Way	
Ain't Givin' Up Nothing	13462
See also I Ain't Givin' Up Nothin'	
Ain't It Good	14096
Ambush	34175
Baby	1940424
Baby I Love You	1912586
Baby Love Me Too	73316
Because You Love Me	97829
Before I Fall In Love Again	100091
Bless Your Heart	123854
Boll Weevil Song	136085
Careless Love	184290
Chariot Wheels	200186
Child Of The Engineer [*alt title:* Engineer's Child]	376130
City Called Heaven	216924
Come On Baby Let's Go	230725
Come On Be Nice	230827
Come On In	231306
Crazy In Love With You	256312
Cross My Heart – *See* Tell (Me) The Truth	
Danger Zone	276157
Deep River	290293
Devoted	298996
Doggone Baby Doggone	314754
Don't Ask Nobody	317078
Don't Call Me I'll Call You	1940426
Don't Walk Away From Me	330438
Doncha' Think It's Time	332699
Endlessly	375657
Engineer's Child – *See* Child Of The Engineer	
Everything	391550
Everything Plus	392299
Everything Will Be Alright	392742
Everytime I Feel The Spirit	393035
Fire	418092
Flat Tire	423812
Flighty	424668
Foolish Enough To Try	430922
For My Baby	433150
Forgot About Me	4542434

Forgotten	437658
Four Thousand Years Ago	439936
Frankie And Johnny	441996
Give And Take	473322
Going Home	488191
Goodbye My Darling	498470
Handshake	1940432
Happy Years	525245
He'll Understand	537824
High School Social	566512
Hold My Hand	574322
Honeybee	581816
How Many Times	594049
Hurtin' Inside	599852
I Ain't Givin' Up Nothin'	601644
See also Ain't Givin' Up Nothing	
I Don't Know	617192
I Got What I Wanted	625805
I Just Dare You	629840
I Just Want To Love You	630756
I'll Meet You After Church Next Sunday	640766
I'll Never Stop Tryin'	642002
I'll Remember Your Name In My Dreams	642516
I'll Step Aside	643225
I'll Stop Anything I'm Doin'	643368
I'll Take Care	643465
I'll Take Care Of You	643471
I'm Coming Back To You	651628
I'm Coming To See You	651843
I Wanna Be With You (Everywhere You Go)	687907
I Wanna Do Everything For You	688190
I Want You Forever	692406
If I Could Cry	701451

If I Could Have Your Love Again	701544
If Only I Had Known	705599
If You But Knew	707454
If You Have No Real Objections	708730
If You Only Knew	709495
If You Think God Is Dead	710258
In A Dream	714651
In Due Time	715857
In The Evening By The Moonlight	719934
Intoxicated Rat, The	729166
It's A Wonder	740069
It's A Worried Man	740127
It's Just A House Without You	744284
It's Just A Matter Of Time	744303
It's So Much Fun	748264
Johnny-O	773938
Just Leave Me Alone	787435
Kiddio	800882
Let Me Fix It	1940423
Lie To Me	865684
Life Is Too Short (For Me To Stop Loving You Now)	867744
Little Ole Girl, Little Ole Boy	882033
Looking Back	902290
Love Me Now	922555
Love Oh Love	923817
Lover's Question	930974
Mark My Word	960754
May I	966700
Mother Nature, Father Time	1014500
My Last Dollar	1035819
My Love With All My Heart	1038498
My Time Will Come	1044130
Ninety-Nine Percent	1068256
No Matter What I Do	1072244
No One To Love Me	1075551
Not One Step Behind	1086316
Nothing	1087509
Nothing In The World (Could Make Me Love You More Than I Do)	1088352
One By One	1118684
One Day I'll Dry Your Tears	1119100
One Love Too Many	1121593
Only Believe	1128056
Our Hearts Knew	1137948
Really, Really	1233860
Remember Remember	1242109
Revenge	1247088
Rockin' Good Way (To Mess Around And Fall In Love)	1263408
Rockin' Piano, Outta Tune Guitar	1263638
Rockin' Years	1263896
Sailor Boy's Love Song	1283204
Same One	1286565
Send Back My Heart	1940428
Sing Your Song	1912585
Sneaky Alligator	1361844
So Close	1363069
Someone To Believe In	1376195
Steal Steal	1407245
Stop Foolin' [*alt. title:* Why Shouldn't We Stop Foolin']	1670891
Substitute	1423627
Take The Hurt Off Of Me	1451950

Tears And Joy	1463200
Tears In My Eyes	1463476
Tell Me Now Or Never	1467714
Tell (Me) The Truth [*alt title:* Cross My Heart]	259206
Tell Me Your Dream	1468810
Thank You Pretty Baby	1476353
That's All I'm Living For	1479356
That's Enough For Me	1479778
That's Love	1480519
This Time Of The Year	1504525
Two Tickets To Paradise	1564325
Unhappy Blues	1573143
Wake Up	1597832
Walkin' Together	1601043
We Can't Believe You're Gone	1614067
What A Kiss Won't Do	1629074
What I Wouldn't Give	1634107
What Is A Woman Without A Man	1634383
Where Do I Go From Here	1654500
Where There's A Will (There's A Way)	1657199
Why Me	1670085
Why Shouldn't We Stop Foolin' – *See* Stop Foolin'	
Will You Tell Him	1676149
With All Of My Heart	1683459
Wrong Number, Right Girl	1698064
You Built A Heaven	1711787
You Can't Get Away From Me	1713502
You Know It Ain't No Sin	1721124
You Precious Thing	1726236
You're For Me	1727775
You're Movin' Me	1729423
You Short-Changed Me	1734092
You've Been Good To Me	1735934
You Went Back On Your Word	1737821
Your Kiss Of Love	1741459
Your Love Alone	1741945

The following titles are registered for copyright with the Library of Congress, but are not listed by BMI:

Work Title	Registration Number	Year
A Worried Man	RE0000416898	1961
Anything For You	RE0000221777	1956
	RE0000234450	1956
Can I Help It?	RE0000221771	1956
	RE0000234448	1956
Double Double-Crosser	RE0000221769	1956
	RE0000234447	1956
Give Me A Sign	RE0000221762	1956
It's Time To Confess	RE0000221753	1956
	RE0000233058	1956
She's A Big Girl Now	RE0000221774	1956
	RE0000234449	1956
Take Care	PA0001799241	2011
	PA0001804403	2011
Tell Me	RE0000325192	1959
What Can I Say	RE0000440935	1961

APPENDIX V

Sheet Music

Philips/Epic

1956
Love Made Me Your Fool

Vik

1957
Kiddio *('Mister Rock And Roll' cover)*

Mercury

1959
Endlessly
It's Just A Matter Of Time
So Close
So Many Ways
Thank You Pretty Baby

1960
A Rockin' Good Way *(with Dinah Washington)*
Baby (You've Got What It Takes) *(with Dinah Washington)*
Fools Rush In
I Do *(with Dinah Washington)*
Hither And Thither And Yon
Kiddio
The Same One

1961
The Boll Weevil Song
Revenge
Think Twice

1962
Hit Record
Hotel Happiness
Lie To Me
Thanks To The Fool

1963
Still Waters Run Deep

1964
Another Cup Of Coffee (Another Lonely Night)
Do It Right
Going, Going, Gone
Too Late To Turn Back Now

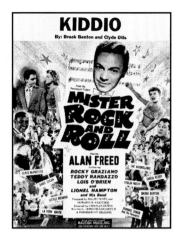

'Kiddio' (1957)

'Endlessly' (1959)

'The Same One' (1960)

'The Boll Weevil Song' (1961)

'Do It Right' (1964)

'Keep The Faith, Baby' (1967)

RCA Victor

1965
Love Is A Many-Splendored Thing

1967
Keep The Faith, Baby

Cotillion

1969
Rainy Night In Georgia

1970
Don't It Make You Want To Go Home

SONGBOOKS

Brook Benton Song Book – A Collection of Hit Songs Recorded by Brook Benton
(Eden Music Inc, Cimino Publications Incorporated, USA)
It's Just A Matter Of Time / This Time Of The Year / Kiddio / The Same One / So Many Ways /
Thank You Pretty Baby / A Rockin' Good Way (To Mess Around And Fall In Love) / Think Twice /
The Boll Weevil Song / The Ties That Bind / So Close

APPENDIX VI

Brook Benton Songs recorded by Other Artists

A Lover's Question
Johnnie Allan
Ernestine Anderson
Johnny Burnell
Johnny Burnette
Chaperals
Lloyd Charmers
Chee Chee & Peppy
Chevrons
Tony Christie
Larry Dean & The Toppers
Dion & The Belmonts
Exciters
Winston Francis
Bill Fredericks
Donny Gerrard
Leroy Gibbons
James Hunter
Jay & The Americans
Ben E. King
Danny Lanham
John Laws
David Linx, James Baldwin &
    Pierre van Dormael
Loggins & Messina
Maurice Long
Ronnie McDowell
Clyde McPhatter
Max Merritt & The Meteors
Bob Mitchell
Tony Orlando
Lou Rawls
Johnnie Ray
Otis Redding
Del Reeves
Lady Saw (with Leroy Gibbons)
Sensations
Sha Na Na
Rocky Sharpe & The Replays
Sly & Robbie
Take Two
Adam Wade
Travis Wammack
Jacky Ward
Cornell Yates

A Rockin' Good Way
(To Mess Around And Fall In Love)
Priscilla Bowman (with the Spaniels)
Chubby Checker & Dee Dee Sharp
Odessa Harris
Arthur Prysock & Betty Joplin
Schurli und die Motorbienen
    (as 'Na, dann tanzen wir doch')
Shaky & Bonnie
    (Shakin' Stevens & Bonnie Tyler)
Ruby Turner
Vernon & Jewell
    (Vernon Garrett & Jewell Whittaker)

Baby (You've Got What It Takes)
Joe Williams *(jazz singer)*

Because You Love Me
Nat 'King' Cole

Before I Fall In Love Again
Clyde McPhatter

Boll Weevil Song, The
Howie Casey & The Seniors

Come On Baby, Let's Go
Ernestine Anderson

Crazy In Love With You
Sam Cooke

Cross My Heart
Jay B. Lloyd

Doncha Think It's Time
Elvis Presley

Endlessly
Pat Boone
Ronnie Butler
Chuck & Dobby
Randy Crawford
Dobbie Dobson
Carol Fran
Dizzy Gillespie
Sonny James
Tom Jones

Clyde McPhatter
'A Lover's Question'

Junior Parker
'Hurtin' Inside'

Bobby Bland
'I'll Take Care Of You'

Sonny James
'It's Just A Matter Of Time'

Nat 'King' Cole
'Thank You Pretty Baby'

Vikki Nelson
'You Can't Get Away From Me'

Bill Medley
Eddie Middleton
Houston Person
Johnnie Ray
Mavis Staples
Nolan Struck

Everything
Roy Hamilton

Fire
Louis Jordan

Flat Tire
Del Vikings
Bobby Johnston
Albert King

Happy Years
Diamonds

High School Social
Clyde McPhatter

Hurtin' Inside
LaVern Baker
Don Gibson
Trini Lopez
Little Junior Parker
Mike Sanchez

I Ain't Givin' Up Nothin'
Priscilla Bowman (with the Spaniels)
Ben Hewitt
Clyde McPhatter
Sonny Wilson

I Don't Know
Little Milton

I Just Want To Love You
Ivory Joe Hunter
Clyde McPhatter

I'll Step Aside
Ruth Brown

I'll Stop Anything I'm Doin'
Clyde McPhatter

I'll Take Care Of You
Bobby 'Blue' Bland
Bobby 'Blue' Bland & B.B. King
Lonnie Brooks
Elvis Costello
Geater Davis
Buddy Guy & Junior Wells
Roy Hamilton
Mick Hucknall
Etta James

Wallace Johnson
Mark Lanegan
Van Morrison
Doug Sahm
Gil Scott-Heron
Statler Brothers
Irma Thomas
O.V. Wright

I'm Coming To See You
Billy Barnes

If You Only Knew
Clyde McPhatter

In A Dream
Roy Hamilton

It's Just A Matter Of Time
Nat Brown
Ruth Brown
Peabo Bryson
Solomon Burke
Glen Campbell
Dick Curless
Leon Daniels & The Venos
E.J. Decker
Aretha Franklin
Mickey Gilley
Roy Hamilton
Sonny James
Tom Jones
Betty Joplin
B.B. King
Benny Latimore
Little Anthony & The Imperials
Gloria Lynne
Garnet Mimms
Liza Minnelli
Patti Page
Persuasions
Charley Pride
Randy Travis
Tammy Wynette
Timi Yuro

It's So Much Fun
Wade Flemons

Kiddio
Big Town Playboys
Teresa Brewer (as 'Daddio')
John Lee Hooker
Johnny Littlejohn (as 'Kitty-O' and 'Kiddio')
Charlie Musselwhite
Doug Quattlebaum
Paladins
Teddy Randazzo
Lou Rawls
Neil Sedaka
Bill Wyman

Lie To Me
Dale McBride
Jimmy McCracklin

Looking Back
Johnny Adams
Inez Andrews
Lee Andrews
Jewel Brown
Ruth Brown
Ace Cannon *(instr)*
Chambers Brothers
Nat 'King' Cole
Eden Brothers
Jackie Edwards
Jerry Foster
Clarence Fountain
Earl Grant
Roy Hamilton
Clarence 'Frogman' Henry
Jan Howard
Ferlin Husky
Original Blind Boys of Alabama
Bonnie Owens
Ray Price
Marty Robbins
Rocky Roberts
Joe Simon
Soul Stirrers
Carla Thomas
Irma Thomas
Conway Twitty
Gene Vincent
Dinah Washington
Mary Wells
Clint West
Don Williams

May I
Johnny Mathis

My Love With All My Heart
Ivory Joe Hunter

My Time Will Come
LaVern Baker

Nothing In The World (Could Make Me Love You More Than I Do)
Nat 'King' Cole
Doris Day
Diane Schuur
Dinah Washington
Timi Yuro

Same One
Jackie Edwards
Roy Hamilton
Persuasions

Sneaky Alligator
Diamonds
Ellis Brothers

So Close
Troy Cory
Carol Fran
Jake Holmes

Someone To Believe In
Randy Crawford
Clyde McPhatter

Tell The Truth
Diamonds

Thank You Pretty Baby
Curley Bridges
Nat 'King' Cole
Troy Cory
Drink Small
Artie White

That's Enough For Me
Clyde McPhatter

Walkin' Together
Reed Harper & The Notes

What A Kiss Won't Do
Johnny Oliver

What I Wouldn't Give
Brown, Ruth

Why Me
Ruth Brown

You Can't Get Away From Me
Vikki Nelson

You Went Back On Your Word
Jerry Lee Lewis
Clyde McPhatter

You're For Me
Five Keys
Clyde McPhatter

You're Movin' Me
Clyde McPhatter

APPENDIX VII

Films, Videos and TV Shows

FILMS

MISTER ROCK AND ROLL • *Paramount* • **USA, 1957** *(B&W)*
Brook mimes to 'If Only I Had Known' (Vik).

MOTHER NATURE, FATHER TIME • *Scopitone S-1046* • **USA, 1965** *(Colour)*
Brook mimes to 'Mother Nature, Father Time' (RCA Victor).

VIDEO

AMERICA'S MUSIC 6: RHYTHM & BLUES 2 • *Century Home Video* • **USA, 1982** *(Colour)*
VHS compilation including live performances of 'The Boll Weevil Song', 'Thank You Pretty Baby' and 'Rainy Night In Georgia' filmed in Hollywood. Orchestra led by Gil Askey. Reissued on DVD in 2010 by Quantum Leap/MVD Visual together with RHYTHM & BLUES 1 as AMERICA'S MUSIC LEGACY: RHYTHM & BLUES.

NOTABLE TV APPEARANCES

THE ED SULLIVAN SHOW • *CBS-TV* • **USA, 12 April 1959** *(B&W)*
Live performance of 'It's Just A Matter Of Time'.

THE ED SULLIVAN SHOW • *CBS-TV* • **USA, 14 June 1959** *(B&W)*
Live performance of 'Endlessly'.

THE ED SULLIVAN SHOW • *CBS-TV* • **USA, 13 December 1959** *(B&W)*
Live performance of 'This Time Of The Year'.

SATURDAY PROM • *NBC-TV* • **USA, 29 October 1960** *(B&W)*
Live performance(?) of 'Kiddio' and 'Fools Rush In'.

DICK CLARK'S
SATURDAY NIGHT BEECHNUT SHOW • *ABC-TV* • **USA, 26 December 1959** *(B&W)*
Brook mimes to 'So Many Ways'.

PERRY COMO'S CHRISTMAS MUSIC HALL • *NBC-TV* • **USA, 14 December 1960** *(B&W)*
Special Christmas edition of *Perry Como's Kraft Music Hall*. Includes live performances of 'Kiddio' and 'Fools Rush In' recorded at NBC studios, New York on 9 December 1960.

Brook guesting on *Dick Clark's Saturday Night Beechnut Show*, 1959.

THE ED SULLIVAN SHOW ● *CBS-TV* ● USA, 4 February 1962 *(B&W)*
Live performance of 'Shadrack'.

THE STEVE ALLEN PLAYHOUSE ● *syndicated* ● USA, 29 October 1962 *(B&W)*
No details.

THE TONIGHT SHOW
STARRING JOHNNY CARSON ● *NBC-TV* ● USA, 30 November 1962 *(B&W)*
Live performance of 'Chariot Wheels' (also recorded onto a 10" acetate disc – see pages 234 and 275). Other guests included Jacqueline Bertrand and Vincent Price.

On *Perry Como's Christmas Music Hall*, 1960.

THE TONIGHT SHOW
STARRING JOHNNY CARSON • *NBC-TV* • **USA, 9 May 1963** *(B&W)*
No details.

VAL PARNELL'S
SUNDAY NIGHT AT THE LONDON PALLADIUM • *ATV* • **UK, 13 October 1963** *(B&W)*
Live performance (unknown titles). This was Brook's UK TV debut. He followed a new group
called the Beatles.

READY STEADY GO! • *Rediffusion* • **UK, 18 October 1963** *(B&W)*
No details.

TEENARAMA • *WOOK-TV* • **USA, 19 November 1963** *(B&W)*
No details.

THE MIKE DOUGLAS SHOW • *ABC-TV* • **USA, 22 November 1963** *(B&W)*
Live performance (unknown titles). While Brook was singing a duet with Roberta Sherwood, the show was interrupted by the anouncement that President Kennedy had been assassinated.

THE STEVE ALLEN PLAYHOUSE • *syndicated* • **USA, 20 December 1963** *(B&W)*
No details.

THE MIKE DOUGLAS SHOW • *ABC-TV* • **USA, 16 March 1965** *(B&W)*
No details.

THE CLAY COLE SHOW • *syndicated* • **USA, 24 March 1965** *(B&W)*
No details.

HOLLYWOOD A GO-GO • *KHJ-TV, syndicated* • **USA, 15 May 1965** *(B&W)*
Brook mimes to 'The Boll Weevil Song' and 'Hotel Happiness'.

SHIVAREE • *syndicated* • **USA, 15 January 1966** *(B&W)*
Brook mimes to 'Foolish Enough To Try' and 'Mother Nature, Father Time'.

HOLLYWOOD A GO-GO • *KHJ-TV, syndicated* • **USA, 22 January 1966** *(B&W)*
No details.

WHERE THE ACTION IS! • *ABC-TV* • **USA, 16 February 1966** *(B&W)*
Brook mimes to 'The Boll Weevil Song'.

WHERE THE ACTION IS! • *ABC-TV* • **USA, 15 March 1966** *(B&W)*
Brook mimes to 'I Wanna Be With You'.

CLAY COLE'S DISKOTEK • *syndicated* • **USA, 9 July 1966** *(B&W)*
No details.

INTERNATIONAL CABARET • *BBC2* • **UK, 31 October 1966** *(B&W)*
No details.

THE JOEY BISHOP SHOW • *ABC-TV* • **USA, 5 September 1967** *(Colour)*
No details.

DEE TIME • *BBC1* • **UK, 2 December 1967** *(B&W)*
No details.

LIVE FROM THE BITTER END • *WOR-TV* • **USA, 1967** *(B&W)*
Live performances of 'Laura' and 'The Glory Of Love' at the Bitter End club in New York.

THE ROLF HARRIS SHOW • *BBC1* • **UK, 6 January 1968** *(B&W)*
Live performances. Brook sings 'Lover Come Back To Me' and 'Ol' Man River'.

THE MERV GRIFFIN SHOW • *syndicated* • **USA, 15 March 1968** *(Colour)*
No details.

ONCE MORE WITH FELIX • *BBC2* • **UK, 16 March 1968** *(Colour)*
No details.

THE DAVID FROST SHOW • *CBS-TV* • **USA, 17 October 1969** *(Colour)*
No details.

THE DAVID FROST SHOW • *CBS-TV* • **USA, 9 July 1970** *(Colour)*
No details.

THE MIKE DOUGLAS SHOW • *ABC-TV* • **USA, 14 August 1970** *(Colour)*
No details.

THE MERV GRIFFIN SHOW • *CBS-TV* • **USA, 28 August 1970** *(Colour)*
No details.

THE BARBARA McNAIR SHOW • *syndicated* • **USA, 18 April 1971** *(Colour)*
Live performances. Brook delivers a fine, moody version of 'Rainy Night In Georgia' and duets with McNair on 'Let Me Fix It'.

THE LARRY KANE SHOW • *KPRC-TV* • **USA, 9 May 1971** *(Colour)*
Live performance. Brook sings 'Rainy Night In Georgia'.

THE MIKE DOUGLAS SHOW • *ABC-TV* • **USA, 25 May 1971** *(Colour)*
No details.

THE DAVID FROST SHOW • *CBS-TV* • **USA, 8 June 1971** *(Colour)*
No details.

INTERNATIONAL POP PROMS • *Granada* • **UK, 13 March 1976** *(Colour)*
Live performance. No details.

INTERNATIONAL POP PROMS • *Granada* • **UK, 18 March 1976** *(Colour)*
Live performance. Brook sings 'Rainy Night In Georgia'.

THE MIKE DOUGLAS SHOW • *KYW-TV, syndicated* • **USA, 27 April 1978** *(Colour)*
No details.

PEBBLE MILL AT ONE • *BBC1* • **USA, 18 November 1983** *(Colour)*
Brook mimes to 'Hotel Happiness'.

LIVE AT SHEFFIELD CITY HALL • *Yorkshire TV* • **UK, 23 October 1984** *(Colour)*
Live performances of 'Thank You Pretty Baby', 'Kiddio', 'Rainy Night In Georgia', 'Endlessly', 'Think Twice', 'So Many Ways' and 'Hither And Thither And Yon'.

THE CANNON & BALL SHOW • *LWT* • **UK, 10 November 1984** *(Colour)*
Live performances of 'Rainy Night In Georgia' and 'Endlessly' – the latter of which is ruined by the hosts joining in.

THE JOE FRANKLIN SHOW • *WOR-TV* • **USA, September 1986** *(Colour)*
Talk show from Secaucus, New Jersey. Four-minute interview with Brook Benton.

NASHVILLE NOW • *TNN* • **USA, 19 January 1988** *(Colour)*
Tony Joe White and Brook Benton sing 'Rainy Night In Georgia' backed by the *Nashville Now* studio band. Repeated 5 September 1988 on *Nashville Now*'s 5th anniversary special.

APPENDIX VIII

Notable Early Live Appearances

26 June 1959
Brook Benton headlines *Dr. Jive's 12th Anniversary Rhythm & Blues Revue*. Other acts: Wilbert Harrison, Shirley & Lee, Nappy Brown, Valerie Carr, Beverly Ann Gibson, Little Anthony & The Imperials, Eugene Church, the Ebonaires, the Shirelles, the Clintonian Cubs and the Cavaliers.

29 January 1960
Brook Benton headlines for a week at the Apollo Theater, New York.

19 March 1960
Brook Benton and the Coasters break the house record during their week at the Howard Theater, Washington, DC.

8 April 1960
Brook Benton opens at the Regal Theater, Chicago.

15 April 1960
Brook Benton headlines the *Easter Parade of Stars* at the Brooklyn Paramount. Other acts: Dinah Washington, Lambert, Hendricks & Ross, William B. Williams, Art Farmer & Benny Golson, Maynard Ferguson and Dion & The Belmonts.

14 October 1960
Brook Benton and the Drifters appear at the Apollo Theater. New York.

28 January 1961
Brook Benton ends a month-long tour in Orlando, Florida.

3 February 1961
Brook Benton, the Shirelles, Maxine Brown and the Dynamics are at the Howard Theater, Washington, DC.

1 September 1961
Brook Benton headlining. Other acts: the Drifters, Betty Carter, Bobby Freeman, Willie Lewis and the Reuben Philips Band.

13 October 1961
Brook Benton headlines *The Biggest Show Of Stars For '61*. Other acts: The Platters, Del Shannon, Dee Clark, the Drifters, Gary 'US' Bonds, Gene McDaniels, the Jarmels, Curtis Lee, Phil Upchurch, the Cleftones, Harold Cromer (MC) and Paul Williams & His Show Orchestra.

12 January 1962
Brook Benton starts a week at the Regal Theater, Chicago.

26 January 1962
Brook Benton headlining. Other acts: Maxine Brown, Shep & The Limelites, the Marcels and Willie Lewis.

12 May 1962
Brook Benton headlines *The Biggest Show of Stars for 1962* at the Forum, Wichita, Kansas. Other acts: Fats Domino, Bruce Channel and Gene Chandler.

14 September 1962
Brook Benton headlining. Other acts: Ruth Brown, the Flamingos, the Blue Belles, Godfrey Cambridge and Erskine Hawkins & Band.

18 February 1963
Brook Benton is at the Riverside Ballroom in Phoenix, Arizona.

5 July 1963
Brook Benton headlining. Other acts: Ruby & The Romantics, Betty Carter, Irwin C. Watson, Paul & Flash Leonard and Jerome Richardson's All Stars.

19-28 October 1963
Brook Benton headlines *The Greatest Record Show of 1963* (UK tour). Other acts: Dion, Trini Lopez, Timi Yuro, Lesley Gore, Ken Thorne & His Orchestra and Jerry Stevens (MC).

14 February 1964
Brook Benton headlining. Other acts: Aretha Franklin, Irwin C. Watson, the Parkettes, Bobby Ephraim and the Reuben Phillips Band.

14 and 15 November 1964 –
Brook Benton headlines *The Big Rhythm & Blues Show* at the Brevoort Building, Brooklyn, NY. Other acts: Major Lance, Tommy Hunt, the Flamingos, the Butterflies and the Charlie Lucas Orchestra.

26 March 1965
Brook Benton headlining. Other acts: Jimmy Reed, King Curtis, Ruby & The Romantics, Dobie Gray and Clay Tyson.

Bibliography

BOOKS

Bloemeke, Rüdiger - *Roll Over Beethoven* (Hannibal Verlag, Höfen, Austria) 1996
Brown, James with Bruce Tucker - *James Brown, Godfather Of Soul*
    (Hannibal Verlag, Höfen, Austria) 1993
Brown, Ruth, & Andrew Yule - *Miss Rhythm* (Donald I. Fine Books, New York, USA) 1996
Bruyninckx, Walter - *Swing Discography 1920-1988 (Volume 11)*
    (Privately published, Mechelem, Belgium) 1989
Cates, Jim - *The Official Picture Sleeve Price Guide*
    (Educational Concepts Corporation, Topeka, Kansas, USA) 1986
Delmore, Daniel - *Fabulous EP's Cover* (Delmore Imprimerie Valblor, Strasbourg, France) 1986
Ertl, Franz - *Soul Diktionär* (Wilhelm Herbst Verlag, Köln, West Germany) 1987
Fox, Ted - *Showtime At The Apollo* (Quartet Books, London, UK) 1985
Gart, Galen - *First Pressings: The History Of Rhythm & Blues (Special 1950 Volume)*
    (Big Nickel Publications, Milford, New Hampshire, USA) 1993
Gart, Galen - *First Pressings: The History Of Rhythm & Blues (Volume 1: 1951)*
    (Big Nickel Publications, Milford, New Hampshire, USA) 1991
Gart, Galen - *First Pressings: The History Of Rhythm & Blues (Volume 2: 1952)*
    (Big Nickel Publications, Milford, New Hampshire, USA) 1992
Gart, Galen - *First Pressings: The History Of Rhythm & Blues (Volume 3: 1953)*
    (Big Nickel Publications, Milford, New Hampshire, USA) 1992
Gart, Galen - *First Pressings: The History Of Rhythm & Blues (Volume 4: 1954)*
    (Big Nickel Publications, Milford, New Hampshire, USA) 1990
Gart, Galen - *First Pressings: The History Of Rhythm & Blues (Volume 5: 1955)*
    (Big Nickel Publications, Milford, New Hampshire, USA) 1992
Gart, Galen - *First Pressings: The History Of Rhythm & Blues (Volume 6: 1956)*
    (Big Nickel Publications, Milford, New Hampshire, USA) 1991
Gart, Galen - *First Pressings: The History Of Rhythm & Blues (Volume 7: 1957)*
    (Big Nickel Publications, Milford, New Hampshire, USA) 1993
Gart, Galen - *First Pressings: The History Of Rhythm & Blues (Volume 8: 1958)*
    (Big Nickel Publications, Milford, New Hampshire, USA) 1995
Gart, Galen - *First Pressings: The History Of Rhythm & Blues (Volume 9: 1959)*
    (Big Nickel Publications, Milford, New Hampshire, USA) 2002
Gart, Galen - *Rhythm & Blues in Cleveland – 1955 Edition*
    (Big Nickel Publications, Milford, New Hampshire, USA) 2003
Gillett, Charlie - *The Sound of the City* (Zweitausendeins Verlag, Frankfurt, West Germany) 1978
Hardy, Phil, & Dave Laing - *Encyclopedia Of Rock* (Macdonald & Co, London, UK) 1987
Hardy, Phil, & Dave Laing - *The Faber Companion To 20th-Century Popular Music*
    (Faber & Faber Limited, London, UK) 1990
Haskins, Jim - *Queen Of The Blues: A Biography Of Dinah Washington*
    (William Morrow & Company, Inc, New York, USA) 1987
Hayes, Cedric J., & Robert Laughton - *Gospel Records 1943-69 (Volumes 1-2)*
    (Record Information Services, London, UK) 1992
Heilbut, Anthony - *The Gospel Sound* (Simon & Schuster, New York, USA) 1971
Hinton, Milt - *Bass Line* (Temple University Press, Philadelphia, USA) 1988
Hoffmann, Franz - *Jazz Advertised In The Negro Press: 1910-1967 (Volume 3)*
    (Privately published, Berlin, Germany) 2001
Hounsome, Terry - *Rock Record 7* (Record Researcher Pubs, Llandysul, Ceredigion, UK) 1997
Hounsome, Terry - *Single File* (Privately published, Rosemarket, Pembs, UK) 1990
Mawhinney, Paul C. - *Music Master: The 45 rpm Directory 1947-1982*
    (Record-Rama, Allison Park, Philadelphia, USA) 1983
McGrath, Bob - *The R&B Indies (Volume 1)* (Eyeball Press, West Vancouver, BC, Canada) 2000
Meeker, David - *Jazz In The Movies* (Da Capo Press, New York, USA) 1981

Merlis, Bob, & Davin Seay - *Heart & Soul* (Stuart, Tabori & Chang, New York, USA) 1997
Neely, Tim - *American Records 1950-1975* (Krause Publications, Iola, Wisconsin, USA) 2006
Nite, Norm N. - *Rock On* (Thomas Y. Crowell Company, New York, USA) 1974
Ochs, Michael - *Rock Archives* (Dolphin Books, New York, USA) 1984
Osborne, Jerry - *Official Price Guide To Records* (House Of Collectibles, New York, USA) 1995
Otis, Johnny - *Upside Your Head!*
   (Wesleyan University Press Of New England, Hannover, New Hampshire, USA) 1993
Pareles, Jon, & Patricia Romanowski - *The Rolling Stone Encyclopedia Of Rock & Roll*
   (Rolling Stone Press/Michael Joseph, London, UK) 1983
Prince, Edward J. - *78 rpm Record Guide 1945-1960* (Privately published, USA) 2007
Reichold, Martin - *Rock & Pop Preiskatalog 2002*
   (Vereinigte Motor-Verlage, Stuttgart, Germany) 2002
Rosalsky, Mitch - *Encyclopedia of Rhythm & Blues and Doo-Wop Vocal Groups*
   (Scarecrow Press, Lanham, Maryland, USA) 2002
Ruppli, Michel - *Atlantic Records (Volumes 1-4)*
   (Greenwood Press, Westport, Connecticut, USA) 1979
Ruppli, Michel, & Ed Novitsky - *The Mercury Labels (Volumes 1-5)*
   (Greenwood Press, Westport, Connecticut, USA) 1993
Ruppli, Michel & Ed Novitsky - *The MGM Labels (Volumes 1-3)*
   (Greenwood Press, Westport, Connecticut, USA) 1998
Ruth, Thermon T. - *From The Church To The Apollo Theater*
   (Ruth Publications, New York, USA) 1995
Sandohl, Linda J. - *Encyclopedia Of Rock Music On Film*
   (Blandford Press, Blandford Forum, Dorset, UK) 1987
Sartre, Jean-Paul - *Was ist Literatur?* (Rowohlt Verlag, Hamburg, West Germany) 1960
Sawyer, Charles - *B.B. King, der legendäre König des Blues*
   (Hannibal Verlag, Höfen, Austria) 1995
Shaw, Arnold - *Die Story des Rock'n'Roll (The Rockin' 50s)*
   (Hannibal Verlag, Höfen, Austria) 1994
Solomon, Clive - *The British Top 50 Charts 1954-1976* (Omnibus Press, London, UK) 1977
Talevski, Nick - *Tombstone Blues* (Omnibus Press, London, UK) 1999
Travis, Dempsey J. - *An Autobiography of Black Jazz*
   (Urban Research Institute, Chicago, USA) 1983
Various - *Record Collector Rare Record Price Guide* (Record Collector, London, UK) 2004
Wallis, Ian - *American Rock'n'Roll: The UK Tours 1956-72* (Music Mentor Books, York, UK) 2003
Whitburn, Joel - *The Billboard Book of US Top 40 Hits* (8th edition)
   (Billboard Books, New York, USA) 2004
Whitburn, Joel - *Bubbling Under The Hot 100 1959-1981*
   (Record Research Inc, Menomonee Falls, Wisconsin, USA) 1982
Whitburn, Joel - *Top Pop 1955-1982*
   (Record Research Inc, Menomonee Falls, Wisconsin, USA) 1983
Whitburn, Joel - *Top Pop Albums 1955-1992*
   (Record Research Inc, Menomonee Falls, Wisconsin, USA) 1993
Whitburn, Joel - *Top R&B Singles 1942-1995*
   (Record Research Inc, Menomonee Falls, Wisconsin, USA, 1996
Whitburn, Joel -*Top R&B Albums 1955-1998*
   (Record Research Inc, Menomonee Falls, Wisconsin, USA) 1999
Wither, Ernest C. - *The Memphis Blues Again* (Penguin Books, New York, USA) 2001
Wölfer, Jürgen - *Das Große Lexikon der Unterhaltungs-Musik*
   (Lexikon Imprint Verlag, Berlin, Germany) 2000

PROGRAMMES

The Biggest Show of Stars, Fall Edition 1961 (Super Enterprises Inc, USA) 1961
The Biggest Show of Stars, Spring Edition 1962 (Super Enterprises Inc, USA) 1962
The Brook Benton Show (The Cash Box, USA) 1959
Easter Parade Of Stars (Sid Bernstein, USA) 1960
1st Lewisham Festival of Jazz (21-26 November 1983)
   Main Auditorium, Monday, 21 November: Brook Benton, Kay Starr, National Youth Jazz
   Orchestra - Sponsored by LBC Radio

Freedom Show (WDAS, Philadelphia, USA) 1965
The Greatest Record Show of 1963 (William Victor Productions, UK) 1963
Living Legends (Mervyn Conn, UK) 1984

NEWSPAPERS & MAGAZINES

Billboard (USA) 9 November 1963 - 'King For A Month'
Billboard (USA) 2 July 1966 - 'Benton's Easy Style Scores In Fast-Paced Nitery Act'
Blues & Rhythm No.5 (UK) December 1984
Blues & Rhythm No.37 (UK) June-July 1988
Blues & Rhythm No.170 (UK) June 2002
Blues & Soul (France) May 1971, 1975, 1976
Cash Box Vol. XX, No.32 (USA) 25 April 1959
Cash Box (USA) 20 October 1962 - 'Happy Birthday Brook Benton'
Cash Box (USA) 2 November 1963 - 'Mercury's King Of The Month'
Cash Box (USA) 23 November 1963 - 'Record Ramblings'
DISCoveries No.125 (USA) October 1988 -
    'The Brook Benton Story & Essential Discography' by Peter Grendysa
Ebony (USA) August 1959 - 'Teen-Agers' Idols'
Ebony (USA) May 1963 - 'Brook Benton – Although Balladeer Is Already Star'
Ebony (USA) May 1978 - 'Brook Benton – On The Come-Back Trail'
Goldmine (USA) 1 October 1993 - 'Looking Back'
Hep (USA) December 1963 - 'Brook Benton – The Man Of The Hour'
Hit Parade Vol.5, No.61 (UK) June 1959 - 'Brook Benton – The New Pop Disc Star'
Jet (USA) - 9 April 1959, 19 May 1960, 1961, 9 April 1962, 9 August 1962, 30 August 1962,
    1 August 1963, 9 May 1963
Juke Blues No.12 (UK) Spring 1988
Juke Blues No.21 (UK) Autumn 1990
K-E-Y Magazine (USA) 5-12 December 1963
Long Island Press (USA) 12 August 1962 - 'No Blues For Brook Benton'
Methadone Treatment Index (USA) 9 July 1974 - 'A Day With Brook Benton' by Eddie Kearney
Melody Maker (UK) 10 November 1962
Melody Maker (UK) 26 October 1963
Melody Maker (UK) unknown date, 1975 - Interview by Max Jones
Music Vendor No.727 (USA) 8 May 1961 - 'Another Hit – Brook Benton'
Negro Digest (USA) July 1966
Nite Lifer Magazine (USA) April 1960 - 'A Singing Sensation on Sunset Strip' by W.E. Barnett
Now Dig This No.212 (UK) November 2000 -
    Interview with Stuart Colman, BBC Radio London on 27 November 1983
Rhythm and Blues (USA) - December 1959 - Brook Benton & Johnny Mathis, April 1960
Rock'n'Roll Musikmagazin No.162, 163, 165 (Germany) 2005-06 -
    'Die Brook Benton Story und Label-Discografie' (Parts 1-3) by Dieter Moll
Rock and Roll Songs Vol.4, No.20 (USA) November 1959
Rock and Roll Songs Vol.5, No.21 (USA) July 1960 - 'All There Is To Know About Brook Benton'
Rock and Roll Songs, unknown issue (USA) 196? - 'The Smooth Mr. Benton'
Rock Revue Magazin No.29 (Austria) October 1978 - 'Mister Rock And Roll'
Sepia Magazine (USA) March 1961 - 'Brook Benton – The Hit Maker' by Dave Hepburn
Sunday News (USA) 2 July 1961 - 'Man With A Voice' by May Okon
Unknown publications, 10 October 1986 and 7 January 1989 -
    Interviews with Clyde Otis by Colin Escott

WEBSITES

Both Sides Now (www.bsnpubs.com)
Callahan, Mike, Dave Edwards & Patrice Eyries - *The Musicor Records Story* - USA, 2006

Marv Goldberg's Yesterday's Memories Rhythm & Blues Party (www.uncamarvy.com)
Goldberg, Marv - *The Sandmen* - USA, 2002, 2009

INDEX OF PEOPLE'S NAMES

Adams, Pepper 88
Adderley, Cannonball 119, 133
Adler, Polly 156
Allen, Steve 148, 151
Andy & The Bey Sisters 119, 121, 122
                    See also Bey, Andy
Anka, Paul 91, 119
Applebaum, Stan 59
Armstrong, Louis 117-18, 124, 130, 133, 134,
                    145, 150, 180, 195
Arnold, Eddy 72
Ashby, Lynn 138
Ashby, Neal 197
Askew, Mary - *See* Benton, Mary
Askey, Gil 140
Atkins, Chet 27
Bacharach, Burt 155
Baker, LaVern 34, 119, 122, 133
Baldwin, John 159
Bankhead, Tallullah 195
Bare, Bobby 80
Barnes, W.M. 115
Barry, Mark 204
Basie, Count 61, 100, 119, 174, 206
Baxter, Ann 155
Beatles 75, 127-8, 129, 153
Bell, Al 104
Belvin, Jesse 119, 122
Benjamin, Bennie 71, 108
Benton Jr, Brook *(Brook's son)* 163
Benton, Gerald *(Brook's son)*
        130, 163, 165
Benton, Mary *(Brook's wife)*
        28, 138, 143, 163-4, 166-7, 170, 196
Benton, Roy Hamilton *(Brook's son)* 163
Benton, Vanessa *(Brook's daughter)*
        58, 142, 154, 163, 169-70, 200, 202
Berlin, Irving 71
Bernstein, Leonard 113
Bernstein, Sid 120-1
Berry, Chuck 34
Bey, Andy 198
                    See also Andy & The Bey Sisters
Bloom, Rube 47
Boone, Pat 129
Borders, Lou 165
Bostic, Earl 134
Boulanger, Nadia 61
Bowen, Jimmy 76, 85, 87
Boyd, Eddie 119, 122
Bradford, Hank 134
Brando, Marlon 160
Brennan, Walter 118, 133, 134
Briggs, Bunny 119
Broonzy, Big Bill 59, 71

Brown, Clarence 'Gatemouth' 119
Brown, James 206
Brown, Maxine 119, 121, 174
Brown, Ruth
        29, 52-3, 119, 121, 122, 139, 157, 197-8
Buckner, Milt 119
Bullock, Sandra 157
Butler, Billy (& The Enchanters) 119
Butler, Jerry 148
Camden Jubilee Singers 24
Campanella, Roy 206
Capucine 155
Carr, Valerie 121
Carson, Jenny Lou 72
Carson, Johnny 151
Carter, Betty 119
Carter, Rev. Julius C. 175, 201
Cash, Johnny 72, 81
Charles, Ray 53, 87, 118, 119, 124, 134,
                    137, 141, 150, 154
Chase, Lincoln 30
Chesnut, Jerry 28, 87
Churchill, Savannah 30
Clark, Dee 119
Clark, Dick 151, 200
Clay, Cassius 132
Clay, Judy 135
Cleary, Duncan 111
Clooney, Rosemary 140
Coasters 119
Colacrai, Cirino 157
Cole, Nat 'King'
        35, 36, 37-8, 47, 48, 66, 81, 82, 117, 130,
        133, 134, 141, 146, 154, 180, 206
Coleman, Ray 44, 127, 129
Coltrane, John 206
Como, Perry 151
Contestable, Paul 72-3
Cook, Bill 28-9, 36, 37
Cooke, Sam 118, 145, 146
Cooper, Joe (Orchestra) 33
Cooper, Morton 181-4, 185
Crawford, Dave 88
Crawford, Joan 195
Crawford, Randy 205-6
Creason, Sammy 88
Crosby, Bing 108, 195
Crosby, Gary 123
Culbreeth, Reese 112
Dandridge, Dorothy 159
David, Hal 155
Davis, Miles 120
Davis, Sammy Jr.
        85, 87, 98, 110, 116-17, 118, 145, 148,
        153, 154, 180, 190, 195, 200, 206

Davis, Skeeter 80
De Jesus, Luchi 68, 69, 72, 74, 123
De Laurentiis, Dino 158-9
Deas, Gerald (Dr.) 176, 178, 202
DeCoteaux, Bert 82
Delmar, Elaine 140-1
Diamond, Neil 187
Diamonds 39
Dickinson, Jim 88
Dillard, Mimi 175
Dion 119, 127
Dixie Flyers 88, 204
Dixon, Willie *(pseudonym)* 36
Dixon, Willie Lee *(Brook's sister)* 25, 36
Dodds, Malcolm 56
Domino, Fats
   66, 119, 130, 133, 145, 146, 150
Donegan, Lonnie 119
Dorsey, George 88
Douglas, Mike 151
Dove, Ian 130
Dr. Jive 121
Drain, Ron 116
Dreyer, Dave 37, 155, 196
Drifters 119, 121, 124
Dupree, Cornell 88
Durante, Jimmy 110
Dylan, Bob 95, 102
Eckstine, Billy 134, 141, 149
Ellington, Duke 195
Ellis, Ray 82
Ephraim, Bobby 121
Evans, Ish 132
Falk, Peter 160
Farmer, Art 119, 124
Feldman, Charles K. 155
Feliciano, José 138
Ferguson, Maynard 119, 124
Fitzgerald, Ella 119, 129, 134, 180, 195, 206
Flack, Roberta 141
Flamingos 119, 121
Floyd, Barbara 153
Fonda, Henry 195
Fonda, Jane 155
Fontaine, Frankie 160
Foxx, Inez 119
Franklin, Aretha 40, 72, 119, 121
Freed, Alan 34, 157
Freeman, Bobby 119, 122
Freeman, Ernie 86
Friedman, Gerald (Dr.) 126
Fuller, Blind Boy 39
Gantt, Harvey 181
Gart, Galen 32
Gentry, Bobbie 86
Gershwin, George 46
Gershwin, Ira 46
Getz, Stan 141
Gilberto, Astrud 140
Gillespie, Dizzy 119

Glaser, Joe 148
Goldberg, Marv 30
Golden Gate Jubilee Quartet 25
Goldstein, Bernard 28
Golson, Benny 119, 124
Goodman, Benny 148
Gore, Lesley 119, 127
Goulet, Robert 182
Grant, Brook *(Brook's nephew)*
   54, 63, 100, 132, 137, 150, 169, 202
Grant, Hugh 157
Grant-Walker Esther 153
Graziano, Rocky 34
Greco, Buddy 140, 141
Green, Irving 23
Griffin, Rex 72
Grimmel, Bernd 96
Hall, Duke 112
Halsman, Marv 29, 31
Hamilton, Andrew 112
Hamilton, Roy 29, 37, 119, 145
Hampton, Lionel 34
Hansberry, Lorraine 154
Harlemaires 26
Harrison, Wilbert 119, 121
Hart, Lorenz 106
Harvey, Laurence 155
Hawkins Singers, Edwin 140
Haynes, Furman/Thurman 29, 31
Henderson, Finis 148
Henderson, Joe 116
Hendricks, Belford C. 37-8, 43, 52
Herman, Woody 140
Herzog, Arthur 71
Hice, Nick 112
Hinton, Milt 'Judge' 206
Hirt, Al 119, 127, 148
Holden, Stephen 141
Holiday, Billie 33, 71, 115, 154, 206
Holly, Buddy 32
Hollywood Strings 87
Hopkins, Linda 33
Horne, Lena 195, 206
Houston, Cissy 88, 92, 93, 204
Hunter, Ivory Joe 39
Husky, Ferlin 34
Illingworth, Gary 88
Ink Spots 29
Inspirational Choir 140
Jackson, Chuck 105, 119, 129
Jackson, Tommy 'Hurricane' 206
Jacquet, Illinois 206
James, Etta 119
James, Jeff 26, 32
James, Joni 119
Jean, Martha (The Queen) 74
Jerusalem Stars 26
Jewison, Norman 154
Jo, Damita 119, 174
Johnson, Billy 169

Johnston Jr, Ernie 201
Jones, Jerry 154
Jones, Quincy 29, 31, 60, 66, 67, 82, 84
Jones, Tommy Lee 157
Jordan, Louis 39
Julian, Don (& The Larks) 139
Junirs, Direoce 153
Kasmiersky, Steve 295
Kellner, Leon (Orchestra) 133
Kennedy, John F. (Pres.) 151
Kerr Singers, Anita 73, 80, 81
Kilgallen, Dorothy 158
Killens, John 159
King, Ben E. 117, 119, 122, 174
King, Carole 66
King Jr, Martin Luther (Dr.)
    179, 181, 184, 187-8
King Curtis 88, 119, 121
Kirby, George 148
Kleiner, Dick 206
Knight, Marie 119
Knox, Buddy 85
Lambert, Hendricks & Ross 119, 124
Lancaster, Burt 31
Lance, Major 121
Landford, Bill (& The Landfordaires)
    25-6, 27, 157
Landford Quartet, Bill 26-7
Lange, Jessica 157
Langford, Bill - See Landford, Bill
Last, James 87
Leadbelly 58
Lee, Curtis 119, 124
Lee, Peggy 141, 148, 195
Leiber, Jerry 88
Lennon, John 102
Lester, Buddy 119
Levy, John 139
Lewis, Bobby 174
Lewis Trio, Ramsey 141
Lewis, Willie 119
Lewitt, Eileen 127
Little Richard 34
Logan, George 125
Logan, Ruth A. 172
Lopez, Trini 119, 127
Louis, Joe 195
Lovin, Scott 108
Lowe, Sammy 105
Mabley, Moms 195
Mack, Johnny 100
Mancini, Henry 80
Mansfield, Jane 175
Mardin, Arif 88, 138
Martin, Dean 85, 87, 108, 154
Martino, Al 133
Masters, Lynn 160
Mathis, Johnny 40
Matsubayashi, Kohji - See Shaolin
Matthew, Brian 129

May, Billy (Big Band) 52, 82
Mayfield, Percy 39
McClure, Tommy 88
McDonald, Adriel 29, 31
McMillan, Allan 195
McNair, Barbara 151, 159
McPhatter, Clyde 34, 36, 134, 157
McRae, Carmen 119, 176
Meadowlarks 119
Meadowlarks Band 139
Mercer, Johnny 47
Mighty Sparrow 141
Miracles 134
Moody, James (Band) 122, 197
Moore, Joanna 155
Moore, Rudy Ray 139
Mulligan, Gerry 119, 141
Newman, Joe 61, 88, 95
Newman, Paul 56
Norman, Fred 135
O'Rourke, Jimmy 88
Otis, Clyde
    24, 31, 34, 35, 36, 37-40, 43, 48, 50-1, 53,
    54, 57-8, 69, 74, 76, 80, 104, 108, 110,
    111, 140, 151, 153, 197, 205
Otis, Johnny 115
Page, Patti 40
Patterson, George 'Paco' 153
Peay, Mattie *(Brook's mother)* 21, 163, 167-8
Peay, Richard *(Brook's brother)* 115
Peay, William *(Brook's father)*
    21-2, 36, 163, 167-8, 193
Penque, Romeo 88
Penquin, The 139
Pfindling, L.O. 137
Philips, Reuben (Band) 121
Platters 119, 124
Poitier, Sidney 160
Pomus, Doc 98
Powell, Benny 88
Presley, Elvis 33, 36, 40, 77, 108
Price, Lloyd 119
Pride, Charley 205
Prima, Louis 123
Pruter, Robert 53, 203
Quinlan, Maureen 140
Raide, William 159
Rainey, Chuck 88
Randazzo, Teddy 171
Rathbone, Basil 160
Ray, Johnnie 119
Redding, Otis 153
Redfield, William 160
Reed, Jimmy 119, 121
Reed, Leonard 119
Reese, Della 119
Richardson's All Stars, Jerome 119
Ricketts, Al 134, 148-9
Riddle, Nelson (Orchestra) 63, 87, 129
Righteous Brothers 119

Robbins, Jerome 159
Roberts, Herman 53
Robinson, Bert 43
Robinson, Edward G. 195
Robinson, Jackie 206
Robinson, Joe 105
Robinson, Sylvia 105
Rodgers, Richard 106
Roker, Wally 108
Rosengarden, Neal 88
Rosenstein, Al 99
Rowe, Izzy 206
Russell, Nipsey 119
Ruth, Thurman/Thurmon 139
Rydell, Bobby 119
Sandmen 29-31
Sasso, J. 60
Saunders, Red (Orchestra) 122
Schiffman, Frank 139
Schuur, Diane 35
Sedaka, Neil 171
Shannon, Del 119
Shaolin (Matsubayashi Kohji) 52, 62-3
Shep & The Limelites 119
Sheridan, Ann 160
Sherwood, Roberta 151
Shirelles 121, 197
Shuman, Mort 98
Siders, Irving 126
Sidran, Lou 46
Silvester, Robert 195
Simon, Paul 136
Simone, Nina 119, 176
Sinatra, Frank 61, 85, 87, 91, 108, 118, 137, 145, 149, 154
Singleton, Margie 64-5
Singleton, Shelby 58, 64, 198
Sledge, Percy 205
Smalls, Clifton 125, 133-4
Smith, Keely 123
Snow, Hank 80
Somerville, Dave 39
South, Joe 44
Southern Sons 25
Springer, Ruth *(Brook's sister)* 24, 29, 169
Springer, Walter *(Brook's brother-in-law)* 29, 31
Stanwyck, Barbara 155
Starr, Kay 140
Starr, Ringo 129-30
Stern, Harold 80, 81
Stevenson, Bobby 157
Stewart, Rod 137
Stoller, Mike 88
Strong, Melvin 125
Stylistics 138
Sullivan, Ed 151, 197
Summers, Myrna 88
Sutch, Screaming Lord 129
Sweet Inspirations 88, 93

Taylor, Jackie 151, 153
Taylor, Robert 156
Thompson, Peter 129
Tillman, Jimmy 151, 153
Townsend, Sandra 41
Troggs 100
Tubb, Ernest 72
Turner, Sammy 122
Upchurch, Phil 119, 124
Utley, Mike 88, 92
Vaughan, Sarah 39, 154, 180
Viglione, Joe 47, 48
Wagner, Robert F. (Mayor) 171
Wagoner, Porter 80
Waller, Fats 206
Warwick, Dionne 75
Washington, Denzel 157
Washington, Dinah 36, 39, 47, 49-55, 73, 119, 124, 127, 129, 130, 153, 154, 157, 195, 204, 206
Washington, Thomas 153
Wassermann, Morris 180
Wassermann, Sally 180
Watson, Irwin C. 72, 121
Wayne, John 195
Weiland, Edward 184-7
Weill, Kurt 48
Weiss, George 71
Wells, Mary 139
Wexler, Jerry 88
Wheeler, Edward 153
White, Tony Joe 90, 93-5, 109, 135, 142, 150, 204, 206
Wiggins, Clarence 139
Williams, George 140
Williams, Jimmy 109
Williams, Joe 90, 119
Willis, Chuck 30
Wills, Bob 72
Wilson, Jackie 118, 119, 126, 146
Wilson, Nancy 119, 130, 140-1
Wilson, Ralph (Orchestra) 33
Wilson, Teddy 140
Winchell, Walter 123
Winters, Shelley 156
Witherspoon, Jimmy 141
Wonder, Stevie 107
Wright, Herbert 126, 148, 154, 159, 184
Wright, Obedia 154
Yisrael, Ammayeh 54-5
Young, A.S. 'Doc' 123
Young, Faron 72
Yuro, Timi 39, 119, 127
Zawinul, Joe 52
Ziegler, Billy 88

INDEX OF SONGS & ALBUM TITLES

Cassette = 📼   CD = ◎   EP title = ▫   LP Title = ▪

Detailed descriptions/discussions of albums appear on pages shown in **bold**.

A Black Child Can't Smile 176, 178, 187
A House Is Not A Home 75, 155-6
A Lovely Way To Spend An Evening 45
A Lover's Question 36, 109
A Million Miles From Nowehere 34
A Nightingale Sang In Berkeley Square
    79, 106
A Rainy Night In Georgia
    See Rainy Night In Georgia
A Rockin' Good Way (To Mess Around
    And Fall In Love) 49, 52, 157, 206
A Touch Of Class 102, 103
A Tribute To 'Mama' 110-11
A Worried Man 59
After Midnight 69
After The Rain 150
▪ *After The Rain* (unissued) **142**, 150
After You've Gone 62
Ain't It Good 35
▪ *Ain't It Good* 35
All In Love Is Fair 107
All My Love Belongs To You 32
All Of Me 61
All Over Again 72, 73
All That Love Went To Waste 102
All Vocal Jingle (Straight Jingle) 100
Alone 99
▪ *Along Comes Ruth* 198
Another Cup Of Coffee 66, 75
Around The World 45
▪ *As Long As She Needs Me* 72
Aspen Colorado 94-5, 204
Baby 90
Baby Won't You Please Come Home
    48
Baby (You've Got What It Takes)
    49, 50, 52, 53, 127, 157, 205, 206
Back In Your Own Back Yard 37
Beautiful Memories 113
▪ *Beautiful Memories Of Christmas* **112-14**
Because Of Everything 50
Because Of You 45
▪ *Best Ballads Of Broadway* **67-8**
Better Times 109
Beyond The Sea 82
Big Mable Murphy 98
Black Rat 23
Blue Decorations 113
Blue Moon 79
Blue Skies 45
Blues In The Night 62

Boll Weevil Song, The
    40, 57-8, 84, 86, 118, 130, 134, 140,
    146, 150, 153, 157
▪ *Boll Weevil Song and*
    11 Other Great Hits, The **57-9**, 74
▪ *Born To Sing The Blues* **69-71**, 72, 186
Born Under A Bad Sign 95, 191-2
Break Her Heart 134
Break Out 89
Breezin' Along With The Breeze 61, 62
▪ *Brook Benton* **102-3**, 105
▪ *Brook Benton At His Best* 31-2
◎ *Brook Benton At His Best* 32, 203
▪ *Brook Benton – The Billy May Way*
    (unissued) **83-4**
Call Me Irresponsible 79
Can't Take My Eyes Off [Of] You 92, 106
Cecilia 37
Chains Of Love 64
City People 100
Cold, Cold Heart 81
Come On, Be Nice 33
Country Comfort 97
Dear Lonely Hearts 37
Dearer Than Life 72
Decorate The Night 114
Desertion 91
Destination Heartbreak 89
Devil Is A Real Bright Boy, The 26
Do It Right 74, 75
Do Your Own Thing 89
▪ *Do Your Own Thing* **89-90**
Doggone Baby, Doggone 35
Doing The Best I Can 96
Don't Do What I Did (Do What I Say) 74
Don't It Make You Want To/Wanta
    Go Home 44, 89, 95
Don't Think Twice, It's All Right 95
Don't Walk Away From Me 35, 157
Doncha Think It's Time 36
Early Every Morning 52
Endlessly 38, 41-2, 45, 193, 205
▪ *Endlessly* **45**
◎ *Endlessly* (Rhino) 76
◎ *Endlessly* (Tring) 104
◎ *Essential Vik and RCA Victor Recordings,*
    The 33, 203
Every Goodbye Ain't Gone 71
Everything Will Be Alright 35
Everytime I'm Kissin' You 72
Faded Love 72, 73

Fine Brown Frame 74
5 O'Clock World 100
Foolish Enough To Try 77
Fools Rush In 47-8, 130, 151
For Le Ann 93, 109, 204
For The Good Times 99
Four Thousand Years Ago 59
Frankie And Johnny 58
Give Me A Sign 32
Glory Of Love, The 86-7, 134, 149
Glow Love 110
Go Tell It On The Mountain 56
God Bless The Child 71
Going Home 56
Going Home In His Name 78, 96
Going To Soulsville 84
Going, Going, Gone 72
■ *Golden Hits* 41
■ *Golden Hits (Volume 2)* 41
Gone 81
Good News 123
Goodbye My Darling 157
■ *Gospel Time* 198
■ *Gospel Truth, The* 23, 78, **95-6**
Got You On My Mind 64
◎ *Greatest Hits* 82
Have I Told You Lately That I Love You? 81
He'll Have To Go 81, 134
He's Got You 81
Heading Home 100
Heaven 139
Hello Walls 81
Hello Young Lovers 68
Here We Go Again 87
Hiding Behind The Shadow Of A Dream 89
Hit Record 63
■ *Home Style* **92-5**
◎ *Home Style* 204
      See also *Today/Home Style*
Honey Babe 58
Hotel Happiness 35, 66, 67, 75
How Many Times 38
Hurtin' Inside 33, 38, 41
I Believe 49-50
I Can Tell 30
I Could Have Told You 29, 30
I Didn't Know What Time It Was 62
I Do 49-50   ■
I Don't Hurt Anymore 72, 73
I Don't Know 157
I Don't Know Enough About You 48
I Don't Know Why (I Just Do) 62
I Dreamed Of A City Called Heaven 26, 96
I Got A Woman 146
I Got What I Wanted 64, 66
I Had It 75
I Had To Learn (The Hard Way) 107
I Just Don't Know What To Do
    With Myself 89
I Keep Thinking To Myself 104, 109

I Left My Heart In San Francisco 86
I Love Paris 61
■ *I Love You In So Many Ways* **46-7**
I Only Have Eyes For You 82
I Really Don't Want To Know 81
I Walk The Line 72, 81, 134
I Wanna Do Everything For You 33
I Was Fool Enough To Love You 31
I Wish Everyday Could Be Like
    Christmas 113
I Worry 'Bout You 69
I'd Trade All Of My Tomorrows 72
I'll Be Around 48
I'll Get By (As Long As I Have You) 61, 62
I'll Meet You After Church Next Sunday 24
I'll Never Be Free 69, 71
I'll Step Aside 72
I'll Stop Anything I'm Doing 35
I'll String Along With You 43
I'll Take Care Of You 29
I'm A Man 187
I'm Beginning To See The Light 83-4
I'm Sticking With You 85
I'm Throwing Rice (At The Girl I Love) 72
I've Got The Christmas Spirit 113-14
I've Gotta Be Me 91, 190
I've Never Been In Love Before 68
If Ever I Would Leave You 68
If Only I Had Known 34, 158
If You Are But A Dream 48
■ *If You Believe* **55-6**, 176
If You Think God Is Dead 95, 96
If You['ve] Got The Time 100
□ *If you've got the time... we've got the beer*
    100
◙ *If you've got the time... we've got the beer*
    100-1
In A Dream 46
Instead (Of Loving You) 87
Intoxicated Rat, The 58, 86
It Started All Over Again 106
It's A Crime 77
It's All In The Game 95
It's Been A Long, Long Time 48, 83
It's Just A Matter Of Time
    23, 29, 37, 38-9, 41-2, 43, 45, 88, 99,
    119, 121, 127, 141, 157, 193, 205
■ *It's Just A Matter Of Time* 30, **43-4**
It's My Lazy Day 58
It's Too Late To Turn Back Now 74, 75
Jealous Guy 102
Jesus Lover Of My Soul 26
Johnny-O 59
Just A Closer Walk With Thee 56
Just As Much As Ever 82
Just Call Me Lonesome 72, 73
Keep The Faith, Baby 84
Kentuckian Song, The 31
Key To The Highway 59
Kiddio 23, 77, 151

Laura (What's He Got That I Ain't Got)
86
■ *Laura, what's he got that I ain't got*
85, **86-7**
Lawdy Miss Mary 29
Lay Lady Lay 102, 103
Learning To Love Again 75
Let Me Fix It 92-3, 204
Let Me Sing And I'm Happy 62
◉ *Let Me Sing And I'm Happy* 204
Let The Sun Come Out 109
Let Us All Get Together With The Lord 96
Letters Have No Arms 72
Lie To Me 64-6, 137
■ *Lie To Me* - See *Singing The Blues*
Life Has Its Little Ups And Downs 91
Lingering On 87
Lonely Street 87
Looking Back 29, 36, 37-8, 66
Lord I've Tried 26
Lost Penny, The 56
Love Is A Many-Splendored Thing 79
Love Is Best Of All 110
Love Look Away 68
Love Made Me Your Fool 32
Love Me Now 75
Love Me Or Leave Me 43
Lover Come Back To Me 48, 83, 134, 149
Lumberjack 74, 75, 115
Make Someone Happy 68
Makin' Love Is Good For You 109
■ *Makin' Love Is Good For You*
108, **109**, 110, 139, 198
Makin' Whoopee 83
May I 35
May I Never Love Again 45
Me And My Shadow 37
Merry Christmas All 113
Message, The 30
◉ *Millennium Collection, The* 203
Mr. Bartender 105, 106
■ *Mister Bartender* 105, **106-7**
Moon River 79, 80
Moonlight In Vermont 48
More 82
More I See You, The 134, 149
More Than You Know 45
Mother Nature, Father Time 76, 77-8, 151
■ *Mother Nature, Father Time* 76, **77-8**
Movin' Day 97, 154
■ *My Country* 73, 76, **80-1**
◉ *My Country/That Old Feeling*
80, 81, 130, 203
My Funny Valentine 106
My Shoes Keep Walking Back To You 72
My True Confession 64, 66
My Way 89, 91
Nearness Of You, The 43, 44
Next Stop Paradise 35
Night Has Many Eyes, The 103

Nightingale In Berkeley Square
See A Nightingale Sang In Berkeley
Square
Ninety-Nine Percent 35, 157
Nobody Knows 71
Nothing Can Take The Place Of You 89
Nothing In The World 35
Now Is The Time 107
Ode To Billie Joe 86
Oh Happy Day 96
Oh Lord, Why Lord 189-90
Oh! What It Seemed To Be 48
Ol' Man River 123, 130, 150
Old Fashioned Strut 110
■ *On The Countryside* **71-3**, 80
On Your Side Of The Bed 102
Ooh 31, 32
Orange Candles 100
Our First Christmas Together 84
Peg O' My Heart 79
People Will Say We're In Love 45
◉ *Platinum Collection, The* 203
Please Help Me, I'm Falling 81
Please, Please Make It Easy 74
Pledging My Love 66
Poor Make Believer 97
Precious Lord 23, 95, 96
Pulling Me Down
See You're Pulling Me Down
Rainy Night In Georgia
75, 89, 90-1, 98, 109, 135, 140, 141,
142, 150, 153, 157, 204, 206
Ramblin' Rose 37
■ *Raw Silk* 205
Remember Me 56
Remember The Good 99, 137
Rest Of The Way, The 35
Revenge 192
Roach Song, The 84, 86
Run On For A Long Time 26
Same One, The 29
San Francisco (Be Sure To Wear Some
Flowers In Your Hair) 86
Save The Last Dance For Me 98
Second Time Around, The 79, 134, 149
■ *Secret Combination* 206
Send Back My Heart 99
Send For Me 66
Sentimental Journey 83
September Song 48
Set Me Free 89
Shadrack 56
She Even Woke Me Up To Say Goodbye
97
She Knows What To Do For Me 89
Shoes 89, 97
Sidewalks Of Chicago 97
Silent Night 84, 112
◉ *Silky Smooth Tones of Brook Benton, The*
204

■ *Sinatra At The Sands* 61
Since I Met You Baby 71
■ *Singing The Blues [Lie To Me]*
64-6, 137
◎ *Singing The Blues*
See *There Goes That Song Again/*
Singing The Blues
■ *Sings A Love Story* **82-3**
Sister And Brother 103
Snap Your Fingers 116
So Close 23, 38, 41, 46
So Many Ways 38, 46, 127
■ *Soft* 108, **110-11**
Somebody To Love 29-30
Someone To Believe In 205
Someone To Watch Over Me 46
■ *Something For Everyone* **99-100**, 137
Song I Heard Last Night, The 78
■ *Songs I Love To Sing* **47-9**
◎ *Songs I Love To Sing* 47
Soul Santa 178, 187
South Carolina 102, 103
■ *Special Years, The* (unissued) 73
■ *Stars Salute Dr. Martin Luther King, The*
187-8
Steal Away 56
Stick-To-It-Ivity 86
■ *Story Teller* **97-8**
Straight Jingle - See All Vocal Jingle
Stroll, The 39
Sun's Gonna Shine In My Door, The 71
Sweet Georgia Brown 82
Sweet Memories 99
Take A Look At Your Hands 96
Take My Hand, Precious Lord
See Precious Lord
Tall Oak Tree 86
Taxi 105, 106
Tell Me Your Dream 43
Thank You Pretty Baby 36, 140, 193
That Old Feeling 79
■ *That Old Feeling* 44, 76, **78-80**, 82
◎ *That Old Feeling*
See *My Country/That Old Feeling*
That's All I Need 30
There Goes My Heart 52, 82
There Goes That Song Again 61-2
■ *There Goes That Song Again* **59-63**, 84
◎ *There Goes That Song Again/*
Singing The Blues 204
There, I've Said It Again 82
(There Was A) Tall Oak Tree 86
These Arms You Pushed Away 104, 110
They Can't Take That Away From Me 48
Things I Love, The 45
This Bitter Earth 35, 54, 74
■ *This Bitter Earth* 35, **73-5**
This Could Be The Start Of Something Big
123
■ *This Is Brook Benton* 105, **106-7**
◎ *This Is Brook Benton* 82, 203

This Is Worth Fighting For 87
This Time Of [The] Year 67, 113, 157
Till/Til' I Can't Take It Anymore 109
Time After Time 45
■ *Today* **90-2**
◎ *Today* 92, 203
◎ *Today/Home Style* 92, 95, 203
Tomorrow Night 66
Touch 'Em With Love 89
Touch Me Jesus 26
Trouble In Mind 62
Trouble Of This World 26, 157
Troubled, Lord I'm Troubled 26, 157
Trust Me To Do What You Want Me To
(And I'll Do It) 110
■ *Two Of Us, The* 46, **49-55**
◎ *Two Of Us, The* 54, 203
Two Tickets To Paradise 67, 130
Unforgettable 82, 134, 149
Valley Of Tears 66
Walk On The Wild Side 155
Walking The Floor Over You 81
Walking Together 35
Wall, The 31, 37
We Have Love 52
We're Gonna Make It 92
Weakness In A Man 87
Weekend With Feathers 106
What Else Do You Want From Me 74, 75
What Is A Woman Without A Man 74-5
When A Child Is Born 114
When I Grow Too Old To Dream
29-30, 61, 62
When Summer Turns To Fall 103
When You're Smiling 37
Where Do I Go From Here 90
While There's Life (There's Still Hope) 78
Whoever Finds This I Love You 95
Why Try To Change Me Now 48
Will You Love Me Tomorrow 66
Will You Tell Him 29
Willie And Laura Mae Jones
93-4, 95, 109, 204
Willoughby Grove 98
Winds Of Change, The 104
With The Touch Of Your Hand 71
Woman Without Love 87, 89
You Ain't Got Faith 26
You Go Around Once 142
You Were Gone 106
You're For Me 157
You're Mine (And I Love You) 77
You're Movin' Me 35
You're Pulling Me Down [Pulling Me Down]
110
You're The Reason I'm Living 86
You've Never Been This Far 104, 110
Your Love Alone 34, 157

INDEX OF FILMS & SHOWS

A House Is Not A Home *(film)* 75, 155-6
A Raisin In The Sun *(play)* 154
All Men Are Liars *(film)* 157
All The Rage [It's The Rage] *(film)* 157
Barbara McNair Show, The *(TV show)* 151
Big Score, The *(film)* 110
Biggest Show of Stars for '61, The *(show)* 124
Boogie Nights *(film)* 157
Brook Benton Story (Just A Matter Of Time), The *(stage musical)* 151
Consenting Adults *(film)* 157
Cool Hand Luke *(film)* 56
Country Music Holiday *(film)* 157
Crossing The Line *(film)* 157
Dick Clark's Saturday Night Beechnut Show *(TV show)* 151
Ding Dong, The Wine's All Gone *(film)* 160
Easter Parade of Stars *(show)* 124
Ed Sullivan Show, The *(TV show)* 151, 197
Father's Day Fashion Show *(Lou Borders event)* 165
Gospel '84 *(show)* 140
Gospel Caravan Show *(show)* 139
Hamlet *(play)* 160
Hareemu Ohgen *(film)* 157
Hurricane *(film)* 157
In The Heat Of The Night *(TV series)* 157
Jazz Greats *(show)* 140
John Reed King Show *(TV show)* 151
Kentuckian, The *(film)* 31
Ladykillers, The *(film)* 157
Live At Sheffield City Hall *(TV concert)* 120. 140, 143
Living Legends *(show)* 140-1
Midnight Jazz Festival *(radio show)* 160, 165
Mike Douglas Show, The *(TV show)* 151
Mister Rock and Roll *(film)* 34, 157-8
Mother Nature, Father Time *(Scopitone film)* 78, 151
My Son The Fanatic *(film)* 157
Nashville Now *(TV show)* 120, 142
Nat 'King' Cole Show, The *(TV show)* 154
Nights In Rodanthe *(film)* 157
Olympic Games *(Bedford-Stuyvesant Youth In Action event)* 172-3
Operation Blue Sky *(film)* 157
Perry Como's Christmas Music Hall *(TV show)* 151
Queen Of The Blues *(stage musical)* 154
Rainy Night In Georgia *(stage musical)* 153-4
Rock, Roll & Remember *(radio show)* 200
Saturday Prom *(TV show)* 151
Skin Deep *(film)* 157
Steer Roast Day *(event)* 124-5
Steve Allen Playhouse, The *(TV show)* 148, 151
Sunday Night At The London Palladium *(TV show)* 127, 130
Teenarama *(TV show)* 151
Tonight Show starring Johnny Carson, The *(TV show)* 151
Two Weeks' Notice *(film)* 157
Untamed Heart *(film)* 157
Walk On The Wild Side *(film)* 155
When Nature Calls *(film)* 157

INDEX OF RECORDINGS

Brook Benton recorded hundreds of songs, many more than once. This index will assist readers to locate the relevant songs/versions within the *Discography*.

The description after each title identifies the parent company for whom the song was recorded, the year the recording was made, and where necessary includes additional information to help readers distinguish between different versions. '*Columbia rec*' (Columbia recording) covers songs that were released on the Columbia, Epic and OKeh labels; '*RCA rec*' (RCA recording) covers songs that were released on RCA Camden, RCA Victor and Vik; and so on.

①, ②, ③, etc after a title indicates the version. Some unissued titles may be versions of earlier or later issued titles, however they are not identified as such except where this is known for certain.

A Black Child Can't Smile *(Cotillion rec, 1971)* 255
A City Called Heaven *(Mercury rec, 1961, unissued)* 229
A Door That Is Open *(RCA rec, 1958)* 222
A House Is Not A Home *(Mercury rec, 1964)* 238
A Lifetime Lease On Your Heart *(Mercury rec, 1965, unissued)* 239
A Little Bit Of Soap *(Cotillion rec, 1969)* 251
A Little Bit Of Soap *(Cotillion rec, 1969, edited version)* 253
A Lovely Way To Spend An Evening *(Mercury rec, 1959)* 224
A Lover's Question ① *(demo, 1956)* 219
A Lover's Question ② *(Ernestine Anderson, Mercury rec, 1961)* 230
A Lover's Question ③ *(Olde World rec, 1977)* 261
A Lover's Question ③ *(Olde World rec, 1977, alt. vocal)* 261
A Man Of Steel *(Mercury rec, 1963, unissued)* 235
A Million Miles *(Mercury rec, 1965, unissued)* 239
A Million Miles From Nowhere *(RCA rec, 1957)* 222
A New Love *(Crown rec, 1956)* 220
A Nightingale Sang In Berkeley Square ① *(RCA rec, 1966)* 242
[A] Nightingale [Sang] In Berkeley Square ② *(All Platinum rec, 1975)* ... 258
A Rainy Night In Georgia – *See* Rainy Night In Georgia
A Rockin' Good Way ① *(duet with Dinah Washington, Mercury rec, 1960)* ... 227
A Rockin' Good Way ② *(solo vocal, Arrival rec, 1982)* 262
A Sailor Boy's Love Song ① *(acetate, Circle, 1965)* 243
A Sailor Boy's Love Song ② *(RCA rec, 1965)* 243
A Sleepin' At The Foot Of The Bed *(Mercury rec, 1965)* 240
A Touch Of Class *(Brut rec, 1977)* 257
A Tribute To 'Mama' *(Olde World rec, 1974)* 261
A Worried Man *(Mercury rec, 1961)* 230
After Midnight *(Mercury rec, 1963)* 237
After You've Gone *(Mercury rec, 1962)* 232
Ain't It Good *(demo, 1956)* 219
All In Love Is Fair *(All Platinum rec, 1975)* 258
All My Love Belongs To You [Kirkland-McCoy] *(Columbia rec, 1957)* 218
All My Love Belongs To You [Glover-Nix] *(RCA rec, 1967, instrumental)* ... 248
All My Love Belongs To You [Glover-Nix] *(RCA rec, 1967, vocal)* 248
All Of Me *(Mercury rec, 1962)* 231
All Over Again *(Mercury rec, 1964)* 237
All That Love Went To Waste *(Brut rec, 1974)* 257
All Vocal Jingle (Straight Jingle) *(Miller Beer rec, 1971)* 256
Almost Persuaded *(duet with Damita Jo, Mercury rec, 1963, withdrawn)* ... 236
Alone *(MGM rec, 1972)* 256
Another Cup Of Coffee *(Mercury rec, 1963, unissued)* 234
Another Cup Of Coffee *(Mercury rec, 1963, edited version)* 234
Any Time *(RCA rec, 1966)* 244

Anything For You *(Columbia rec, 1957)* 218
Are You Sincere *(Cotillion rec, 1970)* 252
Around The World *(Mercury rec, 1959)* 224
As Long As She Needs Me *(Mercury rec, 1963)* 235
Aspen Colorado *(Cotillion rec, 1970)* 252
Baby *(Cotillion rec, 1969)* 251
Baby Won't You Please Come Home *(Mercury rec, 1960)* 228
Baby You've Got It Made *(duet with Damita Jo, Mercury rec, 1963)* 236
Baby (You've Got What It Takes) ① *(duet with Dinah Washington, Mercury rec, 1959)* 225
Baby (You've Got What It Takes) ② *(solo vocal, Arrival rec, 1982)* 263
Bayou Babe *(Olde World rec, 1977)* 261
Be My Friend *(Cotillion rec, 1971, rejected)* 256
Beautiful Memories *(HMC rec, 1983)* 263
Because Of Everything *(Mercury rec, 1959)* 226
Because Of You *(Mercury rec, 1959)* 224
Because You Love Me *(RCA rec, 1958)* 222
Before You See A Big Man Cry *(Cotillion rec, 1970, unissued)* 253
Better Times *(Olde World rec, 1977)* 260
Better Times *(Olde World rec, 1977, alt. vocal)* 260
Beyond The Sea (La Mer) *(RCA rec, 1966, unissued)* 247
Beyond The Sea (La Mer) *(RCA rec, 1966, alt. take)* 247
Big Mable Murphy *(Cotillion rec, 1971)* 255
Blue Decorations *(HMC rec, 1983)* 263
Blue Moon *(RCA rec, 1965)* 243
Blue Skies *(Mercury rec, 1959)* 224
Blues In The Night *(Mercury rec, 1962)* 232
Boll Weevil Song, The ① *(Mercury rec, 1960, unissued)* 229
Boll Weevil Song, The ② *(Mercury rec, 1961)* 230
Boll Weevil Song ③ *(Treasury Department rec, 1963)* 234
Boll Weevil Song, The ④ *(Musicor rec, 1977)* 259
Boll Weevil Song, The ⑤ *(Arrival rec, 1982)* 263
   See also Singing Bug
Born To Sing The Blues *(Mercury rec, 1963)* 236
Born Under A Bad Sign *(Cotillion rec, 1970)* 252
Boy, I Wish I Was In Your Place *(RCA rec, 1965)* 240
Break Her Heart ① *(RCA rec, 1966, unissued)* 245
Break Her Heart ② *(RCA rec, 1966)* 245
Break Out *(Cotillion rec, 1969)* 251
Breezin' Along With The Breeze *(Mercury rec, 1962)* 232
Bring Me Love *(Columbia rec, 1956)* 217
Brook's Christmas Impressions *(HMC rec, 1983)* 264
Bump With A Boom *(RCA rec, 1967, unissued)* 248
But Beautiful *(Mercury rec, 1959)* 223
Buttermilk Sky *(Mercury rec, 1964, unissued)* 238
Call Me *(Mercury rec, 1960)* 227
Call Me Irresponsible *(RCA rec, 1965)* 242
Can I Help It *(Columbia rec, 1957)* 217
Can't Take My Eyes Off You ① *(Cotillion rec, 1969)* 251
Can't Take My Eyes Off Of You ② *(All Platinum rec, 1975)* 258
Careless Love *(Mercury rec, 1961)* 231
Chains Of Love ① *(Mercury rec, 1962)* 233
Chains Of Love ② *(Mercury rec, 1965, unissued)* 240
Chariot Wheels *(acetate, Rockhill, 1962)* 234
Child *(HMC rec, 1983)* 263
Child Of The Engineer *(Mercury rec, 1961)* 231
Christmas Makes The Town (Such A Happy Place) *(HMC rec, 1983)* 264
City People *(Miller Beer rec, 1971)* 256
Cold, Cold Heart *(RCA rec, 1966)* 245
Come Back My Love *(demo, 1956)* 219
Come Back My Love *(Mercury rec, 1961, unissued)* 230

Come Let's Go *(demo, 1956)* 219
Come On Back *(Mercury rec, 1964)* 238
Come On, Be Nice *(RCA rec, 1957)* 221
Completely *(demo, 1956)* 219
Country Comfort *(Cotillion rec, 1970)* 254
Crack Up Time *(Mercury rec, 1963, unissued)* 234
Crazy In Love With You *(RCA rec, 1958)* 223
Crinoline Skirt *(RCA rec, 1958)* 222
Daddy Knows *(Mercury rec, 1963)* 237
Dearer Than Life *(Mercury rec, 1963)* 234
Decorate The Night *(HMC rec, 1983)* 264
Deep River *(Mercury rec, 1961)* 229
Desertion *(Mercury rec, 1969)* 251
Destination Heartbreak *(Cotillion rec, 1969)* 250
Devil Is A Real Bright Boy, The *(Bill Landford Quartet, RCA rec, 1953)* 215
Devoted ① *(demo, 1956)* 219
Devoted ② *(RCA rec, 1957)* 222
Do It Right *(Mercury rec, 1964)* 239
Do Your Own Thing *(Cotillion rec, 1968)* 250
Doggone Baby, Doggone *(demo, 1956)* 219
Doing The Best I Can *(Cotillion rec, 1970)* 254
Don't Do What I Did (Do What I Say) *(Mercury rec, 1964)* 239
Don't Hate Me (For Loving You) *(Mercury rec, 1963)* 235
Don't It Make You Want To/Wanta Go Home *(Cotillion rec, 1970)* 252
Don't Look For Me *(RCA rec, 1967, unissued)* 248
Don't Put It Off *(Crown rec, 1956)* 220
Don't Rob Another Man's Castle *(Mercury rec, 1964)* 238
Don't Think Twice, It's All Right *(Cotillion rec, 1970)* 252
Don't Walk Away From Me *(demo, 1956)* 219
Dreams, Oh Dreams *(Crown rec, 1956)* 220
Endlessly ① *(Mercury rec, 1956)* 218
Endlessly ② *(Olde World rec, 1977)* 260
Endlessly ② *(Olde World rec, 1977, alt. vocal)* 260
Endlessly ③ *(Arrival rec, 1982)* 263
Every Goodbye Ain't Gone *(Mercury rec, 1963)* 236
Everything *(Mercury rec, 1959)* 226
Everything Will Be Alright *(demo, 1956)* 219
Everytime I Feel The Spirit *(Mercury rec, 1961, unissued)* 229
Everytime I'm Kissin' You *(Mercury rec, 1962)* 233
Faded Love *(Mercury rec, 1964)* 238
Fantastic Things *(Mercury rec, 1961, unissued)* 230
Feelin' Good *(Cotillion rec, 1970, unissued)* 254
Fine Brown Frame *(Mercury rec, 1964)* 239
5 O'Clock World *(Miller Beer rec, 1971)* 256
Foolish Enough To Try *(RCA rec, 1965)* 241
Fools Rush In ① *(Mercury rec, 1959)* 225
Fools Rush In ② *(Musicor rec, 1977)* 259
For All We Know *(MGM rec, 1972)* 257
For Le Ann *(Cotillion rec, 1970)* 252
For My Baby ① *(Mercury rec, 1960)* 228
For My Baby ② *(Musicor rec, 1977)* 259
For The Good Times *(part of medley, MGM rec, 1972)* 256
Four Thousand Years Ago *(Mercury rec, 1961)* 231
Frankie And Johnny ① *(Mercury rec, 1961)* 230
Frankie And Johnny ② *(Musicor rec, 1977)* 259
Funny How Time Slips Away *(RCA rec, 1966)* 244
Gee, You Look So Pretty *(Cotillion rec, 1969, unissued)* 251
Girl I Love, The *(Crown rec, 1956)* 221
Give Me A Sign *(Columbia rec, 1956)* 218
Glory Of Love, The *(Reprise rec, 1967)* 249

Glow Love *(Olde World rec, 1978)* 261
Glow Love *(Olde World rec, 1978, alt. vocal)* 261
Go Tell It On The Mountain *(Mercury rec, 1961)* 229
God Bless The Child ① *(Mercury rec, 1960, unissued)* 227
God Bless The Child ② *(Mercury rec, 1963)* 236
God Is About To Do *(Tate download, recorded circa 1987)* 264
Goin' Home *(Bill Landford Quartet, RCA rec, 1953, unissued)* 215
Going Home *(Mercury rec, 1961)* 229
Going Home In His Name *(Cotillion rec, 1970)* 255
Going To Soulsville *(RCA rec, 1967)* 249
Going, Going, Gone *(Mercury rec, 1963)* 237
Gone *(RCA rec, 1966)* 244
Goodnight My Love, Pleasant Dreams *(RCA rec, 1966)* 248
Got You On My Mind *(Mercury rec, 1962)* 233
Have I Told You Lately That I Love You? *(RCA rec, 1966)* 245
Hawaiian Wedding Song *(RCA rec, 1965)* 242
He Gives Us All His Love *(Cotillion rec, 1971, unissued)* 255
He'll Have To Go *(RCA rec, 1966)* 244
He'll Understand And Say Well Done *(Mercury rec, 1961)* 229
He's Got You *(RCA rec, 1966)* 244
Heading Home *(Miller Beer rec, 1971)* 256
Heaven Help Us All *(Cotillion rec, 1970)* 253
Hello Walls *(RCA rec, 1966)* 244
Hello Young Lovers *(Mercury rec, 1963)* 235
Here We Go Again *(Reprise rec, 1967)* 249
Hey There *(RCA rec, 1965)* 242
Hiding Behind The Shadow Of A Dream *(Cotillion rec, 1969)* 251
Hit Record *(Mercury rec, 1962)* 232
Hit Record *(Mercury rec, 1962, alt. take)* 232
Hither And Thither And Yon *(Mercury rec, 1959)* 226
Hold Me, Thrill Me, Kiss Me *(Mercury rec, 1959)* 223
Hold My Hand ① *(Mercury rec, 1955, unissued)* 217
Hold My Hand ② *(Mercury rec, 1959, rejected)* 224
Hold My Hand ③ *(Mercury rec, 1959)* 226
Honey Babe *(Mercury rec, 1961)* 230
Hotel Happiness ① *(Mercury rec, 1962)* 233
Hotel Happiness ② *(Treasury Department rec, 1963)* 234
Hotel Happiness ③ *(Musicor rec, 1977)* 259
Hotel Happiness ④ *(Arrival rec, 1982)* 263
How Many Times *(Mercury rec, 1956)* 218
Hurtin' Inside *(Mercury rec, 1955)* 217
I Believe *(duet with Dinah Washington, Mercury rec, 1960)* 227
I Can Tell *(Chuck Willis & The Sandmen, Columbia rec, 1955)* 216
I Can't Begin To Tell You *(Mercury rec, 1959)* 223
I Could Have Told You ① *(Sandmen, Columbia rec, 1954, unissued)* 216
I Could Have Told You ② *(Mercury rec, 1959)* 223
I Cried For You *(Polydor rec, 1979)* 262
I Cried For You *(Polydor rec, 1979, edited version)* 262
I Didn't Know What Time It Was *(Mercury rec, 1962)* 231
I Do *(duet with Dinah Washington, Mercury rec, 1959)* 225
I Don't Hurt Anymore *(Mercury rec, 1964)* 237
I Don't Know Enough About You *(Mercury rec, 1960)* 228
I Don't Know Why (I Just Do) *(Mercury rec, 1962)* 232
I Dreamed Of A City Called Heaven ① *(Bill Landford Quartet, RCA rec, 1953)* ... 215
I Dreamed Of A City Called Heaven ② *(Cotillion rec, 1970)* 255
I Got What I Wanted ① *(Mercury rec, 1962)* 233
I Got What I Wanted ② *(Musicor rec, 1977)* 260
I Gotta Be Home By Ten *(Mickey & Sylvia, RCA rec, 1957)* 222
I Had It *(Mercury rec, 1964)* 239
I Had To Learn (The Hard Way) *(All Platinum rec, 1975)* 258

I Heard The Preaching Of The Elders *(Bill Landford Quartet, RCA rec, 1953, unissued)* 215
I Heard Zion Moan *(Bill Landford Quartet, RCA rec, 1953, unissued)* 215
I Just Don't Know What To Do With Myself *(Cotillion rec, 1968)* 250
I Keep Thinking To Myself ① *(Stax rec, 1974)* 257
I Keep Thinking To Myself ② *(Olde World rec, 1977)* 261
I Keep Thinking To Myself ② *(Olde World rec, 1977, alt. vocal)* 261
I Left My Heart In San Francisco *(part of medley, Reprise rec, 1967)* 249
I Love Her *(Olde World rec, 1977)* 261
I Love Her *(Olde World rec, 1977, alt. vocal)* 261
I Love Paris *(Mercury rec, 1962)* 231
I Need You So *(Mercury rec, 1962, unissued)* 233
I Only Have Eyes For You *(RCA rec, 1966, unissued)* 247
I Only Have Eyes For You *(RCA rec, 1966, alt. take)* 248
I Really Don't Want To Know *(RCA rec, 1966)* 244
I Still Believe In Rainbows *(Cotillion rec, 1969, unissued)* 250
I Walk The Line ① *(Mercury rec, 1964)* 237
I Walk The Line ② *(RCA rec, 1966)* 244
I Wanna Be With You *(RCA rec, 1965)* 241
I Wanna Do Everything For You *(RCA rec, 1957)* 221
I Want You Forever ① *(Mercury rec, 1955, unissued)* 217
I Want You Forever ② *(Mercury rec, 1959)* 223
I Was Fool Enough To Love You
   (Brook Benton & The Sandmen, Columbia rec, 1955, unissued) 217
I Will Warm Your Heart *(Mercury rec, 1965, long version, unissued)* 240
I Will Warm Your Heart *(Mercury rec, 1965, short version, unissued)* 240
I Wish An Old Fashioned Christmas To You *(RCA rec, 1966, unissued)* 248
I Wish Everyday Could Be Like Christmas *(HMC rec, 1983)* 264
I Worry 'Bout You *(Mercury rec, 1963)* 236
I'd Trade All Of My Tomorrows *(Mercury rec, 1964)* 238
I'll Always Be In Love With You *(Mercury rec, 1963, rejected)* 234
I'll Always Love You *(Mercury rec, 1963, unissued)* 234
I'll Be Around *(Mercury rec, 1960)* 228
I'll Get By (As Long As I Have You) *(Mercury rec, 1962)* 232
I'll Know *(Mercury rec, 1963)* 235
I'll Meet You After Church Next Sunday *(demo, 1956)* 219
I'll Never Be Free *(Mercury rec, 1963)* 236
I'll Never Stop Trying *(demo, 1956)* 219
I'll Paint You A Song *(Cotillion rec, 1970, unissued)* 253
I'll Step Aside *(Mercury rec, 1964)* 237
I'll Stop Anything I'm Doing *(demo, 1956)* 219
I'll String Along With You *(Mercury rec, 1959)* 223
I'm A Man *(Mercury rec, 1964, unissued)* 238
I'm A Man *(Mercury rec, 1964, alt. take, mono)* 238
I'm A Man *(Mercury rec, 1964, different alt. take, stereo)* 238
I'm Beginning To See The Light *(RCA rec, 1966, unissued)* 246
I'm Comin' Home *(Cotillion rec, 1970, unissued)* 254
I'm Coming Back To You *(RCA rec, 1958)* 222
I'm In The Mood For Love *(Mercury rec,1959)* 223
I'm Sure *(Lincoln Chase & The Sandmen, Columbia rec, 1955, unissued)* 216
I'm Throwing Rice (At The Girl I Love) *(Mercury rec, 1964)* 237
I've Been To Town *(MGM rec, 1972)* 257
I've Got The Christmas Spirit *(HMC rec, 1983)* 264
I've Gotta Be Me *(Cotillion rec, 1969)* 251
I've Never Been In Love Before *(Mercury rec, 1963)* 235
If Ever I Would Leave You *(Mercury rec, 1963)* 235
If Only I Had Known *(RCA rec, 1957)* 221
If You Are But A Dream ① *(Mercury rec, 1960, rejected)* 228
If You Are But A Dream ② *(Mercury rec, 1960)* 228
If You But Knew *(Mercury rec, 1959)* 226
If You Have No Real Objections *(Mecury rec, 1961, unissued)* 230

If You Only Knew *(RCA rec, 1966)* 248
If You Think God Is Dead ① *(Cotillion rec, 1970, unissued)* 254
If You Think God Is Dead ② *(Cotillion rec, 1970, matrix CO-20899)* 255
If You Think God Is Dead ② *(Cotillion rec, 1970, matrix CO-22008)* 255
    Matrix CO-22008 and matrix CO-20899 are identical.
If You['ve] Got The Time *(MGM rec, 1972)* 256
Impossible, Incredible, But True *(RCA rec, 1966)* 245
In A Dream *(Mercury rec, 1959)* 225
In The Evening By The Moonlight *(RCA rec, 1966)* 245
In Your World *(MGM rec, 1972)* 256
Instead (Of Loving You) *(Reprise rec, 1968)* 250
Intoxicated Rat, The *(Mercury rec, 1961)* 231
It Started All Over Again *(All Platinum rec, 1975)* 258
It Was Time *(Tate download, recorded circa 1987)* 264
It's A Crime *(RCA rec, 1965)* 241
It's All In The Game *(Cotillion rec, 1970)* 252
It's All In The Game *(Cotillion rec, 1970, alt. take)* 252
It's All Right *(Mercury rec, 1962)* 232
It's Been A Long, Long Time ① *(Mercury rec, 1960, rejected)* 228
It's Been A Long, Long Time ② *(Mercury rec, 1960)* 228
It's Been A Long, Long Time ③ *(RCA rec, 1966, unissued)* 246
It's Just A House Without You ① *(Mercury rec, 1961)* 230
It's Just A House Without You ② *(Musicor rec, 1977)* 260
It's Just A Matter Of Time ① *(Mercury rec, 1955)* 217
It's Just A Matter Of Time ② *(part of medley, MGM rec, 1972)* 256
It's Just A Matter Of Time ③ *(Musicor rec, 1977)* 259
It's Just A Matter Of Time ④ *(Arrival rec, 1982)* 263
It's My Lazy Day *(Mercury rec, 1961)* 231
(It's No) Sin *(Mercury rec, 1959)* 224
It's Too Late To Turn Back Now ① *(Mercury rec, 1960, unissued)* 227
It's Too Late To Turn Back Now ② *(Mercury rec, 1961)* 230
Too Late To Turn Back Now ③ *(Mercury rec, 1964)* 238
Jam Tune *(Cotillion rec, 1970)* 254
Jealous Guy *(Brut rec, 1974)* 257
Jesus Lover Of My Soul *(Bill Landford Quartet, RCA rec, 1953)* 215
Jet *(Polydor rec, 1979)* 262
Johnny-O *(Mercury rec, 1961)* 230
Just A Closer Walk With Thee *(Mercury rec, 1961)* 229
Just As Much As Ever *(RCA rec, 1966, unissued)* 247
Just As Much As Ever *(RCA rec, 1966, alt. take)* 247
Just Call Me Lonesome *(Mercury rec, 1964)* 237
Just Tell Me When *(Crown rec, 1956)* 221
Keep Me In Mind *(demo, 1956)* 219
Keep The Faith, Baby *(RCA rec, 1967)* 249
Keep Your Cotton Pickin' Hands Off My Gin ① *(RCA rec, 1966, unissued)* 245
Keep Your Cotton Pickin' Hands Off My Gin ② *(RCA rec, 1966, rejected)* 246
Keep Your Cotton Pickin' Hands Off My Gin ③ *(RCA rec, 1966, unissued)* 247
Kentuckian Song, The *(Columbia rec, 1955)* 217
Key To The Highway *(Mercury rec, 1961)* 231
Kiddio ① *(Mercury rec, 1960)* 227
Kiddio ② *(Musicor rec, 1977)* 259
Kiddio ③ *(Arrival rec, 1982)* 263
Laura (What's He Got That I Ain't Got) *(Reprise rec, 1967)* 249
Lawdy Miss Mary *(Chuck Willis & The Sandmen, Columbia rec, 1954)* 216
Lay Lady Lay *(Brut rec, 1973)* 257
Lay Lady Lay *(Brut rec, 1973, edited version)* 257
Learning To Love Again *(Mercury rec, 1964)* 239
Let Me Fix It *(Cotillion rec, 1970)* 253
Let Me In Your World *(Olde World rec, 1977)* 261
Let Me Sing And I'm Happy *(Mercury rec, 1962)* 232

Let The Sun Come Out *(Olde World rec, 1977)* 261
Let The Sun Come Out *(Olde World rec, 1977, alt. vocal)* 261
Let Us All Get Together With The Lord *(Cotillion rec, 1970)* 255
Letters Have No Arms *(Mercury rec, 1964)* 237
Lie To Me ① *(Mercury rec, 1962)* 233
Lie To Me ② *(Musicor rec, 1977)* 260
Lie To Me ③ *(Arrival rec, 1982)* 263
Life Has Its Little Ups And Downs *(Cotillion rec, 1969)* 251
Life Is Too Short *(RCA rec, 1965)* 241
Lingering On *(Reprise rec, 1967)* 249
Lonely One, The *(Cotillion rec, 1969, unissued)* 251
Lonely Street *(Reprise rec, 1968)* 250
Long Before I Knew You *(Mercury rec, 1963)* 235
Looking Back ① *(demo, 1956)* 219
Looking Back ② *(Mercury rec, 1962)* 233
Lord I've Tried *(Bill Landford & The Landfordaires, Columbia rec, 1949)* 215
Lord You Know How Men Are *(Olde World rec, 1977)* 261
Lord You Know How Men Are *(Olde World rec, 1977, alt. vocal)* 261
Lost Penny, The *(Mercury rec, 1961)* 229
Love Is A Many-Splendored Thing *(RCA rec, 1966)* 242
Love Is Best Of All *(Olde World rec, 1977)* 261
Love Look Away *(Mercury rec, 1963)* 235
Love Made Me Your Fool *(Columbia rec, 1956)* 218
Love Me A Little *(Polydor rec, 1979)* 262
Love Me Now *(Mercury rec, 1965)* 240
Love Me Or Leave Me *(Mercury rec, 1959)* 223
Love's That Way *(Crown rec, 1956)* 221
Lover Come Back To Me ① *(Mercury rec, 1960, rejected)* 228
Lover Come Back To Me ② *(Mercury rec, 1960)* 228
Lover Come Back To Me ③ *(RCA rec, 1966, unissued)* 246
Lumberjack *(Mercury rec, 1964)* 239
Made Up In My Mind *(Bill Landford Quartet, RCA rec, 1953, unissued)* 215
Make Someone Happy *(Mercury rec, 1963)* 235
Makin' Love Is Good For You *(Olde World rec, 1977)* 260
Makin' Love Is Good For You *(Olde World rec, 1977, edited version)* 260
Makin' Love Is Good For You *(Olde World rec, 1977, edited version, alt. vocal)* 260
Makin' Whoopee *(RCA rec, 1966, unissued)* 246
Mark My Word *(demo, 1956)* 219
May I? ① *(demo, 1956)* 220
May I ② *(Mercury rec, 1959)* 225
May I Never Love Again *(Mercury rec, 1959)* 224
Merry Christmas All *(HMC rec, 1983)* 264
Merry Christmas, Happy New Year *(Mercury rec, 1960)* 229
Merry, Merry Christmas from Brook Benton *(HMC rec, 1983)* 264
Message, The *(Lincoln Chase & The Sandmen, Columbia rec, 1955)* 216
Mr. Bartender *(All Platinum rec, 1975)* 258
Moon River *(RCA rec, 1965)* 241
Moonlight In Vermont *(Mercury rec, 1960)* 228
More *(RCA rec, 1965)* 242
More I See You, The *(Mercury rec, 1959)* 223
More Than You Know *(Mercury rec, 1959)* 224
More Time To Be With You ① *(RCA rec, 1965, unissued)* 240
More Time To Be With You ② *(RCA rec, 1965)* 240
Mother Nature, Father Time *(RCA rec, 1965)* 240
Movin' Day *(Cotillion rec, 1970)* 254
My Darling, My Darling *(RCA rec, 1966)* 243
My Foolish Heart ① *(Mercury rec, 1962, unissued)* 232
My Foolish Heart ② *(Mercury rec, 1963, rejected)* 234
My Funny Valentine *(All Platinum rec, 1975)* 258
My Last Dollar *(Mercury rec, 1961)* 231

My Love Will Last *(demo, 1956)* 220
My One And Only Year Book *(Mercury rec, 1965, unissued)* 239
My Only Year Book *(Mercury rec, 1965, unissued)* 239
My Shoes Keep Walking Back To You *(Mercury rec, 1964)* 237
My Son, I Wish You Everything *(RCA rec, 1965, unissued)* 243
My True Confession ① *(Mercury rec, 1962)* 233
My True Confession ② *(Musicor rec, 1977)* 260
My Way *(Cotillion rec, 1969)* 251
My Way *(Cotillion rec, 1969, single edit)* 253
My Way *(Cotillion rec, 1969, promo single edit, mono)* 253
My Way *(Cotillion rec, 1969, promo single edit, stereo)* 253
Nearness Of You, The *(Mercury rec, 1959)* 223
Never A Greater Need *(Mercury rec, 1959)* 226
Never Like This *(Mercury rec, 1959)* 226
Next Stop Paradise *(demo, 1956)* 220
Next Time I Fall In Love, The *(Mercury rec, 1964, unissued)* 238
Night Has Many Eyes, The *(Brut rec, 1974)* 257
Nightingale In Berkeley Square — *See* A Nightingale Sang In Berkeley Square
Ninety-Nine Percent *(demo, 1956)* 220
No Love Like Her Love — *See* No One (Love) Like Her Love
No One (Love) Like Her Love *(Crown rec, 1956)* 221
Nobody Knows *(Mercury rec, 1963)* 237
Not One Step Behind *(Mercury rec, 1960)* 227
Nothing Can Take The Place Of You *(Cotillion rec, 1969)* 250
Nothing In The World ① *(demo, 1956)* 220
Nothing In The World ② *(Mercury rec, 1959)* 224
Nothing In The World ③ *(Mercury rec, 1959, unissued)* 226
Now Is The Time *(All Platinum rec, 1975)* 258
Ode To Billie Joe *(Reprise rec, 1967)* 249
Oh Happy Day *(Cotillion rec, 1970)* 255
Oh Lord, Why Lord *(Cotillion rec, 1969)* 250
Oh! What It Seemed To Be ① *(Mercury rec, 1960, rejected)* 228
Oh! What It Seemed To Be ② *(Mercury rec, 1960)* 228
Old Fashioned Strut *(Olde World rec, 1977)* 261
Old Man Willis *(Cotillion rec, 1970, unissued)* 252
On My Word ① *(Mercury rec, 1964, unissued)* 238
On My Word ② *(Mercury rec, 1964, unissued)* 238
On Your Side Of The Bed *(Brut rec, 1974)* 257
Once In Love With Amy *(RCA rec, 1966)* 242
Once Upon A Time *(Mercury rec, 1963)* 235
One By One *(Mercury rec, 1959)* 226
One Day I'll Dry Your Tears *(Mercury rec, 1965, unissued)* 239
One Love Too Many *(demo, 1956)* 220
One More Time *(Mercury rec, 1965, unissued)* 239
Only A Girl Like You *(RCA rec, 1965)* 243
Only Believe *(Mercury rec, 1961)* 229
Only Your Love *(RCA rec, 1957)* 222
Ooh *(Brook Benton & The Sandmen, Columbia rec, 1955)* 216
Orange Candles *(Miller Beer rec, 1971)* 256
Our First Christmas Together *(RCA rec, 1966)* 248
Our Hearts Knew ① *(Mercury rec, 1962, unissued)* 232
Our Hearts Knew ② *(Cotillion rec, 1970, unissued)* 254
Partners For Life *(Columbia rec, 1957)* 218
Peg O' My Heart *(RCA rec, 1965)* 243
People Will Say We're In Love *(Mercury rec, 1959)* 224
Please Help Me, I'm Falling *(RCA rec, 1966)* 244
Please Send Me Someone To Love ① *(Mercury rec, 1962, unissued)* 234
Please Send Me Someone To Love ② *(Cotillion rec, 1970)* 253
Please, Please Make It Easy *(Mercury rec, 1964)* 239
Pledging My Love *(Mercury rec, 1962)* 233

Poor Make Believer *(Cotillion rec, 1970)* 253
Precious Lord *(Cotillion rec, 1970)* 255
Pulling Me Down – *See* You're Pulling Me Down
Rainy Night In Georgia ① *(Cotillion rec, 1969)* 251
Rainy Night In Georgia ① *(Cotillion rec, 1969, edited version)* 252
Rainy Night In Georgia ② *(Musicor rec, 1977)* 259
A Rainy Night In Georgia ③ *(Arrival rec, 1982)* 262
Rainy Night In Georgia ④ *(Hindsight rec, 1984)* 264
Rainy Night In Georgia ⑤ *(duet with Tony Joe White, bootleg, 1989)* 265
Really, Really *(Mercury rec, 1961)* 231
Remember Me *(Mercury rec, 1961)* 229
Remember The Good *(MGM rec, 1972)* 257
Rest Of The Way, The *(demo, 1956)* 220
Revenge ① *(Mercury rec, 1961)* 231
Revenge ② *(Musicor rec, 1977)* 260
Revenge ③ *(Arrival rec, 1982)* 263
Roach Song, The ① *(RCA rec, 1966, unissued)* 245
Roach Song, The ② *(RCA rec, 1966)* 247
Rock'n'Roll That Rhythm *(Columbia rec, 1957)* 217
Run On For A Long Time *(Bill Landford & The Landfordaires, Columbia rec, 1949)* 215
Same One, The ① *(Mercury rec, 1959)* 223
Same One, The ② *(Mercury rec, 1959, rejected)* 226
Same One, The ③ *(Musicor rec, 1977)* 259
Same One, The ④ *(Arrival rec, 1982)* 263
San Francisco (Be Sure To Wear Some Flowers In Your Hair)
    (part of medley, Reprise rec, 1967) 249
Save The Last Dance For Me *(Cotillion rec, 1971)* 256
Second Time Around, The *(RCA rec, 1965)* 242
Send Back My Heart *(MGM rec, 1972)* 257
Send For Me *(Mercury rec, 1962)* 233
Sentimental Daddy-O *(RCA rec, 1958)* 222
Sentimental Journey *(RCA rec, 1966, unissued)* 247
September Song *(Mercury rec, 1960)* 228
Set Me Free *(Cotillion rec, 1969)* 251
Shadrack ① *(Mercury rec, 1961)* 229
Shadrack ② *(Musicor rec, 1977)* 260
She Even Woke Me Up To Say Goodbye *(Cotillion rec, 1970)* 253
She Knows What To Do For Me *(Cotillion rec, 1969)* 250
Shoes *(Cotillion rec, 1970)* 253
Sidewalks Of Chicago *(Cotillion rec, 1970)* 254
Sidewalks Of Chicago *(Cotillion rec, 1970, edited version)* 254
Silent Night *(RCA rec, 1966)* 248
Since I Met You Baby *(Mercury rec, 1963)* 236
Since You've Been Gone *(RCA rec, 1965)* 241
Singing Bug *(Mars Broadcasting rec, ca.1964)* 237
    See also Boll Weevil Song, The
Sister And Brother *(Brut rec, 1974)* 257
So Close ① *(Mercury rec, 1956)* 218
So Close ② *(Musicor rec, 1977)* 259
So Little Time *(Mercury rec, 1963)* 237
So Many Ways ① *(Mercury rec, 1956)* 218
So Many Ways ② *(Musicor rec, 1977)* 259
So Many Ways ③ *(Arrival rec, 1982)* 263
So True In Life – So True In Love *(RCA rec, 1966)* 246
Soft *(Olde World rec, 1978)* 260
Soft *(Olde World rec, 1978, alt. vocal)* 260
Some Of My Best Friends *(Columbia rec, 1956)* 217
Somebody To Love *(Sandmen, Columbia rec, 1954)* 216
Someday You'll Want Me To Want You *(Mercury rec, 1959)* 225
Someone To Believe In ① *(Mercury rec, 1959)* 224

Someone To Believe In ② *(Mercury rec, 1959)* 225
Someone To Watch Over Me *(Mercury rec, 1959)* 226
Somewhere In The Used To Be *(Mercury rec, 1961)* 231
Song I Heard Last Night, The *(RCA rec, 1965)* 241
Soon *(Mercury rec, 1963)* 235
Soul Santa *(Cotillion rec, 1970)* 254
South Carolina *(Brut rec, 1974)* 257
Special Years, The *(Mercury rec, 1965)* 239
Steal Away *(Mercury rec, 1961)* 229
Steppin' Out Tonight *(Crown rec, 1956)* 221
Stick-To-It-Ivity *(Reprise rec, 1967)* 249
Still Waters Run Deep *(Mercury rec, 1962)* 233
Stop Foolin' *(duet with Damita Jo, Mercury rec, 1963)* 236
Straight Jingle – *See* All Vocal Jingle
Sun's Gonna Shine In My Door, The *(Mercury rec, 1963)* 236
Sunshine *(Olde World rec, 1977)* 262
Sweet Georgia Brown *(RCA rec, 1966, unissued)* 247
Sweet Georgia Brown *(RCA rec, 1966, alt. take)* 247
Sweet Memories *(MGM rec, 1973)* 256
Sweetest Sounds, The *(Mercury rec, 1963)* 235
Take A Look At Your Hands *(Cotillion rec, 1970)* 255
Take A Look At Your Hands *(Cotillion rec, 1970, edited version)* 255
Take Good Care Of Her ① *(Mercury rec, 1962)* 233
Take Good Care Of Her ② *(Treasury Department rec, 1963)* 234
Tall Oak Tree – *See* (There Was A) Tall Oak Tree
Taxi *(All Platinum rec, 1975)* 259
Tell Me *(Columbia rec, 1957)* 218
Tell Me Now Or Never *(Mercury rec, 1959)* 226
Tell Me The Truth *(Mercury rec, 1955, unissued)* 217
Tell Me Your Dream *(Mercury rec, 1959)* 223
Tender Years *(Mercury rec, 1962)* 233
Tenderly *(Mercury rec, 1962, unissued)* 232
Thank You Pretty Baby ① *(Mercury rec, 1959)* 225
Thank You Pretty Baby ② *(Musicor rec, 1977)* 259
Thank You Pretty Baby ③ *(Arrival rec, 1982)* 263
Thanks To The Fool *(Mercury rec, 1962)* 232
That Old Feeling *(RCA rec, 1966)* 243
That's All I Need *(Lincoln Chase & The Sandmen, Columbia rec, 1955)* 216
That's All I'm Living For *(Mercury rec, 1961, unissued)* 230
That's The Beginning Of The End *(Mercury rec, 1960, unissued)* 227
There Goes My Heart *(RCA rec, 1966, unissued)* 246
There Goes My Heart *(RCA rec, 1966, alt. take)* 246
There Goes That Song Again *(Mercury rec, 1962)* 232
There, I've Said It Again *(RCA rec, 1966, unissued)* 246
There, I've Said It Again *(RCA rec, 1966, alt. take)* 247
(There Was A) Tall Oak Tree *(Reprise rec, 1967)* 249
There's No Fool Like An Old Fool *(Mercury rec, 1964)* 239
There's Still A Little Love Left In Me *(Olde World rec, 1977)* 262
There's Still A Little Love Left In Me *(Olde World rec, 1977, alt. vocal)* 262
These Arms You Pushed Away *(Stax rec, 1974)* 258
These Hands *(Mercury rec, 1963, unissued)* 234
They Can't Take That Away From Me ① *(Mercury rec, 1960, rejected)* 227
They Can't Take That Away From Me ② *(Mercury rec, 1960)* 228
Things I Love, The *(Mercury rec, 1959)* 224
Things That Money Can't Buy, The
    (Lincoln Chase & The Sandmen, Columbia rec, 1955, unissued) 216
Think Twice ① *(Mercury rec, 1959)* 226
Think Twice ② *(Musicor rec, 1977)* 260
Think Twice ③ *(Arrival rec, 1982)* 263
This Bitter Earth ① *(demo, 1956)* 220

This Bitter Earth ② *(Mercury rec, 1959)* 225
This Is Worth Fighting For *(Reprise rec, 1967)* 249
This Time Of The Year ① *(Mercury rec, 1959)* 224
This Time Of [The] Year ② *(HMC rec, 1983)* 264
Ties That Bind, The ① *(Mercury rec, 1959)* 226
Ties That Bind, The ② *(Musicor rec, 1977)* 260
Till I Can't Take It Anymore *(Olde World rec, 1977)* 262
Til' I Can't Take It Anymore *(Olde World rec, 1977, alt. vocal)* 262
Till I Can't Take It No More ① *(Cotillion rec, 1970, unissued)* 254
Till I Can't Take It No More ② *(Cotillion rec, 1970, unissued)* 254
Till There Was You *(Mercury rec, 1963)* 235
Time After Time *(Mercury rec, 1959)* 224
Tomorrow Night *(Mercury rec, 1962)* 233
Too Late To Turn Back Now – *See* It's Too Late To Turn Back Now
Too Much Good Lovin' (No Good For Me) *(RCA rec, 1966)* 245
Touch 'Em With Love *(Cotillion rec, 1969)* 250
Touch Me Jesus *(Bill Landford & The Landfordaires, Columbia rec, 1949)* 215
Trouble In Mind *(Mercury rec, 1962)* 232
Trouble Of This World *(Bill Landford & The Landfordaires, Columbia rec, 1949)* 215
Troubled, Lord I'm Troubled *(Bill Landford & The Landfordaires, Columbia rec, 1949)* 215
Trust Me To Do What You Want Me To (And I'll Do It) *(Olde World rec, 1977)* 262
Try A Little Tenderness *(RCA rec, 1965)* 242
Try To Win A Friend (When It's Over) *(Army Reserve rec, 1974)* 258
Two Tickets To Paradise *(Mercury rec, 1962)* 232
Unclaimed Heart *(Mercury rec, 1964, unissued)* 238
Unforgettable *(RCA rec, 1966, unissued)* 247
Unforgettable *(RCA rec, 1966, alt. take)* 247
Valley Of Tears ① *(Mercury rec, 1962)* 233
Valley Of Tears ② *(Mercury rec, 1965, unissued)* 240
Wake Up *(RCA rec, 1967)* 247
Walk On The Wild Side *(Mercury rec, 1961)* 231
Walking The Floor Over You *(RCA rec, 1966)* 244
Walking Together *(demo, 1956)* 220
Wall, The *(Columbia rec, 1957)* 219
Way I Love You, The *(Cotillion rec, 1970, unissued)* 253
We Need What We Need *(Olde World rec, 1977)* 262
We're Gonna Make It *(Cotillion rec, 1969)* 251
Weakness In A Man *(Reprise rec, 1967)* 249
Weekend With Feathers *(All Platinum rec, 1975)* 258
What A Kiss Won't Do *(demo, 1956)* 220
What A Wonderful World *(Cotillion rec, 1969, unissued)* 251
What'cha Gone – *See* Won't Cha Gone
What Else Do You Want From Me *(Mercury rec, 1964)* 239
What Is A Woman Without A Man *(Mercury rec, 1964)* 239
When A Child Is Born *(HMC rec, 1983)* 264
When I Fall In Love *(Mercury rec, 1959)* 223
When I Grow Too Old To Dream ① *(Sandmen, Columbia rec, 1954)* 215
When I Grow Too Old To Dream ② *(Mercury rec, 1962)* 231
When Summer Turns To Fall *(Brut rec, 1974)* 257
When The Light Goes On Again *(Cotillion rec, 1970, unissued)* 253
When We Were (Friends) *(RCA rec, 1966, unissued)* 245
Where Do I Go From Here? *(Cotillion rec, 1969)* 251
Where Does A Man Go To Cry ① *(RCA rec, 1966, unissued)* 245
Where Does A Man Go To Cry ② *(RCA rec, 1966)* 246
Where There's A Will (There's A Way) ① *(Mercury rec, 1964, unissued)* 238
Where There's A Will (There's A Way) ② *(Mercury rec, 1965)* 239
While There's Life (There's Still Hope) *(RCA rec, 1965)* 241
Whoever Finds This I Love You *(Cotillion rec, 1970)* 253
Whoever Finds This I Love You *(Cotillion rec, 1970, alt. take)* 253
Why Don't You Write Me *(Mercury rec, 1963)* 236

Why Try To Change Me Now ① *(Mercury rec, 1960, rejected)* 228
Why Try To Change Me Now ② *(Mercury rec, 1960)* 228
Will You Love Me Tomorrow *(Mercury rec, 1962)* 233
Willie And Laura Mae Jones *(Cotillion rec, 1970)* 252
Willie And Laura Mae Jones *(Cotillion rec, 1970, alt. take)* 252
Willoughby Grove *(Cotillion rec, 1970)* 254
Winds Of Change, The *(Stax rec, 1974)* 258
With All Of My Heart *(Mercury rec, 1959)* 223
With Pen In Hand *(Cotillion rec, 1969)* 250
With The Touch Of Your Hand *(Mercury rec, 1962)* 233
Woman Without Love *(Cotillion rec, 1969)* 250
Won't Cha Gone *(Crown rec, 1956)* 221
Won't Cha Love – *See* Won't Cha Gone
Yaba-Daba-Do *(duet with Damita Jo, Mercury rec, 1963, withdrawn)* 236
You Ain't Got Faith ① *(Bill Landford & The Landfordaires, Columbia rec, 1949)* 215
You Ain't Got Faith ② *(Bill Landford Quartet, RCA rec, 1953)* 215
You Can't Get Away From Me *(demo, 1956)* 220
You Should Have Told Me *(Columbia rec, 1957)* 218
You Take Me Home Honey *(MGM rec, 1972)* 256
You Were Gone *(All Platinum rec, 1976)* 259
You'll Never Know *(Mercury rec, 1959)* 224
You're All I Want For Always *(Mercury rec, 1963, unissued)* 235
You're All I Want For Christmas ① *(Mercury rec, 1963, 1 voice, unissued)* 235
You're All I Want For Christmas ① *(Mercury rec, 1963, 2 voices, unissued)* 236
You're All I Want For Christmas ② *(Mercury rec, 1963, 1 voice)* 236
You're All I Want For Christmas ② *(Mercury rec, 1963, 2 voices, unissued)* 236
You're For Me ① *(demo, 1956)* 220
You're For Me ② *(RCA rec, 1957)* 222
You're Mine (And I Love You) ① *(RCA rec, 1965, unissued)* 240
You're Mine (And I Love You) ② *(RCA rec, 1965)* 241
You're Movin' Me *(demo, 1956)* 220
[You're] Pulling Me Down *(Olde World rec, 1977)* 262
You're So Wonderful *(RCA rec, 1965)* 241
You're The Reason I'm Living *(Reprise rec, 1967)* 249
You've Never Been This Far *(Stax rec, 1974)* 258
Your Eyes *(Mercury rec, 1960)* 228
Your Love Alone *(RCA rec, 1957)* 221

ILLUSTRATIONS & PHOTO CREDITS

Ads on pages 34, 370 and 372 courtesy Music Mentor archive; ads on pages 84, 308, 374, 376 and 378 courtesy Hans Maitner; ad on page 152 courtesy Benton Family collection.

CDs on page 293 courtesy Herwig Gradischnig; bootleg CD on page 312 courtesy Music Mentor archive.

Download image on page 295 courtesy Music Mentor archive.

EP sleeves on pages 277 (top left, middle left), 316 (bottom right), 317 (top left, top right, middle left, bottom right) and 328 (bottom right) courtesy Music Mentor archive; EP sleeves on page 277 (top right, middle right), 316 (bottom left) and 317 (middle right, bottom left) courtesy Terry Kay; EP sleeves on pages 277 (bottom left, bottom right) and 304 courtesy Hans Maitner.

Front cover photo by Chuck Stewart, courtesy Mercury Records/Benton Family collection.

Funeral order of service on pages 207-210 courtesy Herwig Gradischnig.

Labels on pages 26, 29, 30, 266, 315 (top left) and 328 (bottom left) courtesy Konrad Nowakowski; labels on pages 52, 269 (all except top left), 270 (all except top left), 273 (top right, middle left, bottom left, bottom right), 274 (top left, bottom left, bottom right), 315 (all except top left), 316 (top left, top right, middle left, middle right), 326 (top left, top right, middle left, middle right), 331 (top right, middle right, bottom left, bottom right), 334, 338 (top left, top right, middle left), 342 (bottom), 347, 352 and 355 courtesy Music Mentor archive; labels on pages 353 and 359 courtesy Roy Rydland.

Letters on pages 173 and 174 courtesy Benton Family collection.

LP sleeves on pages 43, 45, 46, 47, 49, 55, 57, 59, 64, 67, 69, 71, 73, 77, 78, 80, 82, 86, 89, 90, 92, 95, 97, 99, 102, 110 and 188 courtesy Hans Maitner; LP sleeve on page 106 courtesy Music Mentor archive; LP sleeves on pages 107, 109 and 112 courtesy Herwig Gradischnig.

Miller Beer promos on pages 100 and 101 courtesy Hans Maitner.

Newspaper cuttings on pages 22, 76, 169 and 177 courtesy Benton Family collection.

Photos on pages 5 and 190 by James J. Kriegsmann, courtesy Hans Maitner; photos on pages 25, 38, 65, 70, 85, 120, 121, 122, 128, 131, 132, 136, 144, 145, 146, 149, 156, 164, 166, 167, 168, 187, 195, 394 and 395 courtesy Benton Family collection; photo on page 27 courtesy Brook Grant; photos on pages 50 and 51 by Chuck Stewart, courtesy Mercury Records/Benton Family collection; photo on page 63 courtesy Mercury Records/Music Mentor archive; photo on page 117 by Forshee, courtesy Benton Family collection; photo on page 118 courtesy Konrad Nowakowski; photo on page 139 by Hans Maitner; photo on page 211 by Brook Grant; photo on page 382 courtesy Hans Maitner.

Picture sleeves on pages 302, 368 (top left, middle left, middle right) and 369 (all except top right) courtesy Hans Maitner; picture sleeve on page 326 courtesy Konrad Nowakowski; picture sleeves on pages 331 (middle left), 333, 335, 338 (middle right, bottom left. bottom right), 347 (top right, bottom left, bottom right), 357, 368 (top right, bottom left, bottom right) and 369 (top right) courtesy Music Mentor archive.

Poster on page 157 courtesy Hans Maitner.

Programme on page 124 courtesy Konrad Nowakowski; programmes on pages 125 and 400 courtesy Hans Maitner.

Sheet music on page 368 (all except middle left) courtesy Hans Maitner; sheet music on page 368 (middle left) courtesy Music Mentor archive.

Singles on pages 104 and 390 courtesy Hans Maitner.

Tapes on pages 296 and 298 courtesy Hans Maitner.

SONG LYRIC CREDITS

Extracts of the following songs are quoted by kind permission of the copyright owners:

24   I'll Meet You After Church Next Sunday *(Brook Benton-Clyde Otis)*
Clyde Otis Music Group Inc. (BMI)

31   The Wall *(Ormay Diamond-Cliff Owens-Dave Dreyer)*
Vanessa Music Corp. (ASCAP)

62   There Goes That Song Again *(Sammy Cahn-Jule Styne)*
Skidmore Music Co. Inc. (ASCAP)

68   Hello Young Lovers *(Richard Rodgers-Oscar Hammerstein II)*
Williams Music Co. (ASCAP)

79   A Nightingale Sang In Berkeley Square *(Eric Maschwitz-Manning Sherwin)*
Colgems EMI Music Inc./Shapiro, Bernstein & Co. Inc. (ASCAP)

91   Rainy Night In Georgia *(Tony Joe White)*
Combine Music Corp. (BMI)

93   For Le Ann *(Tony Joe White)*
Combine Music Corp. (BMI)

93-4   Willie And Laura Mae Jones *(Tony Joe White)*
Combine Music Corp. (BMI)

94   Aspen Colorado *(Tony Joe White)*
Combine Music Corp. (BMI)

111   A Tribute To 'Mama' *(Clyde Otis-Duncan Cleary)*
Clyde Otis Music Group Inc./Utopia Unlimited (BMI)

113   I've Got The Christmas Spirit *(Susan Collins-Michael Barbiero-Jimmy Maelen-Paul Shaffer)*
EMI April Music Inc./Ring Bearer Music Inc. (ASCAP)

114   Decorate The Night *(Dobie Gray-Bud Reneau-Wray Chafin)*
N2D Publishing Co. (ASCAP)

142   You Go Around Once *(Brook Benton)*
Unpublished?

178   Soul Santa *(Gerald Deas-Brook Benton)*
Benday Music (BMI)

187-8   I'm A Man *(Neil Diamond)*
Tallyrand Music Inc. (SESAC)

189   Oh Lord, Why Lord *(Phil Trim)*
EMI Longitude Music (BMI)

190-1   I've Gotta Be Me *(Walter Marks)*
WB Music Corp. (ASCAP)

191   Born Under A Bad Sign *(Booker T. Jones-William Bell)*
Cotillion Music Inc./Irving Music Inc. (BMI)

OTHER TITLES FROM MUSIC MENTOR BOOKS

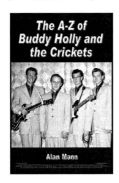

The A-Z of Buddy Holly and the Crickets
Alan Mann
ISBN-13: 978-0-9547068-0-7 *(pbk, 320 pages)*

The A-Z of Buddy Holly and the Crickets draws together a mass of Holly facts and info from a variety of published sources, as well as the author's own original research, and presents them in an easy-to-use encyclopaedic format. Now in its third edition, it has proved to be a popular and valuable reference work on this seminal rock'n'roller. It is a book that every Holly fan will want to keep at their fingertips. It is a book about a musical genius who will never be forgotten.

American Rock'n'Roll: The UK Tours 1956-72
Ian Wallis
ISBN-13: 978-0-9519888-6-2 *(pbk, 424 pages)*

The first-ever detailed overview of every visit to these shores by American (and Canadian!) rock'n'rollers. It's all here: over 400 pages of tour itineraries, support acts, show reports, TV appearances and other items of interest. Illustrated with dozens of original tour programmes, ads, ticket stubs and great live shots, many rare or previously unpublished.

Back On The Road Again
Dave Nicolson
ISBN-13: 978-0-9547068-2-1 *(pbk, 216 pages)*

A third book of interviews by Dave Nicolson in the popular *On The Road* series, this time with more of a Sixties flavour: Solomon Burke, Gene Chandler, Bruce Channel, Lowell Fulson, Jet Harris, Gene McDaniels, Scott McKenzie, Gary S. Paxton, Bobby 'Boris' Pickett, Martha Reeves & The Vandellas, Jimmie Rodgers, Gary Troxel (Fleetwoods), Leroy Van Dyke and Junior Walker.

The Big Beat Scene
Royston Ellis
ISBN-13: 978-0-9562679-1-7 *(pbk, 184 pages)*

Originally published in 1961, *The Big Beat Scene* was the first contemporary account of the teenage music scene in Britain. Written before the emergence of the Beatles, and without the benefit of hindsight, this fascinating document provides a unique, first-hand insight into the popularity and relevance of jazz, skiffle and rock'n'roll at a time when Cliff Richard & The Shadows were at the cutting edge of pop, and the social attitudes prevailing at the time.

British Hit EPs 1955-1989
George R. White
ISBN-13: 978-0-9562679-6-2 *(pbk, 320 pages)*

Fully revised and expanded second edition of the only chart book dedicated to British Hit EPs. Includes a history of the format, an artist-by-artist listing of every 7-inch hit EP from 1955 to 1989 (with full track details for each record), a trivia section, the official UK EP charts week by week, and much more. Profusely illustrated with over 600 sleeve shots.

The Chuck Berry International Directory (Volume 1)
Morten Reff
ISBN-13: 978-0-9547068-6-9 *(pbk, 486 pages)*

For the heavyweight Berry fan. Everything you ever wanted to know about Chuck Berry, in four enormous volumes compiled by the world-renowned Norwegian Berry collector and authority, Morten Reff. This volume contains discographies for over 40 countries, plus over 700 rare label and sleeve illustrations.

The Chuck Berry International Directory (Volume 2)
Morten Reff
ISBN-13: 978-0-9547068-7-6 *(pbk, 532 pages)*

The second of four volumes in this extensive reference work dedicated to rock'n'roll's most influential guitarist and composer. Contains details of bootlegs; radio albums; movies; TV shows; video and DVD releases; international tour itineraries; hits, achievements and awards; Berry's songs, roots, and influence on other artists; tributes; Chuck Berry in print; fan clubs and websites; plus annotated discographies of pianist Johnnie Johnson (post-Berry) and the ultimate Berry copyist, Eddy Clearwater.

The Chuck Berry International Directory (Volume 3)
Morten Reff
ISBN-13: 978-0-9547068-8-3 *(pbk, 608 pages)*

The third volume in this award-winning reference work dedicated to rock'n'roll's most influential guitarist and composer. Contains details of over 4,500 cover versions of Chuck Berry songs including many rarities from around the world. Alphabetical listing by artist (brief biography, comprehensive details of recordings and relevant releases, illuminating commentary and critiques), plus dozens of label and sleeve illustrations.

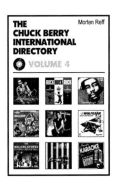

The Chuck Berry International Directory (Volume 4)
Morten Reff
ISBN-13: 978-0-9547068-9-0 *(pbk, 546 pages)*

The fourth and final volume of this groundbreaking work contains an A-Z of cover versions of Chuck Berry songs, details of hit cover versions, cover versions in the movies and on TV, over 900 Berry soundalikes, a 'No Chuck' section (non-Berry songs with similar titles), games, and even a brief chapter on Chuck Berry karaoke! Also over 100 pages of additions and updates to *Volumes 1, 2* and *3*, plus useful indices of Berry's releases by title and by label.

Cook's Tours: Tales of a Tour Manager
Malcolm Cook
ISBN-13: 978-0-9562679-4-8 *(pbk, 324 pages)*

Throughout his 44 years in the entertainment industry, Malcolm Cook met and worked with some of the biggest names in show business. In this humorous, fast-paced biographical account, Cook lifts the lid on what it takes to keep a show on the road and artists and audiences happy. It's all here: transport problems, unscrupulous promoters, run-ins with East German police, hassles with the Mafia, tea with the Duke of Norfolk, the wind-ups, the laughter, the heartbreak and the tears. A unique insight into what really goes on behind the scenes.

Elvis & Buddy – Linked Lives
Alan Mann
ISBN-13: 978-0-9519888-5-5 *(pbk, 160 pages)*

The achievements of Elvis Presley and Buddy Holly have been extensively documented, but until now little if anything has been known about the many ways in which their lives were interconnected. The author examines each artist's early years, comparing their backgrounds and influences, chronicling all their meetings and examining the many amazing parallels in their lives, careers and tragic deaths. Over 50 photos, including many rare/previously unpublished.

The First Time We Met The Blues – A journey of discovery with Jimmy Page, Brian Jones, Mick Jagger and Keith Richards
David Williams
ISBN-13: 978-0-9547068-1-4 *(pbk, 130 pages)*

David Williams was a childhood friend of Led Zeppelin guitar legend, Jimmy Page. The author describes how they discovered the blues together, along with future members of the Rolling Stones. The climax of the book is a detailed account of a momentous journey by van from London to Manchester to see the 1962 *American Folk-Blues Festival*, where they got their first chance to see their heroes in action.

Jet Harris – In Spite of Everything
Dave Nicolson
ISBN-13: 978-0-9562679-2-4 *(pbk, 208 pages)*

As a founder member of the Shadows, and a chart-topper in his own right, bassist Jet Harris scaled the heights of superstardom in the 1960s. A helpless alcoholic for most of his adult life, he also sank to unimaginable depths of despair, leaving a string of broken hearts and shattered lives in his wake. In this unauthorised biography author Dave Nicolson examines his eventful life and career, and how he eventually overcame his addiction to the bottle.

Last Swill and Testament
– The hilarious, unexpurgated memoirs of
Paul 'Sailor' Vernon
ISBN-13: 978-0-9547068-4-5 *(pbk, 228 pages)*

Born in London shortly after the end of World War II, Paul 'Sailor' Vernon came into his own during the 1960s when spotty teenage herberts with bad haircuts began discovering The Blues. For the Sailor it became a lifelong obsession that led him into a whirlwind of activity as a rare record dealer, magazine proprietor/editor, video bootlegger and record company director. It's all here in this one-of-a-kind life history that will leave you reaching for an enamel bucket and a fresh bottle of disinfectant!

Let The Good Times Rock!
– A Fan's Notes On Post-War American Roots Music
Bill Millar
ISBN-13: 978-0-9519888-8-6 *(pbk, 362 pages)*

For almost four decades, the name 'Bill Millar' has been synonymous with the very best in British music writing. This fabulous book collects together 49 of his best pieces – some previously unpublished – in a thematic compilation covering hillbilly, rockabilly, R&B, rock'n'roll, doo-wop, swamp pop and soul. Includes essays on acappella, doo-wop and blue-eyed soul, as well as detailed profiles of some of the most fascinating and influential personalities of each era.

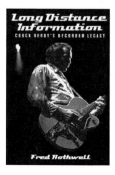

Long Distance Information
– Chuck Berry's Recorded Legacy
Fred Rothwell
ISBN-13: 978-0-9519888-2-4 *(pbk, 352 pages)*

The lowdown on every recording Chuck Berry has ever made. Includes an overview of his life and career, his influences, the stories behind his most famous compositions, full session details, listings of all his key US/UK vinyl and CD releases (including track details), TV and film appearances, and much, much more. Over 100 illustrations including label shots, vintage ads and previously unpublished photos.

Mike Sanchez: Big Town Playboy
Michael Madden (Foreword by Robert Plant)
ISBN-13: 978-0-9562679-7-9 *(pbk, 314 pages)*

The compelling story of one of the foremost exponents of authentic rhythm & blues and rock'n'roll in the world today. Author Michael Madden has been given full access to a vast archive of material charting Mike Sanchez's journey from his Spanish roots through an eventful 35-year musical career that has seen him progress through the ranks of the Rockets, the Big Town Playboys and Bill Wyman's Rhythm Kings to fronting his own band and performing with some of the biggest names of the rock world including Robert Plant, Eric Clapton, Mick Fleetwood and Jeff Beck.

More American Rock'n'Roll: The UK Tours 1973-84
Ian Wallis
ISBN-13: 978-0-9562679-3-1 *(pbk, 380 pages)*

The long-awaited follow-up to *American Rock'n'Roll: The UK Tours 1956-72*. Like its predecessor, it's crammed full of information about every American or Canadian rock'n'roller who visited Britain during the period covered. If you love rock'n'roll, you will wish to relive memories of all those nights spent in hot, sweaty clubs amongst the honking saxes, pounding pianos and twanging guitars. It is 'the greatest music in the world', and all those wonderful memories can be found again within these pages.

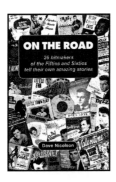

On The Road
Dave Nicolson
ISBN-13: 978-0-9519888-4-8 *(pbk, 256 pages)*

Gary 'US' Bonds, Pat Boone, Freddy Cannon, Crickets Jerry Allison, Sonny Curtis and Joe B. Mauldin, Bo Diddley, Dion, Fats Domino, Duane Eddy, Frankie Ford, Charlie Gracie, Brian Hyland, Marv Johnson, Ben E. King, Brenda Lee, Little Eva, Chris Montez, Johnny Moore (Drifters), Gene Pitney, Johnny Preston, Tommy Roe, Del Shannon, Edwin Starr, Johnny Tillotson and Bobby Vee tell their own fascinating stories. Over 150 illustrations including vintage ads, record sleeves, label shots, sheet music covers, etc.

On The Road Again
Dave Nicolson
ISBN-13: 978-0-9519888-9-3 *(pbk, 206 pages)*

Second volume of interviews with the stars of pop and rock'n'roll including Freddie Bell, Martin Denny, Johnny Farina (Santo & Johnny), the Kalin Twins, Robin Luke, Chas McDevitt, Phil Phillips, Marvin Rainwater, Herb Reed (Platters), Tommy Sands, Joe Terranova (Danny & The Juniors), Mitchell Torok, Marty Wilde and the 'Cool Ghoul' himself, John Zacherle.

Railroadin' Some: Railroads In The Early Blues
Max Haymes
ISBN-13: 978-0-9547068-3-8 *(pbk, 390 pages)*

This groundbreaking book, written by one of the foremost
blues historians in the UK, is based on over 30 years
research, exploration and absolute passion for early blues
music. It is the first ever comprehensive study of the
enormous impact of the railroads on 19th and early 20th
Century African American society and the many and varied
references to this new phenomenon in early blues lyrics.
Includes ballin' the jack, smokestack lightning, hot shots, the
bottoms, chain gangs, barrelhouses, hobo jungles and more.

**Music Mentor books are available from all good bookshops
or by mail order from:**

**Music Mentor Books
69 Station Road
Upper Poppleton
YORK YO26 6PZ
England**

Telephone: **+44 (0)1904 330308**
Email: **music.mentor@lineone.net**
Website: **http://musicmentor0.tripod.com**